MASQUERADE!

Captain Adam Falconer sailed the *Wild Sweet Witch* but a different enchantress held him under her spell.

She tempted him as the amber-eyed headstrong English missionary girl, Caroline Wyeth.

She seduced him as the sensual exquisite Tahitian maid, Teura—whose taboo passion inflamed his tempestuous desire.

She bewitched him as the wanton harlot aboard the Chinese pleasure boat—and his lust showed the darker side of his soul.

But it was through the magic of her love that Caroline Wyeth captured his heart and united their passions in a rapture as engulfing and all-consuming as the South Pacific itself!

Araby Scott

AVON
PUBLISHERS OF BARD, CAMELOT AND DISCUS BOOKS

AVON BOOKS
A division of
The Hearst Corporation
959 Eighth Avenue
New York, New York 10019

First Avon Printing, May, 1981

❦ CHAPTER ONE ❧

The woman finished fastening the bodice of her low-cut silk gown. It was 1805, and although this was Montego Bay, and Jamaica a British colony, the high-waisted, slender-skirted dresses of Napoleon's Empress Josephine were the fashion on both sides of the Atlantic. The woman's waist was narrow and supple, her hips invitingly rounded, and her overripe breasts seemed to strain for escape from the confines of the emerald-green silk.

She glanced back at the velvet-canopied bed she had occupied until some minutes before, and at the man who lay there, watching her. She gave a soft excited laugh.

"You *are* ready for me again, Adam." Her eyes lingered on the rumpled sheets, and the evidence he made no effort to hide. The tip of her tongue touched and moistened her rouged lips. "How can you expect me to leave now?"

The man's eyes crinkled into a slumbrous smile, and lamplight caught a wicked glint of his white, even teeth. The eyes, like the tousled hair above them, were black. "You knew damn well what you were doing, Esmé. You're bloody insatiable! And it must be nearly dawn."

"Why, Adam," she protested with mock innocence, "all I did was comb my hair—and put on my clothes."

"And in that order, too! Such wasted effort. Now you'll have to take them off again."

Esme's overblown lips curved provocatively, then pushed themselves into a pout. "I'm too tired, Adam. All those nasty little fastenings and stays! Surely you can think of a better way? I've always hated this dress."

In seconds he was across the room, his body long and lithe and well-aroused. "She-devil!"

As he tore the fabric, Esmé's ripe body spilled from its gown, and moments later they fell together on the

1

opulent carpet, too impatient to return to the abandoned bed.

Clanggggg!

The sound exploded into Adam Falconer's consciousness. He came animal-alert, his hand reaching for nonexistent weapons almost before his body had time to jerk to a sitting position.

"Damn your eyes, Noah, that's no way to wake a man." Adam's long lean frame began to uncoil, to lose its tenseness. He pushed himself up against the silken pillows and glowered at the squashed face of the man called Noah. "You're taking an awful risk! I might have killed you."

"Jest slipped my hand, Capn. Aye! Reg'lar butterfingers I am this morning." Noah Mapes stooped to retrieve the large brass tray from the floor. He had the face of a monkey and the agile bowed legs to go with it. At the moment, his bird-bright eyes were angelic.

Several steaming silver-lidded dishes, carefully removed from the tray, sat on the mahogany table beside the bed. "But dammit, Noah, it's too early for breakfast. You might have let me get some sleep."

"Ain't me is to blame, Capn. Some others is mighty determined to keep a man from his nat'ral eight hours." Noah Mapes allowed his mouth to crease with pretended disapproval. "Now if we was back at sea, you'd a been up near five hours. It's past eleven o'clock."

"Eleven o'clock?" Adam Falconer winced. What time had Esmé finally left?

"Ain't right for a man to sleep all day, Capn. Now there's folks works by night—our hostess for one. Lady runs a gamblin' establishment, she's used to night work. Madame Esmé, I spotted her scurryin' for her own rooms not three hours ago, wearin' a man's nightshirt an' gown that looked mighty similar to some I seen. Now I wonder what could a kept her up till then?"

"Damned if I know." Falconer stifled a yawn and reached for the damp towel that Noah, good manservant that he was, had brought with the breakfast. He rubbed it over his face and his unruly black hair.

The face was tanned to teak, all but the rather paler feathering of lines about his eyes—laughter lines, perhaps, or the kind of lines a man gets from squinting long hours into a far horizon under a harsh sun. The lines

2

made him appear older than his twenty-nine years, but it was also part of what women saw when they looked at his face—that, and the near-blackness of his eyes that sometimes held hints of mockery, and sometimes something else, something smoky and dangerous and not quite understood. Pride, perhaps? Certainly there was pride in the mouth and a sensual quality, and traces of something that could be cruelty or ruthlessness. But women, even experienced women, forgot that when he smiled—just as they forgot that they had known at once he was a man who would be faithless to any mistress but the sea. Surely there were ways to change a man's mind!

"How's the wind, Noah?"

"Prevailin' trades, fair to middlin'. Sailin' weather—a man should be on the seas!" Captain Falconer's last ship had sunk under them not a year ago in a terrible Cape Horn storm, when they were heading from the Pacific. Only two hands lost—a miracle, that, and a credit to the captain. But with the ship had gone all his master's hard-earned investment. Noah gazed longingly at the sweep of Montego Bay that lay beneath the window, and wished there were some way out of here. "Should a never come to Jamaica. Pacific's where we belong—Pacific's where we should a stayed."

Adam Falconer yawned and stretched, gladdened by the good December weather in the tropics. He, too, longed to be back in the Pacific, but he was prepared to take each day as it unfolded. "Patience, Noah! We'll get back there soon enough. You know why we came here. Now, throw me my trousers, will you, Noah?"

"Aye, an' a cockeyed reason too." Noah found the discarded trousers and carried them to his master. "Turrible bad piece o' property it turned out to be! Might a known that man you won it off weren't on the up an' up."

Falconer made a face. The man was someone he had tried to forget, without success. He put his feet over the side of the bed and started to pull the trousers over his long-muscled swimmer's legs. "I never was convinced he was telling the truth. But we had to see for ourselves, didn't we? Remember, Noah, he was desperate."

"You ain't still blamin' yourself! Man commits suicide, he ain't doin' it over a worthless piece o' property. Acres an' acres, an' you'd not give a bucket o' sheep-dip for the lot! He knew it, too. Deed ain't worth the paper it's writ on. Muckin' liar!"

"We know that now, Noah, but three months ago it seemed reason enough to come to Jamaica." Adam busied himself with his belt buckle. "And don't berate the dead. What's done is done—no use getting angry."

In a strange way, the fact that the Jamaican property had turned out to be worthless had been a mixed blessing; at least it had made Adam feel less responsible for the man's death. He had won the land on a turn of the cards. The ten thousand acres existed, true enough, but it was in that inhospitable part of Jamaica known as Cockpit Country, a haven for slaves freed by the Spaniards more than two centuries before. A decade back, the British had taken an expedition into Cockpit Country and defeated these men—the Maroons, as they were called. Cockpit Country had in turn defeated the British. It still teemed with fiercely independent blacks who somehow scratched a living from the pitted and unfriendly territory. Locals called it "The Land of Look Behind"—and for good reason; Adam and Noah had barely escaped with their lives. The property deed Adam owned—one the British had handed out a decade ago as a reward for service—was only paper.

"Time we moved on," grumbled Noah. "Costs an arm an' a leg, it does, to stay in this fancy house! You could a earned your keep at the gamin' tables, too, if you wasn't so stubborn. Might a taken in enough to buy yourself another sweet little piece o' timber. An' another thing—"

"You know I'm through with gambling, Noah. It's like liquor—best if you can leave it alone. And dammit, I've decided to leave it alone! Now stop nagging me. You're like an old woman this morning. We'll leave when we can find a ship bound for the States."

But the ships that lay in Montego Bay were mostly Liverpool merchants loading sugar and rum. News of the Third Alliance against Napoleon had filtered across the Atlantic several months before, and now American ships' captains were running shy of British ports, even here in the West Indies. With the Declaration of Independence still fresh in men's minds; with Jefferson president and favoring the French; with British warships daily seizing and searching American vessels, and often impressing

4

their crews into the British navy; with growing murmurs about restriction of neutral trade, Great Britain and the infant United States were hardly on nodding terms. Merchant ships still traded between the countries, but at their own risk.

Falconer went on: "No way we're sailing out on any of those ships in harbor—and there's been nothing new in for days, except that British man-of-war."

"No? Well," said Noah with a slight smirk, for he could not resist the sly dig at his master, "if you'd not lie slugabed like some shore dandy, you'd be knowin' better."

Adam's eyes widened. He strode across the room and drew back the heavy silken drapes. The high sun streamed in the window, and it took a moment for his eyes to adjust to the sparkling turquoise waters of the bay. In the harbor lay several fat-jowled merchant ships, each a beehive of activity as men hoisted casks over the side. A few untidy cutters, typical island trading vessels with patched sails the color of old paper, threaded slowly toward the horizon. In deeper waters the lone wall-sided warship, a frigate, swung forlornly at anchor, temporarily without masts, even though flame-coated marines drilled on deck, like tiny red ants at this distance. But Noah was right: something new had been added to the scene.

"Baltimore-built and -rigged," murmured Falconer, recognizing at once the lines of the large schooner that had found anchorage earlier this morning. The ship had the slightly raked masts, the yards where beautifully cut square topsails would stretch taut to the wind, giving her a speed no ordinary schooner would have. She was of the type known as a Baltimore clipper. "She's a beauty. Why didn't you wake me when you saw her come in, Noah?"

"Cain't say as I didn't try, Capn. 'Twere just after eight—not long past when I saw some *other* folk headin' for some *other* folk's own quarters. Came in an' tried to tell you. Cursed me right roundly, you did."

Falconer grinned. "Did I, now?" He gazed at the harbor once again and asked, "What's her name?"

"The *Sweet Witch.*"

"Mmmm—yes, suits her. Nice clean lines, saucy little thing. I'd like to see her under sail."

"Rips off the knots in fine fashion, she does. But she ain't so little, nor so clean."

"Oh? In need of vinegar and holystone, is she? Well, not every ship's captain cares, more's the pity. Out of where?"

"Out of Bristol. Aye, she's British now—but she's Baltimore-built right enough, one of two sister ships seized by the Limeys a few years back."

Falconer pushed aside the twinge of disappointment. "Who's her captain?"

"Beau Blore, Capn Beau Blore by name. Saw him come ashore, I did. Built like an oak tree, he is, an' eyes like a toad! He owns this 'un, the *Sweet Witch*—an' the sister ship too, the *Bristol Witch*. This ain't his reg'lar port o' call."

"What is?"

"Loo-siana. New Orleans. He put in here for a saw-bones—ship's doctor died on the high seas. An' now he thinks he may offload here instead. Aye, he said Jamaica looked like his cup o' tea. What with the new mess o' things, Capn Blore seems keen to change to a Brit-ish port o' call, an' mebbe even put down some roots, for he ain't too happy 'bout this whole war with the French-ies. Interferes with a man's nat'ral right to make money, he says! Aye, he's a bad 'un—got a sharp eye for the main chance."

"Haven't we all?" sighed Falconer. "Anyway, well done, Noah. I'll go and see this fellow Blore this after-noon. If he sails on to New Orleans, perhaps we can book passage with him."

"Count me out, then," said Noah sourly.

"Noah! Whatever for?"

Noah turned to face his master, and this time the dis-gust was written plain on his wrinkled walnut face. "*Sweet Witch* is a slaver, Capn. You still be wantin' to meet with this Blore bloke?"

Adam Falconer turned away from the window, sick-ened. A slaver: the pitiful half-naked bodies, the whip-marks and raw running sores, and the awful, indescribable stench . . . no wonder the *Sweet Witch* needed a doctor. "You're right—I won't be wanting to meet Captain Blore."

"May not get your wish, Capn, less'n you're ready to move out of your lady friend's pricey quarters here. Capn Toad-Eyes jest came in the door downstairs, an' asked for rooms. Says he heard that Madame Esmé's here is the

6

place for high-stakes gamblin'—an' he's looking to find hisself a game tonight."

Falconer grinned. "Well, well. I wonder if he knows that Esmé's a quadroon?"

For a moment deviltry returned to Noah's eyes. "He'll never know it to see her, will he now? Spite of them full-blown red lips and them snappin' black eyes. Aye, she'll have it in for a slave-capn! Any luck, she'll take him for everything he's got, an' happy to, considerin' his perfession. Now if she was to get him at the faro tables . . ."

"I must buy Esmé a present," said Falconer reflectively, in answer to nothing in particular. "How much money do we have left, Noah?"

"Near on nine hunnerd pounds, British, Capn, and six hunnerd good United States currency. Plus some loose change. You ain't broke by a long ways, but—"

"Good. Keep the dollars; we'll need them soon enough. But fetch me the nine hundred, will you?"

"Capn! Ain't no ways you can spend that kind o' money on any skirt—don't care how many times she's lifted it up for you."

"Don't be disrespectful, Noah. Madame Esmé is a lady, for all that she runs a gaming house. And I'm not intending to spend it all on her. There's a ruby necklace she's been admiring. It'll cost no more than a hundred pounds. A nice going-away present."

"Then a hunnerd pounds'll do," said Noah firmly. "I'll be mindin' the rest, same as usual. Which lodgings you thinkin' o' moving into?"

"Did I say we were moving to other lodgings? And I'll need all nine hundred, Noah. While you're at it, dig out my diamond studs, and the sapphire stickpin—the ones I won in Macao. Damn good thing I didn't sell them last year! They'll be just the thing for tonight. And Noah —my good jacket too, the plum velvet."

A slow puckish grin spread over Noah's features. "So you'll be gamblin' again! Aye, an' taking on that cursed slavin' sea-captain! Well, it's time he got his come-uppance. An' you're the man to give it to him."

"Maybe," said Falconer noncommittally. His eyes were closed now, and Noah could read nothing there. "I've a job for you this afternoon, Noah. Make the rounds of the grogshops and see if you can find some likely-looking young sailors. Deserters if you must—that British warship's got a bucko mate, heavy on the whip hand. Half the men are impressed anyway, and they're treated like dogs. They'll skip ship—can't even rightly call it deserting. Careful who you pick. Half a dozen will do, skeleton crew only. Tell them with luck we'll be sailing out of here tomorrow."

"An' will you be so kind as to tell me how?" asked Noah, although he already knew Falconer's intentions.

"In the *Sweet Witch*, of course. While you're out and about, Noah, buy some vinegar—and any medicines you think we may need."

Noah's grin broadened almost to his ears. So he had been right. Just how the Capn planned to win the *Sweet Witch* he was not sure, but if anyone could do it, his master could. "About time you got back to the gamblin'! Knew you couldn't stay so cursed straitlaced forever, Capn. Aye, an' this time the winning'll be a double pleasure, God's truth!" Noah looked at his master admiringly; he was convinced that there was no man alive who could get the better of him. No, nor woman either!

"Who said anything about winning?" Adam Falconer's voice was mild, but his eyes came open and crinkled into the beginnings of a smile; and Noah saw an unholy black gleam that he recognized only too well. "I'm going to lose tonight, Noah. I'm going to lose nearly everything I've got."

CHAPTER TWO

Five thousand miles across a restless Atlantic, it was much later in the day. A dying sun lay pale on the low walls of old-gold Cotswold stone and the tilted tile roof that capped them. Frost fingered the ancient window-panes, and smoke whispered up from a squat chimney, for it was cold, even though it was nearly snowless in this part of England. Only a few thin drifts of powdery white lay in shadowed patches of the land. Even in their winter nakedness, the Cotswold hills were gentle, worn soft by centuries of grazing sheep—and the house, though it stood alone, did not look lonely.

Jonah Wyeth could hear the front door slamming; could hear the breathless silvery sound of a young voice; could hear the housekeeper in the hall beyond the library door, worrying at his sister like a mother hen, and thinking he could not hear:

"Why, Miss Carey, where have you been! Grime all over your hems—and look at your hair! Where *is* your bonnet? Riding with that young Cavendish boy, I'll be bound, hatless, and on a cold day like this! Here, quickly, give me your cloak—and take off those shoes, you've near torn the heel off. Well, you picked the wrong day to stay too long, for your brother's waiting— yes, he's here! Now don't go all excited, for he won't want to see you looking like that, after coming all the way from London two days early, just to be with you. This Christmas maybe he'll stay a little longer and make the trip worthwhile—that stagecoach costs a pretty farthing, you know! And now you'll have to keep him waiting longer, for you'll need to change into something decent. And wash your face! La, you'll never make a lady, Miss Carey, for all those fine lessons you take. You should be having a tutor for deportment, instead! Off you go, and be quick about it, or your brother will think I haven't been looking after you properly!"

But instead of running up the stairs, the girl burst in at the library door, her flyaway hair looking as though the summer sun was still tangled in it, despite the silver frost that patterned the windows today. Flyaway gold—and cheeks rosy with the nip of the English winter, and brown eyes sparkling amber with excitement and pleasure.

"Oh, Jonah—Jonah!" Carey Wyeth flung herself impetuously across the room at the brother who was eleven years older than herself, and more like a father. "How good to see you! It's been so long. I didn't expect you until Christmas Eve."

"Caroline!" Jonah allowed his sister to hug him, although he was alarmed to see how much she had changed in the year he had been away from home. Everything about Jonah Wyeth was pale and brown—pale brown hair, pale brown eyes, sallow sunless skin. He looked older than his twenty-seven years—as though he could, indeed, have been Carey's father. Now, with a frown, he held her at arm's length. "You've grown. An inch, I think. But, Caroline—"

"Two," she reported. "And all of it last spring. I've stopped now! You see what happens when you stay away so long? You left a little girl and you came back to a lady. I'm seventeen now, Jonah, near as old as you were when you went to London!"

"You're not seventeen yet," he corrected her. Carey's birthday was on Christmas Day: three days hence.

"As good as, though," she scoffed, and then smiled at him again. With the smile and the excitement lighting her face it was possible to see that Carey Wyeth would be quite beautiful some day, for the bone structure was there, and the warm curve of the lips, and the straight little nose. And if, in repose, the face still seemed all oversized eyes and spiky lashes and a stubborn little chin—well, it would mellow, someday, into something worth looking at. But that was not what Jonah Wyeth saw when he looked at her.

"And as for being a lady, Caroline, Mrs. Sutton was right. You look disgraceful! What *have* you been doing?"

"Riding," she admitted after a fraction of hesitation, for she knew Jonah was going to object. "Miles Cavendish brought a horse over for me this morning—a little roan

10

mare. Poor thing, I do hope she's not hurt! She's such a gentle mount, but she slipped on a patch of ice, and—"

"I can see you've had a fall," frowned Jonah disapprovingly. "There's grime on your skirt. It's no occupation for a girl! And why weren't you wearing your bonnet? Yes, I heard Mrs. Sutton ask about that!" he said, at her guilty look. "At seventeen you're too old to be out in public with your hair flying about your back, Caroline."

"But as you pointed out, I'm not seventeen yet! Anyway, I did have my bonnet when I started out. In this weather, I needed it. But the horse trampled it. It's quite wrecked, and I haven't another."

Jonah shuddered slightly—but whether it was with the thought of the trampled bonnet, or the thought of what might have happened to his sister, no one could have been sure. "You're not a child now, Caroline. Such dreadful behavior! And out with young Miles Cavendish, unchaperoned. Perhaps I should have forbidden you to see him long ago."

"Jonah, you wouldn't!" Carey's eyes grew larger and went sooty-brown with consternation. "Miles is the only young person who lives anywhere near—except for Mrs. Sutton's nieces and nephews, and there's not one of them over twelve years old! In any case, *they're* allowed to go to school in the village, and I'm *not*. Miles and I have been friends for five years, and—"

"And he's turned sixteen now, and hardly a fit companion for a seventeen-year-old girl!"

"Sixteen," she retorted mulishly.

"Caroline, I had no idea what was going on here! I can't think why Mrs. Sutton has been allowing this to go on—and why she hasn't written to let me know!"

"What do you mean—allowing *what* to go on?"

"This riding . . . why, who knows what might happen between a boy his age and—" Jonah shuddered again. He did not yet tell Carey what had brought him here, post-haste, two days earlier than expected: the letter from Squire Cavendish that had chastised him for allowing his sister too much freedom. Had he been too lax? He had not thought so, until the letter. Today was Saturday, the only day of the week that Caroline was permitted any freedom at all. Sunday was a day of contemplation and study, the day when Mrs. Sutton took his sister to church, in the otherwise-forbidden village. The rest of her week, he knew, was taken up with French lessons, German lessons, Greek lessons, Spanish lessons, Italian lessons. Some nine years ago, when Jonah had first been converted to Calvinism and had gone to London to pursue his own studies, he had engaged a tutor, a kindly white-haired professor of languages who had retired to a cottage not far from here. It seemed that Caroline had a gift for languages. Jonah had been pleased, for it was an appropriate field of study for a young girl. But she was a young girl no longer! Well, at least her talent for languages would be put to good use now.

"Can't we stop talking about me, Jonah?" Carey was impatient to leave the subject. "I want to hear about you —about your plans. Are they still talking about sending you to that place called Otaheite—or is it Tahiti? I hope not! What would I do with you halfway around the world? Can't you be a missionary in some closer place, like Africa? And why don't you ever write? Are you still—"

Jonah interrupted the tumble of questions, firmly. "First go and change into something respectable, Caroline. Truly, I shudder to think of the way you let yourself be seen in public! If I have news, it can wait until you've put on a pair of shoes and a clean dress."

"But I don't need to change!" She tossed her head, inadvertently drawing attention to the tangle of gold.

"And do something about your hair! Do it now, Caroline." It was the tone of voice that was more father than brother, and Carey knew she must obey. But she grimaced, all the same, as she left the room, when Jonah could not see it. If turning seventeen meant tidy knots in her hair, and no horses, and none of Miles's good-natured company, she wasn't going to like it at all!

Well, thought Jonah, as his sister left the room, Squire Cavendish had certainly been right. Caroline did look like a young thing only half-tamed; and if she had not quite filled out to womanhood, she was very near it. Well, Mrs. Sutton should have been more careful with her charge. Perhaps he had made a mistake in choosing Mrs. Sutton as housekeeper nine years ago. But he had been only eighteen then, when he had made the choice, and at the time, with his sister only seven, it had seemed important to hire someone of warm and affectionate disposition. And now, did it make any difference, as he intended to take Caroline under his own wing again?

Of all the people who knew Carey, only Jonah called her by her proper name. He had always called her Caroline. Perhaps it was because he alone remembered the day of her birth, Christmas Day, nearly seventeen years ago. The frost on the windowpane brought it back . . .

His mother lay in the large fourposter bed where she had spent most of her pregnancy. Jonah had been startled at first to see the mound of her stomach no longer visible beneath the sheets. Her body seemed shrunken, her eyes large and luminous, her lips bloodless. Jonah had looked at the small bundle that lay beside her and wondered how that scrunched-up bit of ugliness could occasion such happiness.

"She takes after your father," his mother had murmured in a voice that scarcely stirred the air.

"She's nice," Jonah had lied staunchly, hoping to please his mother. "What's her name?"

"Caroline," his mother said faintly. "I thought of it when I heard the carolers last night. They comforted me."

"Oh."

"You will love her, won't you, Jonah?"

He hesitated no more than an instant. "Of course."

His mother had closed her eyes over a tired smile. "You're a good, brave boy, Jonah," she had said, and his heart had swelled. Then his father had appeared, and Jonah had been ordered out to play. He had never seen his mother alive again.

The girl-child thrived. Her fine baby-down hair changed to the burnish of old polished gold; she did indeed resemble his father in coloring. But she had his mother's finely-drawn bones and overlarge eyes, and some of his mother's vulnerability. She would cry over foolish things, sometimes even when she was happy; yet at other times, miraculously, she would display his father's fierce stoicism. Jonah remembered one time when she had been punished for some long-forgotten misdemeanor. Whatever the offense, she had denied it at first stolidly, then tempestuously: her small golden head tilted in rebellion, her tiny jaw thrust at a mutinous

13

angle. Then the strap: there had been one long, enraged, mind-wrenching howl as the belt first descended. After that, her small face had gone pale and screwed itself into a knot, as though she were trying to pretend she was somewhere else. There had been no tears. Four times the strap had descended, and at length Jonah himself, unable to bear it any longer, had run forward and begged his father to stop. No, she had not cried then, nor a month later when their father had died. She had a way of keeping those hurts inside. A commendable trait; if only she were more controlled in other ways . . .

Within minutes Carey returned, hair hastily but neatly knotted, cheeks now paler with the return of warmth. The sensible brown of her unfashionable dress did nothing to fulfill the promise of beauty. But Jonah eyed her with satisfaction: "So! You can look like a lady, after all."

Carey concealed the beginnings of a smile. She hated the dress, but she had worn it to please Jonah. The years of missionary study had made Jonah much too stern and proper for her liking; she preferred the memory of the brother who had defended her when she was little. In nine years, she and Jonah had grown apart.

"Now tell me about yourself, Jonah. You look quite worn out! As though you've been studying in that little room of yours without ever seeing the sun—burning oil all night long."

It was not so very far from the truth, but Jonah made a deprecating gesture. "Not quite all night; I couldn't afford that! But I have been studying hard. I've been trying to learn Tahitian. I wish I had your ear for languages."

"So it's true! They're planning to send you to Tahiti." Her face fell. "Oh, Jonah—"

"Yes, it's been decided. But not Tahiti—Tahiti already has missionaries. There are other Pacific islands that need me. I'll be sent to one of them."

"Jonah, that's dreadful! Well, dreadful for me—I know it's what you want. But it won't be for at least another year, will it? You *did* say that. And by then—"

Jonah interrupted her. "I'll be going next month, Caroline. I've already booked passage. There's a ship leaving for Tahiti and I must be on it, for it's hard enough to find passage to that part of the world at the best of times. Right now, with this dreadful defeat at Austerlitz, and so soon after Lord Nelson's death—why, who knows how long the seas will stay safe?" Austerlitz and defeat had followed close on the heels of Trafalgar and triumph. The news had arrived only days ago; England was still reeling with shock.

"Next month!" Surprise widened Carey's eyes. "Oh, Jonah, it can't be! Why, I may never see you again, or not for years."

"Yes, you will, Caroline," he said unsmilingly, for he knew his next words would upset her. "I've taken passage for two."

"Passage for—" Carey's heart stopped for an instant. But of course, she must have misunderstood him. She laughed, and shook her head as if to straighten her thoughts. "What do you mean?"

"You're coming to the Pacific with me."

"The Pacific!" Carey's head swarmed with dismay. She loved Jonah. But even more, she loved Mrs. Sutton, who had cared for her needs for nine years; and she loved the gentle golden Cotswold countryside; and she loved the fine quiet English air; and she loved Saturdays, on horseback, racing with Miles against the wind . . . "Oh, no, Jonah!"

"Caroline, you're coming." Jonah's expression was uncompromising. "There's work for both of us. It was meant to be! Why else did God give you the gift of languages? You know the story of the talents! You have a calling, Caroline."

"*You* have a calling, Jonah! I have none. I belong here, in England—oh, I'll miss you, truly I will. But—"

"We'll be leaving next month, from Bristol."

"You can't be serious! I won't go."

"Caroline! Need I remind you that I am your guardian, and will be for four more years?"

"But there's Mrs. Sutton," said Carey with growing desperation. "I can't leave her."

"I told her before you arrived. She'll have a small pension, and move in with her sister's family until she finds another position. She's quite content."

"And the house—"

"Caroline—. You've reached the age when I can't leave you unchaperoned. If you were older, perhaps you could stay in England. But as it is—"

"There's nothing you can say that will make me go to the Pacific—nothing! Why, I couldn't leave this house. I've lived here all my life. You can't make me go!" But in the turmoil of her thoughts Carey knew that Jonah did, indeed, have the power to make her go. But how *could* she go and leave her beloved home? The mellowed stone, the windbreak of beeches, the way it nestled into the hills— houses needed to be loved too; and the thought of it standing empty, perhaps for years . . . "I won't leave, Jonah! You can't be so cruel."

"You'll have to, Caroline. I've sold the house."

"You couldn't! It's half mine."

"I have the right to make such decisions until you're twenty-one. Your half of the money will be put aside for you, never fear, with a firm of London lawyers."

"I don't care about money! How could you have sold it? There have been no buyers to see it—nobody's come near! I'd have heard about that."

"All the same, it's sold—to Squire Cavendish. I signed the papers this afternoon."

And for a moment Jonah half-regretted his decision, for looking at the way his sister's face had gone white and pinched, he was reminded of the other time, the time she had not cried.

CHAPTER THREE

"Another round of rum for everyone! This time charge it to me." Beneath the games table, the man's heavy knee surreptitiously nudged that of his hostess—a signal that he no longer wished his drinks to be thinned with cold tea. He leaned back, expansively, against the opulent velvet-covered chair. Against his solid wrestler's shoulders, the lank brown hair, tied into a pigtail, looked vaguely incongruous. Despite the evident satisfaction in the man's face, one look at his massive bull neck and small gem-hard eyes told you he was someone to be reckoned with. All through tonight's gambling he had remained tense, cautious, menacing—but now, with the evening's winnings piled high on the green baize of the table top, he seemed ready to relax somewhat.

"Dolores! Irma! Don't just stand there! Captain Blore is celebrating. This time, bring a bottle of the very best— my private stock!" Madame Esmé, in mauve silk with a low ruched bodice that more than emphasized her ample charms, put away the cards that had just been used in the baccarat game. She leaned forward toward the third person at the games table. Lamplight gleamed on his skin. "Are you sure you're all right, Captain Falconer?"

She was answered by an inebriated groan. "Still don't b'lieve it," slurred a voice that bore only the murkiest resemblance to Adam Falconer's usual devil-may-care tones. "Gotta gi' me a chance, Blore. Gi' me chance to win it back."

Captain Beau Blore smiled in a way that didn't stir his jeweled lizard's eyes. "I've played long enough, Falconer." He fingered the property deed that had already been tucked into his pocket, quite separate from the cash and the diamond studs that still lay on the table. Ten thousand acres of good British colonial territory! Earlier, when Falconer had lost everything else, and his manservant had gone off to fetch the deed, Esmé had warned Blore that he should check on its validity. A local official had been rustled out of bed, and had testified that it was indeed a good British land title, proper in every respect. "Aye, I've had enough gambling for tonight! I know when to mucking well stop, Falconer! I'm through with work for tonight. Time for pleasure now." Blore hoisted his refilled glass to his lips, and downed half the amber liquid in a single draft. "Here's to our hostess! Best baccarat banker this side o' New Orleans."

"Bes' for you," came Falconer's muzzy voice. "Oooh—"

"Are you sure you wouldn't like to be taken to your rooms, Captain Falconer?" asked Esmé anxiously. "Perhaps with some small consolation to take your mind off your losses? Irma and Dolores do some very interesting things, especially if you were to hire both of them."

"Capn Falconer ain't able to afford it, now." From the gloomy background of the room, Noah scurried forward. "No ways! Turrible for a man to lose his whole inheritance. Cain't think what he'll do now—but a bed full o' naked female flesh ain't about to solve his problems. Best drink no more, Capn—here, I'll take him upstairs."

Falconer pushed aside the hands that came out to help him. "Lea' me alone, Noah." He slumped in his chair and began to mutter incoherently.

"Another drink for Captain Blore, Irma—and this time fill it to the top of the glass!" Esmé snapped her fingers, and then turned to tonight's winner with a radiant smile. "Worthless girls! Always thinking about their own pleasures. If it weren't for their other talents I'd soon send them packing."

Blore leaned forward and stuffed several oversize British banknotes down the front of Esmé's dress. He allowed his square hard fingers to linger rather too long. His head was beginning to feel pleasantly addled with the warmth of the liquor. "I'm sure they haven't the talents of our hostess."

Esmé laughed throatily, and pushed the bills a little deeper into her dress. "I'm afraid I go by your own credo, Captain. Business and pleasure don't mix! But I'll see you're properly attended to. I suggest—let me see. For you—I think Dolores. She likes men."

"I'll take Irma, too." Blore thrust two more banknotes toward his hostess, and drained his glass. Immediately, it was refilled. "What's that Falconer fellow muttering about?"

By now, Adam's head was lolling against the table, and he appeared too drunk to take part in the conversation. But his voice droned on.

Esmé dismissed him with a gesture. "Oh, he's still worrying about the property. Says he has no reason to stay on in Jamaica now. He's mumbling something about selling his slaves."

"Slaves?" But of course, thought Blore—Falconer must have hundreds of slaves on an estate of ten thousand acres. It would take a lot of bodies to run a plantation that size. Although Blore had won the land, he had not won the blacks to work it. For a moment, despite the warmth of the liquor coursing through his system, he frowned. It was a matter he hadn't considered in the first flush of victory; this was going to be something of a problem. He pushed his drink away. "How many slaves?"

"How many, Noah?" asked Esmé, turning to Falconer's manservant, who still hovered in the shadows beyond Adam's shoulder.

"Seven, eight hunnerd," replied Noah. "Cain't hardly work a property that size without! Specially with cane-cuttin' time around the corner. Ain't exackly sure o' how many, though. Allus birthin' and dyin', they are. But don't you worry, Capn Blore, we'll round 'em up and get 'em off the land, soon's Capn Falconer can fix it to sell 'em. He'll be needin' to now, for he'll have to go back to his reg'lar perfession. Told him he shouldn't leave the sea, I did, when his uncle died an' he came into that piece o' land. Aye—sea capn he was born, sea capn he should a stayed!"

"Sell 'em," mumbled Falconer against the green baize tabletop. "Sell 'em all."

Esmé clucked her tongue, and moved Falconer's drink farther away from the hand that threatened to knock it over. "Your master's in no condition to be worrying about this tonight, Noah. You can arrange for him to see his agents first thing in the morning. I'm sure they'll manage to dispose of the slaves right away. But tonight he's too drunk to think about it. Now why don't you take him to his rooms?"

"Wait a moment," said Blore. "Perhaps I should be given first refusal on the lot."

"I dunno about that," returned Noah dubiously. "Worth a fair chunk o' money, they are. Too much for one man to rightly afford. Aye, that number o' blacks'd have to be split up an' sold separate, specially as Capn Falconer'll be in a hurry for the cash."

Falconer's head came up and leered across the table. "Let 'm make 'n offer, Noah."

Blore did some rapid mental calculations. Seven or eight hundred slaves at an average of—conservatively —a hundred pounds each. Probably closer to two hundred pounds, for these would be seasoned plantation hands who spoke English, not like those wretched lice-ridden Ivory Coast troublemakers aboard his own ship. Yet there was no way he could raise capital for such a purchase on short notice; it would take at least two months for a bank draft to come through from England. In the meantime, the sugarcane would be rotting in the fields. Damn. It would have been so easy to let the game of baccarat continue. Tonight, with a genuine winning streak aided by the bribe he had slipped to Madam Esmé before the game started, he could not have lost . . . But now it was too late; the cards had already been put away. By tomorrow night his opponent would be sober, and hung over, and much more cautious. The man had intelligence in his eyes and on his forehead—Blore had seen that earlier in the evening. Tomorrow, Falconer would prob-ably refuse to play at all. But what was ten thousand acres without the slave-power to run it? "I'll trade you your slaves for the slaves on my ship, Falconer."

Falconer just hiccoughed and laughed, and seemed to sober a little. " 'M drunk, Blore, but 'm not that drunk." Falconer's hand retrieved the drink Esmé had taken from him a short time ago. "Wager there's no more'n a hundred blacks on your ship. Nearer dead 'n alive, too, by god."

It was true; but Blore had not really expected the offer to be accepted. He was aware that, drunk or no, Fal-coner would never agree to such an uneven bargain.

"Come, gentlemen, enough talk for tonight." Esmé smiled charmingly at her more sober guest. "Captain Blore doesn't want to think of business now! Irma— Dolores—go up and prepare Captain Blore's bed at once. And take a bottle of good rum up with you! A present from the house."

"One moment," Blore said, as Irma and Dolores left the

room. "Business before pleasure! I'll be needing those slaves. Perhaps we can come to some agreement."

"See m' agents," mumbled Falconer.

"I'll trade you my ship for your slaves."

"Thass an idea. Less see—"

"Hold your horses, Capn," Noah broke in. "No ways you can afford to buy a cargo if you trade off all them hunnerds o' good strong blacks for just a ship. Put 'em up on the block, an' let the highest bidder take 'em! They'll bring in more'n enough to buy ship an' cargo both—an' a tidy sum left over. Now come to bed— if Capn Blore's int'rusted, he can see your agents tomorrow."

Falconer drained his glass and allowed himself to be helped to his feet. He lurched toward his hostess in a drunken parody of a bow. "G'night, ma'am."

"Goodnight, Captain Falconer. So nice to have you staying with us." Esmé's half-lowered lids revealed nothing. "Do have a good sleep. The tables in this house have been unkind to you tonight . . . perhaps the beds will be less so."

Falconer leaned over and deposited a kiss on the proffered hand, and allowed Noah to drag him toward the door.

"Ship and cargo both, Captain Falconer! Ninety-seven slaves in the hold—good strong males, every one! No women, no children."

Falconer reeled back to the game table. "Howzzat, Blore?"

"Ship and cargo both, in exchange for all your slaves. Last offer, Falconer!" Blore's raisin eyes betrayed no glint of the satisfaction he felt. He knew he had Falconer hooked now; if only he could get it settled tonight . . . "Pen and paper is all we need, Falconer. We can make out an agreement right now. Tonight! Think of it—no commissions to pay, no slave auctions to go through! This way, you can get back to sea at once. Otherwise, it may take you weeks to dispose o' those friggin' niggers."

Esmé's smile hardened perceptibly, and for one dreadful moment Adam Falconer thought she was going to lose her head and jeopardize everything.

But Noah intervened: "Capn Falconer ain't about to sign nothin'! He's too drunk."

Esmé took Blore by the arm. "Isn't this rushing things

a bit, Captain Blore? You know what they say! Act in haste, repent at leisure."

Blore silenced her with a poisonous glance. Sweet Jesus, after all the money he'd shoveled down her dress tonight, couldn't she hold her tongue? Where were the woman's brains—in her bosom?

Seeing Blore's expression, Esmé allowed her tug of caution at his sleeve to change into a conspiratorial squeeze. "Pen and paper? I'll fetch them at once," she smiled. "We wouldn't want to leave Irma and Dolores alone together for too long, would we?"

Captain Beau Blore stepped cautiously into the longboat that was to take him out to the *Sweet Witch*. This morning his tongue felt like soggy ship's biscuit with weevils in it; his stomach roiled; his eyeballs ached; and his head felt as if a blacksmith was shoeing horses inside. In spite of all that, he was pleased with himself. The hangover was a small price to pay for the good piece of business he had done last night.

He was heading out to the *Sweet Witch* to retrieve some of his belongings, and to inform the crew that they'd be sailing on under a new captain. Hangover or no, he was still functioning today; he was sure Falconer was not. Yes, by God, it had been a good night's work!

The longboat pulled alongside the *Sweet Witch*, and Blore's aching eyes came open. There was an odor in the air—what was it? Blore's nostrils were wholly accustomed to the slave-ship stink; but this was something different—*vinegar?*

Was it possible that someone other than the regular crew might be aboard the *Sweet Witch?* The face of Falconer's manservant, that little monkey of a man who'd been so difficult last night, appeared over the rail. His squashed-in features registered consternation.

"You ain't aimin' to come aboard, by some freak o' fate?"

"And why not?" The freeboard of the *Sweet Witch* was low amidships, and Blore, strong of arm, managed to hoof his way up with a minimum of help from the men in the longboat. "Why in God's name not, you insolent—"

Blore's insult stuck in his throat. He looked about him with amazement. Not his own trusted crew, but men he

22

had never seen before, were moving hastily about the ship, making preparations to sail at once. Preposterous! If he had not had his back turned coming out from shore, he'd have seen the signs several minutes before.

And Captain Falconer, over there on the quarterdeck, issuing a stream of crisp orders—dammit, the man looked positively bright-eyed this morning!

Blore shoved Noah aside and strode across the deck. The first seeds of a terrible suspicion were germinating in his head. He was nobody's dunce; he knew the look of a winner. And Falconer, right now, looked like a winner.

"What the devil is going on here, Falconer!"

"And what the deuce are you doing on board? Get back to your longboat. We're making sail at once."

But the longboat was already departing, and in any case Blore had no intention of leaving until he found out what was happening.

"You can't sail!" he exploded.

"Can't I? Sorry I can't stand and chat, Blore. Better get off or you'll be sailing with us." Falconer shouted an order to two sailors heaving at the giant capstans. Blore could hear the creak of metal; he knew the great bower anchor was being raised.

"Falconer! Where's my crew?"

"*Your* crew is ashore. The *Sweet Witch* is mine now, Blore—signed, sealed, and delivered. Check that splice, Alden!" he called out to a copper-haired lad, no more than sixteen years old, who was working at the rigging.

"Falconer, I aim to find out what's afoot here, and I don't aim to be put off with any fancy words! I'm not saying I've been cheated, and I'm not saying I haven't been. But I am saying it's possible. Dammit, man, have you done it to me or not?"

"As you say, it's possible. Now if you'll excuse me—"

"Is that land deed good or no?" roared Blore.

"Yes, it's good."

"Are there any mucking slaves on it or no?"

"Blacks, yes—slaves, no. Now get off my ship, Blore! As you see, we're in a bit of a hurry."

Falconer's eyes had flickered away for an instant; Blore, noting it, followed their direction. From the side of the British warship a whaleboat was putting out, crammed with blue-jerseyed sailors and armed red-coated marines. So that was where Falconer had picked up his

23

crew—British deserters! No wonder he was in a hurry to be off. Blore flung himself to the side of the *Sweet Witch* and started to holler at the distant marines. He had a voice like a bullhorn, and the wind was with him.

"They're here! Those sodding sons-of-bitches are here! Your godrotting deserters are here!"

And then Blore could shout no more, for something iron-hard and well-aimed had connected with the back of his neck, and his world exploded into blackness.

Adam Falconer, rubbing the firm weapon-edge of his right hand, wasted no more time. The whaleboat was turning; the Britishers had heard Blore's cry.

"Sheet fore and main tops'ls! Let go aft!" Men scurried to do his bidding. "Easy away for'ard!"

Manned by a dozen oars, the whaleboat skimmed in its new direction across the water's surface, toward the now-moving *Sweet Witch*. But already the schooner's sails were filling and billowing to the wind. Slowly at first, then more rapidly, she gathered speed.

"Can't catch us now," exulted Noah, watching the distance grow as the *Sweet Witch* left its anchorage, and the whaleboat, behind.

"We're away, Noah! By god, we did it."

"You did it, Capn. An' I'm still not sure how."

"We all did it. You, me, the new crew. And Esmé . . . by the lord Harry, she earned her necklace," said Adam fondly.

"An' Blore here, what're you going to do with him?" Noah prodded the heavy-set supine figure with his toe, disgustedly, as he might have prodded a snake. "Instead o' knocking him cold, should a just turfed him over the side."

"I didn't know if he could swim, Noah, or I would've done just that. We didn't have time to hang about and fish him out again."

Noah grinned at his captain wickedly. "An' who said aught about fishin' him out?"

Two days later, on Christmas Day, the schooner *Sweet Witch*, Captain Adam Falconer commanding, dropped anchor less than a mile from the hot and dusty town of Port-au-Prince. Beyond lay the lime-green hills of Haiti—for so it was now named; just a year ago Saint Dominique (later Santo Domingo) had won its independence from

Napoleon's fever-decimated armies. It took several hours to make the necessary arrangements with the port authorities before the unloading of the human cargo could start.

At the moment, a doctor—a renegade Frenchman who had somehow survived the bloodbath of 1802—was checking over the unchained blacks for signs of infectious disease, a necessity before they could be allowed ashore. The man Blore, surly and silent, was bound to the mizzenmast nearby; and he too was waiting—with a terrible hatred in his heart.

"Be a proper load off, when this is done," sighed Noah to his master. "I ain't sayin' I won't be relieved when we put this place behind us, an' the cargo. Poor devils—sores all over, an' lice somethin' fierce. Half-starved too, with that pig slop Blore's been dishin' out! They've been through livin' hell, an' that's God's truth."

"It won't be easy for them here, Noah, but at least they'll be free men."

The French doctor emerged from the hold and gave clearance to put ashore. Despite the wretched condition of the men below, there were no infectious diseases. Noah took charge of the longboat that was to start transferring blacks to Port-au-Prince.

"Noah! Take Blore on the first boat, will you?" Adam Falconer frowned at the burly figure bound to the mast. "It might sweeten the air around here."

"Why, you—"

"Aye, Capn, an' glad to see the tail end o' him! You—young Alden—give me a hand, will you? We'll truss him good an' proper."

"No need to tie him, Noah," Falconer broke in. "If he escaped, where is there for him to go? And he won't escape. He'll be with a boatload of men who have very little love for him—one false move and they'll rip him apart with their bare hands. You know that, don't you, Blore?"

Blore's thick neck reddened with fury. "You can't put me ashore!"

But if there was hell's own fire in Blore's eyes, it was more than matched by the hard glint of disdain in Falconer's. "I'm not taking you to New England, Blore. You'd contaminate the place."

"You aim to let those mucking niggers kill me, Falconer

—to have them do your dirty work for you! Curse your rotten eyes!"

"I'd be praying, not cursing, Blore, if I were you. Now get in the boat. Take my advice and sit close to Noah. You may need protection."

"Protection!" Blore spat viciously, near Falconer's feet. "What kind of protection is it to put me ashore in Haiti? It's no place for a white man! They'll flay me alive!"

"That's something you know a lot about, isn't it, Blore? Who knows—maybe you can teach them a thing or two about techniques." A muscle worked in Falconer's jaw. "Maybe you'll live, Blore, maybe you won't. A man can survive whippings—ask those poor devils down in the stinking hold! How many died on the way across the Atlantic? A third—half? I'll give you the same odds."

"I know my rights, Falconer. I've broken no laws. Slaving's still legal, in spite of those prissy-faced abolitionists and all their ranting. I refuse to go in that boat and that's that!"

But Noah and the young copper-haired English sailor and several other deckhands pinned his arms and lifted him bodily over the side into the already-loaded longboat. Blore, in spite of his massive strength, struggled in vain.

"Stand by the oars!" called Noah as he clambered spryly into the coxswain's position, aft at the tiller. Blore had been shoved unceremoniously into a seat nearby. "Give way!"

Blore was on his feet at once, legs like treetrunks planted firmly in the longboat, even though it was already streaking toward shore.

"God rot you, Falconer! You know they'll kill me!" He shook his powerful fist at the receding silhouette of the *Sweet Witch,* and the detested dark-eyed captain who leaned over her rail, watching. "Blast you, let me out of this boat at once!"

A slow smile crinkled its way up to Falconer's eyes. "Noah! Alden!" he shouted across the growing space, "let him out of that boat at once!"

"Aye, *aye,* sir!" responded Noah with unrestrained glee; and in the next instant, with a shove from Noah and a sudden sweep of Luke Alden's oar, Blore found himself flying helter-skelter over the side.

He came up sputtering, treading water, choking with impotent ire and a mouthful of Caribbean salt. The tie that knotted his hair at the nape of his neck had come loose, and straggling brown locks streamed wetly over his eyes and into his mouth.

"Not too fast, Noah!" yelled Falconer, as soon as he could see that Blore was not about to drown. "Let the bastard swim for shore—but don't let him sink! Drowning's a sight too good for him!"

"I'll see you in hell, Falconer! You'll pay for this!" The ex-captain of the *Sweet Witch* pushed the stringy hair from his hate-filled eyes. The tearing rage in his lungs gave him the strength to shout out in spite of the waves that crested into his mouth and the wet clothes dragging at his limbs. "You've not heard the last of me! I don't die so easy, Falconer—and neither will you! Neither, by God, will you!"

⚔ CHAPTER FOUR ⚕

In January of the year 1806, under a grieving sky, the barkentine *Speedwell*, Captain Joshua Paxton commanding, left behind the hunched houses of Bristol and struck southward on a voyage that was to take more than half a year.

Joshua Paxton had been trading between England and Pacific waters for more than twenty years. Only last year he had lost an eye and part of a leg to a fearful Cape Horn storm. Now he found it difficult to manage aboard ship—although, on his stumpy wooden peg, he had learned to do so well enough on dry land. Tahiti was his destination, and he planned, once he was back in the Pacific, to sell the *Speedwell* and settle there.

As the ship lurched southward on the arduous nine-thousand-mile stretch to Cape Horn, she was at first beset by storms. The crew grumbled at this, for it was considered unlucky amongst the brotherhood of sailors to carry any missionaries. This ship carried two—although one was hardly more than a slip of a girl, and by her own account not really a missionary at all.

But then the storms abated, and with them the complaints. The journey across the Atlantic remained uneventful.

On any other ship, the men might have grumbled, too, about the unluckiness of having a woman aboard. The men of the *Speedwell*, however, were quite used to serving on a hen ship. The officers often sailed with their wives, space permitting, and until recently the captain's own daughters had graced the decks. And, of course, there was the captain's wife—slender, indomitable Mercy Paxton.

After the first two thoroughly miserable weeks aboard a pitching ship, Carey had found her sea legs—and she had not lost them again, despite the roughening weather as the *Speedwell* drew closer to the dreaded Horn.

"It's so *cold*. Is it usually this bad, Mercy?"

"It's always cold near the Horn, yes. More so at this time of year, for their summer season is past. But this isn't so bad. We're on deck, aren't we? And not quite frozen to death. When we double the Horn I doubt you'll be able to come up for air at all."

"You mean it gets worse?"

Mercy laughed. "Never worry about what might happen until it happens! But you won't see much calm water between here and the Pacific."

"Calm water . . ." To Carey, it sounded heavenly. "Is the Pacific calm?"

"Usually."

"It's strange to think my future is bound up in a part of the world I've never seen—or Jonah tells me it is, and he believes in predestination."

"Do *you* believe in it?"

Carey hesitated, then admitted the truth, although she knew that Jonah, Calvinist to the core, would have considered it blasphemy. "No. I don't. But until I'm older, I'm not free to do as I wish. Jonah may be predestined for the Pacific, but I don't feel that I am."

"Neither did I, once." Mercy's eyes traveled to the horizon and lingered there, and for a few moments she was silent. When she spoke again, it was as though she had forgotten Carey's presence. Memories tumbled back to her, crowding in upon each other, memories of all the years at sea, the good years and the bad, and most of all, memories of the Pacific. "It's so big . . . so very big. It's hard to explain to anyone how big it is. Sometimes for days on end there's nothing but the ocean and the sky, stretching away until you think you'll scream. But you don't scream, and in time you learn to accept . . . When it's placid for too many days you long for a storm, for an island, for another ship, for a shark, for a coconut floating in the water—anything to break the awful monotony. I've seen men's eyes grow hollow and red-rimmed with the sameness of the fine blue days. Men in the Pacific do things they wouldn't do elsewhere . . . Oh, it's hard to comprehend, for someone coming from a tame, safe, sane place like England. But in the Pacific the sky is larger and the colors are stronger and the men have to be stronger, too, or they won't survive . . .

"The Pacific does strange things to a man. The strong ones grow stronger, and the ones who aren't strong enough go mad, or die, or go back to nice soft civilization, and try to forget the things they've seen. They're the casualties. The others are the survivors—and there's very little in between, for the Pacific is still too raw for most men. It's only twenty years since the sealers came; and the whalers, fifteen years ago. I suppose some day there'll be more white men come to settle on the islands, men who'll try to change things—as your brother will be trying to do. I don't know if it can be done. Will he change the Pacific or will the Pacific change him? I wonder . . ."

Mercy shook herself, and gave an apologetic little laugh. "Do I scare you? I don't mean to. For all my words I love the Pacific, or I wouldn't want to settle there."

And Carey, too, pulled herself back to reality. Because for a few minutes, although she had been standing on a pitching deck and staring out at a gray and lumpy Atlantic, she had seen the golden hills of the Cotswolds in her mind's eye.

For the next three weeks, as the *Speedwell* pitted its frail hull against the Horn, Carey was convinced that she would be a casualty of the Pacific before she saw it. Here, at the southernmost tip of the Americas, where the two mightiest oceans in the world clashed and thundered against each other, there was a monumental never-ending battle of such elemental force and fury that it seemed no man-made vessel could survive. The ship became a plaything of Titans—a purgatory of cracking canvas and groaning timbers, a world of wildly clashing wave trains and sickening troughs and mountainous combers; and through it all coldness, perishing coldness, made all the worse by the fact that everything on board was soaked. Jonah, for much of the three weeks, had to be tied into his bunk; and once Carey, too, submitted to this—for at least it prevented the worst of the bruises and contusions. "A Cape Horn snifter," Mercy called it, and she seemed to remain cheerful enough, heartened by her husband. Captain Paxton was determined that the *Speedwell* would not be beaten by the Horn. Other ships—Bligh in the *Bounty,* for one—had had to concede defeat and scurry back the breadth of the Atlantic for safer passage via the Cape of Good Hope, a defeat which added half a year to any trip. The *Speedwell* had never yet had to surrender; she would not do so now.

In the end, Captain Joshua Paxton's determination paid off. The Horn was now no more than an evil memory. The eight weeks of good weather since, as the ship worked its way across the sleeping giant of the Pacific, restored even Jonah to some semblance of normality. He was not a good sailor; he would never be that—but at least, now, some of his meals managed to reach their destination and stay there.

It was when the *Speedwell* was somewhere south of Mangareva that catastrophe of a new kind struck. A small whale-oil lantern was dropped by one of the hands in the early predawn hours, and the spilled oil ignited.

Fire: that most dreaded of all occurrences at sea, for even with an ocean-full of water, there was little that could be done once the flames had taken hold. This time the *Speedwell*'s luck held. With the help of a sudden driving squall, the fire was doused—but not before there had been considerable damage amidships, where Carey and Jonah and some of the officers of the crew slept.

The sails remained lowered all through the day that followed as the men of the *Speedwell* worked feverishly to repair the worst of the damage. Despite the fact that all signs of smoke had long since disappeared below, buckets of water were still being poured on blackened wood. Half-ruined cargo was dragged on deck; so were the trunks, Carey's and Jonah's. Some of the contents were found to be scorched, the rest soaked. It was while Carey was still occupied in sorting and throwing ruined clothes overboard, and wondering where she and Jonah would sleep tonight, that the cry came from the foredeck.

"Sail on the starboard beam!"

Carey could hear Captain Paxton calling orders to the deckhands, and within moments a nimble-footed sailor had scrambled aloft. The shout came down: "Schooner, sorr, three-masted, with square tops'ls! She's hull-down now, but she's headed this way, and making good knots!"

Carey, who had stopped her unpleasant task at the first cry, now watched as the sail that had been no more than a white pin-prick grew effortlessly out of the blue sea. It

31

was like a bird, she thought—a graceful white-plumed bird. At a safe distance from the *Speedwell* the other ship hove to; and now that the two ships were lying parallel, Carey was able to see the cloud of canvas and the proud jut of the schooner's prow. She could not remember having seen a ship just like this before, with back-swept masts and big square sails set above the large triangular ones.

The schooner lowered a tiny boat over the side. Soon four men were straining at the oars, and in moments it came alongside the crippled barkentine. Captain Paxton, square and solid and optimistic despite everything, stumped over to the rail, joined by Carey and Mercy and others of the crew. Even Jonah, pale and miserable with this return of inclement weather, edged his chair closer to the rail.

"*Sweet Witch*, an' it's Capn Falconer's command," came the shout from the water. "Saw your bare poles, we did! You in trouble, by chance?"

"We were," called Paxton. "Fire in the midships—but she's under control now. I'm Captain Paxton commanding the *Speedwell*, out of Bristol. Aren't you out of Bristol too? Seems I've heard of the *Sweet Witch*—thought she was a slaver, running the Guinea trade."

"Aye, she was that! But no more. She's out o' nowhere now, 'cept the Pacific, although Capn Falconer's a Yankee. Sails where he pleases, he does, an' trades as he pleases."

Carey, leaning over the rail, liked the face of the man who spoke. Surely he had not been in the slave trade? He was a wiry, feisty little man with a pushed-in nose and a stretched-out smile, and a rather pugnacious look about his jaw. Now, at Paxton's invitation, the newcomer came over the side, and the conversation ceased to be a shouting match.

Noah looked about the desk, taking note of the scorched timbers and the remains of goods that had been brought up from below, and now lay strewn around the deck. "My name's Noah, Noah Mapes. Call me Noah—ain't a soul, man or woman, calls me Mr. Mapes. I'm here to convey Capn Falconer's compliments. He says if you're in trouble an' there's aught we can do, jest ask. Less'n it's to do with food—we're a mite low on that ourselves. Jest some tea an' porridge an' sauerkraut, and that's the whole of it. 'Cept for some coconuts an' some giant crabs

—them as robs the coconut trees. Picked up a good lot of 'em not two days ago, on a flat flyspeck of an island. That's why we're in the gig. Longboat's full up with a load o' the big devils, caged in. We could spare some o' them—meaty and mighty tasty, too, they are!"

"Our food stores survived, thank God," returned Paxton. "Some cargo damaged, as you see, but we're carrying mostly tinwares, or the fire would have been a lot worse. Our main problem is sleeping space. Where are you headed?"

"Macao—but afore that, we're bound for Tahiti or one o' them islands on the way. We been scrounging here an' there, but now Capn Falconer has a mind to take on a proper lot o' food." Noah didn't mention that his master knew he could get supplies in Tahiti without money. Metal, especially nails, was more valuable than currency in the islands, and the *Sweet Witch* had several barrelsful.

"Are you sure it's not you who need help?" asked Paxton dryly. "At least we've got food. We can give you some."

"Nay, Capn Falconer'll see us through." Noah knew that his master could not offer to pay. "You be in need o' any lumber—or nails?"

"Thank you, no. But there is one thing you could do. Do you have any room for passengers?"

"How many passengers?"

"Two."

"Bound for where?"

"Tahiti. Their cabins were burned out in the fire, and we've no empty bunks aboard, nor after today a square inch to squeeze a mattress in. I'd pay, of course. A fair portion of their passage money . . . plus some ship's biscuit we can spare."

Hard cash! thought Noah, and his eyes lit up. Aye, the Capn would like to see some o' that, an' the ship's biscuit too!

"We ain't really got a spare bunk ourselves," admitted Noah regretfully, seeing the dollar signs fade before his eyes. "Well, cept . . ."

"Anything would do. It can't be worse for them than if they stay here. Several of the crew have had their quarters burned out too, and we'll be doubling up as it is, or sleeping on deck. For the crew, I don't mind, but for the Wyeths . . ."

"Well," conceded Noah dubiously, "there is a small part o' the ship ain't in use. Capn Falconer aimed to fill it with extra stores next trip, but . . ." This time, there had not been enough money for extra stores of any kind. "Bunks in there too, if you can call 'em that. Planks, more like! Sick-room for the slaves, it was. Any o' the poor devils took on anythin' real catching, like, that's where they'd put 'em so's it wouldn't spread. It ain't no lap of luxury—though we could fix it up some, proper mattresses an' all. An' jury-rig a partition if needs be. All been cleaned out real good, too—every inch o' the ship scrubbed down a dozen times, with vinegar an' elbow grease an' good strong lye soap."

"What do you say, Mr. Wyeth?" Captain Paxton turned to Jonah, who was sitting nearby in patent discomfort.

"A slaver?" Of all the things said, Jonah had fastened on that.

"She ain't a slaver now! Capn Falconer don't hold with slavin'."

To Jonah, who longed only for dry land, the thought of trading one pitching ship for another had no particular appeal. And the idea of climbing down into that tiny rowboat that had practically vanished in the swell of the waves on its way over . . .

Noah peered at him. "Ain't got your sea legs, is it? Well, well. We'll put that to rights aboard the *Sweet Witch,* for I've some medicine that'll be jest the thing. Laudanum —ain't nothin' better for the heaves, for it makes a man sleep like a baby."

"We'll go," gasped Jonah.

And so it was that fifteen minutes later, damp trunks repacked and goodbyes said, Jonah and Carey found themselves in a small boat bound for the side of the *Sweet Witch,* with nightfall not an hour away.

Capn Falconer ain't going to like me bringin' mission folk aboard, Noah thought—not at all! The brother was bad enough—but the girl! An' a mousy little thing she looked to be too, with her churchy little bonnet an' her touch-me-not high collar. But the Capn had said to help, an' he weren't one to have his orders disobeyed. Besides, Capn Falconer wouldn't a turned down an honest penny

—or would he? Noah was not sure, for he knew how his master felt about Bible-thumping folk, and female ones in particular.

As the bucking boat approached the *Sweet Witch,* wind whipped Carey's skirt up around her ankles. She knew that Jonah, sick though he was, would lecture her later if he thought her conduct unbecoming now. As if a few inches of ankle more or less made a difference! All the same, she looked to her feet, and clenched the skirt determinedly with her hand to prevent the wind from having its way. And then, with half a dozen helping hands, she came over the side.

The first thing she saw when she glanced upward was a pair of eyes staring down at her with cold disbelief, and more raw dislike than she had ever encountered in her life . . . and with them went a face that sent her wits skittering for safety. What was it Mercy had said? The Pacific does strange things to a man. Like turning eyes into black ice . . .

Slowly, her wits returned. The man had pulled Noah aside a few paces, and the two of them were talking quietly. With a still suffering Jonah, she waited, feeling ill at ease.

He must be the captain—of course. He had that air about him. And a thoroughly disturbing sort of captain he looked to be—not at all like nice, dependable Captain Paxton! Of course this captain was a lot younger, and taller, and fitter. He didn't look to be much over thirty. And less formal than Captain Paxton too, for he wore no jacket—only a loose white shirt with a pleated neckcloth, and dark trousers of narrow cut. Maybe he would not be so bad, after all . . . his eyes had crinkles that said he had a sense of humor. But he wasn't smiling now, even though another man had just arrived to speak to him.

"Miss Wyeth—Mr. Wyeth? I'm Captain Falconer. Captain Adam Falconer. And this is Mr. Lovell, the first mate. When I'm not on deck he'll be in command. We're a small crew and we don't stand much on ceremony. You can approach him directly if you need anything."

Jed Lovell was a kind-eyed man of stocky build and middling height, with a face like a balding cupid. Carey was to learn, later, that he was totally, transparently honest; his ears reddened when he was angry or embarrassed or upset.

Introductions completed, the dark-eyed man she now knew was Captain Falconer continued: "Noah's arranging to have a partition jury-rigged for your quarters. It won't be comfortable, probably not up to your standards. But it'll be private and adequate, and a sight better than when this was a slave ship."

"Anything," muttered Jonah, who had gone quite green, "if I could only lie down. Mr. Mapes said he had some medicine . . ."

Falconer looked at Jonah Wyeth with a pensive frown. "I wouldn't take too much of Noah's medicine if I were you. He's a wizard with a bandage, but he's a little too heavy-handed with some of his remedies. A good shot of rum, that's what you need."

Whether it was the thought of rum, or the motion of the ship as it began to gather way, Jonah ran to the rail and spent several wretched minutes relieving himself of the day's meals.

"You stay here, Miss Wyeth." Adam Falconer beckoned to one of the seamen, and strode to Jonah's side. "Take him below at once, Alden. Tell Noah to give him some drops, just for tonight—but not too bloody many! Mr. Lovell, may I see you for a few minutes?"

While Captain Falconer issued a stream of instructions, Carey made use of the time to look about the ship. Its appearance did not confirm the twinges of misapprehension she had felt, for some reason, on first seeing its captain. The deck was clean-scrubbed, the lines neatly coiled or flemished, the few guns polished to a fault, brasses gleaming. It had the look of a creature cared for, as though it were really the *she* that men of the sea insisted on calling a ship.

Then she noticed, further along the deck, the longboat Noah had mentioned, with something that looked like a latticework lid over it. Would that be to confine the giant crabs Noah had spoken about? She glanced back toward the helm where Captain Falconer and Mr. Lovell were still talking. Beyond them, someone was setting a taper to the binnacle light. Carey could see, by the purplish dusk that had settled over the ship, that nightfall was not far off. Soon it would be too dark to see anything. Giving in to the impulse of curiosity she felt, she started to move along the deck toward the longboat.

On the *Speedwell*, Carey had several times seen the

star-swept tropic sky, but it happened that she had never witnessed the actual coming of night. Expecting a long soft English twilight, she was unprepared for the suddenness of what happened next, before she had even reached the longboat. One moment everything was bathed in intense purple gloom: the next, it was instant night. All at once she was swallowed in black velvet, disembodied, disoriented, alone on a lonely sea . . . The rise and fall of the deck beneath her feet added to the peculiar sensation of unreality. Although her eyes, as yet unaccustomed to the dark, could not see the Pacific, she knew it was out there, waiting, immense, reaching for her in the dark . . .

"Miss Wyeth! Now where has she gotten to?—damn!"

Panicking, Carey turned and started to run toward the one island of sanity in all this mindless ocean—the yellow pool of luminescence cast by the swaying binnacle light.

"Oh, dear!" Her skirt caught against something hard and cold and metal. She gasped and started to fall—but in the dark, a pair of hands shot out and caught her, gripping her by the shoulders. Her own hands, stretched out for the fall that never came, connected squarely with something warm and firm and human: a man's chest. And through the thin fabric of his shirt, she could feel little ends of hair prickling at her fingertips. Relief flooded her; and then, following swiftly on its heels, embarrassment. She snatched her hands away, and her pulses raced. She did not have to be told who this was; she knew.

"Are you all right?"

"I—yes," she answered breathlessly. Now she could see his dark shape, outlined by the binnacle light some thirty feet away.

"What were you doing over here?"

"You were busy and—I was curious."

"Well, come to the quarterdeck, and mind your step." She could hear a rough impatience in his voice.

"I can't. My hem's caught on something—a piece of metal."

He kneeled down, and for a few moments she was overwhelmingly conscious of his hands moving about at her hemline. At length he stood up. "It's no good. I'll have to rip it, or fetch a lantern. It's caught on a gun mounting."

"Please don't rip it! It's the only dress I have right now. My others were all scorched, or soaked."

"Lantern it is, then." He turned on his heel, and in moments he had returned with a swinging whale-oil lamp that revealed, only too clearly, the hills and hollows of his face, and the night-black eyes. Wordlessly, he kneeled again, and this time the dress came free.

"Do you always disobey instructions?" he asked, as he came to his feet.

Carey was quite honestly bewildered. "What instructions? I don't remember any instructions."

"I said to stay where you were."

"But I thought you meant I was to stay on the deck—not to go below with my brother. I didn't suppose you'd mind if I looked about."

"In the dark?"

She could hear the dry sarcasm in his voice, and reacted. "It wasn't dark when I set out, and I only went forty or fifty feet. Even my brother Jonah doesn't put me on a leash."

He was silent for a moment. "Is your brother always so seasick?"

"He was managing all right until today. But the fire, the confusion, the squall . . . it's been a terrible day altogether, and—"

The voice cut through her words. "Will he be back on his feet tomorrow?"

"No. Not unless the sea calms down."

"Well, it won't likely do that. We're in for a blow, I think." His frown, in the yellow light, was unsettling. "It would be better if your brother were around to look after you, but as he's not likely to be, I'll have to ask you to be responsible for your own conduct aboard this ship."

"I'm used to looking after myself. Are you worried about my behavior? I assure you it will be perfectly proper!"

"I'm sure it will," he returned sardonically. "It's not your behavior I'm thinking of. It's the crew . . . they're a good lot, but they're sailors, and they're human, and they haven't seen a female for nigh on four months. Nothing they'd like better than to catch a young lady on the deck in the dark."

"You seem to have very little faith in your crew."

"They're a damn good crew, and by now I know them

well enough to trust them with my life, or yours—but not necessarily with your virtue. Even those who behaved in New England won't necessarily behave here, for there's a saying that a man hangs his conscience on the Horn when he sails into the Pacific. If I had known them longer, I might not be so cautious, but this is the first time most of them have been with me. So remember it and act accordingly, Miss Wyeth."

Carey, conscious of his antipathy, flushed. "Why do you dislike me so, Captain Falconer?"

Surprise registered in his dark brows. "Direct little thing, aren't you?" Adam Falconer was annoyed with himself, and her. Had he really let his prejudices show so blatantly? "I suppose I must tell you, then, that in letting you come aboard I've made an exception to one of my rules."

"Rules? I'm not sure what you mean."

Was she going to be difficult? Probably—this type always was. A stiff-spined little virgin—perhaps a bit of shaking up would do her good. "Only one type of female allowed aboard this ship," he drawled, expecting her to understand, "and you're not the type."

Carey noticed the way his eyes had gone slumbrous and wicked, but her sheltered life had not prepared her for men like Captain Adam Falconer, and she had no idea what he meant. She blurted out: "What is the type, then?"

"My mistresses," he returned bluntly, without batting a lash. "Or ladies like 'em—for the men, after they've had a long dry spell at sea." He paused a moment to let it sink in. "Look, Miss Wyeth, nice little virgins and hardened sailors simply don't mix. But you're here and there's no help for it, and now I'm concerned only that you get to Tahiti all in one piece. Stay away from the men and stay off dark decks, and there'll be no trouble . . . Now come along, for your cabin's ready, and Noah's waiting to take you down."

Carey followed the swinging lantern along the gloom-shrouded deck. Captain Falconer had some kind of grudge against her, that was evident, for he was finding fault and looking for problems where there were none. Why should there be any trouble aboard this ship? *She* hadn't hung *her* conscience on the Horn!

⟨⟨ CHAPTER FIVE ⟩⟩

"Ice? I don't believe it." Carey, wilting and sticky in her high-necked dress of gray linsey-woolsey, could hardly credit what she had just heard. The temperature here on deck, in spite of the blustery wind, must be near eighty degrees. How could this ship be carrying ice to the Orient? She stared disbelievingly at the young copper-haired sailor who had just answered her question about the cargo. Their shared nationality had created an instant bond between them on this ship crewed mostly by Americans, and they had been making friends on and off for three days, since Carey had come aboard.

"I'll show you if you like." Seventeen-year-old Luke Alden had remained with Captain Falconer ever since Montego Bay. Now he grinned back at the slender pixie-faced girl before him. Nice eyes, he thought—if only she weren't wearing those atrocious confining clothes and that hideous little bonnet that almost hid the color of her hair. But she was young and English, and he had discovered that she had a sunny smile that seemed to light up her face. "I'm not on watch now, and I don't suppose anyone will mind. I'm usually sent down to the hold every day, anyway, to check if there's been any melting. Come along, Miss Wyeth, I'll take you."

Carey followed him eagerly, glad of the diversion. "Is it cool in the hold?"

"It's cool, but it's dark. Do you mind getting sawdust on your shoes?"

"Not at all." She accepted the arm that steadied her down the ladder. From below, the faintly musty aroma of damp jackpine sawdust wafted upward like a cool embrace, in shocking contrast to the tropic heat of the deck. Carey found her footing on the ladder and in moments was ankle-deep in soft wood particles. Her eyes, unaccustomed to the darkness, saw little at first. Even the square patch of sky seen through the open hatch, although it looked blindingly brilliant, did not shed much light.

"Here, I'll show you, Miss Wyeth." With sweeps of his arm, Luke started to push aside a small mountain of sawdust, uncovering the block beneath. In the darkness he guided Carey's hand to the frigid surface for a moment.

She savored the sensation. And to think that two months ago she had wanted never to feel cold again!

"How did you come to be sailing with an American ship, Luke?" Carey did not try to pull her hand away from his. It was a pleasant feeling, holding hands, and little question marks tingled at her skin. Would he try to kiss her? What would it feel like, to be kissed—with a man's mouth covering hers? What did people do with their *noses?*

"It's because—"

But a shadow had come over the one source of light into the hold, and there was the sound of a voice muttering: "Now who the hell left this hatch open?" A lithe long outline swung itself onto the ladder, and descended. Guiltily, Carey snatched her hand away.

"It's me, Luke Alden, Captain Falconer. Just checking the cargo."

"I checked it myself, Alden, earlier today. You might —is that someone there with you?" Falconer squinted into the darkness, picking out the unfamiliar shape. Good God: was that the mission girl? What had she and that Alden lad been doing?

Carey's voice stuck in her throat, but Luke spoke for her. "It's Miss Wyeth, sir. I was showing her the cargo."

Falconer uttered an oath that Carey didn't understand. "Get up top, Alden. And in future if you want to talk to Miss Wyeth do so in a public place."

"Yes, sir." But Luke hesitated, and looked toward Carey's shadowy form. "I'll see Miss Wyeth to her cabin."

"On the double! I'll take care of Miss Wyeth."

"Yes, sir."

Carey made as if to follow Luke's retreating form, but a steely hand barred her escape. "Not so fast, Miss Wyeth. I'll have a word with you." He paused until Luke was well out of sight, and then went on. His voice held

41

an impersonal chill. "Perhaps you misunderstood me? I told you to stay away from the men, and I meant all of them. That includes Luke Alden, even if he is a countryman of yours. I want no trouble aboard this ship."

"Surely you're not suggesting that Luke and I were doing something improper, Captain Falconer? In any case, Luke isn't one of those hardened sailors you talked about. Why, he's hardly more than a boy! Our birthdays are no more than a month apart, and—"

But Adam Falconer's voice broke in bluntly. "He's old enough to get you in trouble. And trouble's exactly what you'll find yourself in, if you insist on pursuing your friendship in dark corners."

"We haven't done any such thing! This is the first dark corner I've been in, and I feel perfectly safe here— or I did, until you came down. And as for Luke, why Luke *wouldn't*—"

"Wouldn't he? Young Alden has all the working parts, Miss Wyeth. And I'm sure you have too."

In the darkness Carey flushed, and a ripple of indignation reverberated up her spine. "I only came to see the ice. You talk as though you think I'm a woman of—of easy virtue."

"No, I don't think that. Good Christ, if you were that kind of a woman d'you think I'd give a damn whether any of the men took you for a tumble in the sawdust? Or all of them, in pairs, for that matter?" Adam Falconer rumpled a hand through his hair, and began to feel irritable. What a cussedly stubborn girl! Did she not know, did she really not know, how sex-starved men became after months at sea? Well, perhaps shock tactics were in order. "No, Miss Wyeth, I don't think you intended a damn thing. But there are two dozen men aboard this ship who haven't taken a woman to bed in months, although they've been talking about very little else ever since we doubled the Horn. You might be thinking of no more than a chaste kiss in the dark, but—"

"We weren't kissing!" Carey cut in quickly, all the more indignant because she had been thinking of exactly that when he had come on the scene. "Why, I've never—"

"What, never been kissed?" Falconer's voice was dry. "Oh God, I suppose you think kissing is some nice friendly thing done between two closed pairs of lips.

Well, it's not. It's teeth and tongues and the whole damn thing, and—anyway, it isn't kissing the men have on their minds. Or holding hands either! You're thinking about kissing, I'm talking about sex. Sex, Miss Wyeth— or haven't you heard the word said out loud before? It's what a man and woman do together in the dark. Even a prim English girl like you must have heard of that sort of thing at some time—or did you close your ears?"

Carey practically choked; people didn't talk like that! "No! I mean—oh, I'm not used to people being so crude."

"And I intend to be, Miss Wyeth, for I think you need to be shocked out of your complacency. You're not in safe, civilized England now. This is the Pacific—and men get quite primitive here. So stay away from dark holds and secluded corners, or one of the men will try something—and you'll find out he's got something to offer that you can't handle."

"Luke Alden tried nothing," she protested. "He's a gentleman, which is more than I can say for you."

"I've never laid claims to being a gentleman, Miss Wyeth, and in all my life no one's ever accused me of being one." In the darkness the light gleamed only faintly on the whiteness of his teeth. Without seeing the eyes, she could feel their mocking expression. "You're in as much danger from me as you are from any of the others. I've had four frustrating months at sea, too, and with any encouragement I might even forget that I have a built-in hatred for lemon-mouthed little church brats who pretend to go all indignant at the very thought of a man taking a woman to bed."

"Pretend to—oh, you are vulgar! Please let me pass." She tried to shake away his restraining hand. "I've heard quite enough of this. No matter what you may think, Captain Falconer, I'm quite capable of taking care of myself."

"Are you sure?"

"I most certainly am! I've got lungs, and I can scream. And if anyone on this ship bothers me, that's exactly what I'll do—scream."

His voice went soft, but she did not know him well enough to recognize the danger signals. "Is that so, Miss Wyeth? Well then, take care of yourself now."

Suddenly, too swiftly for her to know how it had hap-

43

pened, she found that her feet had been knocked out from beneath her. With a gasp and a muffled thud that knocked her breath away, she landed on the blanket of sawdust. Before she could give voice to her cry of outrage, a hand was over her mouth, and the sound that emerged from her throat was no more than an impotent gurgle. All in the same moment, her heavy skirts were thrust upward to her waist and his other hand was between her legs, clamped possessively over the cotton undergarment that alone stood between his hard hand and her innocence . . .

Panic-stricken, she struggled, but his powerful knee came over her legs, and in the damp sawdust she felt as though she were floundering, sinking, suffocating.

Then he laughed. "Stop struggling, my little English wren. I don't intend to do a thing, not a damn thing. If I did, d'you think that thin little undergarment would have stopped me just now? You don't appeal to me, not in the slightest. I just wanted to show you how easy it is, that's all. I warned you before, and you chose to ignore my words. This is to show you they weren't just words! I'll remove my hand—*both* my hands—as soon as you signify you're not going to scream. Just move your head to show you promise."

Carey's struggles gradually diminished. At last, desperate and choking with helpless rage, she made the signal. His hands came away slowly, and his knee; but she could still feel the press of his body against her side. He came up and leaned over her, his head a dark close shape. The light from the hatch revealed her face, concealed his.

"Stay away from the men, Miss Wyeth, and stay away from dark corners! Your brother's not up and around to look out for your interests, and I'm damned if I intend to follow about after you like a nursemaid, or pick up the broken pieces should some horny seahand take it in mind to rape you."

"I have more faith in the seahands than I have in you!" Her body, trembling all over, betrayed the aftermath of shock.

"You're lucky this time. I don't even intend to kiss you. And for all your air of outraged innocence, I think that's exactly what you came down here for—a little experimentation in the kissing line. And maybe you'd even let me—for that pink little tongue-tip of yours is moistening your lips and making them quite . . . Agh, get up and go away, Miss Wyeth." Disgusted with himself, he rolled quickly to one side, and set her body free. "Get out of my sight. But if you make any more trouble on this trip, you'll spend the rest of it confined to your cabin."

Heart pounding, Carey scrambled to her feet and angrily brushed the sawdust from her skirts and her bonnet. "If I've learned any lesson, Captain Falconer, it's that there's one man *not* to be trusted on this ship—you!" With a dry sound that was half-fury, half-frustration, she grabbed her skirts and vanished up the ladder.

Adam Falconer lay face-down in the sawdust for a few more minutes, cursing the betrayal of his body, until at last the throbbing in his groin became bearable.

The news of Carey's encounter traveled fast, in that mysterious way that gossip has of spreading about a ship. It was not long before every man aboard had heard some version of the goings-on down in the hold. That all of these versions were inaccurate bothered neither the tellers nor the listeners. It was a diversion—and after the weeks of empty sea and sky, it was a better weapon against boredom than the ten-times-told tales of old salts yarning in the fo'c's'le.

"Hear she fair kicked him in the shins, she did! Jest shows there ain't no knowing what's inside a book, less you peek under the cover."

"Think the Capn was peekin'?"

"Or pokin'!"

"Nay, not a chance. From the little that Nate Gordo overheard, the Capn was layin' down the law. 'I ain't no nursemaid,' he says, 'an' you ain't to be kissin' no muckin' seamen aboard this ship.' That's us, Jack! Us tars that ain't tetched a pair o' lips since 'Tucket Sound! Course Gordo couldn't see a thing. Too dark, it was, and he could hardly butt hisself in. So he jest stayed near the hatch cover an' caught the odd word. But it all took place not five minutes after that young whippersnapper Luke Alden came trundlin' up the ladder, sawdust all over the seat of 'is pants."

"That Alden could tell us a thing or two!"

"Aye, but he won't. He ain't talkin', an' he never will, for he's a close-mouthed keep-to-himself kind of lad, for all that he'll make a good sailor one day."

"What else did Gordo hear?"

"Not much, for the voices was too low. Fair soaks up the sounds, that sawdust. But she did pipe up once, an' Gordo heard 'er tell she had more stock for us common rub-a-dubs than she did for him. Real poison-voiced, too."

"Mebbe the Capn's got her dead to rights—mebbe she's been makin' eyes at young Alden. For all her high-chinned dress, she's got a nice little figger—bumps in all the right places. An' a great big pair o' eyes— brown, but kinda gold too, an' sparkly."

"Oho! So you been lookin' already. Well, I'd a been more inclined to look if it was a great big pair o' somethin' else. She's too skinny by half."

A few more raucous jokes followed, but the men had not yet deserted this fascinating new topic.

"Anyone seen under that pokey bonnet o' hers? Hair looks to be fair gold about the edges, an' it ain't no bottle job either. Her a mission girl an' all."

"I seen it once, but you ain't likely to have the same priv'lege. For all that brother o' hers is groanin' around his bunk and laid out from this spell o' weather, he's mighty concerned that she gets herself bundled up decent-like before she comes on deck, heat or no. Heard it meself, one day when I took his meal down. An' that's when I saw her hair. Aye, it's pirate's gold! But it's all fussed into a little knot behind her neck. Couldn't help wonderin' what it would be like if she loosened it up."

And then the men fell to wondering what it would be like if she loosened up in other ways. In all the conversation, nothing was resolved; but the next day, when Carey Wyeth came on deck, there were at least a dozen pair of eyes that looked at her with anything from stirring interest to open hunger, despite the drab gray clothes and the dreadful little felt bonnet.

Adam Falconer might have proved a point—but he had proved the wrong point, and to the wrong people.

Noah was not above listening to ship's scuttlebutt, except when it had to do with his captain. The other men, knowing this, and not wanting to incur Noah's righteous wrath, never discussed the captain's doings in his presence. But the mission girl was another matter—and Noah, like nearly everyone else aboard, had heard and savored the new wave of conjecture about Carey Wyeth, although he had no idea what, exactly, had triggered it. By now, in the telling, what had started as speculation had become unshakable fact.

"Kissin' and suchlike, eh? Well, I'll be blowed. An' her such a proper-looking little thing." He aimed a measuring look at the girl in question, who was standing aft at the rail, quite alone, seemingly unbothered by the bucking of the ship as it ran before a gusting wind dead astern. Her a flirty thing? Didn't seem hardly likely—but you never knew. And he went off, shaking his head, to the longboat where the giant robber crabs were kept. With the help of another seaman, Tom Huggins, he was about to fish out one of the large angry-eyed creatures for tonight's dinner. Each of the men had a long-handled gaff, or boathook, for the task; for unless handled properly, the crabs could be quite dangerous. Most of them spanned a yard or more, and their giant claws were quite capable of crushing a man's foot into pulp.

"Mind your fingers there, Huggins! Them crabs is our dinner, not t'other way around. Easy does it, now." And together, they removed the large wooden pegs that held the trapdoor in the latticed covering. With his gaff Noah started to maneuver one of the larger crabs into position, while Huggins prodded the remaining crabs safely to the far end of their temporary home in the longboat.

Suddenly, there was an outcry from one of the other men, and a scramble as several sailors flung themselves aft toward the starboard quarter. Noah glanced up, still staving off the pincers that were making angry passes at his boathook.

"It's all right, Miz Wyeth! I'll get it, right enough!" shouted a sailor, making a dive for something small and gray and a-flutter with the ribbons that had, until recently, held it in place. The mission girl's bonnet, by the Lord, realized Noah, as it skittered toward his own feet, caught in a new gust of wind. He slammed down the cover of the crab's prison—"Watch it, Huggins!"—and made a leap for the swiftly vanishing bonnet, for he

47

could see that the other crewman could not possibly catch it, and it might easily blow overboard.

His hand clutched for it, and half-caught a ribbon—but a new flurry of air tore it from his fingers. The bonnet swirled upward, out of reach, and connected with the stays'l; and there it clung, trapped against the bellying canvas by the press of the wind. By now at least ten sailors had joined the chase, and Mr. Lovell, at the helm, was calling out to find what was going on.

"Oh, dear! I'm sorry." Carey, too, had sped forward in pursuit of her lost apparel, and now she was looking anxiously up at the sail. "It doesn't matter, really. I don't—"

"I'll get it for you, Miz Wyeth," said the crusty long-armed sailor named Nate Gordo—but in spite of his reach, and even with a boost from his able-bodied companions, he was unable to retrieve the bonnet.

By now the pinnings of Carey's hair, ripped at by wind and unprotected by the confines of gray felt, were working their way loose. Honey-color hair spilled over her shoulders, and tumbled down her back—and the men, starved for just such a sight, could see that it was near waist-length, and syrupy-soft, and by jingo, the girl was quite a looker with the wind and the excitement whipping color into her face.

"Give us that gaff, there, Noah! That'll snag the pesky thing, by damn—er, pardon the French, Miz Wyeth. By *darn*."

"Ain't nobody puttin' a gaff near that sail, 'cept it's me!" Now Huggins, truly alarmed, hurried forward from the longboat. He was bow-legged and wrinkled like a prune, and he moved with the true rolling gait of a man who has been at sea for all of his life. As sailmaker and mender for the *Sweet Witch,* he wanted no one to put a hole through the stays'l with one of the long-handled iron hooks. "I'll fetch it down, don't you fret, Miz Wyeth." And with his own gaff, he reached up toward the elusive hat, and snagged it.

But just then, the schooner took an unexpectedly deep plunge into the trough of a wave. Huggins, with his eyes upward toward the sail, lurched forward a step and swiftly recovered his balance—but not before the gaff had made a small tear in the canvas. The dislodged bonnet, trailing ribbons, was whisked away into the sea. Half a dozen experienced deckhands ran to the rail and watched it swirl away in a crest of foam.

"God rot the luck!" cursed Huggins, staring in frustration at the tear he knew he would have to mend before the day was through, and preferably before Captain Falconer saw it.

"Hey! Lookit those crabs." It was Nate Gordo who spoke, boggle-eyed. "Gawdamighty, Noah, how'd they get out?"

Noah turned and gaped, and so did others. The latticed trapdoor stood open, and a half dozen huge and ugly creatures now scuttled across the deck in a desperate search for safety.

"Oh Jesus! Now the Capn'll have his dander up, for sure," moaned Huggins, racing across the deck and slamming shut the lid on the longboat to imprison its several remaining occupants. Now, on all sides, men were occupied in a new pursuit, as they snatched whatever weapons came to hand, and tried to corner the escaped and very belligerent crustaceans. Out of instinct, one quick-moving specimen grabbed for the mainmast with its enormous claws, and in seconds it had scuttled up with all the skill of a born tree-climber, and now hung near the top, glaring down balefully, daring all comers.

"Heave to!" cried Mr. Lovell. "Trim sails!" And in moments the *Sweet Witch* had turned to windward, and was coming to and falling off with shortened sails, as the men coped with this new emergency.

Carey, huddling wide-eyed against the rail, felt sick at heart. What trouble one little bonnet had caused—and she would have been so happy to see it vanish over the side, right at the start!

Suddenly, from somewhere in the distance, came a voice over the babble:

"What's going on here? Noah, what the *hell's* going on here?" It was Captain Adam Falconer, and Carey could see, when she turned and wiped the whipping hair out of her face, that his eyes were blazing-black with fury and disbelief as he stared up at the crosstrees where Nate Gordo clung. Above Gordo, the giant crab hung on for dear life with one claw, and sparred valiantly with the other.

"Well, Capn, it's a long story . . ."

And then Noah could not even complete his answer, for just at that moment Nate Gordo, with a yelp of dismay, lost a small chunk out of his ear—and Noah had to run for the bandages.

It was some time before order was restored, and only then did Adam Falconer get a full and coherent—as coherent as could be expected—account of what had happened. Noah, sheepish, told him everything, right from the beginning. They had moved down to the captain's cabin, for Adam wanted to hear the whole story in private before making any judgments.

"Damn." So she'd paid no attention to his warnings. Even allowing for the ship's gossip mill, there had to be some truth to this, or the men would not have been goggling at the girl instead of paying attention to their duties. Well, she had been warned that she would be confined to her cabin; now he'd have to do it. "All the same, Noah, I hold you responsible for those crabs getting loose. As if it wasn't enough that one of our good men had half his ear nipped off! And Ah Chin, cornered behind the stove in the galley, fencing off a crab with a frying pan—"

"Leastways, that 'un got paid off in the supper pot," said Noah with the beginnings of a grin.

"I'll laugh tomorrow, Noah, but right now I'm too damn angry. By God, that girl has turned this ship on its beam ends, with all the men gone witless into the bargain. Golden hair be damned! Fetch her down to my cabin at once—and don't dawdle along the way, or I'll think you've gone as soft-headed as the rest of them."

By the time Carey, led by an apologetic Noah, worked her way toward the captain's cabin, her hair was once more fastened in a tidy and uninspiring knot at the nape of her neck—this time braided for good measure, before it was coiled. There was no longer a bonnet to conceal its new-minted glint, but all the same she looked demure and proper—and hardly the girl to have stirred up such a commotion on deck.

"I hear you've been making trouble," Adam Falconer said tightly, when Noah had backed out the door and closed it behind him. "I warned you what would happen, and I don't make threats I don't intend to keep."

"I'm sorry." Carey's lowered eyes studied, without really

seeing it, the pattern in the opulent Oriental carpet that covered much of the floor. On first entering, she had had an impression of polished woods and gleaming brass and simple solid comfort, and light filtering through a grating in the ceiling. But at the same moment she had seen the captain's face, and the surroundings had dimmed by comparison. Now, she was tremblingly aware only of the chill in his voice, and of the looming shape that stood facing her, halfway across the swaying cabin. Out of the corner of her eye she saw the long dark-clad legs, the white shirt front open to reveal a dismaying amount of skin, the arms folded and accusing.

"Be as sorry as you like, Miss Wyeth, but you'll have to be sorry in your own cabin. When Noah takes you back there, that's where you'll stay. You're not to come on deck for the rest of the trip. You'll stay below with your brother."

"But that's not fair!" Her eyes came up to his, sparkling amber. "Surely you can't confine me to my cabin just because I lost my bonnet to a gust of wind? I've done nothing to deserve that, and it's so dark and uncomfortable down there. With Jonah it's different; he's seasick, and Noah's been giving him laudanum to settle him. But the weather doesn't bother me, and—"

"You were told your quarters would be dark and uncomfortable when you came aboard." Adam cut across her words of protest. "I'm sorry for that, but I can't afford any more disturbances up on deck." He turned on his heel, and went over to a cluttered teak desk. His voice, when he spoke again, was offhand and abrupt, as if he had already dismissed her from his mind. "That's all, Miss Wyeth. You can go."

Impotent with rage in the face of his cool dismissal, Carey started to leave. Oh, how she'd like to get under that infuriatingly indifferent surface of his! And perhaps this was why she turned, at the last minute, after she had opened the door, and said to him, not without a touch of spite in her voice:

"You're wrong about one thing, Captain Falconer! Kissing doesn't have to be the way you described it. Not at all!" The chaste lip-brushing had taken place the previous evening, when Luke Alden had found her on deck under the stars. It had been his first kiss, too, although Carey did not realize that. "At least now I know how a *gentleman* kisses!—I found out, last night, in the *dark!*"

Falconer looked up and tilted a dark eyebrow quizzically. "Do you really want to tell me with the door open, Miss Wyeth?"

"Yes! And what's more, I quite enjoyed it. *Lips closed.*"

"Oh?" returned Adam Falconer dryly. "Well, I suggest you keep them that way, from now on. That little tidbit will probably beat you up to the quarterdeck. Goodday, Miss Wyeth."

Carey slammed the door behind her, and came up full tilt against Noah's ear-to-ear grin.

⨯ CHAPTER SIX ⨯

Neither Carey nor Jonah surfaced again before Tahiti: Carey, because of Adam Falconer; Jonah, because he was in too much agony. Noah, realizing belatedly that he had led the young preacher into a mild addiction, had refused to issue any more of the opium-based drops, even though laudanum was at that time a nostrum in many a conscientious mother's medicine chest.

If Jonah suffered in his way, so did Carey in hers. But where Jonah's private hell led him through tortured nightmares of a lost and forbidden Elysium, Carey's was centered on a pair of mocking eyes that haunted her dreams. How she hated the glint of them, the black ungodly light that disturbed her so . . . Even in her waking hours, Adam Falconer preoccupied her thoughts.

But soon Carey would be leaving the *Sweet Witch* forever. The ship was about to anchor in Matavai Bay, and already, earlier this morning, Luke Alden had been down to uncleat the trunks and carry them up on deck. Within a day or two—perhaps even before the *Sweet Witch* weighed anchor and left Tahiti—Carey and Jonah would be on their way to whatever island the local missionaries saw fit to assign them to.

Oh, if only she had Jonah's unswerving sense of duty, if only her spirit did not rebel so at the thought of the years that stretched ahead . . . but no, she must not think like that. She must take each day as it came. Who knew what might happen before she reached the golden goal of twenty-one?

Now, Luke had come below again, to see them to the deck. Jonah was making a quick last-minute check of Carey's partitioned-off part of the cabin, and was for the instant out of earshot. Carey, properly attired for the deck and already wilting in her hot long-skirted gown with her hair wrapped in a woollen scarf, looked at Luke with real affection.

"You've been very good to us, Luke. I don't suppose we'll meet again, but I won't forget you."

"Carey—"

But just then Jonah returned.

"What is it, Luke?" Carey asked.

What could he have said to her, even if her brother had not arrived? He was seventeen and penniless, and he had nothing to offer. "I wish you were staying in Tahiti, Miss Carey. That way we might meet again."

Jonah looked at the pair suspiciously, but saw nothing untoward. "If you're back this way, Mr. Alden, you can always ask the local missionary where we are. Rivers . . . his name's Mr. Rivers."

"I'll remember."

"Shall we go?"

Luke hesitated. Should he warn them of the things he had seen, just before he came below? Of the dozens of outriggers and canoes putting out from shore, filled with dusky-skinned, bare-breasted girls; of the sailors waving and shouting obscenities and jostling for position at the rail amidships? But surely they must have been told about Tahiti . . .

"What's the matter, Luke?"

He sighed. "Nothing. Nothing at all."

And so, when Carey and Jonah came on deck, they were totally unprepared for the scene that greeted them. Neither of them noticed the mountains of Tahiti that jutted imposingly against the sky; nor the distant black coral beaches; nor the spume breaking on the reefs; nor the sweep of primitive color that, under other circumstances, would have assaulted their senses.

Jonah, his eyes riveted by the first bare-breasted girl he had ever seen, went gray. He had been told to expect nakedness in this heathenish country, but somehow he had not expected this—this *excess* of nakedness. Already, on this starboard side that lay toward shore, several girls had climbed on deck, clad in no more than flimsy skirts of cloth or grass, hitched casually over their hips. Sailors were pawing them quite openly, and leading them away toward the fo'c's'le or the foredeck. Even as Jonah watched with horrified eyes, one dark-skinned beauty in an approaching canoe doffed her single skimpy piece of cloth and dove in to swim the last twenty yards to the *Sweet Witch*. Several more laughingly followed her lead with an unmistakable show of enthusiasm.

Oh, wickedness, wickedness; fire and brimstone; Sodom and Gomorrah! And Jonah, remembering that this was why he had come to Tahiti, found strengths he had not had five minutes before. Regaining his wits, he hastened to the rail and ran from sailor to sailor, alternately shouting and pleading and bullying and wishing down the wrath of God, and accomplishing nothing at all.

Carey, too, had paled at the sight. But she was more resilient than Jonah, and might not have reacted so strongly if she had not spotted that tall familiar figure, some distance from the others. Adam Falconer was lounging on the afterdeck, elbows resting easily on the rail, his long frame bent and relaxed as he peered over the side. Even at this distance and in all the babble Carey could hear the disturbing echoes of his voice. Calling encouragement, no doubt, to some approaching swimmer! How could he, he who had dared to question her own mild flirtations! The thought swarmed angrily in her head, and without really thinking things through, she ran abaft and looked over the rail. A naked girl, agile as a monkey, was working her way up the anchor chain. Two others, equally nimble and nubile, were using a hawser line, no doubt thrown over at the last minute—the rope secured by a belaying pin. In the water immediately beyond, half a dozen canoes milled about, laden with men and women, waving, shouting in pidgin, bearing gifts of fruit and flowers.

Carey noted all this only vaguely, for she was too furious to think straight at the moment.

"How could you? How *could* you?"

Adam Falconer looked up with mild surprise. Oh, no, not her again! Couldn't someone have seen to putting her ashore already?

"Alden! See to getting a boat ready on the port side. Miss Wyeth and her brother are going ashore at once. Try Huggins. I think he's past his prime for this sort of diversion."

And Luke turned to do his captain's bidding with a will, for he had seen the expression on Carey's face, and at the moment he wanted nothing more than to take her away from here.

"Now look, Miss Wyeth—" Adam started patiently enough, for he wanted only to be rid of her for once and for all. The Polynesian girl who had been on the anchor chain had just rolled over the side not three feet away, and there she stood, naked and dripping, red flowers twined into her streaming black hair, and a smile on her face whose invitation could not be mistaken. And there were more coming: Adam glanced beyond the rail and then turned back. "I think you'd better go with Luke Alden."

But Carey was not to be diverted. "Don't you think you should practice what you preach?" Her voice shook with rage.

"I don't remember preaching. I leave that to your brother. The vahines—the girls—are a fact of life in Tahiti, Miss Wyeth. Eight years of missionaries haven't cured them, and neither will you. Best go now, and forget what you've seen."

"Forget *her?*" Carey made an angry gesture at the tall vahine who had just draped herself over Adam's shoulder. From one of the canoes, someone had thrown the girl's pareu aboard, and she had refastened it around her still-wet hips—but the breasts were unashamedly naked, and gleamed bronze beneath little drops of water.

Adam felt a surge of irritation. Oh, *damn* all primfaced mission girls with their accusing eyes and their militant virginity! Then, quite deliberately and perhaps more openly than he would have done at another time, he moved his arm around the vahine and let his hand fall casually and possessively over the half-naked hip. The girl, squirming against his side, began to take possession of the few things she found in his pockets.

"Go away, Miss Wyeth. You're out of your depth here —can't you see that?" And with a smile at his new companion, Adam Falconer turned back to the rail.

Carey was beside herself with impotent fury. Almost without conscious decision, she snatched for the belaying pin that held the hawser line in place. The pin came away in her hand. There was a scream—and sounds of splashing, as the freed line fell into the sea with its burden of Polynesian beauties. Adam Falconer's head snapped around.

"What the hell d'you think you're doing?" He stared at the belaying pin in Carey's hand. He shook the vahine from his arm, and seized Carey's shoulders roughly. "Are you trying to create an incident—turn the natives unfriendly?"

Without letting go, he leaned over and shouted an apology at the water, in pidgin, for he knew only a half-dozen words in Tahitian, and none of them fitted the occasion. There was a stunned ugly lull in the nearest canoes—a lull that was beginning to spread to other canoes, farther away. One of the fallen vahines had banged her head against the topsides of the *Sweet Witch*'s hull; no one yet knew how badly she was hurt. Was this Big Canoe friendly—as Captain Cook's had been nearly two generations ago, and the *Bounty* after that? Or had it come to plunder and pillage and cheat, as some of the white men's canoes seemed prone to do?

Something had to be done—and fast; Falconer could see that. Not forty years ago the men of HMS *Dolphin* had fought their way ashore in Tahiti, killing a number of natives. Memories were long in the islands. And there had been trouble elsewhere, with smaller provocation than this hot-headed English girl had given just now.

"Sorry about this," Adam said through clenched teeth. Then he seized Carey by the waist and turned her bodily, backside-up, over the ship's railing, and thrust her skirts over her head. From the canoes and from the deck of the *Sweet Witch,* all those who could see watched.

"You can't do this! Stop at once! Jonah, help me— Jonah! Oh, stop!"

But the flat of Adam's hand had already landed smartly and squarely on its goal. A laugh rippled up from the water, and it was echoed on the ship, to the accompaniment of a few cheers.

By the time a few more sharp smacks had been delivered, Carey's face was flaming with rage and hurt and humiliation—and hatred for the man who was responsible.

Then, further along the deck, the sailor Nate Gordo flung a handful of nails across to the canoe nearest him. This was more valuable than money in a part of the world where coin of the realm meant nothing; a gesture of true friendship—and at once the vahines were again laughing and jostling and shinnying over the sides, all insults quickly forgotten.

Falconer turned his attention back to the sputtering, squirming girl he still held doubled over the rail. Gradually, he allowed her to slide back down to the deck, without releasing her. Her fists and her feet continued to pummel at him. The Polynesian girl watched with lively interest.

"Give up, little one," Adam said to Carey. "You're fighting a losing battle, you and your brother."

His hands came away, releasing her, and she turned to face him. Too late he realized that it was not submission he saw in her eyes—for in the next instant, a slender hand flashed up and cracked across his face.

"That's for running a bawdy ship—and for being unfair—and for daring to punish me in public, with everyone looking!"

Ruefully, he rubbed his jaw where the imprint of her hand was beginning to come up red. At the instant of contact his eyes had gone opaque; but now there was something else in them—a strange black light, Carey noted, as little warning bells rang in her head, something quite heathenish and primitive and seen only too often in her dreams.

But his voice, when he spoke, was no more than a soft drawl: "When I punish, Miss Wyeth, I don't use those methods. That wasn't punishment, it was prevention. And as for everyone looking—" He glanced down the length of the ship, "—there's not a soul with their eyes in this direction now, except for our Tahitian friends here. And they're used to seeing all kinds of things. I usually make a point of not kissing people goodbye, but in your case, Miss Wyeth, I'll be willing to make an exception."

And with that, he seized her head between both his hands, and his mouth came down on hers—hard. She tried to push him away, but he had crowded her against the rail; and now his hand on her chin was taking advantage of her involuntary gasp to drag her unwilling mouth open. His lips and his tongue and his teeth took her by storm, penetrating her defenses, assaulting her brutally—and then, when she thought she would surely faint, he suddenly let her go.

Senses swirling, Carey let out a choke of fury and ran, as fast as her confining gray skirts would allow, over to the port rail, where Luke, who had seen none of this, was putting out the gig.

And as the small rowing craft headed toward shore some minutes later, she did not even look back to see if Captain Adam Falconer was still on deck, or if he had vanished below with the half-naked vahine on his arm. She didn't want to know—for she fervently hoped she would never, ever see him again!

ℭ CHAPTER SEVEN ℵ

How strange, thought Carey—Christmas half a world and a whole existence away from England. Was it only a year ago that her entire being had rebelled at the thought of following Jonah to the ends of the earth? She was content now; she had accepted and even grown to love this island of Mahi Mahi, where she and Jonah had been sent by Mr. Rivers, the missionary on Tahiti. She was fond of the blithe-spirited, buoyant islanders, and she loved Mamma Ruau, the enormous, warm-hearted Polynesian woman—an early convert of Mr. Rivers's—who had come with them from Tahiti, to help them with the language and customs of their new home.

Mahi Mahi was beautiful, an emerald jewel of an island, its lush foliage startlingly green against the lapis lazuli of the Pacific sea and sky. Like Tahiti, it had black coral beaches and a rimming reef that caught the breakers and sent them flying skyward, so that much of the time there was a necklace of white spume surrounding the calmer waters of Mahi Mahi's luminous lagoon.

A cloud clung to the high end of the island—a cloud that had served as a signpost in the sky to Polynesian mariners for hundreds of years; for whenever the trade winds prevailed, as they did for most of the year, the cloud remained the same. It wisped, and grew pink with sunset, and wept torrents of water upon the round crest of the mountain that breasted it. As on many other Pacific islands, the rain seldom fell into the valley where the Polynesians' nipa huts were clustered, nor on the surrounding black sand beaches. Nor did it fall here, on the rising tail of land where Carey and Jonah and Mamma Ruau lived, and where Jonah had built his frail grass-walled church. The cloud spilled its riches to the islanders in the form of waterfalls that coursed down the mountainside toward the island's central valley, and made Mahi Mahi a green and earthly paradise.

Paradise—but today, with memories of other Christmases in her mind and because it was her eighteenth birthday, Carey felt the empty ache of homesickness. There should have been sparkling frost on the windowpanes, and mistletoe, and roasting chestnuts, and the distant familiar echo of carolers—but instead the sun blazed down on the nipa huts, and the scent of ripe bananas and the faint pervasive smell of sea-things—mollusks and salt and seaweed—were heavy in the air, along with the near-tuneless warbling of Mamma Ruau's rich round voice, as she sang the words she had learned in Tahiti:

"Me belong Number One Fella,
  Me belong Pickaninny Jesu Keristio . . ."

Like many Tahitians, Mamma Ruau was incapable of coping with the "k" sound. It came out not as Keristio at all, but as Teristio.

Nor was Mamma Ruau able to cope with the sound of Carey's name, though she spoke and understood English perfectly well. Carey had asked Mamma Ruau to choose for her a Polynesian name close to her own, and Mamma Ruau had settled on the name Teura. All the islanders now knew her as Teura, or as Missee Teura— not to be confused with the title *misi*, which meant missionary, and which they had conferred on Jonah.

"For you, Missee Teura!"

"Why thank you, Mamma Ruau! What a beautiful comb." Carey accepted the handsome tortoiseshell piece, and hugged the Polynesian woman who was easily twice her size. Earlier, Carey had handed over her own present to Mamma Ruau, a sampler painstakingly worked with the letters of the English alphabet, which she had been teaching not only to Mamma Ruau, but to the children of the island. She had not yet tried to teach them English. Until now, working with the Tahitian dictionary compiled several years before by one of the sailors from the *Bounty*, she had been teaching the islanders to read and write in their own language, while she learned to speak it herself—for, as she had pointed out to Jonah, how could they be expected to read and write in English when they could not read and write in their own tongue?

61

Now, seeing Carey's evident pleasure in her gift, Mamma Ruau's broad face creased into a dazzling smile, and her mountainous body shook with delight. She touched a hand to Carey's hair—hair whose tendrils, under cloudless tropical skies, had become a paler gold around her sun-honeyed face—although the long bulk of it still nested in a coiled braid at the nape of Carey's neck. Carey had filled out somewhat in the five months on Mahi Mahi, and although she was still very slender, it was now the slenderness of womanhood. She was no longer the same girl with pinched face and overgrown eyes who had been aboard the *Sweet Witch*. The promise of beauty was beginning to be fulfilled, although Carey was not fully aware of this.

"Too nice hair, Missee Teura! You comb it out now, hey?"

The word comb sounded like "tome," but Carey by now understood Mamma Ruau perfectly well. "No, I won't comb it out now, Mamma Ruau. Jonah wouldn't want me to. I'll use your comb in a short while, at bedtime. I can't let my hair out until then."

"Why—when all-a-same God gave you hair?" Mamma Ruau sighed, for the ways of the misi—all misi —were strange. Such hot heavy clothing they wore; and why should misi Wyet' want his sister to hide her hair, when it was the color of dawn on a cloud's underside? But he was a good man. He cared for the islanders when they were sick, and taught them things about planting crops, and kept them from abandoning girl-children to the sea, and from making human sacrifices to the Great God Ta'aroa. And he was bringing to Mahi Mahi all the better things she had learned about Christianity, back on Tahiti. A good man—but strange, like the other misi, for he grew apoplectic at the free-loving ways of the islanders—and what was wrong with a man and girl vanishing together into the bushes? How could a young girl learn how to please a husband, unless the older men of the island first instructed her? The ways of the misi were indeed beyond comprehension.

All the same, Mamma Ruau had never regretted her conversion to Christianity. For some years, before the coming of the first misi to Tahiti, she had lived with a sailor, a deserter from the *Bounty*—one of the few who had not vanished with Fletcher Christian to some mysterious and unknown fate. The sailor had given her many nails, one blue-eyed child, a large fine mirror which she still prized above all else, and much prestige in the eyes of the other Tahitians. He had left some years later, on another ship, without saying goodbye; the passions of her youth had been spent; the child had died. By then only the mirror remained to show her that her lithe youthful form had long since vanished beneath vast folds of flesh. Mamma Ruau did not mind that; to Polynesians, fat was beautiful. But she had never forgotten the fine blue-eyed boy child she had adored with every fiber of her being—and when the misi came, and told tales of the pickaninny Jesu Keristio, her heart had filled once again with an all-encompassing warmth. She pictured baby Jesu as having eyes like the sky he had gone to; and ever since becoming a Christian she had been filled with a wonder of love that had been sadly lacking in her life since the death of her own child. For what was life without children?

"Where is Jonah, Mamma Ruau? I want to show him my comb. I haven't seen him since we had our Christmas dinner—and that's more than an hour ago now." Christmas dinner had been dorado, cooked with shredded coconut, and lobster and baked breadfruit and yams.

"Misi Wyet' down at beach. Go see big ship—big ship all-a-same stay. Aué! No go way."

Carey frowned, disturbed by the news. She could not see the large vessel that lay anchored some distance beyond the reef, for a rise of land and a stand of banyan trees intervened. It was a Spanish ship from the Philippines, Jonah had told her, bound, with soldiers, for Alta California. The ship was too large to breach the coral reef; only small craft could do that. The Spaniards in their longboats had spent the last two days cutting and loading wood, and refilling their water casks, and accepting gifts of fresh fruit. But they had finished with all their provisioning some hours ago, and they had still not left. It was worrisome.

"Chief Tetaheite send vahines, big ship walkalong soon enough, you see!"

"Oh, Mamma Ruau, you mustn't say such things!" Jonah had worked hard to teach the islanders some sense of sin—and in that he had had somewhat more success than Mr. Rivers back on Tahiti. Not that their promiscuous ways had all been cured, by any means. But at least, when the ship had been sighted, Chief Tetaheite, goaded by Jonah, had ordered all the young girls of Mahi Mahi to the mountains. There had been grumbling, and many wistful backward glances, but they had gone. Carey knew, as Jonah did not, that they had crept back under cover of night to sleep in their own dry and comfortable huts, only to vanish again before dawn. Jonah would have been disturbed if he had known that —just as he would have been disturbed if he had heard Mamma Ruau's very un-Christian suggestion that the girls be brought back to satisfy the Spaniards.

"Vahines like white men," Mamma Ruau said, as if that forgave everything. "White men make fine babies." Her eyes misted with the memory of her own.

Carey sighed. If Mamma Ruau, a convert of several years, could not understand, how could Jonah ever hope to instill a sense of decency into the young girls of the island? Somehow she knew that if she and Jonah left Mahi Mahi tomorrow, the rickety church that was built of matting and palm fronds might survive for a time, but their teachings would vanish without trace, washed away like so many footprints in the black sand beach.

"Help me set out the lights, Mamma Ruau, so Jonah will be able to see his way home." She made her way toward the pile of coconut lamps that lay heaped near the doorway of the two-roomed nipa hut they shared—Jonah in one room, she and Mamma Ruau in the other. "It will be dark soon—and there won't be a moon tonight. I wish that ship would leave!"

Lieutenant Diego Fuentes stood at the taffrail of the Spanish ship *San Felipe* and glowered at the island that rose up against the horizon, caught in the rays of a rapidly sinking sun. Its beauty gave him no comfort, for he was in a foul rage, and it showed in his narrow, overlong face, in the tightness of skin over bone, in the pitiless ice-blue of his eyes.

His bad temper had started months before, back in the Philippines. Fuentes had been given instructions to take a contingent of men halfway around the world to some pesthole of a presidio in Alta California—dog's leavings, that, for he had been told it did not even have the comforts of New Spain! And he suspected that the real reason behind his posting was that his superior officer had developed more than a passing interest in the lissome Filipino girl whom he, Fuentes, had found cowering behind a convent wall, and taken to mistress.

If he had had a promotion to go with the posting, he might have accepted with more grace—but he had not.

Perdición! And then there had been the other news, about the humiliating defeat at Trafalgar, a defeat the Spaniards had shared with those abominations of Frenchmen. Even though Trafalgar had taken place more than a year ago, the thought still rankled. The very mention of the hated English victors filled him with a cold fury once again.

To think that he had been forbidden to go ashore by the capitan of this moth-eaten ship—Madre de Dios! He, a lieutenant in the service of His Most Imbecilic Majesty Charles IV—in Spain a man served not the king but that slut of a queen, Maria Luisa, which really meant serving her lover Godoy, who had been largely responsible for Spain's woes. How had a despicable army officer like Godoy managed to attract such royal attention when he, Diego Fuentes, had not even been rewarded for his years of service with the lowly rank of capitan?

The ship's Capitan, Ortiz, son-of-a-puta that he was, had insisted that only the sailors could go ashore on their watering and wooding parties—while his own men, restless and champing at the bit for a taste of Polynesian flesh, had been compelled to stay on board. The capitan had at first promised that he would bring girls out to the *San Felipe*, but he had brought none. He had said there were none to be found—not that Fuentes believed him for one minute.

These stories of an Anglo missionary—spit on the English!—who had sent the women to the hills—this was too much to be borne! Of course Ortiz might not be lying about the missionary, for there was a large grass building on the rise of land to the south that could be a church. But that it should be those heretical English, who had defeated his countrymen at Trafalgar . . .

He swung around on his heel, boots clattering against the decking, and issued a crisp order to several of his men who stood nearby. Together they strode to the quarterdeck of the *San Felipe*.

"Capitan Ortiz! I must ask you to put out a longboat

65

immediately. We're going ashore at once—all my men."

"As I said, your men can put ashore tomorrow, now that the provisioning is safely completed. But you will find it is as I said—"

"I know what you said. But perhaps your elusive island girls will not be so elusive after dark, no!" Thin lips bared the lieutenant's teeth in something that passed for a smile. "Or have you just been saving them for yourself and your own men?"

"Teniente—there are no girls! Only fat ancient women like cows, and some very young children, mostly boys. Surely it is not young boys who interest you? If it is, there is one of your own soldiers . . ."

"I am not here to be insulted! I have told you what I want—what my men want."

"There are no girls," repeated Ortiz with strained patience.

"Liar!" Fuentes's face contorted and his hand moved to his sword-hilt.

The captain's eyes flickered, but he had no intention of displaying cowardice in front of this sneering bully. Girls? A man at sea had to learn to do without them, and although he was not immune to the charm of flashing female eyes and whispering mantillas, he could wait. There were always men like the young soldier in Fuentes's contingent.

Fuentes's expression, when he finally turned away, was one of cruel satisfaction, for he had heard the order given to put out the longboat.

Carey prepared herself for bed shortly after darkness fell. Here there were no clocks, only the sun—and the little coconut lamps did not shed much light for sewing or reading. Mamma Ruau was already curled up on a pandanus mat asleep in the little room she shared with Carey.

Carey slipped into her nightshift and located the new tortoiseshell comb. It was quite exquisite, really, decorated with shells in an artful island design she had seen repeated on other ornaments, and even in the tattoos that decorated the men's ankles. Well—it had been a good Christmas, after all! Who needed carolers and crackling fires and crisp English winters? And next year would be even better, for by then the homesickness would have passed entirely. She pulled out the clip that had fastened her hair into its tight knot, and unplaited the braid. Gold spilled over her shoulders and breasts, for her hair was as long as a Polynesian's. She combed it now, idly watching her own warped reflection in Mamma Ruau's badly desilvered mirror.

The mirror: she stared into it now, transfixed, and her heart beat a wild warning tattoo against her ribs. There was a face staring back at her from the doorway—and it was not Jonah's, and it was not a Polynesian face. From across the distance of the room she saw it in the mirror—long, narrow, lustful, taut skin drawn over the bone in such a way that she could almost see the skull beneath . . .

The lips that were pulled back in a thin cruel curve were not really smiling. "Madre de Dios! So there *are* English here." The words, silky-dangerous, were spoken in Spanish; and Carey, whirling around from the mirror as the man closed in across the room, responded unthinkingly in the same language.

"Who are you—what are you doing here? My brother . . ."

"So you speak Spanish, too! Your brother, where is he? I hear he has been ill-advised enough to think he can hide the island girls from my men. Well, I assure you—"

Just then, Mamma Ruau woke up with a great piercing wail—"Aué!"—and wallowed to a sitting position.

It was as if the wail were a signal, for suddenly there was a confusion of noise outside. Carey could hear the shouts of many rough voices, the scuffling of feet, the clink of armor—and through it all, Jonah's voice coming from the clearing where the church stood. She darted past the man who stood now, arms akimbo, in the center of the room, and ran to the door of the nipa hut. The man gave a nasty laugh, but made no particular effort to catch her.

"Do not think you can escape me so easily, my pretty one. Yes, look out the door—I think you'll find my company preferable!"

One glance told Carey why he was so confident. A half-dozen soldiers, swords drawn, were milling about near the entrance to the hut. At the moment their eyes were turned upward toward the church clearing, where there were perhaps ten others—some with torches, some with muskets, some with swords. Two soldiers were dragging Jonah, his face wild and pale, from the church. In the torchlight, Carey saw it all like a scene out of hell.

"No—no! You can't! This is a house of God!" Jonah screamed in English to a man who was approaching the grass-walled church with a flaming rush torch in his hand.

"The women—where are they?" The voice answering Jonah spoke in English, heavily accented.

"There are no women!"

There was a curse, and the torch moved. "Here's what we think of your English god!" The fire took hold, and licked its way greedily up the dry reed side of the edifice, and in moments the whole landscape was bathed in an unholy light.

"I ask you again—where are the women? Answer!"

A sword swept through the air and Carey realized with a shock of unspeakable horror that where Jonah had had an ear there was only a great gash weeping red over his shoulder. He screamed and clutched at his head. Carey started to dash forward, but hands came up and held her—Mamma Ruau's hands, for the Polynesian woman had pushed her way into the door behind Carey. She had seen scenes like this before, and knew it was better to do nothing.

"That will teach you to use the other ear better! Where are the women?"

"There . . . are . . . no . . . women." The voice was muffled agony now but Jonah, reeling, was still on his feet. And Mamma Ruau's hands were like a steel vise, dragging her backward through the door; and the flames, leaping higher, gleamed red on faces and on swords . . .

"Look," said a soft voice in the darkness not far from Carey. "Qué es esto?"

Several men turned and saw the women standing in the doorway. Their eyes fastened not on the enormous Polynesian woman, but on the slender girl she was clutching. The girl's face was nearly as pale as her nightgown, her hair spilled like syrup over her shoulders, and her wide shocked eyes stared toward the church so that she did not even see them . . .

But even as their rough hands caught at Carey's nightshift, the tall figure of their lieutenant thrust its way through from behind the women, and their grins faded.

"This one's mine. Hands off! Look elsewhere for your

pleasures." The snarl was a command, and the men started to back away. "You—Manuel—stay! Take the big one under guard, outside the hut."

"And mount her. If you can!"

There was a ripple of ribald laughter, but the men were not really amused at being cheated of their find—especially Manuel, who could see all his evening's entertainment frustrated by the lieutenant's unfortunate choice. For even as he took the Fat One from the doorway, shouts and screams from the valley below told that girls had been found in some of the grass shacks and bushes, and were being dragged from their hiding places by the soldiers who had gone to search the village.

"Would you rather I returned you to their tender mercies?" The lieutenant's oily voice penetrated Carey's shock. "Pah—animals! They would spread your legs and stake you to the ground—believe me, I've seen it done before! No, my little beauty, I have other methods. I'm in no hurry—not like those savages out there, who'll be through almost before they have time to adjust their clothing. Efficient, believe me, but hardly the way to take the most pleasure out of the situation. So you see, my dear, you're really better off in my hands." Lieutenant Fuentes unbuckled his sword unhurriedly, his eyes like blue hoarfrost never leaving the girl for an instant. Her heaving chest and horrorstruck expression told him she was already terrified beyond imagining, and that was how he liked it. Por Dios, he'd take his time with this one! She'd be a virgin too—this type always was. Let her fight and claw for a time; it helped arouse him and only made the eventual surrender sweeter. And surrender she would, just as the little Filipino girl had surrendered at last, cowed and cringing, worn out by her struggles. It was no good if a girl was too willing, for what was the pleasure in that?

He hoped this one would not be too easy. She had already retreated across the room and now stood, frozen, where he had first seen her. She looked as though she was too shocked to understand what was happening—and that was no good; she had to understand. At least she spoke Spanish!

"Take off your nightgown," he commanded, knowing she was too paralyzed to obey. He didn't even want her to obey. "Take it off, and spread your legs for me."

She didn't stir, and he moved toward her, panther-like. "Take it off!" His hand cracked across her face, not too hard yet—that would come later. All the same the jolt drove her head to one side. She gasped but didn't scream as he might have wished; but he smiled, partly satisfied, for the brown eyes were kindled for a moment with points of golden flame. She was not in a state of shock, not yet.

He let his long-boned fingers slide through hair still rippled by the braid that had fastened it during the day. The fingers lingered, tangling in a strand that cascaded over one breast. "Castilian gold," he murmured. "I wonder if it is the same all over?"

And with that his hand moved to the ribbons that fastened her collar. Slowly, deliberately, he undid them—and then, taking his time to draw out his enjoyment of the expression he saw in her eyes, his fingers insinuated themselves beneath the cloth and found the flesh. The valley between, the young round rise, the nipple . . . Suddenly, viciously, he twisted the flesh, and heard her sharp intake of pain.

That was when they usually started to fight in earnest —why was this one not fighting? Why did she just stand there, her little fists clenched until the knuckles showed white?

"Take off your nightgown," he ordered again, his voice like iced butter. "There are men who would rip it from you—shall I do that? Before I take, I intend to see— yes, and to have you turn before me in the lamplight, too! Have you never undressed for a man? Ah, I see you have not, for your soft little breasts still shrink away from me. Is my touch so repugnant to you? And will you shrink from my fingers when they touch you else-where, I wonder? Such modesty!" And with that, he wrenched abruptly at the virginal white cloth of her nightgown. It parted with a sudden rending sound, and then—taking his time again—he pushed it aside to reveal the body beneath. Why was she not fighting? *Why?*

"Gold all over, I see," he sneered, and let his hand slide between her legs for just an instant. Then, without warning, when she still did not respond, the hand came up and cracked again across her face, harder then be-fore. "Puta! English puta!"

The stunning force of the blow knocked her off balance. She fell to her knees. But then she looked up at him with eyes like a cornered cat, and clawed herself to her feet.

Good, he thought for one fleeting moment, she is going to fight back! Then he saw a face coming at him, a cruel distorted death-mask of a face, and too late he realized it was his own face—and his world exploded into a thousand shards of pain and light, as Mamma Ruau's large and treasured mirror crashed full into his eyes.

Nothing was left of the church now but embers. Mamma Ruau sat in the dark outside, cradling her huge body and rocking back and forth in anguish at the sights that greeted her eyes from the valley below. Aué, such misery! that the soldiers should be taking so forcibly what should have been given so freely! And the poor little girl, Teura, inside the hut with that cruel-looking popaa, the white man—no good had come of sending the vahines to the mountains, no good at all! Tears coursed freely down her great fat cheeks. The church was gone and the misi Wyet' had already perished, mutilated beyond recognition, and with him the beautiful altarcloth. And what if her own life ended tonight? If she died then it must be the will of the Great Gods Ta'aroa and Tane, whom she must have offended mightily by listening to the Christians. She realized it all now, too late, for this scene was one wrought by the white man's god—and it was evil, all evil!

She paid no attention to the soldier who stood beside her, sword drawn, nor he to her. He had long since decided she was too fat to pose any real danger—three hundred pounds if she was an ounce, and slow, like a great waddling turtle. His eyes were moody as they drifted over the carnage below. Lucky dogs, those other soldiers that had not been made to stand guard! In the distance he could hear their raucous voices, their shouts of triumph. But he was really listening for the sounds inside the hut, sounds that might tell him when the lieutenant had had his pleasure of the girl, for with luck she might be given over to him.

He had been expecting cries for some time, and he was instantly alert when he heard the blood-curdling howl that issued from inside. For a flash he thought it was the girl, breached at last, but then he realized that

71

it had not been a woman's voice. He hurtled to the door of the hut and flung aside the matting that covered it—and there was the captain, clutching at his bloodied face. And the girl, now near-naked, standing over him almost dazedly, holding a handsome wooden frame and the remains of what had once been a mirror.

The next thing Manuel knew, some inexplicable force knocked the wind from his lungs, and he himself was thrown to the floor. His sword skidded away, out of reach, and something enormously heavy landed squarely on his shoulders.

"You hurt, Missee Teura?" Mamma Ruau looked anxiously at the white girl from her perch atop the stunned soldier.

For a moment the words were bottled in Carey's throat. Then she found her voice. "Yes, I—"

"Mamoo—no talk," warned Mamma Ruau, dipping her head at the Spaniard who was now on his feet and staggering around, blinded by the blood that streamed over his face. He was no longer screaming. Instead, weird retching sounds issued from his throat as he clawed bits of glass from around his eyes.

But Carey had still not recovered her wits, and she said in a stupid strange choked voice: "I broke your mirror."

The Spaniard, like a blinded enraged bull, lunged toward the direction of her voice, but Mamma Ruau shouted a warning, and Carey moved a few inches, just in time. Fuentes crashed against the wall of the hut, knocking out one of the support posts and falling to the ground in a tangle of plaited matting.

"You broke him good, too," grinned Mamma Ruau, ebullient now that the Spaniards were being paid in kind. It seemed that Ta'aroa had given her another chance, after all, and perhaps she would be allowed to live until tomorrow, but they must get away from here and hide at once, while the other soldiers were busy below. She knew of a little cave not far away, near the banyan grove—no one would find them there. Later, she would tell Missee Teura about her brother. "Hurry," she said needlessly, for Carey, working feverishly now, had already started to shred her torn nightgown into long white strips that could be used to tie the men.

The soldier beneath Mamma Ruau had started to

struggle and issue strangled sounds. So she reached over and snatched a piece of the ripped cloth, and stuffed it in his mouth. Then she bounced once or twice, happily, to the accompaniment of cracking ribs.

Terrible things had happened—oh, terrible! As for the mirror, her most prized possession—well, there would be time enough to weep for that tomorrow.

⊱ CHAPTER EIGHT ⊰

Adam Falconer sat cross-legged on the sand, waiting, as he had been waiting nearly thirty hours—ever since dawn of yesterday morning. His face was impassive, betraying none of the concerns, none of the misgivings that gnawed at him. For several hours now he had hardly moved a muscle, except to take a few brackish drops from his water flask, and even that was dry now. The noonday sun was scathingly hot, the black stretch of sand was like a blast furnace. And it was becoming apparent that his patience was not going to bear fruit.

The six other crew members ashore were showing signs of restlessness and heat exhaustion. They wanted to return to the *Sweet Witch* and make sail at once, in search of a friendlier anchorage. He could not find it in his heart to blame them. But Falconer knew only too well that, in this part of the Pacific, there were islands where not even a longboat could put ashore without being dashed to death on the rocks; others where the coral reefs were totally impregnable, affording no channel for even a small boat to pass; and some where there was no fresh water—none at all.

The *Sweet Witch* was desperately in need of water. There had been no rain for weeks, not since they had doubled the Horn, and the little that was left in the water casks was covered with a greenish slime, almost undrinkable.

At least this island—Mahi Mahi, it was called on the charts—had water. Unfortunately it had inhabitants too, hostile inhabitants. Yesterday morning the unfriendly faces of spear-carrying men had barred the way to the waterfall that tumbled down the hills not a quarter mile distant.

So, yesterday afternoon, he had had his men spread gifts on the beach, and all night and all day the islanders had been creeping closer to the strip of sand where an incongruous collection of chamber pots, china dishes, mirrors, and odd pieces of metal lay strewn around Falconer in a vast semicircle. Every once in a while a near-naked bronze-skinned figure would dart from behind some cocopalm or banyan tree, and the semicircle would grow a little smaller. Adam pretended not to notice, as he pretended not to notice the passage of time.

Time—that was the thing. Very soon his men would start to die. Perhaps they would be scooping up handfuls of Pacific brine to quench their thirst—but madness and more thirst would be their only reward.

He came to a sudden decision, and called quietly across to the waiting longboat.

"Noah!"

Noah Mapes moved, less spryly than usual, across the burning black coral sand. He reached his captain's unmoving figure and waited for instructions without speaking. His tongue already felt unreal and swollen from the parching heat of the sun, and his water bottle, too, was dry.

It took well over an hour to comply with the instructions he had been given, and it was with relief that Noah saw his master sitting, still unharmed, as the longboat pulled once more into shore. The circle of gifts had diminished, visibly.

Noah trudged back to where Falconer sat. "Where d'you want 'er put, Cap'n?" He pointed at the unwieldy metal object that weighed down the longboat. "Like to sink us, it did—almost down to the gunwales."

"Bring it here, on skids. But first start a fire, close to the boat, to warm some water. Not too hot, mind."

It took four men and all of the half-hour that the water was heating to wrestle the enormous claw-footed cast-iron piece out of the longboat and up the beach to where the captain was sitting. At length it was ready.

"Crazy notion," grumbled Noah, tipping the last huge kettleful of hot seawater into the bathtub, to top up the buckets that had previously been carried up from shore. "Here's the soap—and the scrub brush."

"Well done, Noah. You can go now." Adam Falconer calmly started to strip off his clothes. He laid them ostentatiously on an empty water keg, some distance from the tub. Then, without allowing himself even a surreptitious glance toward the trees, he stepped into the hot bathwater.

Long before the first party of islanders actually arrived at Falconer's side, Adam knew that his ruse had worked. By now, thank goodness, the water had cooled somewhat: it had been warmed not for comfort, but for dramatic effect—because he had wanted to build the suspense of what he was doing.

For nearly half an hour men had been abandoning the shelter of the trees, and edging closer, inch by inch. They were confident, now, that the white man was unarmed, for they had seen him quite naked and defenseless. Nevertheless they stayed in a wide wary circle, each waiting for some braver soul to make the final move.

When it came, it was not from any of the encircling men, but from a party that marched straight out from the woods, without preliminaries. Falconer registered no surprise. He continued to scrub his back with the long-handled brush, but he took good note of the newly arrived group out of the corners of his eyes.

There were seven or eight of them, all men, except for one enormously fat woman who must have weighed nearly three hundred pounds. All but the woman and one other man were armed—and he, as imposing in his bulk as she was in hers, appeared to be the chief. Adam knew this not only from his size, his age, and the richness of his feathered garments, but from the marvelous intricacy of the tattooing that covered his arms, his legs, his chest, and indeed every visible part of his body. Birds, fishes, sharks, cocopalms, and crabs sprouted on every available inch of skin, in a display that was a testimony to the patience of the artist and the endurance of the recipient. Falconer paused in his scrubbing and inclined his head, gravely.

The party circled the tub. Then the chief, as befitted a man of bravery, touched it—and all at once, men were stroking the rims, sliding their hands over the ornate fruit-and-flower patterns sculpted in the metal, trying in vain to lift the edges, dipping in to feel the water and splash it tentatively with their fingers, all the while chattering in a garble of Tahitian that Adam could not understand at all. He wondered if they were debating the possibility of trying to drag the tub, contents and all, into the woods. Indeed, he was not far from the truth.

"It will not be so heavy without the Tall-Man-from-the-Big-Canoe," pointed out one venturesome warrior. "Let us tip it over, and spill out the water. Then we can run with it to the trees."

"It is heavy for running," observed another man, less optimistic by nature. "But we have many spears. Let us kill him."

"No." It was the chief who spoke. "The men in the Little-Canoe-with-Oars may have firesticks. And we all know what firesticks can do. They will surely leap to defend their leader. Then others will come, from beyond the reef."

"Their leader is unarmed," pointed out a man who had just appropriated Adam's clothing and searched the pockets. "Perhaps they too are unarmed. We have seen no firesticks."

"The white man has many weapons," judged the chief in his wisdom. "Some firesticks are no larger than a conch-shell, and they might easily be concealed in the Little-Canoe-with-Oars."

The other men fell silent. Their chief had been to Tahiti in his youth, and knew many imponderable things.

"It is true," nodded Mamma Ruau sagely; and the men listened, for although she was only a woman, she too had seen much that lay in the far reaches of this ocean they knew as Moana-Nui-o-Kiva, the Great Ocean of the Blue Sky. Moreover, she even spoke the language of the popaa, the white man.

"We will trade for it," announced the chief firmly, and nodded to Mamma Ruau. "Proceed."

Mamma Ruau turned to the tall white man in the tub. Adam was still scrubbing doggedly at his water-logged skin, and wondering how much more saltwater punishment he could take.

"This one veree fine bathtub, *tane*," she started. Unlike most of the other islanders, she had seen this kind of contrivance before, and knew what it was called.

So that's why she's here with the men, thought Falconer: she speaks English.

"A very fine tub," he agreed solemnly, lathering his armpits for the twentieth time.

Mamma Ruau pursed her lips, and her eyes narrow.

The chief would not thank her for appearing too eager. Better to let this dark-haired popaa be the first to mention the possibility of barter. "Men have much trouble to bring tub to Mahi Mahi. Why for you bring tub?"

"I have a bath in this tub every day," explained Adam truthfully enough. "Why must I do without my bath, just because the great chief of Mahi Mahi wishes to keep me waiting before he barters?"

"Every day?" Mamma Ruau was astonished. She did not think white men bathed daily, as Polynesians did. Her sailor-lover of many years ago had not had a bath every day—no, not even every month. Perhaps that was because he had had only a wooden tub, not a fine iron one like this. But she must pretend not to be too impressed, or the price of the tub would go up. "Why—when there is ocean to swim in, all-a-same?"

"It is a very special tub," lied Falconer. "It has much mana. It once belonged to Captain Cook."

Mamma Ruau translated some of this and the men around her sucked in their breath, unable to conceal their awe and admiration for this truly important piece of news. The great Captain Cook—or Toot, as they pronounced it—was by now a demigod, a legendary figure even in the most remote islands, as this was. There was a buzz of voices, and at length Mamma Ruau turned back to the tall stranger in the tub. She was a trifle hesitant about this request she must now translate.

"Chief Tetaheite says veree good to sit in tub of Great Toot."

"Tell him he may sit in it if he wishes." Adam stood up, dripping, and bowed in the chief's direction with a dignified sweep of his arm. Then he stepped out of the tub, and with much ceremony handed the scrub brush to the chief, whose attendants were already winding him out of the length of tapa cloth that encircled his ponderous middle.

With equal aplomb, Chief Tetaheite, clad in no more than his feathered headdress and his tattoo marks, climbed into the now-tepid bath. Some of the water, displaced by so much bulk, sloshed over the side. He lathered himself all over as he had seen the white man do—as he had done himself once, many years before, in Tahiti. Solemn-faced, he tickled his toes with the long-handled brush. Everyone watched, fascinated. He made a circle of his fingers and blew a fat shiny bubble through it. Gasps of delight greeted this astounding feat. Even the white man had not done this!

Oh, this was fine! thought Chief Tetaheite. He must have the tub, and some soap with it. He spoke a few words to Mamma Ruau.

"Chief Tetaheite say tub veree fine, a good tub for a chief." She made no further efforts to beat around the bush. "What you want for tub?"

Falconer stroked his chin, gravely, knowing the serious bargaining was about to begin. He wished he had his clothes now; it would add to his prestige. But he could not ask for them yet. And he could not let the islanders suspect how desperately his own men were in need of water. Chief Tetaheite was nobody's fool. He might decide to procrastinate until the sailors thirsted to death, then seize the bathtub anyway.

"The tub is not for trading," Adam began.

Mamma Ruau did not believe him, yet. "We have plenty breadfruit, fine young chickens—"

Falconer shook his head.

"Bananas, coconuts, tapa cloth—"

"Not for trading."

"Oyster-seeds?" Surely the prospect of pearls would arouse this tall fine-looking popaa, with his body as straight and strong as the tamanu tree. But no, he only turned away and stared out into the distance, unconcernedly. Mamma Ruau's face crumpled at the prospect of failure, and she turned to confer once more with the chief.

"He is interested in nothing," she said.

Chief Tetaheite thought for a moment, and rubbed his enormous belly with what was left of the cake of soap.

"Every man wants something," he pronounced shrewdly, and men about him nodded their concurrence. "Offer him some vahines. That was what the other white men wanted, ten moons ago."

She turned and made the offer, which was greeted with silence. Adam was gauging the success of his ruse. If the chief was offering girls, it meant some measure of trust had been established. Girls would be welcome, they were always welcome after the long celibate months at sea—but water was the urgent need.

"Eight vahines—no, ten," pressed Mamma Ruau, as

79

Chief Tetaheite held up his fingers behind Falconer's back. At least the tall white stranger seemed to be wavering. "They walkalong in Big Canoe, sail with you."

Under other circumstances it would be tempting, but . . . "Tell Chief Tetaheite his offer of vahines is very generous, and I am honored," returned Adam regretfully. "But I cannot trade the tub for vahines. I am sailing to Tahiti. I cannot return the vahines to Mahi Mahi."

To Adam's surprise, Chief Tetaheite agreed with alacrity that the girls need not be brought back to Mahi Mahi, if only a trade for the tub could be arranged. So the old chief was that anxious . . . well, he would have no trouble getting water now.

"Tell Chief Tetaheite that the tub is not for trading," Adam repeated after a moment's reflection. "But I might make a gift to the great chief of the island of Mahi Mahi. A gift of the tub of Captain Cook."

Mamma Ruau expelled her breath in an explosion of relief. So it *was* vahines the captain wanted! She told the chief, who at once gave the order to send a runner into the hills.

She gave the news to Falconer, and told him the girls would come to the shore at dawn tomorrow. But there was more business to attend to. "How much soap you trade?"

"You told of other things we shall want, if I am to trade soap. If you give these other things, I will fill the tub with soap twice over." Fortunately, there was a large supply aboard the *Sweet Witch*.

Mamma Ruau's round face grew suspicious. Surely he would not want vahines—and pearls besides! She knew pearls fetched a great price now in Tahiti; white men killed for them; and there were very few pearls on Mahi Mahi. Now, she regretted that she had mentioned them earlier. "What things?"

"Breadfruit, bananas, coconuts, young chickens, pearls," Falconer reeled off, and when the fat woman started to look alarmed, he added with a satisfaction he did not let her see: "But if you are short of pearls, you may fill our water casks instead. And return my clothes."

Mamma Ruau agreed and looked pleased, and so did the chief when he was told. What a fine bargainer for a woman, he thought to himself, looking up from his bathtub with admiration. He had often noticed what a truly splendid-looking specimen she was, regal in bearing and mountainous in size as a chieftain's wife should be. And now to discover she was wily as a shark besides! An important chief, as he was to be with this new possession, would surely need another wife.

"Tell the popaa he must also take the misi vahine," Tetaheite ordered, for it occurred to him that if he were to take Mamma Ruau into his hut it would be necessary to get rid of the white girl who lived with her. In his royal residence, she would only be an encumbrance.

The tall stranger's face registered surprise.

"Misi?" Was that why they'd had such a cold reception here—because the missionaries had been at work? And a female at that! Well, he'd tangled once with a mission girl, the one he'd delivered to Tahiti a year and a half before—strong-willed, tempestuous little chit that she had been! But he kept his voice calm, and revealed none of this to Mamma Ruau. "With vahines aboard, ma'am, I can hardly carry a misi."

Chief Tetaheite, watching him, observed that for one fleeting instant the stranger's eyes became black and turbulent, like the clouds that sometimes came with the Great Wind. He did not wait for Mamma Ruau's translation of Falconer's words.

"Tell him it is not necessary," broke in Chief Tetaheite, for he did not want anything to jeopardize the bargaining that had just taken place. And anyway, he had a plan. It would be fun to trick the white man.

Happily, he wriggled his toes and watched the ripples shiver across the surface of the water.

Carey had seen the *Sweet Witch* arrive and anchor beyond the reef. She had recognized the ship at once—and memories of its dark-eyed captain had made her acquiesce, only too readily, when she had been told to go up into the hills with the island vahines.

Jonah had died from the wounds inflicted by the Spaniards—Jonah, and four of the vahines, and nearly sixty of the island's men—almost half the male population. The sorrowing islanders had built a new hut for Carey to share with Mamma Ruau, and donated some valuable lengths of tapa cloth; and these she now wore as the Polynesians did, wrapped and tucked around her body like a pareu or kind of sarong. The only difference was that, where the island girls draped theirs over the hip, Carey wore hers above the breast. Some taboos died hard.

When the first days of grieving passed, she had started to rebuild her life. She had learned to swim, taught by a child half her age, in a part of the lagoon that was sheltered and private. She had learned to avoid the deadly and beautiful fire coral; she had learned where to find shellfish, and which species were poisonous. She had learned to husk a coconut, and to eat fish half-raw, sprinkled with seawater and cooked only by the heat of the sun on a rock. She had learned to pretend indifference, as Jonah would not have done, when island couples vanished into the bushes—and when they emerged, minutes later: the girl with her pareu hastily rehitched, the man proudly displaying on his face and on his shoulders the deep scratches that told of the swift, furious love-making that Polynesians call Maori style. She had learned a great deal more of the native language in the past ten months than she would have believed possible. She had learned how to bake a whole pig in a buried earth-oven built of hot stones; she had learned which roots were edible, and how to prepare them. She had learned to survive.

The night, the soft black insidious night, was the worst. She woke often, nightmare clashing with the night-darkness, the memory of blood and violence strong upon her. It clutched at her throat and she could not cry out to dispel the awful dreams. It was only when, in the dark, she found the solid comforting shoulders of Mamma Ruau, sleeping on the mat beside hers, that the nightmare would give way to reality—and then, gradually, peace of a kind would seep back into her soul.

So she had been astonished and afraid when Mamma Ruau explained what she was expected to do. "But Mamma Ruau, I can't! In the first place, I can't speak Tahitian that well."

"Yes, can do! White man no know."

"But my hair, my skin—"

"Mamma Ruau fix, you see." Already the vahines were out searching for the roots and tree-barks that would conceal Carey's fairness, dye the long golden hair, and stain the skin to a believable shade of brown. She explained all this to Carey.

But Carey was far from ready to agree. "I don't have Polynesian eyes!"

Mamma Ruau pursed her lips and thought about the problem. Then her eyes lit up. "I catch one white baby, long time. Other vahines all-a-same catch white baby. You white man's baby. French sailor's baby, hey?" She was enormously pleased with her solution.

"But Mamma Ruau! They *have* to know that I'm different."

Mamma Ruau understood at once. Missee Teura did not want the white men to think she was aboard for their pleasure, as the other girls were. But Chief Tetaheite had already thought of that.

"We tell 'em you tapu," she said proudly.

Carey considered the prospect. Tapu—or taboo—was a fearful interdiction among the islanders, but would it hold water with a group of hard-bitten sailors? She thought not. "It won't work, Mamma Ruau."

"Yes, all-a-same work! Big boss white man, he say one vahine tapu—no touch."

So Captain Falconer had agreed. Somehow Carey thought he was a man who would keep his promises—although why she was not sure, remembering those hellfire-and-damnation eyes. All the same . . .

"I won't do it, Mamma Ruau."

Mamma Ruau looked crestfallen. It was very important for her to convince Missee Teura that she must go. Much depended on it.

"Too much bad, Missee Teura. Aué!" And with that she burst into tears.

"Mamma Ruau, whatever is the matter?"

And with that it all came out. Mamma Ruau wanted to go and live in Chief Tetaheite's hut—but she felt she could not do so without taking Carey. The chief would take Carey into his compound, but she would have to sleep in a hut alone. How could he share his pandanus mat with Mamma Ruau, and a white girl, too? And what would happen in the night, when those dreadful nightmares started? Unless Carey went back to the mission house in Tahiti, all Mamma Ruau's hopes would be dashed. Such an opportunity would not come again.

"But if there are to be other girls aboard," Carey objected weakly, "they will gossip. Perhaps one of the

83

sailors will understand enough Tahitian to find out the truth about me."

"No-good vahines all-a-same say nothing! Chief Tetaheite tell 'em that tapu. No talk!" Mamma Ruau didn't bother to explain to Carey why she was so positive the other girls would not talk. Chief Tetaheite had threatened to call down the vengeance of the Great God Ta'aroa upon the sons and the son's sons of the very first offender. For good measure, and to show that he meant it, he intended to bury all the now-living relatives of any such loose-tongued vahine with the cornerposts of the very next royal residence, which was to be started within the next two moons. And the cornerposts would need, as everybody already knew, four living bodies to hold them up. "No talk, you see!"

"All right, Mamma Ruau, but I hope the captain keeps his promise."

The tears vanished like magic, and sunbeams took over Mamma Ruau's face. "He keepem, you see! Chief Tetaheite send plenty vahines, good vahines! No man see you." And she believed it, for why would any man worth his salt choose this scrawny thing when he could have a tall, sturdy Polynesian girl skilled in the arts of love? Especially when the golden hair and honey-colored skin were dyed to the prescribed shade of darkness? And even more especially since Chief Tetaheite had told her he planned to send twenty girls, not just the ten he had promised? That way there would be plenty of vahines for all sailors—and it would solve the problem of having too many females on the island, which had caused not a little trouble since so many of the men had been killed last year. Oh, he was a fine clever man, was Chief Tetaheite, and he would bring her much mana in her old age!

The black velvet star-filled night had long since fallen when Falconer finally returned to the *Sweet Witch*. He had remained wakeful and watchful as the natives rolled the full water-casks down to the shore; as they brought heaping baskets of breadfruit and bananas, and great piles of coconuts, and a coopful of scrawny chickens.

The night of sleeplessness and the two days of sitting in the full blazing sun, near-waterless, had taken their toll. Every fiber of Falconer's being was exhausted, and he had fallen gratefully into his comfortable bed, not long before dawn, without even removing his clothes.

In spite of this he was instantly alert when he heard the commotion on deck at first light next morning. Adam tumbled out of his bed, yawning, and made his way to the deck.

"You can't have her, I tell you!" To his surprise, Falconer recognized the voice of the first mate, Jed Lovell. Lovell, of all people! Not like him to make a scene over a woman. Adam moved forward and the men, seeing their captain, fell aside to give him passage.

"Beggin' your pardon, *Mister* Lovell, but she's mine." The answering voice was barely civil, in spite of the seeming politeness of the words. Falconer recognized first the voice, then the small cranium and great meaty hands of a sailor who'd shipped on several months before to replace the ship's carpenter who had come down with cholera. He had not liked Starbuck even then—but he'd had no choice; there were no other ship's carpenters available, and it was a vital post on a long sea voyage. During the weeks they had been at sea, he had grown to like Starbuck even less. Now, the man's fleshy fingers were fastened over the arms of a Polynesian girl. The girl, unwilling, was shrinking from him. She seemed slighter, finer-boned, less durable than the rest of the girls, several of whom stood nearby, watching the proccedings with a lively interest. Many of the vahines, already chosen in the straw drawing that was going on, had scattered to other parts of the ship with their new tyos, or mates.

Falconer's voice broke across the babble. "What's going on here?"

The men fell silent at their captain's words, all but one. Starbuck had staked his claim; and he stubbornly kept his hands on the Polynesian girl.

"She's mine, Cap'n! I won the draw, fair and square—'twere my choice next! But Mr. Lovell, he's got his eye on this 'un, I'll wager. Ain't right that she ain't in the choosing."

Falconer made no judgments, not yet. "What's the other side of the story, Mr. Lovell?"

"She's the one who's taboo, Captain. I told them all not to choose this one."

"Taboo!" Starbuck spat over the rail contemptuously, taking care to give good clearance to the spotlessly scrubbed deck, or the captain would have had his hide. "I spit on their taboos."

"There's no call for that, Starbuck." Falconer kept his voice crisp and level, but he frowned. Starbuck was a born troublemaker, but this was not the time for a show-down. "These taboos are very important to the islanders. She may be the daughter of a chief. They're not given the same freedoms as the other girls."

"Fat chance o' that! She's a sailor's by-blow, an' no mistake . . . *Captain* Falconer." Starbuck was furious that Falconer had arrived on deck. He had thought he was going to win this altercation with Lovell. Sure, he'd heard that son-of-a-sewer-rat first mate tell the men not to pick this particular girl—which was exactly why he had done so. He was certain the hated mate wanted her for himself, and the memory of many slights, real or imagined, had given him the impetus for this small piece of revenge. "Taboo be blowed! She ain't no chief's daugher."

"It's true," came another voice, "the fat one said 'er pa was a Frenchie, a sailor went on the beach in Tahiti. She ain't even one of the locals. Look at 'er eyes."

Falconer did—and saw flecks of gold sparking back at him. The eyes were brown, but amber-brown, not the soft coffee-brown eyes of an islander.

"Eyes or no, she's not to be touched. I've given my word."

"But—"

"Get your hands off her, Starbuck. Choose again."

The mutinous expression on Starbuck's face deepened, then schooled itself. At last, with a muffled oath, he dropped his hands and turned toward the remaining women.

But Lovell had seen the expression on Starbuck's face. He pulled Falconer aside, and lowered his voice. "I don't think we've seen the last of this, Adam. I don't trust that Starbuck any more than I'd trust a shark. He'll take the girl if he gets half an opportunity."

Falconer glanced at her again. She had moved to the ship's rail now. Her eyes were turned away, toward shore. In spite of the heat of the morning, she appeared to be shivering in her skimpy pareu. Why was she taboo? Was it some foolish island superstition? Unfortunately, he'd never spent enough time in these islands of Polynesia to learn the customs. Most of his time in the Pacific had been

86

spent around Macao, and before that, whaling in the waters north of Hawaii.

"D'you know her name, Jed?"

"Teura . . . the fat one called her Teura. Seemed to be mighty concerned that we would look after her properly."

"And why the taboo?"

"She didn't say. Just that it was a very powerful one, and if the girl was molested in any way there'd be trouble, big trouble, when we got to Tahiti."

"Better keep her well away from Starbuck, then. And the other men too. They're a good lot, but dammit, they're no angels. Does she speak any English? Pidgin?"

"Not a word."

"Damn. Well, somehow you'll have to get it across to her that she can't stay with the other girls. She won't be safe in the fo'c's'le—nor on deck."

"Where shall I put her, then? There's no space in the hold this trip. If you'd not had those plank beds taken out to make more room for stores, we could have jury-rigged something. But as it is—"

Falconer clucked his tongue impatiently. "Get rid of her now, will you, Jed? Put her anywhere safe—lock her in my cabin for all I care. But get her out of harm's way, and then get back up top. We're making sail at once."

Then, bringing his voice back up so it could be heard across the deck: "Ah Chin! Get that food below, will you?"

CHAPTER NINE

When Mr. Lovell led Carey below, she went with him readily enough. She had learned on the trip out to trust the kind-faced New Englander, and she was relieved to be away from the desk; relieved, too, that Noah had not been present; that young Luke Alden had drawn a long straw, and been one of the first to vanish with an admiring Polynesian vahine on his arm. And most of all, she was relieved that Captain Adam Falconer had not recognized her—but why would he? Their encounters before had been few, and mostly in dim places. When Mamma Ruau had finished her work yesterday, she had smiled with satisfaction. "Mai tai! Veree good! No see white vahine now!" Carey's long golden hair was now jet black, her skin dyed a deep copper color. Mamma Ruau had heated a dark mixture made up of roots and barks and berries, and while Carey soaked in it, the same mixture was applied to her face. When Carey had looked in an old piece of mirror in the chief's hut, she had not recognized the dark-skinned native girl that stared back at her. She saw also, with some surprise, that she had changed since her earlier sojourn on the *Sweet Witch*: her face and body had filled out to more womanly contours. It seemed she would get away with it.

But now, Carey could not prevent the shiver of alarm that touched her at the sound of the key in the lock. The captain's cabin—*his* cabin. She could not avoid facing those mocking black eyes again—oh, they had not been mocking a few moments ago on deck, but she knew how soon they would be if Captain Falconer were to find out the truth about her! Should she beat on the door—beg to be put back on Mahi Mahi? But there were no sounds of sailors moving beyond the bulkhead; and soon the creak and groan of timber and the new pitch of the ship told her that the *Sweet Witch* had put out to sea. It was too late to do anything but wait, and hope. And at least the cabin was quite dark. It would be hard for the captain to get a good look at her in this dim light.

She amused herself by inspecting the furnishings—the fine inlaid sea chest, brass-bound; the comfortable chairs; the heavy teak desk strewn with navigational charts and papers. The large captain's bed—she preferred not to look at that, and turned her eyes away forcibly, for memories of its disturbing occupant came tumbling back.

By the door there was a huge brass urn, scrolled with characters that looked to be Chinese. And in the far corner a large wooden tub, which looked out of place amidst the simple solid luxury of the rest of the cabin. She guessed that it had been brought in as a hasty replacement for the monstrous claw-footed metal one; like everyone on Mahi Mahi, she was well aware of the story of the bathtub.

A tall, substantial locker in one corner opened to reveal his wardrobe. The clothes were mostly plain and dark, and all well cared for. There were drawers full of faultlessly laundered white shirts, some of the finest silk—most simple in style, but a few ruffled or finely plaited. Another drawer pulled out to reveal a good gold timepiece, scissors, a razor and strop, some onyx-studded buttons, some mathematical instruments. What did it tell her about the man? So little . . . The only thing that looked as though it might have meaning to him was an American copper coin, a one-cent piece some ten years old, with a flowing-haired Liberty image on one side. The coin had been drilled with a hole so that it hung on a length of plaited silk. A good-luck piece?

By the time Adam Falconer made his way wearily back to his cabin, he had long since forgotten about the morning's exchange with Lovell. It had been a busy, confusing day up top, but at last order had been restored. The supplies had been cleared from the decks; the island girls had mostly vanished below to the fo'c'sle, or sat in quiet clusters on the foredeck, gossiping and giggling. The sailors had reluctantly returned to their appointed watches, their bellies full of sweet water and their brains full of an even sweeter contemplation of the off-duty hours to come. Falconer, for his part, was too tired as yet for any such diversions. In forty-eight hours he had managed only three of sleep—and it was sleep he needed now, more than any woman. Tomorrow he'd choose one . . .

He was a little surprised to find his cabin locked. But he decided Noah must have done it, as a precaution against the light-fingered vahines on board. Just as well, for navigation would be impossible without his chronometer and sextant and some of the other all-too-tempting instruments inside. He turned the key, and stepped into the cabin.

"What the deuce—!" he swore softly, under his breath, as he saw the outline on his bed. Then he remembered. Christ, couldn't Lovell have put her somewhere else? With a flash of irritation he recalled that he himself had suggested his cabin—and in truth, where else was there?

Damn Noah's eyes anyway, for not warning him she was here! He could have ordered a makeshift bunk to be rigged up—could have had a hammock swung from the bulkheads, for there was plenty of room. Then he realized that his manservant had not been present this morning, had not witnessed the scene on deck.

The girl was asleep, quite soundly asleep by the looks of things. She had not disturbed the sheets, but lay on top of the cover. She was lying face-down, one hand thrown above her head and curled trustingly, like a child's. In spite of his bone-weariness he felt a quick regret. Teura—that was her name, wasn't it? Yes, Teura. She was quite lovely, really—liquid curves scarcely hidden by her pareu; why did she not wear it as the other girls did, he wondered? Slender brown limbs, finer-boned than one would expect of a Tahitian; impossibly thick lashes that, fanlike, cast shadows over her high cheekbones; long black hair that appeared to be softer-textured than that of most of the Polynesian girls he'd seen. The French blood, he supposed. The hair looked as though it would wind like spun silk around his fingers. It would be easy enough to wake her, to find out if she was willing . . .

He thrust the thought from his head. She was taboo, and he had given his word. God knows what trouble might land on his doorstep if he violated her innocence!

He quelled the momentary surging of desire and without looking at her again, he extinguished the lamp and stepped out of his clothes. It was late; he was tired; and if the girl was sleeping in his bed—taboo or no taboo—she'd have to sleep beside him. To a Polynesian girl it would mean nothing. He eased the sheet from under her body, and placed it over her. She stirred in her sleep, and made a small sound. He slipped in beside her, and with the habit of years at sea, he was asleep in moments.

The dream started as it always started. There was darkness and a great void, and she was running until the breath exploded in her lungs and the sweat streamed into her eyes and over her naked breasts. But fast as she ran, she could not seem to move forward; she was rooted to the spot. All at once someone was standing before her. She knew it was Jonah. And she knew he had been there all along. She turned her face to him with a smile of relief, and Jonah smiled back—which was horrible, for his mouth was no more than a gaping red wound, and blood streamed from the side of his head, and his body was fearfully mutilated . . . but the smile, and the eyes, were Jonah's. Gruesomely, appallingly, Jonah's . . . Terrified, she tried to run again. Then she realized she was not running at all, or even standing, but was pinned into place on the ground, panting with a truly nameless terror. The eyes that looked into hers glazed over and went blue, iceberg-blue, and they were not Jonah's eyes at all; and the face grew long, and the fingers which were really skeletons reached down and touched her in intimate places, and her body started to tremble all over. The eyes, the cold blue unforgiving eyes came closer, wanting something, some essential and untouchable part of her, something she knew it would kill her to give . . .

Adam woke in the dark to hands clutching at his shoulders, and instantly all his senses came alert. The girl's hair streamed across his face, and her mouth uttered little whimpers, meaningless whimpers, soft incoherent sounds. He tensed and then his arms came about her, enclosing her, whether for comfort or for some other reason he could not have been sure. His nostrils filled with the scent of her, a subtle compelling scent, like crushed herbs or hidden mosses. His mouth touched her forehead and moved against it, muttering soothing things, discovering the taste of her; brushing away the little beads of moisture that had gathered on her brow.

For a moment she seemed to relax against him, to cling. His body responded, and she did not move away. He thought: she's Tahitian, and for a Tahitian to make love is as natural as sunlight and birdsong, as inevitable as the lapping of the tides on the coral reef. His mouth moved down and found the hollows of her eyes, the lashes spiky against his lips; and suddenly, hardly aware of what he was doing, he had shifted and her body was beneath his. Tiredness, taboos, promises—all were forgotten, and there was only this, this urgency in the night, this meeting of flesh-on-flesh, this melding of softness and hardness, the smoothness of her skin under the scar-roughened texture of his, this surging of his body and the yielding suppleness of hers.

When, in the dark, the hands eased her back against her own side of the bed, Carey woke with the flooding sense of relief that always came when she realized that this had been, after all, no more than a dream. Mamma Ruau was here; she was safe; the nightmare ebbed. She nestled against the pillow and sighed with something like acquiescence, so that Mamma Ruau would know that she was all right now.

But the hands did not go away. And that was the first confused realization she had that this was not Mamma Ruau whose broad comforting shoulders she had found in the night. What was happening? Where was she? Who was this beside her? Was it the dream, continuing—and was this the Spaniard whose hands were moving against her skin, in a way that Mamma Ruau's hands had never moved—in a way that was as intimate as if they had been her own hands?

Oh God—the hands were unfolding the pareu from her body. It was the dream, it must be the dream! A knee nudged her legs apart, and suddenly there was a heavy weight poised over her, and there was a head buried in the hollows of her neck. She whimpered again, and her feet tried to move as they had so often tried to move in the nightmare, but once again she was helpless, pinned in the black void as she had so often been pinned before.

She gasped, a single soft gasp, as something warm and moist and hard sought the secret places of her thighs, found its goal, forced the first difficult part of the entrance. All at once she knew this was no dream. She knew where she was—and she knew who he was. This was different, this was real, this was happening. And he was doing the thing she had been fleeing in her dream . . . She lurched sideways, then, wildly, upward, in a desperate attempt to escape. A dagger-thrust stabbed through her core. Oh merciful heaven! What had he done to her—*what had he done?* A spreading stickiness slid over her thighs, as pain shot through her loins and became a fire in her lungs, and she could no more cry out than she could stop this torture that drove deeper into her with every thrust of his hard maleness.

And by this time Adam Falconer, after nearly four celibate months at sea, could not have stopped himself either.

He had realized almost at once that she was a virgin, as soon as he had started to breach the passage. But by then it had been too late. Moments before, he had heard the sigh of acquiescence, had sensed the sleepy acceptance of her body as he placed her against the pillow. By then his long-starved body had been on fire for her. Surely she had not been unaware of what her actions would lead to—she had seemed very eager to lose her virginity! Her hands came free, clawing, and found his face. Or was she fighting?

"Oh Christ! So it's Maori-style you want." But he had no wish to have his face marked in this quick violent style of island love-making, as many of the sailors' faces would be marked by tomorrow. So he paused, poising his full weight against her hips, and trapped both her hands in his. He pulled them upward, above her head, and snared them against the pillow with one of his. His other hand traveled back to her thrusting breasts—Lord, what a wildcat!—then down to her arching hips, grinding them against his own until the storm in him crashed and climaxed, and then, at last, abated.

Afterwards, he spoke to her gently, needing, somehow, to reach her in the darkness. He wanted to light the lamp, to see her body before him all at once, unclothed—the body that had given him so much: pleasure, and release, and innocence. But somehow he sensed that she would not want the lamp lighted. She had turned away from him in the night and lay, quite still now, saying nothing. His hand drifted down her spine, trying to soothe away the tenseness he felt in her. Dammit, he should have been able to control himself better—should have been able to wait until she, too, had been readied for the ending. Curse these long sea voyages, they did that to a man . . .

He spoke to her softly although he knew she would not understand. He expected no answers, and got none.

"Teura—what a pretty name. Almost as pretty as that slender little body of yours feels. What soft skin you have! A back like a baby's—no, don't move away from my hands. See, they can find you even in the dark. There"—his fingers slid to her hip—"no, don't cringe. Did it hurt very much, my dark-skinned beauty? It sometimes does, the first time. But it won't next time, you know. Next time it will be beautiful for you, too. What a passionate little hellcat you'll be once you're truly awakened—and how I'd like to be around to see it! But you'll have to sheathe those claws of yours." He firmly put away a hand that threatened to impede his progress. "That's the Polynesian in you, sweet. God in heaven, how did you reach womanhood intact! It must have been a very powerful taboo—"

His hand, fondling her hip, moved over the barrier and started toward her thighs. She pulled right away from him and cringed against the bulkhead, at the very farthest edge of the bed.

"So you understood something I said, did you, my little Teura? Well, it's too late for taboo, do you understand that—too late! I am sorry, but what's done is done. No, I'm not sorry. I'm glad it was me. I'd do it all over again —even if I knew in advance you were a virgin." His searching hand found the hair that had fanned out behind her on the pillow, closer to his touch. He smoothed it, then wound his fingers into its cornsilk texture. Not like Tahitian hair at all . . .

His voice went on, wooing her with its gentle tones. "Do you know you're doing it again, you little witch? I'm on fire for you already—and I'm not even touching you now! I wonder if you're ready yet—or if it still hurts. Oh, Teura, there are things I could teach you that wouldn't hurt at all—not at all, not even now! I'm sure you'll have a talent for it. You have a very intriguing little mouth, you know. A very French mouth. And quite remarkable eyes for an island girl . . ."

His hands had started to move, very slowly, over the curve of her shoulder, and his lips were still murmuring things into her hair, things she hardly heard for the tumult in her brain. She huddled her arms about her breasts, protectively—oh, if only he would leave her alone, if only he would go to sleep so she could think! From her youth she remembered overheard whispers, after church meeting-time, between two matrons: they had left her with the impression that men did that sort of thing—took you and then fell asleep, snoring. Perhaps if she stayed very still and pretended to be asleep herself he would do just that. If he went to sleep she would be safe for a time. So she lay unmoving, unprotesting, feigning slumber, forcing her body to grow limp and unresisting under his touching hands.

How else could she stop him? Fighting seemed to do no good. He understood no Tahitian; she already knew that. And she could hardly speak English to him: that would most certainly give her away. Could she bear for him to discover who she really was? No! The very thought of it made her body feel as if it were blushing all over with shame. He thought he had taken an island girl—let it stay that way. Perhaps, if she had been wakeful enough to protest earlier, before she had lost what he was determined to take from her, it might have helped. But now it was too late. She was no longer a virgin, *he* had made sure of that. Let him not also have the satisfaction of gloating over her when he discovered who she really was! He had said some moments ago that she was arousing him again, and now she knew what it meant—it meant that *that* part of a man's body became a weapon, a weapon for entering and probing and punishing. Would he—heaven forbid, would he rape her *again*, even knowing the truth? None of these were possibilities she wanted to face. No, he must not find out who she was! She could not speak to him, could not stop him, could not tell him to take away his hands that were inching forward, insinuating themselves beneath the arms that protected her breasts, stroking her skin with surprising gentleness. Sleep, pretended sleep: that was her only defense.

"Teura, ma petite, ma belle . . ."

She could not hide the involuntary start, this time, at the sound of his voice. He spoke French! And very well too, for now he went on, with an excellent accent:

"So you're not asleep, my little one! I didn't think you would be."

And she was supposed to be half-French, the product of a seafaring deserter who had gone on the beach in Tahiti. It would not be extraordinary for her to answer him in the same language. He would never, never recognize her voice, for she spoke French quite fluently and the inflections were entirely different. Perhaps somewhere in that rakehell heart of his there was enough gentleman left that he would obey her wishes, and remove the persistent and marauding hands that were tracing tingles across her skin.

"Je ne veux pas, monsieur," she whispered in a throat-catching voice, and then, continuing in the same language: "Please don't touch me."

"So you do speak French!" He laughed softly, but his hands did not move away. Instead they caught at her shoulders and pulled her unwilling body in a half-turn toward him. He rose up on one elbow, leaning over her. She could see his silhouette in the darkness, lit by the silver moon that had risen high enough, now, to shine through the skylight's grating. "I thought you might speak your father's tongue."

She saw his shoulders, broad and uncompromisingly masculine, bend toward her in the quarter-light; saw the way the muscles rippled under the skin still a-sheen with the exertions of minutes ago. She felt the tingle of his furred chest against her bare breasts. His face was in darkness, but she could almost imagine the expression in his eyes—triumphant, self-assured, the all-conquering male—oh, how she hated him at this moment! She wanted to weep, to storm, to rail at him, but something stopped the words in her throat. She shivered, in spite of the warmth of his body against hers, and tried to pull the sheet between them.

"Je ne veux pas," she repeated in a husky whisper. "Monsieur, please do not touch me—I hate you to touch me! Please leave me alone. I am not—"

But his mouth came down over hers, gently this time, opening and closing over her lips, trailing soft messages that were new to her experience. This was not how he had kissed before. This, too, was an assault, but a different kind of assault. When she gasped, his tongue probed, but with none of the violence, none of the harsh earlier compulsion to invade and vanquish. If he felt passion this time, it was a more controlled passion. He was using none of the animal strength she knew he possessed. Why, now, did she feel unable to stop him? What were these strange feelings rioting through her veins, surging across the secret places of her skin, like messengers that traveled even before his following hands?

"Teura, sweet Teura," he murmured against an ear that seemed, for the moment, to have found silky nerve-endings she had not known existed. Her limbs felt like water, her lungs like an explosion, and the soft words of love spoken in French did nothing to restore her sense of balance. "Now it's your turn, Teura. I'm sorry I couldn't wait before—oh God, what continence does to a man! It's been so long, so very long. And a virgin too—if I'd known that, I'd have made myself wait, I'd have taken more trouble to arouse you. I'm too used to taking what I want, and too damn used to women who know what that is—"

She protested again, breathlessly, but her feeble protests were lost somewhere in the whirlpool of feeling between them. And how could he pay attention to protests when her hands, clinging to his shoulders like the hands of a drowning swimmer, gave all her protests the lie? Yes, she was drowning—drowning in the discovery of the new and startling sensations that were taking over her body, all the more violent as they were unexpected. Nothing in her experience had told her she could feel like this. Reason and propriety had flown; sensation had become everything. Sensation was a pulsating knot somewhere deep in her belly that ached for—what?

And yet, groaning and nearly beside herself, she made the effort to pull away when his lips moved down and sought her breasts. The breasts felt hard, engorged, sensitized—oh, what was his mouth doing to her? It played over the nipples, teasing them, touching them, lifting away . . . then came down again to claim her moistly, greedily, as a hungry suckling child might claim a mother's breast.

"Please, oh please," she moaned, but whether to deter him or to beg him to go on, she no longer knew herself.

"What a shy little body you have! It doesn't know what to do yet, does it? Open your legs, my sweetheart—no, don't push me away. It doesn't still hurt there, does it?"

No, it didn't hurt now, not in the way it had hurt earlier —but still, the trespassing hand had restored her to some of her senses. What was she doing, what was she letting him do? When she twisted away, horrified, he did not insist, not yet. His hand traveled instead to her belly, smoothing, soothing, gentling her against her sudden alarm. And his other hand went to her hair, moving in her scalp, comforting.

Were those really the same hard male hands that earlier had hurt, bruised, punished? That had pinned her struggling arms and scorched her breasts . . . these hands that now traveled over her skin so lightly, so surely, with such devastating gentleness?

"Non, monsieur, je vous en prie . . ."

But moments later, when his hand once more stole lower and broached the forbidden triangle of her thighs, fingertips barely brushing against the flesh, his mouth covered all pleas and protests she might have uttered. And her own mouth, self-willed, opened to let his tongue plunder as he wished. This time, when his fingers sought and parted the softness of her thighs, she made no effort to close her legs against him. Her very being seemed, now, to be concentrated in the mound of flesh that submitted to his stroking fingers and she wanted—what did she want? She wanted something that made her hips strain upward against his hand, that made her once-reluctant legs obey when he eased them ever farther apart, that made her whimper low in her throat when his fingers found and felt and buried themselves in deeper flesh. There was no pain this time, only an exquisite agony of the senses, an inevitability of something that must come now now now . . .

And he, feeling her body arch upward beneath his hands, feeling the compelling convulsions of her loins that he had not expected so soon because of the instinctive shyness of minutes before—he knew that she could not be contained for the mounting he now, once again, desired so urgently. So he increased the tempo and the rhythm, and plunged his fingers deeply, deeply . . . and let her go without him. She crested, dry wrenching sobs shattering her newly awakened body, and shuddered into stillness.

"Oh Teura, Teura, my beautiful one, my sweet . . ."

And she, floating and falling back to reality, could hardly believe what had happened to her. Could it be true? Had she really felt those things; had he really been able to make her forget—everything? Forget all the constraints, all the proprieties of her upbringing, forget what she was and where she had come from? Forget that she did not even *like* him? And was this the thing she had been running away from in her dreams? Oh, it could not be!

And as reason returned, so did a confused sense of guilt. What she had done was wrong. She knew it was wrong; it had been drummed into her through all of her formative years. Yet how could it be wrong? The vahines of Mahi Mahi did not consider it wrong—and at last she understood what it was that lured them, laughing, into the bushes. It was too beautiful, too strong, too natural, too instinctive to be wrong! Yet in her own world, it was wrong.

But she was not in her own world. A small inner voice said it to her, soundlessly, seductively, sinfully. She was thousands of miles away from her own world, a world which in any case no longer really existed, for Jonah was dead, and she had no other living relatives. She was in a world where it did not seem so very strange for a man and woman to meet and mate, strangers in the night, casually and without the giving and taking of vows—a world where the fact that a man's hands were still unashamedly exploring her nakedness seemed to be quite unrelated to any prudish thing she had ever been taught.

Who would ever know? The wing-flutter of newly discovered sensuality circled the notion and found it irresistible. Who would ever know? Not Mr. Rivers, the missionary in Tahiti—he didn't even know, yet, what had happened on Mahi Mahi. Certainly not a soul in England. Not even this sea-captain whose experienced fingers and sensual mouth were already stirring her body anew. *He* thought she was a brown-skinned island girl, and in the week or so it took to get to Tahiti she would take care that he found out nothing else. Strangers in the night, a chance encounter. And when he sailed on . . .

But she was thinking too far ahead. There was only the now, only this moment in time, only the male-hard body that was poised again over her own upward-surging limbs. Oh, she wanted him, she wanted him . . .

He penetrated, and all else was an illusion but the meeting and the melting and the way he was filling her, fulfilling her; imprisoning her senses, and setting them, finally, free.

What was this thing he had taught her about her own body? That she could be as wanton, as shameless as

99

any island girl . . . that she could be as much on fire for a man's body as he was for hers. Did it matter that she didn't love him, when this was only to be for one stolen week out of her life? Did anything matter any more?

"Teura, my beautiful Teura, turn and kiss me." She could sense the sleepiness, the completeness in his now-slaked body. Idly, his hand stroked the firm hollow of her stomach—his hand brown as her belly; his arm, unsunned above the wrist, a paler brown, hard-muscled, hair-roughened, a stranger's arm.

"Teura, speak to me. Look at me. Do you mind very much not being a virgin any more? Do you still hate what I've done to you?"

Tentatively, she placed her slender hand over the larger one that rested on her skin, and the movement sealed her decision. The part of her that was Carey Wyeth half-hated him for what he had done, what he was doing, what he would do, what *she* would do. But the half of her that had been born on Mahi Mahi, and here in the captain's cabin of this ship, turned and saw his eyes—eyes that, strangely, held none of the triumph she had expected to see. She smiled at him—and beneath the shyness, it was a languorous, age-old island smile.

"Je suis contente, monsieur," she murmured.

CHAPTER TEN

The seas and the skies were mild, in the days that followed. There was little wind, and at this rate it would take the *Sweet Witch* at least a week to reach Tahiti. It was as well, thought Adam—for his thoughts were no longer on the running of the vessel, which was schooning idly and uneventfully to the northwest, but on the girl who waited in his cabin below. And now dawn had spilled its pink-gold glory over the ocean; his watch was over, and Jed Lovell had arrived on deck to relieve him.

"Take over, Mr. Lovell." Adam started to go, then swung back. "By the way, any more trouble with that Starbuck fellow?"

"No—not since the other day. Although he's still got an outsize chip on his shoulder! I'm afraid he's had it in for both of us ever since the first day we asked him to lift a hammer. He's a lazy good-for-nothing, to tell the truth—and he'd like to stick a knife in my back, or yours."

A frown creased Falconer's brow. "We'll put him off in Macao, Jed. He's a nasty customer."

"Good. We'll all sleep a little easier. Why not in Tahiti?"

"Not enough ships call there yet. He'd have trouble shipping out again—and we'd have no chance of hiring a replacement. But if he makes trouble again, let me know at once."

"Aye, I will that, Captain."

"And, Jed—take over for the rest of the day, will you? I have some paperwork to attend to below. I could use some hours without interruption."

It was true enough: Adam was behind in his paperwork. If only Teura were not so distracting! Sometimes he thought it would have been better if she were not able to speak French so fluently. Then he could have forgotten her more easily, between times. Or if she were less devoid of artifice, less innocent . . .

How had she remained so innocent—Tahiti-bred, even with a French father? She was all innocence, yet all worldly-wise, child and woman all at once, seductive yet pure, sensuous yet untouched. Her moods were endlessly fascinating to him. It was like watching a beautiful butterfly as it emerged from its chrysalis and spread its wings to dry and shimmer in the light of day. Her initial shyness, her timidity had been partly overcome, but there were inhibitions still to be shed, and selfishly, he wanted to be the person to make her shed them. There were so many things he wanted to do with her, someday. To swim with her by starlight in a still lagoon, and make love to her under the water's silky caress. To kiss her slowly, all over, under a blinding cruel sun, on a white hot stretch of beach—someplace where he could see her, really see her, instead of in a confined near-sunless space like his cabin. To teach her to watch, as she had still not learned to watch, while she aroused the passions in him, artlessly, with her body and with her hands. To see her move about unclothed, as the other vahines did, doing homely familiar things—naked, and all unashamed of her nakedness.

But none of this should be occupying his thoughts this morning—the paperwork had to come first. And, damn her, she didn't want the paperwork to come first.

"No, Teura, don't do that—it's too distracting."

"But it's only your ear. You don't write with your ear." Her disobedient lips continued their exploration.

"Nor can I write if you nibble it!"

"It tastes nice—like salt and soap. Your chin tastes nice too."

"Um. Va-t-en, you little baggage. Go away."

"Kiss me and I'll go away."

"Kiss you nothing!" He delivered a well-aimed smack to her pareu-clad bottom.

"Ouch! That hurt!"

"I hardly touched you. If I ever decide to spank you, you'll know it."

"*Would* you ever spank me, Adam?"

"Yes, in about ten seconds, if you don't leave me alone! Un-deux—"

"You wouldn't!" But she knew he would, and already she was halfway across the room.

For a few minutes it seemed enough just to watch him: to watch the way the shadows fell across his face, the way the concentration creased his brow and added tiny lines around the edges of his mouth, giving it a hint of cruelty that told nothing of the gentleness and ardor she knew it could hold. To watch the way his shoulders pressed against the thin stuff of his shirt, the way the dark hair of his chest prickled at the cloth, in a texture she could almost feel with her eyes . . . oh Lord, how *could* he keep working at those interminable papers?

"Adam . . . ?"

"Yes?"

"Qu'est-ce que c'est que tu fais?"

"Nothing you'd understand—trigonometry. It all has to do with charting a ship's course."

"And how long will it take you to do it?"

"All morning—this and other things. Now be quiet."

"All morning—! But it's already been two hours."

"One."

"Three!"

"You silly chatterbox! Do something to amuse yourself. Find a book. There are some in French—on the top shelf. Can you read?"

"Of course!" She reached for one at random, and held it ostentatiously upside-down. "Comme ça?"

Adam looked up, and saw, and tore his eyes away, and fixed them determinedly back on the task at hand. "Yes—like that. Now read!"

"It looks funny like this. Are you sure?"

"That's just because you need more practice reading. Now be quiet and start practicing."

"I was lying, Adam, I can't read."

"Then learn. Keep looking at it—and close your pretty little mouth, or I'll have to put a gag in it."

"Gag, Adam? What's 'gag'?"

"Teura! One more word and you'll get one."

"One what, Adam?"

He closed the distance across the cabin in two seconds. It took a little longer—what with the wriggling and the laughing, and the finding of a clean handkerchief to stuff in her mouth and another to tie over it—to fulfill his threat. And even when the threat had been carried out, it

103

took him more than another half-hour to get back to his work.

"Teura, ma petite sotte, you're very naughty." Adam had finally put away the papers and the instruments and the charts, and now, at last, he could let his attention be totally taken by the thing that had never left his mind this morning, not for an instant . . . damn her for being such an engaging little witch! It had taken twice too long to get the work done.

"Naughty, Adam?" But in spite of the innocence in her voice, her eyes gleamed gold and satisfied and not at all repentant.

"Yes. This morning you kept me from getting my work done."

"It's done now."

"Now it is. But if it hadn't been for you I'd have finished before noon."

"I'm sorry. Will you forgive me?"

Of course I forgive you, you island sorceress . . . "Ah —maybe. See this coin? I'll toss it in the air. If it lands heads-up I'll forgive you."

"And if it doesn't?"

"I'll take my revenge."

"Revenge? I don't trust you! What kind of revenge?"

"I'll decide."

"But I want to know now! Promise me it won't be a spanking?"

"I promise."

"Or a gag?"

"You liked that."

"Well—not really. Not *that*. But please—I want to know before I agree."

"Hmm. Well then, I'll give you a job to do."

"What kind of a job?"

"Persistent devil, aren't you? You could—tidy up. Put one or two things away for me, in my sea chest."

"That's easy! Throw the coin."

It rose, spun, landed, was slapped on the back of Adam's hand. His eyes crinkled into a smile. "Ha! I won."

"I knew it! I'm never lucky. What do you want me to put away?"

"Your pareu."

"Adam!"

"Teura, you didn't have to hide your head under the sheet when Noah brought dinner."

"But I'm naked—he'd see me!"

"Noah's seen girl's heads before."

"It's only that—I'm embarrassed."

"Embarrassed? When there are twenty near-naked girls up on deck? Teura, if it weren't for your dusky skin I'd swear you were a shy little French convent girl."

"If you'd let me have my pareu back I'd feel better."

"Sorry. I've lost the key."

"I don't believe it!" Triumphantly, she seized the trousers he had just removed. "I saw you put it in your pocket."

"Stay away from those pockets! Don't you dare— Teura, I swear . . . Now look what you've done!"

"I'm sorry. I'll pick it all up . . . Adam! What's this?" In her hand was the coin he had used earlier; she turned it over in her palm.

"Let me have that!"

"Two tails!" Her chin tilted at him rebelliously. "Oooh—je te déteste, monsieur! Cheat, fraud, swindler!"

"Go ahead and hate me, then—you look beautiful when you hate, all sparkle and spirit. Come here and tell me you hate me."

But she had fled across the room, and turned her back to him. "No!"

He came up behind her. She could sense the nearness of him, the height of him beyond her shoulder, even though he had not touched her. "Teura, look at me."

"I can't. I'm upset."

"About the coin?"

"No—not really."

"What, then? It wasn't so bad, was it—going naked?"

"I—well, no. I'm not sure."

"Don't tell me I have to leave that rag locked up!"

"No."

Now his hand tangled in her hair, but she refused to turn to his touch. His voice was soft: "You'll take it off whenever I ask you, then?"

"No."

"No! God's blood, girl, you're stubborn. All I want to do is feast my eyes once in a while."

"That's just it! You've been feasting your eyes all day and—and—I don't think it works. Nothing's happened since I took my pareu off. I don't think I even excite you anymore."

"How can you be so sure? You won't even look at me."

There was a silence, and Adam pulled her around to face him.

"Look at me, Teura. No, don't look away so fast . . . I'd swear you were blushing under that dusky skin of yours." His hands in her hair directed her head, gently. On his mouth and in his eyes, the smile was warm. "If anyone blushes it should be me. I can't hide a thing."

❧ CHAPTER ELEVEN ❧

Carey slid into the large wooden tub, as she did each day at this time, with a sigh of content. Her body felt good, alive all over, vibrant and glowing in a way she would not have believed possible four days ago. She soaped herself slowly, luxuriantly, with a new-found sensuality, watching as the bubbles shimmered over her skin and into the warm water.

How marvelous that felt! If only she could wash her hair—but Mamma Ruau had warned her that she must not do so during the few days it would take to reach Tahiti. The stain on her body had been applied by a soaking of several hours in a compound of roots and barks and berries that would fade only with time. The same solution had been used on her already-tanned face, in many painstaking layers, for she had been unable to hold her head under water for that part of the treatment. But the dark solution that colored her hair held no such permanence; the long tresses were pinned high out of harm's way, quite safe for the moment.

At length she put the soap aside and lay in the tub, dreaming. Dreaming of Adam—Adam, who filled her hours, her minutes, her nights and her days. Adam, whose sheen-black eyes sometimes lit with little points of fire, then grew smoke-black, storm-black, with passion. Adam, whose lips could be an exquisitely soft caress or a cruel torture—and sometimes both, at the same time. Adam, who had taught her to be bold with her body and with his, who had taught her to touch and to hold and to arouse him with her fingertips. Adam, who could be funny and tender and kind and very very wicked . . .

She had fallen in love, desperately in love, with the tall dark-eyed sea captain, and she could no longer even remember why she had once hated him. Hate . . . love?

They were two sides of a coin, and like Adam's coin, both sides were the same.

England was a dream and the shadow of a dream; and the substance was this—this space where she slept, woke, walked sometimes naked, spoke French, ate, sang, laughed, made love. She refused to think of the future. Tahiti was time enough to think of the future and, thanks to a lazy lulling wind, Tahiti was still a few days away. For now, there was no future; only today. There was no Carey; only Teura. There was no sin, so sun, no moon, no world—only Adam.

At length, shaking away her daydream, she stood up and reached for a towel. It was then that she noticed the lock of hair that had somehow come loose. It fell in a curtain over her shoulder, its ends sodden and accusing —and, unmistakably, no longer black.

Her heart hammered. When would Adam be returning? It could be at any minute, and he would notice—he couldn't fail to notice! What was she to do? Could she tell him the truth? No, never! Her English soul writhed at the very idea.

Her eyes raced around the cabin. And at that moment she was not Teura, she was only Carey—Carey, desperate for concealment. The india ink, in the inkwell on his desk, could be her answer. But there wasn't enough of that; she knew, because she'd used it yesterday, to touch up a few telltale roots. There was nothing else, unless . . .

She flew to the wardrobe and found the scissors she had seen a week before. With unsteady hands, she slashed away the revealing inches. She checked in the large mirror, and removed a few more stray wisps, putting them carefully together with the first. Then she unpinned the rest of her hair and chopped off just enough to even the ends. In all, it was nearly eight inches that she had had to lop off. Adam could hardly fail to notice! But at least it was done—except for one small problem.

How was she to get rid of this mound of part black, part honey-colored pile of hair-cuttings? Adam's trash basket was hardly a safe place because its contents were collected by Noah for burning. If Noah discovered the hair he would be sure to tell Adam. But if she hid it anywhere else in the cabin, Adam would find it, sooner or later. If only he would allow her to go on deck she could dispose of it easily. But with the man Starbuck aboard,

Adam had made her promise to stay here in his cabin, until Tahiti at least. She had agreed, eagerly—for she had not wanted to go on deck to the curious stares of the crew. Nor did she want to now. And Adam, if he saw her on deck, would be furious.

But what else could she do? Smuggle it out? Yes, of course—smuggle it out! In the food garbage. Carey knew, from other times at sea, that waste food was dumped overboard to the sharks. It would be scraped into a large container and tossed holus-bolus into the sea. No one would ever know, if she wrapped it carefully in the skin of a baked breadfruit, or a chicken carcass.

But until the right meal came along, the evidence must be hidden. There must be someplace Adam wouldn't look, for at least a day or two. Again her eyes darted around the cabin, seizing and discarding the possibilities. Most spaces were too small, or too much in danger of drawing Adam's attention. Then she saw the solution: the large Chinese brass urn, on the floor by the door. Adam never used that; it would be the very thing. She wrapped the hair into a fold of paper from the desk, then lowered it cautiously into the depths of the urn. She was about to deposit her small package when her hand connected with something, and there was a clinking sound—metal-on-metal. Her fingers fastened on something cold and hard.

"Oh, drat!" Carey's face registered her disappointment. The clank had been a keyring: she pulled it out and looked at it. This must be a master set of keys for everything around the ship—the weapons chest, the food supplies, the liquor stores. Probably even for this cabin —although that was of no particular import now since Adam no longer locked the door. But she could not leave the hair in the brass urn; Adam might need this set of keys at any time.

At length, finding no better hiding place, she slid the package beneath the edge of the mattress; and that night at the evening meal, it found its way undetected into the carcass of a demolished Mahi Mahi chicken, before Adam even returned to the cabin.

The day had brought one small nagging problem after another, and it was already dark by the time Adam was able to come below. He was not in the best of moods;

he'd hoped for an idle afternoon with Teura. Teura, with her witchery and her shy sideways glances and her liquid limbs . . . that was what he needed to soothe him after a difficult day.

He was unprepared for the sight that greeted him, and for the flare of anger inside himself. Anger was something he'd taught himself to conceal, but it was a lesson hard-taught, and at times something primitive surfaced. Despite the best of intentions, his mouth tightened with disapproval. "Why the devil did you do that to your hair!"

"I didn't cut it all off—it's still very long." But the guilty knowledge of why she had done it remained in Carey's voice, and gave it more asperity than usual.

"Not long enough! Merde! You've chopped off eight inches at least."

"Don't swear at me! And I don't need your permission to cut my hair." She tossed what was left of it, angrily.

"You do now, by God." Why did she make him feel this way—what the *hell* was she doing to his self-control?

"Oh—!" Carey stamped her foot in an uncharacteristic gesture. "And what gives you *that* idea?"

"Because you belong to me now."

How dare he sound so autocratic, so feudal? "Belong to you! I don't belong to anyone."

"Yes, you do—every sweet, maddening, goddam, velvet inch of you! And that includes your hair."

"You, you—"

"Huff and puff all you want to, Teura, but from now on don't do anything to that pretty body of yours without asking me. I suppose next time you'll turn up with tattoomarks from top to toe!"

"—bâtarde!" Somehow, in French, the word came easier to her tongue—but all the same, she was breathless with her own daring even before he grabbed her shoulders, the flame leaping higher in his eyes. "No, Adam, no, I didn't mean it—I take it back."

Gradually his eyes smouldered and went smoky, for the touch of her skin was a powerful narcotic to his senses. It was like satin—like soft brown satin. Why did she have the power to get under the surface of him as no other woman had ever done?

"Coward," he said in a gentler voice. "You can fight me if you want—it might be fun."

"I don't want to fight. I'm sorry about the hair, Adam. I didn't think you'd mind." Something inside her went tremulous, expectant, for now all the cruelty had left his mouth, and she had seen his softening eyes.

"Well, I do mind. Why did you do it?"

"I was bored."

"That's not a good enough reason."

"Well then, because I thought you'd like it. It used to hide my breasts."

"That's a better reason. Take off your pareu and let me see. Um, well, yes, it does improve the view. Turn this way—now that. Now if you'll just stand still—" His hands guided her toward the large mahogany-framed mirror mounted on the bulkhead.

"Adam, I can't look at myself!"

"Yes, you can." His palms brushed against the nipples, hardening them and paving the way for the fingers that now caught at her, half-playfully. She turned away from her own reflection and pulled him, with her, onto the bed.

"I'd rather look at you . . . oh, yes, Adam!" she murmured a little breathlessly, for already his teeth and his tongue had found a breast. He closed over it, hungry for the taste of her. Her hands clung to his sinewed shoulders, tangled in his hair; and now the madness was upon her—the madness that would not end until his flesh had become one with hers. His tongue trailed kisses down her body, and the touch was a fine agony to her nerves.

"My love, my love, please oh please," she groaned. Liquid fire over the flat of her stomach, and below. "—Oh!"

Suddenly she was sitting bolt upright, senses spinning at the thought of what he had so obviously intended. "Adam! Don't do that."

"How do you know what I was going to do? You didn't let me do it."

"I know what you were going to do! And I—I won't let you!"

"Why not?"

"It's not right!" Oh, how could he even want to? It was indecent, improper, the kind of thing she knew would be done only by ladies of the night—she knew this, despite the fact that she had never even suspected that such a way of making love might exist.

"It's right, Teura. Let me do it to you. You'll like it."

"I won't like it! And I won't let you do it."

"Never?"

"Never! Nice ladies wouldn't do things like that—and if you were a gentleman, you wouldn't either."

Adam lifted a dark brow. "You sound like a priggish middle-aged matron from my home town. Not like my little island temptress."

"I don't care, I can't do it."

"Polynesians do it all the time."

"I'm not—" She caught herself in time. "I'm not interested in what the—the rest of my race does! I wouldn't enjoy it."

"I would," he said in a soft wheedling voice, while he rained tiny kisses against her shoulder, her breast, her waist. "Let me do it, Teura. I want to kiss you there."

"I don't care what you want to do! You have no right to use my body as if—as if you owned it! You don't own my, my—that part of me—any more than you own my hair. Kiss me here instead." With new-found confidence she took his head and placed it to her breast.

He pulled away, and his eyes teased her, but there was something serious in them too. "No, Teura. I don't like to be ordered."

"Oh, Adam! Stop being so domineering. Kiss me!"

"As I want to?"

"No! I don't care what you want."

He swung his feet over the edge of the bed.

"Where are you going?"

"Does it matter? I don't feel very welcome here."

"Adam, come back! I want to make love."

"Usually I care about what you want, Teura—but tonight, dammit, I'm not so sure."

"Well then, sleep on the floor for all I care!"

He shrugged. "As you wish."

"I hope it swallows you up!"

Adam found a blanket and pillow, and threw them on the floor beside the bed. "In that case I'll stay down here until you invite me back up."

"I won't! You're a brute."

"Tsk, Teura," he said mildly, settling the bedding under him. "If I were a brute, you could have said no a thousand times, and it wouldn't have made any difference. I can outclaw you any time. I'd be up there right now—with my head between your legs."

"Oh—!" she gasped, and buried her flaming face into the pillow.

She thought she could outwait him, that he would be back at her side within the hour. But an hour came and went, and then another. She knew he was still awake, for although he lay without stirring, his breathing was not regular, as it would have been in sleep. She smiled to herself, and settled her head on the pillow. She could wait all night if necessary. How had the silly fight started anyway? Not merely because she had refused to do as he wished; surely that could have been settled without rancor. No, it was more than that. A battle of wills, maybe . . .

She began to drift. Suddenly, she realized his breathing had grown even. Once more she was wide awake, taut with anger. How could he go to sleep, when she herself had been unable to do so!

She rolled over to the edge of the bed and touched his back, with her hand. He didn't stir.

"Adam . . . !" But the hissed whisper aroused no response. She jabbed a finger at his spine more cruelly, but he only groaned and muttered in his sleep and turned over, restlessly. Now she could see his face, the mouth slightly parted, the breathing, after a few irregular moments, once more quiet and slow. For an instant her anger and her resolve melted. She had watched him before in sleep, and loved the way it tempered the angles of his face, giving him an almost boyish look, the way the thick lashes lay over the closed eyes, the way the black tousled hair fell across his forehead. If there was sometimes harshness or hardness in the waking face, it was lost now, in slumber.

He was most certainly sleeping, and deeply too. And no, she would not let him! She sat up with an annoyed cluck, and dropped her feet over the side of the bed.

"Adam!"

She pushed at his chest with her toes, then drew back to aim a kick.

It seemed he had not moved; and yet suddenly his hands were around her ankles.

"Kicking, Teura? Nice ladies don't do things like that," he mimicked.

"You've been awake all the time!" She squirmed, but could not free her ankles from his iron grip.

"Of course." His eyes mocked her, slate-black, amused.

"But you pretended to be asleep!"

"How else could I get you to make the first move? And you were about to go to sleep. I couldn't let you do that." He lifted one of her feet, and his tongue touched its instep.

"Oh, you, you—"

"No more names, Teura." He nibbled experimentally at a toe. "I don't really want to stay on the floor all night. Why don't you invite me back up?"

"I don't trust you," she declared, but she was appeased, for she thought she had won.

Adam hauled himself to a sitting position, cross-legged, and his lips tingled across her ankles. "Come on, Teura, we haven't got all night. Or rather, we have got all night, but I'm damned if I want to waste it this way. Ask me back up."

How she wanted to, but . . . "Not until you promise."

His hands moved in leisurely fashion up her legs, stroking and stoking the fires. "Promise what? Loosen up, Teura, your knees are as tight as a granny knot."

"Promise you won't ask me to, to—you know."

"Mmmm—I'll think about it."

"Promise!"

"All right—I promise."

"What *exactly* do you promise?"

"I promise I won't ask you to do anything you don't want to do."

"Never again?"

"Never again."

She relaxed, smug that she had won, and he nudged her knees a little further apart.

"Oh, Adam, I thought you'd never give in! It's been so lonely up here—"

When he moved, she was off guard, and before she had time to resist, her thighs had been thrust wide against the bed and pinned beneath his forearms. In the same sweep of movement, he flung her torso flat and shackled it with his hands.

"Adam, you promised!" she howled, and tried to wrench her body away from its prone position—but it was too late.

"Be quiet, you long-legged little witch." Already his

114

mouth was nuzzling experimentally, sending shock waves through that hidden part of her. "You've talked too much already. Why couldn't you be a nice easy female who enjoyed being mastered? Damned if I'll let myself be run by any woman, even you . . . Now stop fighting me."

"Let me go!" Oh shame, shame, shame that his lips should be touching her as they were touching her now! Shame and something else—something that was growing beyond her control.

"Not yet," he murmured huskily, and burrowed against her skin. "Now stop talking. I can't answer."

"Adam—don't! Oh Lord, please don't. No, no, I can't bear it—oh please, not that! Have pity!"

But his probing tongue was an exquisite torture, and already the struggling and the writhing had turned into a wild reaching for the sensation she now knew so well. When he at last hoisted her legs over his shoulders, and moved his hands to cup her pointed breasts, she still groaned and begged and twisted, but she no longer wanted him to listen to her words—no longer tried to push away the invading head, no longer wanted the fiercely seeking tongue to stop its sweet and terrible incursions. And when she could bear the torment no longer, she twisted her fingers into his hair and clenched him close, close, close, as though she wanted him never to stop.

Afterward, when he had found his own deliverance, they lay together in the darkness, and on his lips she tasted the memory of what she had once thought so wrong.

"You broke your promise," she murmured against his mouth.

"Do you mind?"

In the night-blackness she could sense the soft laughter in his eyes, although she could not see it. She hedged: "Yes . . . no."

"Anyway, I didn't promise I wouldn't *do* it. I promised I wouldn't *ask*. And I'll never ask again."

"That's quibbling!"

"No, it's not. How else was I to get you where I wanted you—short of tying you to the bed?"

"Adam!"

"Shocked again? Aren't you the prim and proper one!"

"I'm not!"

"Good. Because I don't like prim and proper people."

"I won't be one then, ever again." Now why had she said that? It was Teura talking but soon, very soon, prim and proper Carey Wyeth would have to take her place . . .

"Is that a promise?"

There was a pause, a very long pause. At last she spoke, in a small voice.

"Yes, it's a promise."

After that, for the three days it took to reach Tahiti, she refused him nothing, no matter what he asked. For she knew these were the last times they would share together. Her hair would soon give her away, and she couldn't take the risk.

❧ CHAPTER TWELVE ❧

Luke Alden sat on the afterdeck, watching the lazy wake of the *Sweet Witch* and occasionally throwing another offering out to the sea. It was his last assignment before he went off watch, half an hour from now, and he was in no hurry. As the youngest member of the crew, this part of the galley duty was often left to him. Unlike some of the other men, he didn't mind. It had become a challenge, almost, to see how soon he could attract the sharks —how soon, with their unerring instinct, they would come, tailfins knifing through the water. Sometimes they came alone, sometimes in groups, sometimes not at all. Once, when he had thrown over a whole slaughtered pig that had been found diseased and inedible, one small shark had been wounded. The fresh blood in the water had attracted more and bigger sharks, and a fierce feeding frenzy had followed. The sight had not attracted him; since then he'd taken more care to feed the garbage out slowly, luring the sharks to follow in the ship's wake without awakening their indiscriminate voraciousness.

Now, his hand dipped into the bucket of damp fish entrails and came up with something different—a chicken carcass. The captain's dinner from last night, no doubt. No such luck for the common seamen! But he was unresentful, for Falconer was a fair captain and it was a good life aboard the *Sweet Witch*—bliss compared to the first two hellish years after the press gangs had seized him in the name of His Majesty King George III.

Luke was about to toss the carcass overboard when he noticed the dark stain over his palm. He shifted the wet chicken bones to his other hand—and that, too, came up streaked with black. Curious now, he reached inside the cavity. He had no notion of what he would find, or whether he would find anything.

117

When he discovered and opened the wrapped package inside, he could hardly credit what he saw.

Golden hair. A woman's hair, he was sure, for there was too much of it to be a man's. Eight inches of hair, at least. But who on this ship had hair of this honeyed color? No one. And no one had cut their hair that he had seen. It had been colored black, that was evident, although much of the black had washed away by now. What did it mean? Was there a *blonde* woman aboard ship? And where—in the captain's cabin? It must be, for this refuse was from the captain's dinner. Now, he almost wished he had listened to the men and their gossiping. He knew that much of the tongue-wagging this trip had centered around the goings-on in the captain's cabin, but he'd paid little mind to what he'd heard. He did recollect something about a taboo, and he did recollect seeing the girl for moments only, the first day she had come on board. He had not seen her since, for his duties never took him to the captain's cabin.

In truth, it was none of his business—or anybody else's. Thank God it had not been one of the other men on garbage detail, or what a bombshell would have exploded in the ship's grapevine! All the same, it was curious, it was curious . . .

It was late morning, and Adam, off watch for the moment, was lying back against two plumped pillows on the bed, reading a book. Carey, nestled into the crook of his arm, was restless. At other times like this, she would often, without seeming to do so, read the pages as he turned them. But this was a manual of some kind about navigation, and she had no particular interest—such a dull, heavy tome! Did ships' captains really have to know such things?

For the past half hour she had been cautiously unbuttoning Adam's shirt, and he hadn't noticed. Now, she slid her hand through the opening, very slowly, and her fingertips touched the rough hair on his chest.

"Read me some words, Adam." She wanted to hear the sound of his voice, wanted to fix it in her memory. Tahiti was so close—Tahiti, and the future she had tried to push from her mind.

"You wouldn't understand them."

"I don't care. I like to hear your voice. Please won't

you read me that sentence?" She jabbed at something that started: "The shoals in the northwest channel of the . . ."

"All right, but they're in English."

"I don't mind. Read the English."

He gave her shoulder a tweak. " 'And then he said to her, you are an enchanting little piece of baggage, and if you don't stop distracting me I'll never get this book read.' Satisfied?"

"Translate it for me—into French."

"If you insist. 'The shoals in the northwest channel of . . .' "

"Never mind. In French it sounds very dull. Can you read me some more—in English?"

"Just a few more words, then. 'Those fingers of yours are driving me mad and if you don't take them away from my chest at once I may throw you back against the bed and rape you.' "

"That sounds nice—the English, I mean. Go on."

"Teura, I *have* to read this book. So please—"

The disobedient fingers delved in a little farther. "First teach me to say some words in English."

"If I teach you to say something in English, will you go away and leave me alone?"

Reluctantly, she promised.

"All right then. What words shall I teach you?"

"Teach me some English words to say when we make love."

"Eh bien, you can say, 'I love you, my darling.' Try it: 'I love you, my darling.' "

" 'I love you, my . . .' " She clipped the words deliberately, giving them a strange foreign sound, and pretended to forget the ending.

" '. . . my darling.' That wasn't too good. Try again—with a little more feeling."

" 'I love you, my darling.' "

"That's better."

" 'I love you, my darling.' What does it mean?"

"It means—er—'Thank you very much.' "

"That's nice. 'I love you, my darling.' It sounds much better than 'merci beaucoup,' don't you think?"

"Much better."

" 'I love you, my darling.' "

"No more now, Teura. Go sit in that chair over there

—you promised. You can say it later tonight, as often as you want." And well satisfied that he had tricked her so easily into saying the words he had been wanting to hear, he turned back to the book.

Reluctantly she withdrew her hand, and left the bed. But she would not let him off so easily. "In the meantime, I'll practice it," she announced airily.

"Good." Adam didn't look up.

"I can say thank you whenever you kiss me."

There was no answer.

"Or when you put that book down."

Still no response.

"And I can thank the sailors when they bring my bath-water."

"Teura! You'll do no such thing!"

"When do you estimate we'll make Tahiti, Captain Falconer?" Jed Lovell's voice was businesslike, for they were standing on the quarterdeck, and at the moment there were several seamen within earshot. For now, the formalities of shipboard must be observed.

"Tonight about dusk. We'll lie hove-to for the night, outside the reef, and make anchorage tomorrow morning. And, oh, by the way, can you step along here for a moment, Mr. Lovell? I'd appreciate your opinion on some of the splices in the running rigging."

Lovell's round face registered surprise, for he'd checked the running rigging himself not two days ago. But he knew better than to question his captain's sharp eyes, so he followed.

"Where are the weak splices, Captain?"

"Relax, Jed. The rigging's fine. I wanted to talk to you about the girl."

"The girl?"

"You know who I mean. Teura."

"What about her?" Lovell sounded guarded.

"Has there been any talk about her? I know some of the men have the odd word of Tahitian—and language barrier or no, they always manage to communicate, one way or another. Perhaps they've heard something from the other vahines."

"Well—yes, there's been some talk." Lovell tried to hide his embarrassment. "You know the kind of thing. You've spent a lot of time in your cabin this trip."

"God's blood, Jed, you know I don't give a tinker's damn for that kind of gossip. I mean—anything about why she's taboo."

"So you do think there'll be trouble." Lovell's face creased into the lines of concern.

"I don't know. We'll only spend one night at Tahiti, just in case. And we'll keep the other girls on board till the last minute, so they won't be spreading tales. But it would help if I knew exactly what this taboo is all about."

"Why don't you ask her, Adam?"

"She won't talk about it. What have you heard?" he persisted. "Speak up, Jed, for God's sake! I don't put any stock in superstitions—and I'm not going to put her ashore anyway. You can tell me."

"Well, the vahines have been very reticent about it. But one thing keeps cropping up. The men all think it's something about—about being buried alive."

A premonition as fleeting as a wing-brush seemed to stir the air, and for an instant Adam Falconer's unsuperstitious soul went cold.

Later that night, after they had made love, Adam listened to the words he had taught Teura, words he had since told her were a special kind of thank-you, to be used only between lovers. Replete and drowsy, she curled up against him in the night. But he was wakeful. She sensed it—and saw it, for the moon, shining through the grating of the skylight, gleamed darkly in his eyes.

"Why are you so wide awake, Adam? When your muscles are all knotted up I can feel it. It keeps me awake too."

"Then I'll try to relax." He turned his back, and pretended. Her lips found his shoulders, and soothed them; her slow fingertips tried to ease the tensions away. Ten minutes crept by, and another ten, and still she could feel his tendons taut beneath her hands.

"It's no good, Adam. I can still feel it. Talk to me, if you like. It might make you relax."

"It's too late for conversation, Teura. Forget about me. Go to sleep."

"I can't." It was true; his wakefulness had infected her. "But please, I only want to hear your voice. Speak to me in English . . . put me to sleep."

" 'I love you, my darling.' "

"No, not just that—more."

So he started, his voice very soft so as to lull her to sleep. "There are so many words I want to say—and not just in English. But I can't say them. Not yet . . ."

"Go on," she urged gently after a few moments, in French.

"You called me a bastard the other day, Teura, and you were right—not just in the way you meant it, but in the other way too. Not that that would mean anything to you—but you weren't born in a god-fearing New England town, as I was. Born on the wrong side of the blanket, they used to say.

"Buried alive . . . that's what they did to my mother, with their words and their looks and their scorn. He broke her heart, and they broke her spirit. I understood that from the time I could walk the length of the main street. You learn to walk alone when no one will walk beside you. You learn to fight with your fists and your feet and your teeth, if necessary . . .

"I was nine when my mother died, although she'd been dead a long time before that, inside. And then I found out who he was. She'd kept his letters, his loving, lying letters. He'd married someone else when she was three months pregnant. He had tried to give her money to leave town, and she had thrown it in his face. Pride! She couldn't give me much else, but she did give me that. Even though she had to do things in those last years, just to keep us alive . . . things that still make my skin crawl when I think about them. Things I've never told a soul. And after the men would leave, she would weep . . .

"By then he was a pillar of respectability, damn his whoring soul! And his wife was one of the worst. Prim and proper and poison in every wag of her tongue, all church-charities and no charity, the kind who wouldn't hand out her laundry to someone like my mother in case it came back soiled. Oh, God . . ." he paused, remembering, probing into that part of his mind where painful memories were kept.

"I learned to wait in those days. And to hate. He was a trustee of the orphanage where they put me. I saw him sometimes. I used to watch him . . . and I saw in his eyes that he knew who I was. I watched, and I grew older waiting and hating . . . And in time I stalked him. I was twelve years old and I stole a kitchen knife from the orphanage kitchen. I would have murdered him too, if the knife had been sharper or longer. At the time, I thought he had died, or I would have finished him with my bare hands.

"They hunted me for days. For weeks I lived like an animal. I hid and I went hungry and I stole food and I learned to live by my wits. And with the knowledge that I had killed my own father. Funny, it was only after I thought he was dead that I began to think of him as my father.

"They don't ask too many questions when you sign on to go to sea. They're too damned glad to have a body, man or boy, that hasn't had to be dragged aboard. And they don't care much about your nationality—war or no. Spaniards, Swedes, French, British, Portuguese, Americans, I've sailed with them all. There are no good nations and no bad nations, only good ships and bad ships. My first ship was bad. But you learn to avoid the floggings if you keep your eyes open and your mouth shut and don't let anyone see that you're afraid, bone-afraid, the first time they order you to climb to the crosstrees in a gale, when the mast's taking wild hundred-degree swings and the canvas is cracking like a whiplash.

"After that it was better. I got on one of the first whalers doubling the Horn into the North Pacific, up past the Sandwich Islands. He was a hard man, that captain. Tough as the devil! But he made me learn. Crammed it into my head! Gave me books to read and lessons in trigonometry, and tongue-lashings and extra time in the yards if I didn't learn fast enough. Said he was going to drag me up by the bootstraps if it killed me. I cursed him for it at the time, and after that it was too late to do anything else . . .

"He died. Killed by a Malay. And that was the day I really killed my first man, although I thought it was the second. The Malay was from Cochin China, a gentle funny little fellow with those soft eyes they have. Fearless, too—he'd jump on a dead whale's back and balance there, water sloshing about his ankles, stripping off blubber with his flensing knife while the giant hooks pulled it aboard—and sharks tearing at the carcass inches away from his feet. I liked him. But he ran amok and a Malay amok is a different man.

"The deck was slippery with his blood and the blood of the captain and the three other men he'd killed. And he should have been dead, too, by then . . . but he came at me and he kept coming, and his eyes didn't even know who I was. I killed him with a flensing knife—the flensing knife he'd taught me to use, stripping blubber. I still see his eyes sometimes, not the way they were when he died, but before. It's not the killing that's so hard, it's the re- membering.

"I went back, in time, to my home town. Back to the scene of what I thought was my first killing. I'd grown up some; I was a young man by then. What was I looking for? I don't know. I walked around for a while, expecting someone to recognize me. No one did. The shack where I'd lived as a child was gone. The orphanage was gone, moved to a bigger town. But the local emporium was still there, the store that my father had owned. I went in . . . To exorcise my personal devils, I suppose. I bought some- thing, I can't remember what. The girl gave me change— a penny too much. I started to give it back, knowing it would be taken from her own salary—she probably didn't earn more than a dollar or so a week. And then a man came through the door from a back room. It was him. He hadn't died at all—although he had a bad limp from his wounds, and had to walk with a cane. He looked at me. Just looked at me. Not with fear, not with recognition, just a kind of empty look, sad around the edges. And he said: keep the penny, maybe it'll bring you better luck than I've had. And I knew he knew . . .

"Not to be a murderer! For years I'd had an ugly black cloud hovering over me. It was as though a great wind came and cleansed away all the ugliness . . . I couldn't even hate him any more. What the hell had he done that I hadn't done, too, by then? My heart was as black as his . . . blacker. You've only seen one side of me, Teura —pray God you never see the other. I've cheated and I've lied and I've whored—as he did. I've slept with more women than he ever shook hands with in his puritanical New England existence, and I've given some of them short shrift—for I've never wanted to let myself be trapped into marriage. I've never wanted to be tied to a woman, so I've used whores and I've used ladies who are free with their favors—and now I've used you.

"But I've never taken a woman under false pretenses,

or promised anything I couldn't give. And that's why I won't say the words now . . ." And then, in French, for he no longer felt her breath fanning his spine: "Teura? Are you still awake?"

There was no answer, and when he turned, he saw only that she appeared to be asleep, for the moon had now moved along the sky, and no longer silvered the tears that lay on her lashes.

CHAPTER THIRTEEN

"No shore leave—not for anyone. Captain's orders! We're standing out to sea again tomorrow."

There was some grumbling among the men, for most of them had not set foot on solid land for over four months. Now that they lay anchored in Matavai Bay, with the Tahitian shoreline not two miles distant, it was disappointing to learn that they would not be staying long enough to sample the island's all-too-seductive charms.

"When do the vahines go ashore, Mr. Lovell? If we can't leave ship, like—"

"They'll stay on board tonight. So enjoy yourselves, lads, while you can! Tomorrow we make sail for Macao."

Lovell turned away from the small cluster of seamen. "Noah!" he called. "The bos'n is about to take a longboat in to shore. Captain Falconer requests that you go with him—stop those canoes that are putting out from the beach. Tell them we've got vahines aboard, that we don't want any more."

"Aye, Mr. Lovell."

"And then you can take your party ashore. You've checked to see what supplies we need?"

"Aye, I've done that."

"Good." Lovell's voice dropped, and he pulled Noah apart from the others. "While you're at it, Noah, you're to see what you can find out about the girl Teura. She used to live here. Do it quietly. The captain doesn't want to stir up any interest in the fact that she's on this ship. Not that the taboo means anything, but—"

Noah was offended and made no bones about showing it. "Cap'n Falconer could a asked me that hisself!"

"I know, I know, but there were other men around when he was talking to you last."

Noah's ruffled feelings were not soothed. "Anything partic'lar his mightiness wants to know?"

"He didn't elaborate. Just said he trusted your discretion."

Noah was only partly mollified. What kind of a pass were things coming to? Ever since his master had become besotted with that shy-faced Polynesian thing who couldn't even look a man in the eye—leastways, she'd never looked *him* in the eye—ever since Mahi Mahi, the Capn had been a man possessed. An' now to use the mate as a go-between! Noah sniffed. "Aye, well, I'll ask about. Shouldn't be too hard. No more'n a handful o' white men ever lived on Tahiti. A Frenchie sailor? Well, I'll look into it. But he should a asked me proper-like."

"Do what you can, Noah. And report back to the captain as soon as you're able."

"Stop pacing the cabin, Teura. You're skittish as a colt."

"Can't I go on deck and see Tahiti?" Carey knew she must make her decision soon: whether or not to tell Adam the truth. Just the knowledge that the journey's end was out there had made her more Carey than Teura, and brought back the full frightening realization of all that had happened.

She knew that if Adam were to learn who she was he might do what Jonah would have called 'the proper thing' by her. But how long would it take before he grew to hate her? *I've never wanted to be tied to a woman,* he had said. She was sure he had some affection for Teura: but Teura didn't exist, not really. And even if by some miracle she could continue to be Teura, what would her future be with him? Would he want to take her on to Macao? How long would his infatuation last? In any case, she could not continue the pretense any longer. She had tricked him a thousand times over. She had allowed him to talk about himself, thinking she could not understand, in a way that she knew he would not have wanted anyone to hear. It was something he might never forgive. And yet, and yet . . .

Perhaps the sight of solid land would help her make the impossible choice. *"Please* can I go on deck?"

"Yes, you can go on deck and see Tahiti—tomorrow."

"What time tomorrow?"

"Tomorrow afternoon."

"When does the *Sweet Witch* sail?"

"Tomorrow afternoon."

Her heart stopped for a fraction of time with the implications of what he had said, made all the more clear by the way his eyes were crinkling at her, amused and tolerant. But she wanted to hear him say it in so many words. "What if I want to go ashore right now—leave the ship today?"

"*Do* you want to leave right now?"

"No."

"No! And yet she sounds so miserable about it . . . come here, you adorable wench, and I'll cheer you up."

"No, please, Adam—" and she twisted away from his hands.

He started to follow her, for he knew something was wrong. But just then there was a knock on the door of the cabin.

"Who is it?" he called, reverting to English.

"Me. Noah. Noah *Mapes,* if you need remindin'."

For a moment Adam almost called out for Noah to go away, for he wanted to pursue this matter with Teura. But Noah sounded as if he had his dander up about something too, and besides he might have news from shore that would be important in his own plans for Teura.

"Come on in, Noah. What d'you have to report?"

But Noah had decided he would punish his master a little, for using the mate as an intermediary earlier. "Well, the watercasks is full again, an' we've taken on all the fruit an' firewood we can store."

"No, not that—Christ, Noah! What did you find out?"

"I found places for all the vahines to shack up. Spoke to the local bigwigs, I did. An' I'm here to hand on a formal Re-quest from their Highnesses that you come callin', tomorrow morning."

"I'll do that. But that's not what I mean, Noah. I want to know about the girl."

"Oh, the girl! Might a known you'd have your mind on the *girl.* Aye, she's fair rarin' to see you."

"What?" said Falconer with some confusion. "Who?"

"Name of Parea—you shacked up with her for a spell, last time you was in Tahiti. Surely you ain't forgotten? Hot and heavy to see you, she is!" Noah grinned wickedly. "You told her you'd be back—bring her a bolt o' Chinese silk."

"Christ! Well—it's true. And I did bring it. It's some-

128

where about. In my sea chest, I think. She can have it later."

"Ain't no time like the present." Noah's eyes were wide and angelic. "She's up top, an' champin' at the bit fer you-know-what."

"Noah, you—" Adam stopped himself. There was no point getting angry with Noah; and he did owe the girl Parea something. "Tell her I'll—no, have her wait. I don't want any unpleasantness. I'll tell her myself that she'll have to go. In a few minutes."

"Aye, Cap'n." And Noah, having finally put paid to his umbrage, smiled a Cheshire-cat smile.

"Now tell me what you found out about this one. Don't use her name. I don't want her to know we're talking about her."

"Nothin' much. There was a French sailor living over t'other side of the island some years ago, gone native-like. Lived with one of the local vahines, had a couple o' brats."

"What happened to them?"

"Ain't nobody seems to know. Packed his family up and took off, kit an' caboodle. Seems he was in hot water of some kind—stealin' from the natives."

"That's a switch," said Falconer dryly. "Any mention of taboos—anything that could cause trouble on shore?"

"Nay—'less it's to do with the stealin'."

"Could be," said Falconer thoughtfully. "Any friends, any relatives at all?"

"None as I could find."

Adam smiled to himself, satisfied for the moment. There might be trouble tomorrow, but then there might not. More important, there was no one to tell him no if he wanted to marry the girl—as he intended to, tomorrow, once he had contacted the local misi. Who knows, perhaps it would be that sallow-faced fellow he'd carried here on his last trip—the one with the stiff-spined little sister who'd been such a thorn in his flesh.

But Carey, who had no inkling of Adam's intentions, imagined to herself something quite different. Adam was looking for her supposed relatives: a place for her to stay, despite what he had implied to her not ten minutes before. Even as Teura she meant nothing to him, in spite of all that had happened. She was no more to him than any other girl, someone he had lived with for a time—to be bought off, no doubt, when he tired of her. Someone to be forgotten as swiftly as he had forgotten the girl named Parea . . .

"All right, Noah, you can go."

"Aye, Cap'n. Oh, one other thing. There's a ship's cap'n on shore sends you his compliments. Knew him the moment I clapped eyes on him—although you ain't had the pleasure."

"Who is it?"

"Name's Paxton. Sold off his ship an' cargo, an' settled on Tahiti not more'n a month after we was last here." Carey heard—but for the moment did not absorb fully.

"I remember. The ship that put off those missionaries. Captain Joshua Paxton."

"Aye, that's him. Says he'd be mighty proud to meet with you now, time permittin', an' it ain't no particularity to him if your countries ain't on speakin' terms. Big white house up the hill—no ways you can miss it, ain't another wooden building in sight."

"Thanks, Noah. Maybe I'll look in on him in the morning. Oh, by the way, can you arrange for the missionary to come aboard tomorrow afternoon?"

Noah was astonished. "The preacher? Sufferin' jibstays, why?"

Adam considered telling him and decided against it, although it might mean putting Noah in another huff, when he did find out, tomorrow. But Noah would only lecture him, and he didn't want to be lectured right now. So he said dryly: "Tell him we can all use him after the last ten days."

Finally, when Noah had gone, Adam turned back to comfort Teura for whatever had been troubling her before. But there was no need, after all, for when he put his arms around her, all her inner agitation seemed to have vanished. She turned to him with a serene smile, all perturbation resolved, and rested her head against his shoulder.

"Teura, ma chère. I can't keep up with your moods. Now you've gone all pensive."

"Perhaps you'll understand me some day."

"I doubt it." He whacked her on the bottom, none too gently. "Now go over to my sea chest, will you? See if you can find a bolt of silk at the bottom of it. I have to pay off a debt—I'll be on deck for a while."

"Do you have to go?"

There was something wistful in her voice, and he looked at her again, more closely. But her eyes told him nothing.

"You're sad that you can't see Tahiti right now—that's it, isn't it?"

"No. I can wait until tomorrow." She laughed, a musical little half-laugh, and tiptoed up to kiss his ear, lingeringly, as she had been taught.

"You little vixen! You want to make love. Don't you ever think of anything else?"

"Sometimes. But not tonight. Please don't be long."

"In that much of a hurry, are you?"

"No. Tonight I want to make love slowly, Adam. Very slowly—I'm not in a hurry at all."

When he left the ship next morning, Adam did something he had not done since Mahi Mahi. He locked the door to his cabin. And if he had been asked why, he would have said it was because he had very little understanding of the island taboos—and he had no intention of risking Teura's safety. But in his heart he knew there had been something else, something that worried him—a poignancy in Teura's lovemaking, almost as though it were for the last time.

Yet she had seemed to be quite herself this morning—a little gayer than usual, if anything. Was it because he had finally told her, when they lay sated last night, that he had no intention of putting her ashore in Tahiti? He had told her no more, yet, for he wanted to speak first to the missionary and make sure he would not refuse to marry them. For all their fine talk, sometimes preachers frowned on a white man entering into union with an island vahine.

"Shall I bring you a present from shore, Teura?" he had said as he prepared to leave.

"Of course! I love presents. Doesn't every island girl?"

"You're not every island girl."

"You won't let me go ashore with you? I promise I won't follow you around. I'll—I'll make myself scarce."

"Sorry."

She pouted prettily. He kissed her nose, and started to do the same to her mouth, but she twisted playfully away from him.

"Come here and kiss me properly, Teura."

"I kissed you properly last night."

"You kissed me very improperly last night, and you know it." But he smiled at her, and did not insist.

And then he was gone.

Carey looked around the cabin that had become her world, and her throat ached with unshed tears. She knew she must wait until Adam was well ashore, in case he stopped to chat up on deck. But an hour from now he would be with the local chieftains; she would leave in an hour.

So much to be engraved on her memory: the silly wooden tub where she had watched him bathe . . . the desk covered with his notes, his letters, his mementoes . . . the books she had read over his shoulder . . . the large brass-bound sea chest . . . the bed. She could not bear to look at the bed. She turned her eyes away, but it mocked her from the mirror, the mirror that alone had witnessed all that she must now try to forget.

Scarcely conscious of her own intent, she walked to the wardrobe where Adam's clothes were kept. In a bottom drawer she knew he kept small things, bits of jewelry, keepsakes. Surely there would be something she could take—something he would not miss. She rummaged through the drawer. Something small—a ring, perhaps, or some other trinket. Her eye fell on the large copper penny she had seen once before. By now she knew its significance. Would Adam mind very much if she took it? He never wore it, and at least it did not have any great intrinsic value. She took it from the drawer and hung the plaited silk cord around her neck. She knew already, for she had tested it yesterday, that there was a key to the cabin on the master ring. She unlocked the door now and placed the ring back in the urn. With luck she would soon be swimming to shore if the beach were not too far; she knew she could swim no more than a mile at most.

Before she closed the door behind her, she turned back to look, for the last time.

"Goodbye Teura," she whispered to the empty air. The ghosts of lovers hovered in the half-light of the cabin, half-sensed, half-seen, beckoning her back. "Goodbye, Adam."

✂ CHAPTER FOURTEEN ✂

Hutiti readied his outrigger for the trip back to shore. He was well satisfied with the past half-hour's work at this great ship anchored in Matavai Bay. He had traded off all his coconuts, all his shellwork and beads, and nearly all his baskets. He could have traded away all his mats, too, for several sailors had wanted to buy the last few; but at the moment they were serving a more lucrative purpose: they, along with his indispensable fishing nets, concealed the popaa, the big-shouldered white man.

The popaa was a deserter; Hutiti knew that. Sailors were always deserting in Tahiti. That was why this one had paid so handsomely for the two-mile trip back to shore—far more than any normal passenger would have paid, and ten times the worth of the cheap mats that covered him. Ah, it was good to think the day's work was done already, with the sun not yet in mid-sky. Yes, and the month's work too, for with the nails and the rope and the bits of white man's clothing he had collected, he would be able to lie under the cocopalms for many weeks, making love and drinking kava.

He was about to set sail when he saw the girl's head over the rail. She was not a full-blooded Tahitian, he could see that at once—and perhaps that was why she chose her words so carefully.

"Can you take me to shore?" she asked in imperfect Tahitian.

Hutiti considered the request. He had been told by one of the off-island vahines aboard this ship that they would all be going ashore soon. Those vahines had seemed in no hurry to leave. Why was this one in such a hurry? Had she managed to make off with something of value?

"Have you stolen many nails?" he asked with a disarming smile—for he could hardly request that a vahine pay for something as simple as a trip to shore. "Or something even more valuable?"

"I have nothing," she replied—but he did not believe her. She was looking back over her shoulder, as if afraid that someone might see her. Although the two or three sailors that were standing about seemed to be watching her with some curiosity, they made no move to interfere. But of course they could not understand the conversation. Perhaps the girl's theft had not yet been detected?

Hutiti was about to tell her to come aboard, when she reached for something that hung around her neck.

"I can give you this." She indicated a round piece of metal, pierced and strung onto a cord.

He heard the note of desperation in her voice, and responded at once. "Climb in, then—but do not walk on that pile of mats and nets. And do not let the popaa see your haste, or they will surely search my small canoe." Then, louder, in pidgin, so that the sailors might understand, he went on: "This one fella veree good, you see! This one fella good tyo—vahine like this fella! Plenty good jig-a-jig, you see!"

From the lowest point of the freeboard amidships, Carey managed without too much trouble to drop into the waiting canoe. She avoided the pile of mats, as she had been told, found a clear space in the bottom of the outrigger, and huddled low into it.

Hutiti at once turned his sail of matting to the wind, anxious to be off—for he had seen the way she crouched, as if in hiding, and now he had begun to suspect that the girl might have done something really serious, like murder her lover. Aué! That would be trouble for her, big trouble—and perhaps big trouble for him too. Not that he could blame her if she had killed one of the white men! Some of them behaved like sharks in a feeding frenzy when they were with girls. Pah! It was enough to turn one's stomach—and so unnecessary, for when one wanted a girl, one had only to smile and make a suggestive gesture—and the girl was sure to follow you into the bushes. White men! They were beyond understanding.

About the same time Carey came up from below, Luke Alden had been dangerously occupied high above deck, replacing some worn sheets—the corner ropes that held the square tops'ls taut to the yardarm. Yesterday a new wave of rumors, that the captain had no intention of putting his lissome tyo ashore in Tahiti, had gone about the ship.

She was the only vahine on board that he had never seen—or at least, had seen for moments only—and she was unusual in several ways, he thought. She spoke French. She was modest. She covered her breasts with her pareu; none of the men had seen her unclothed, even when fetching and carrying bathwater. And there was even a rumor, courtesy of the ship's laundry, that she'd been a virgin—although the captain had made short work of that. A Polynesian virgin? Hard to believe. But if she were, indeed, a white girl, as he had every reason to suspect . . .

He was shinnying his way back down to the deck, spare lines slung over his shoulder, when he overheard the voices of some crewmen passing by.

"You sure that was the Capn's little piece?"

"That it was. You seen her before—the first day."

"Aye, but she weren't one to catch my eye! Ain't hardly enough of her for a man to get his arm around."

"Depends on your tastes."

"Me, I like 'em stacked."

"Aye—two at a time!"

"Think he knows she's leavin' ship?"

"Mebbe yes, mebbe no. We ain't got orders to stop her. Capn's taken off ashore—same with Noah Mapes. An' the mate—well, he ain't nowhere to be found. If the Capn wanted to keep her aboard, he should a locked her in, or tied her to—Halloa, what d'ye think got into that young fellow Alden? Jest took off—an' dropped them bloomin' sheets like he was expectin' some ancy-fancy lady's maid to pick up after 'im! An' to think I been callin' him a likely lad. Lord-a-mercy!"

Luke reached the rail just in time to see the claw-shaped sail of the outrigger catch the wind. There was a dark-skinned girl just settling herself into the bottom of the canoe. Her hair swung over her face, concealing it for the moment, but he saw as he stared at her that the hair was about eight inches shorter than the other girls'. It was gold beneath the black, he felt sure of it now. Then she turned. The hair swung back to reveal her features. And for one heart-stopping second—for he al-

ready held quite a different coloring in his mind's eye—
he looked into the eyes and the face of the girl he still
held in his heart.

Carey turned her attention to the shoreline. Already
she could see her goal, the white frame house, high on
a hill, that must belong to the Paxtons. Mercy would
hide her; Carey was sure of it.

But they were not heading directly for the shore. Instead, the outrigger had veered off, and was beating its
way toward a distant point of land.

"Where are you taking me?" she asked of the young
Tahitian who owned the boat. She felt no particular
alarm; he looked as though he might be trusted.

Hutiti smiled easily. He wouldn't tell her about the
deserter—not yet. "You do not want the popaa to find
you. I can see that. I, Hutiti, will take you where the
popaa will not find you—a village some miles along the
shore, where you can hide until the white man sails
away."

Carey thought, Yes, perhaps it would be safer to land
at some distance from Matavai Bay, where there was always a chance of encountering Adam. She could easily
walk back later. She nodded acquiescence. Then she
remembered her promise, and took the coin from around
her neck. "Here, Hutiti, this is yours."

Hutiti bit the coin to make sure it was metal. Coins
were of no particular value, but the metal they contained was of great worth. He was satisfied, and was
about to tuck it into the folds of the lava-lava he wore as
a loincloth, when he saw the look on the girl's face.

"It is a very good piece of iron," he said regretfully,
handing it back to her, "but Hutiti does not take payment from a vahine, especially since I can see it is the
only thing you stole."

"I didn't—" But Carey halted her denial, realizing
that what he thought was true. She *had* stolen it. And
when Adam discovered its loss, would he think her any
better than any of the other vahines? . . . *Don't think
about Adam.* That way lay madness; time enough for
madness in the night. Now she must numb her brain to
thoughts of him; and the man Hutiti was still waiting,
with interest, for her answer. "I didn't have a chance to
steal more."

"Then why were you so anxious to leave? Did you kill your lover?"

"Kill him?" Carey puzzled to herself: now why would he think that? "No, I did not kill him. I killed no one."

"Was he cruel, then?"

The ache in her heart begged for tears—tears she would not shed. "Cruel?" A bolt of silk . . . yes, he had been cruel in a way, unwittingly. "Perhaps. But I think he meant to be kind."

Hutiti prodded the pile of pandanus mats and fishnets with his big toe. Starbuck knew it was safe to emerge now. He pushed aside the stifling covering, without losing hold of the musket he had kept beside him, and stretched his cramped limbs—then looked to see which of the vahines it was that he would have to kill.

"You—!"

A slow grin took hold of his face. The captain's little tyo! So it would be a pleasure, after all. Ever since he had heard the woman come aboard, back at the *Sweet Witch*, he had been hoping it was not one of the several vahines who had entertained him so obligingly since Mahi Mahi. It was one thing to kill a man you hated, quite another to kill a woman you had enjoyed—even if only for a few hours.

But this one was different. So he would have his revenge not only on that son-of-a-whore Lovell, but on the captain too! And revenge would be sweet indeed.

But it would have to wait. For the moment he needed the man to take him to safe shelter, and find him food, for he had not eaten since last night. And if he killed the girl, the native might not cooperate.

He ignored Hutiti now, and concentrated on the girl, who was staring at him with profound shock in her eyes. "Aye—an' I wonder if your high-an'-mighty Capn knows where his little doxy's gone? Ain't his nose going to be out of joint!"

Starbuck gave a nasty laugh. "I'd like to see his face when he finds you've hightailed it with your new Tahitian loverboy!" Of all the words spoken back at the *Sweet Witch* and during the voyage since, he had understood only Hutiti's few words of pidgin. "Or will he think you've run off with old matey Starbuck? That's an even better one! An' he'll never know, will he? For you ain't going to be tellin' no tales—nossir, not ever!"

It was then that Carey knew what his intention was. Her heart stopped for an instant, and she hid her consternation by smiling at him, a fixed and silly smile.

"Oho! Tired of your new fella already, eh? So you recognize me—but you don't hold no grudge. Well, Starbuck ain't got time for your flirtations. Not now, leastways." His eyes turned to scour the shoreline, and he fell silent; but he kept his musket over his knee.

"Byemby come place," said Hutiti pleasantly enough—for he thought that the white man must be watching for signs of the village.

"Shut up," snarled Starbuck, but Hutiti did not understand the expression, and started to speak again.

"Mamōō," warned Carey in Tahitian, and all three fell silent. She wished she could catch Hutiti's eye—warn him, somehow, for she was growing certain that Starbuck intended a swift end for him, too.

More minutes ticked by. At length Starbuck saw what he had been looking for. "Here—we land here." He jabbed his musket at a deserted stretch of beach, encased and isolated by high surrounding cliffs, and made signs to show Hutiti that he must head to shore.

Hutiti, astonished, looked at the inhospitable cove and shook his head.

"Here, goddam you!"

"Do as he says," murmured Carey in Hutiti's language.

"But it is a bad place," objected the puzzled Tahitian. "It can be reached only from the sea—and look how the cliffs overhang. There are falling rocks here. Why would any man land in this place?"

"What the hell are you two talking about?" growled Starbuck suspiciously.

"Smile, Hutiti, pretend to be happy. He plans to kill us." Carey finished her bald statement with a tinkly laugh, so that Starbuck's misgivings might be set to rest.

Hutiti believed her. He did not think it strange that she understood the white man's tongue. Obviously, Tahitian was not her true language. And he had seen the fear in her eyes when the popaa had emerged from his hiding place. This must be one of those bad white men—aué, that he had taken such a passenger on his canoe!

"Agh, stow your stupid lingo—put in here." Starbuck

jabbed the musket again, and Hutiti, obedient this time, followed its directive.

"If he gets off first, then we must push to sea at once." Hutiti tried to sound as though he were telling a joke. "If not, we must bide our time." Hutiti laughed hugely, and Carey joined in. Starbuck scowled at them, although he was pleased to see that they suspected nothing.

Hutiti sailed the little outrigger smoothly in to shore, and paddled the last few feet until he had found a good landing place for his craft. Then he waited for Starbuck to step out.

But Starbuck motioned with the gun. The other two obeyed the gesture, and stepped ankle-deep into the water. Starbuck, following, indicated that Hutiti should beach the boat behind a large boulder, where it could not be seen from the water.

With luck, thought Starbuck, only one man would be in the boat when it put out again.

By the time Adam Falconer returned to the *Sweet Witch* from his obligatory visit to the local chieftains, it was early afternoon. Adam was anxious to see Teura at once: he had been told this morning that the local missionary was a man who had no objection to performing marriage rites between white sailors and island vahines. Now, at last, he could ask Teura if she was willing. He waved the longboat back to shore to fetch the missionary, and came aboard.

But something was wrong on deck: he could see that immediately, for as soon as he came over the side several of the men started to speak at once.

"Down in the hold, he was."

"Blood all over him—"

"Couldn't find him nowheres, all through the watch."

"Thank Christ you're here, Capn!"

"What's all this about?" Falconer stilled the agitated babble and singled out one man. "You, Huggins, tell me what's going on."

"It's the mate, Capn. Murder—somebody's tried to murder 'im."

"Mr. Lovell—Christ! Is he dead?"

"No, not dead. Throat's slit, near ear-to-ear, but the knife didn't go too deep. He's alive."

"How bad?"

"Can't say, yet. Noah's with 'im now—an' the second mate too. He's lost a lot of blood. Whoever done it left him for dead in the dark—mebbe couldn't see to finish off the job."

"Who did it?"

"Dunno—we just found 'im, not ten minutes ago, jammed in a big crate, back of the weapons chest."

"Line the men up on deck, at once." Falconer's mind raced. He wanted to see Lovell, to see how he was—but Noah would be doing everything possible belowdecks; at the moment it was urgent to find the would-be murderer before he escaped. "And fetch the second. You, Ah Chin," he ordered, picking a man he trusted implicitly, "you get below and help Noah."

Adam's mind checked off and mentally discarded the men in the longboat. They were all trusted deckhands, or he'd not have chosen them to go ashore today. He had his suspicions, but you could not convict a man on suspicions.

"Who's missing here?" called the second mate once the men were all together.

"I ain't seen Gordo."

"I'm here," grumbled the just-named man in his own defense. "Lord-a-mighty, did you think it was me? You should be frettin' about Ah Chin's whereabouts."

"Ah Chin's below, with Mr. Lovell."

Falconer watched until he was sure. Finally he spoke to the second mate, quietly; and the question was shouted out.

"Anyone seen Starbuck recently?"

There was a silence as each man looked at his neighbor. Then the voices began. No—nobody had seen Starbuck, not since before dawn, at the changing of the watch, the same time Mr. Lovell had gone off to his bunk. Somebody remembered seeing them together; remembered that Starbuck had been foul-mouthed about the lack of shore leave.

"Search the ship. He must be hiding somewhere. It's too far to swim to shore, and I don't think Starbuck can swim anyway."

"We already did, Capn, whiles lookin' for Mr. Lovell. Ain't an inch where a man could be hiding, truck to keel."

"He must have gone ashore, then. Any native canoes here this morning?"

"Aye, one—a trader. A Tahitian. He hung around for a while, till he'd traded off everything. Then he took off."

"To shore?" asked Falconer.

"I didn't see."

"Nor me."

"They went in that direction, Captain Falconer."

Falconer turned to the new voice. It was that young English fellow, Luke Alden. So at least one of the men had been observant.

"They?" Adam Falconer had caught the implications of the plural. Had Alden seen more than one person in the outrigger?

At that moment the returning longboat pulled in beside the *Sweet Witch,* and the inquiry came to a temporary halt. Two men went to help at the rail; and in moments the missionary, a hollow-chested ascetic man clad in unsuitably heavy black alpaca clothing, climbed aboard, panting.

"Ah, I see you already have the men assembled!" Mr. Rivers beamed broadly as he wiped the sweat from his brow. He very seldom got requests for his services from the ships that pulled into Matavai Bay. An iniquitous lot, sailors! But this ship's captain must be a god-fearing man—in spite of the boat-loads of girls who had come ashore not two hours ago. "My name's Rivers—Mr. Rivers."

"This is another matter, Reverend," frowned Falconer. "I'm afraid our business will have to wait for a moment."

"No hurry," returned the missionary good-naturedly. "I can wait."

Falconer turned back to the seamen. "Well then, this Tahitian traded everything, did he—his canoe was quite empty?"

"All but a few mats an' some fishnets."

The same thought occurred to everyone at once, and the men looked at each other sheepishly.

"We didn't think to search before he left, Cap'n. We was too busy watchin' the girl."

"The girl?"

"They left together—she and the brown man," said a brave soul.

"Which girl?"

The men fell silent and shuffled their feet, for nobody wanted to be the first to tell him. Adam felt something cold clutch at his entrails, for he knew—without being told, without even looking in his cabin, he knew. He spun on his heel and aimed toward the hatch.

Mr. Rivers caught at his elbow. "Captain Falconer! When shall I—"

"Damn you, let me go!" Adam tore his arm away with another curse so filthy that even the hardened second mate blanched to think a man of god should hear it. Then, without a backward glance, he flung himself down the companionway.

The missionary stood agape and uncomprehending, watching the captain vanish. Then he regained his composure: he must not forget his duty and his mission. He turned back to the assembled men, and forced a beatific smile to his face.

"Well then—shall we proceed without him?"

Starbuck found it hard not to drowse while he sat in the shade of the cocopalms and watched the others at work. He knew he must kill them at nightfall, or he would not be able to sleep safely. And nightfall was only minutes away.

The man Hutiti was up in a cocopalm, a small distance away, gathering green drinking coconuts as well as ripe ones, and dropping them down to the ground. The girl had been ordered to husk the growing pile of coconuts with a sharpened stake. Starbuck sat with his musket across his knees. He didn't imagine there would be trouble—they knew he was armed. His eyelids began to droop; it had been more than twenty-four hours since he'd slept. A moment later he forced them open and to his astonishment found Teura looking at him with a strange expression. Before he could react, a coconut caught him a glancing blow above the ear, dazing him for the moment. Then another coconut—this one spun the musket from his hands, driving it several feet away. He dove for it, and missed as the girl kicked it aside with her bare feet. With a curse he caught the girl's ankle instead, and rolled, plowing her into the ground. She screamed something he could not understand, in Tahitian. He rolled again, using her body as a shield against the shower of coconuts Hutiti was hurling down, and at that moment a coconut connected with her head. She struggled in his grasp for another second, then suddenly collapsed against him, a dead-weight over his body.

In a trice Hutiti was down from the tree. The girl had said to run for help—and she was right; there was little either of them could do against the white man's fire-stick. It was bad luck that that last coconut had caught her, instead of the man . . .

As he cleared the distance to the water, Hutiti could hear the white man's shouts, as he ran after him. There was no time to get the boat. He plunged into the waters to the sound of a musket firing.

"Come back, damn you!"

With a strength born of desperation, Hutiti's well-muscled arms struck out and left the shore behind. Then, he felt an explosion of pain . . .

"Damn, damn—Christ, damn your filthy black eyes!" Starbuck pounded his musket angrily against the sand. The swimmer was out of range now, his dark outline nearly swallowed by distance and the swiftly advancing tropic sunset. Starbuck had used two shots, but there'd be no third now. It took too long to reload a musket—and in any case, he had dropped the rest of his musket-balls in the scuffle a short time ago. Damn! If he'd reached the shoreline seconds sooner he would have been right on target, though he had seen the man Hutiti lurch in the water, had seen the blood spurting. Well, let the sharks deal with him. It was a long, long swim to the next cove; a wounded man would never make it. All the same, thought Starbuck murderously, if only he had not been still half-dazed by that first blow, if only his musket had not been knocked away, if only he had not had to struggle out from under the girl's inert body.

Remembering her now, he knew he must deal with her at once, before she came to her senses. With fury in his heart for the way these slow-witted Polynesians had duped him—the way *she* had helped dupe him—he turned away from the water and made his way back up the now-dark beach to the grove of cocopalms.

Already it was too black to see properly. He stumbled over a few stray coconuts and finally, falling to his knees, searched for her body with his hands without finding it.

Still clenching his musket, he searched more carefully as his eyes grew accustomed to the dim light. There was no trace of her . . . nothing to indicate where she might have gone.

Good Christ, she'd taken his musket-balls! He threw the gun down in disgust. But he still had his hands, like giant mallets, that had been weapon enough for him many a time. How he'd like to get them around her brown neck!

Carey crouched in the darkness, in a crevice in the cliff-side where a small waterfall slivered its way downward, and where rockslides on either side formed a little grotto that afforded some protection. She was safe here, she thought, at least while it was dark. She had no great hopes that Hutiti would return with help before daylight. She had seen his body spin in the water, caught by musket shot and spurting blood. Hutiti might be dead by now, from the wound or from the ever-present sharks.

No, she could not count on Hutiti for help. Nor could she expect to live long after dawn. Starbuck would kill her as soon as he could see her—perhaps even before dawn, when the moon rose. And she did not want to die.

What could she do? She had nothing—no weapon at all. Only the sharpened stake she was to have used in the husking of coconuts. It was little enough defense, for she knew she would not have the strength or the accuracy to drive the stake into any man's ribs, any more than she would have the strength or the accuracy to take aim and break a coconut. Break a coconut . . .

The stake was never driven into a coconut. The nut had to be smashed against the half-buried stake. Smashed against the stake . . . could it be done?

In the darkness she marked off an area with her hands, about the length from a man's feet to his chest. Very carefully, working in silence, she buried the blunt end of the stake in a few inches of sand. Her fingers searched for loose rocks and found a few of the right size; and these she rolled into place, very slowly, until the stake was securely wedged between them, its point angled slightly toward the grotto's entrance.

But she must make him trip, somehow . . . she was not strong enough to push him. Perhaps on a stone? No—

he might see some indefinite outline by starlight, or feel it with his foot. The musket-balls! She spread them around the entrance, silently. Then she remembered Adam's coin that she had taken this morning, and the plaited silken cord that held it about her neck. The silk had seemed very strong, and perhaps it could be made long enough. Thank goodness Hutiti had not taken it! A good-luck coin, after all! She removed it, and sawed the tied end silently against a sharp stone until it parted. Then her fingers set to work to unplait the silk. She re-tied the three strands into a single longer cord, and then —breath held lest she make any noise—stretched it tautly across the grotto's entrance, and tied and wedged the new ends with rocks, low in the shadows, ankle-high.

She stood up, about to make the noises she hoped would bring Starbuck. She took one last look over her shoulder at the grotto's entrance—and froze. The moon had risen, a quarter-moon, and now its light gleamed, palely but unmistakably, on the white silken cord.

She sat down again and buried her head in her hands, wanting to cry. Oh Adam—Adam! If only he knew where to look for her; if only she had not been too proud or too foolish to tell him the truth; if only he had seen through her disguise.

Slowly, surely, the idea grew in her head. Her dis-guise. It was her last weapon . . . her only remaining weapon. And there was water at hand—not much, but enough, in the thin trickle that came over the cliff. For one thing, she could darken the silk and the wooden stake with the color from her hair. She removed her pareu and crept silently over to the waterfall.

Starbuck was nodding, fighting the fatigue that gripped his entire body. But he jerked back to alertness immedi-ately when he heard the sounds of rocks sliding, another noise as of someone falling, and the muffled gasp in the night. So she was not in the grove of cocopalms after all! She was further away—over by the rockslides. She must have been trying to climb the cliffs in her desperation. He smiled to himself. He could make short work of her now. So he would be able to sleep tonight, after all!

Stealthily, by the now-risen moon, he crept across to the place where the noise had seemed to come from. He could see the outlines of obstacles well enough to avoid them. He could see the heavy boulders; then the darker gap between the two rockslides . . . she must be in there. He heard another noise, a tiny noise, but enough to tell him he was right.

For a moment he saw nothing but a dark crouching shape. Then all at once she rose to her feet, seemingly dazed. For some reason she had wrapped her pareu around her head, and her skin glistened, brown and naked in the moonlight. Her nakedness meant nothing to him; he'd seen too many naked Tahitian girls recently to give it more than a moment's thought. His feet edged carefully forward, for he knew perfectly well it could be a trap. He thought he felt musket-balls beneath his feet . . . damn her, was she trying to make him slip?

Then she pulled her pareu from her hair. He stood for a moment in stupefaction.

"Omigawd!" he gasped, as he stepped forward.

The hair—the cascading, moonlit, *golden* hair—that was the last thing he saw as his ankles connected with the taut dark cord, and he plummeted downward toward the waiting stake.

Three days later, when some of his strength returned, the man Hutiti crawled and clawed his way to the top of the cliffs in an adjoining cove, and worked his way along their crest. He could see at once his canoe was gone.

By now the wound had healed enough that he knew he would not trail fresh blood in the water, so he climbed back down the cliffs by the same difficult route, and, after resting for a few moments, swam around the long tongue of land.

He had expected to find a body—but not this body. Obviously the man had not died right away, for he had crawled some feet from the stake, toward where the girl must have been waiting. His great ham of a hand, grown rigid in death, was still clenched over the girl's pareu. Hutiti was glad she had escaped. He was also astonished that she should have been so ingenious—for he had noted at once that she was not very skilled at the simple tasks the white man had assigned her.

She would be in trouble now, bad trouble. The white man did not rest when one of his own was killed, even if that one was a deserter. And perhaps he, Hutiti, would be in bad trouble too—for who would believe that the girl alone had done this thing? He thought of dragging the white man's body out to sea, where all secrets would soon be devoured; but without his boat, and with the wound in his side only half-healed, he knew he would not have the strength. So, for a few minutes, he moved about at the base of the rocks, rearranging the evidence.

By the time he reached the adjoining inlet, an hour later, he was near collapse. He had to wait until the following morning to climb the cliff once more, and finish the task.

The same morning, an exhausted Adam Falconer trudged up the hill to the white house overlooking Matavai Bay, and introduced himself to Captain Joshua Paxton. But Paxton could not help him; he had heard no rumors of a white deserter ashore—nor, for that matter, of a dark-skinned island girl named Teura. As for the young invalid who was upstairs recuperating under Mercy Paxton's care—well, if Paxton happened to mention that, Adam didn't notice.

The following day, Hutiti's boat was found, empty and deserted, not far from Matavai Bay. It held no clues—except that, strangely, the sail was gone. It remained unclaimed.

It was nearly six weeks before Hutiti himself was found—six weeks during which the *Sweet Witch* stayed anchored in Matavai Bay; the first mate recovered slowly but surely; and Adam Falconer grew gaunt. The men had learned to avoid him, whenever possible, for his eyes had grown haunted and his temper uncertain, and the faint hint of a cruel line about his mouth had deepened into something ugly. Only Noah seemed unafraid to face him. The others preferred not to approach him all, even with the best of news.

And this was not the best of news.

"Blast your mealy mouth, Noah—out with it! How did you find this man Hutiti? Where? Was she with him?"

Noah hesitated, for even he was none too willing to hand over the information. "He was up in the hills, makin' hisself scarce. Like as not waitin' till the *Sweet Witch* weighed anchor. No, she weren't with him. First, he kept his mouth tighter'n a clam, wouldn't admit nothin'. But we knew 'twas him on account of this." He handed over the copper coin, with its gaping hole. The cord was gone. "Paid him for the ride, she did. An' it's true—for the men say she was showin' it to him afore she climbed on his canoe."

"Go on." Falconer's voice was grim; his fist clenched white over the coin.

"Seems that Starbuck was wavin' a musket about. Forced this man Hutiti to put 'em all three into a deserted cove. Bad piece 'o land if ever I saw one! Hutiti took us there. Cliffs all about—no way out, 'cept by sea. Starbuck kept 'em there for a day. Then Hutiti got his wind up . . . decided Starbuck aimed to kill 'em both. He made a dash for it an' swam off. Starbuck was havin' none of that—he took a shot at this fella; turrible bad wound it looked to be, too! But Hutiti got away."

"Go on—get to the others. Any sign of them at the cove? Any clues? Does this Tahitian fellow know any more?"

"Hutiti went back a few days later, to see if they was still there. Found Starbuck's body squashed flatter'n a pancake—musta been hit by a rockslide. We saw the remains."

"And the girl—Teura? God, man, get to the girl!"

"Well, Hutiti had a good look-about for her—an' he finally sighted the edge of her pareu, under a pile o' the big boulders. Showed us, he did. Blood on it an' bits o' bone here an' there—but most of her musta been under the rockslide. An army couldn't move them stones! She musta been buried alive."

⚔ CHAPTER FIFTEEN ⚔

Aboard the *Sweet Witch*, the men were at first speechless with disbelief, but not for long. They found their voices soon enough; and news of the captain's unexpected marriage raced through the ship like fire along a short fuse.

"Pulled the wool over his eyes, she did—tricked him good an' proper!"

"An' her such a re-fined looking little thing."

"Gordo says she ain't so re-fined without 'er clothes on!"

"Course, the Capn were drunker'n a skunk. Still is, for that matter! An' still swillin' the rotgut like it was going out o' style. If Mr. Lovell weren't back on his feet, ain't no way we'd a sailed this morning."

"Drunk or no, never thought we'd see the day any woman'd make him toe the line."

"Toe the line? Wait'll he sobers up! He'll give her the heave-ho, soon enough."

"Where to? Can't heave-ho a lady into the drink. D'you think it's true—that he got into 'er, back on Tahiti, like she said?"

"No doubt. The Capn just stands there, he does, rufflin' his hair, an' the fair sex lines up fer a share."

"Aye, but the Capn don't even like this one. Heard him tell Noah, a coupla weeks ago, to keep her away from him. Said he couldn't bear the sight o' her, that she was pure poison. One o' them flirty virgins, he said, all promise an' no delivery."

"Sounds to me like he got the delivery!"

"But a mission girl—"

"Mission girls got something between their legs, too! Ain't no reason she'd be unsusceptible—for all that she wears those stiff little dresses, an' looks like butter wouldn't melt in 'er mouth."

"Weren't she aboard once before?"

"Aye, before you signed on with the *Sweet Witch*. Scarce out o' the cradle, she was. But she took 'im on then too, although she weren't no match for the Capn. Paddled her rear end proper, he did, an' it weren't no more'n she deserved."

"All the same, don't like to think of 'er down in that cabin with Capn Falconer fair out of his mind with drink—for she seems like a nice, friendly little thing. An' quite a looker, with that hair an' those eyes, if she'd fill out a bit more."

"Nice? Well, I'll grant you that. But when the Capn comes to from his bout with the bottle, she'll be out on her ear. That marriage won't stick, nosirree! Wouldn't give 'er half the chance of a snowball in hell."

And only Luke Alden, who, unable to listen, had walked away at the beginning of the conversation, knew any part of the truth. He, unlike Falconer, had gone to see Mr. Rivers weeks ago, and confirmed his suspicions. He knew where Carey Wyeth had been; he knew the girl Teura had survived. He knew why Carey had wanted to trick Adam Falconer into marriage—or he knew at least a part of the reason; he didn't know she was pregnant. And knowing all this, he began to hate Adam Falconer.

Falconer groaned and stirred. His head felt like a loose spar had been smashing around inside, and there was a bilge pump in his innards. His eyes opened, and Noah's face swam into focus.

"Go away, Noah. You look like a bad dream."

"This time I ain't goin' till you eat."

"Eat?" He groaned.

"You ain't had a bite to eat for six days, Capn—not since we put Tahiti behind us. Reckon you'll feel better if you eat."

"Something to drink, that's what I need. Get me something to drink."

"Nay, Capn, no drink." Noah could be firm when he had to, and now he had to. The captain's private liquor supply had at last run out, and it was time to put an end to the binge.

"Dammit, man—" But Falconer had not the strength to argue, and collapsed weakly against the pillow.

"An egg'll give you strength."

"An egg! Ooooh . . ."

"A soft-boiled egg. That's what Miz Falconer ordered. And some lemon juice."

"Mrs. *who?*"

"Miz Falconer. Here, take a mite spoonful. Then in a while I'll shave your beard, as your hand ain't too steady for the job."

Falconer knocked aside the spoon and struggled to a sitting position. The cabin reeled and tilted nastily, then gradually came into focus.

"Mrs. Falconer! What the hell are you talking about?"

"Your wife."

"My wife! What wife?"

"She's been mindin' you ever since we left Tahiti—but she's up top right now. I reckoned it was best, seein' as how there ain't no bottle within reach this time, an' no tellin' what you might do."

Falconer's head spun. What had happened during this past day—or was it days? His hand encountered a week's stubble on his chin, and told him part of the answer. Wife! Yes, he remembered a woman, some vague shadowy woman, moving about the cabin, helping him once when he stumbled and fell to the floor. What woman? He had known it was not Teura, and that was all that had seemed important at the time.

"Who in God's name did I marry?"

Did he really not know? thought Noah, when they've been shacked up in this cabin together for nigh on a week? He shook his head disbelievingly. "That slip of a mission girl—Miz Carey."

"Oh God." Not her! Not that man-chasing minx—he must be drunk still! It couldn't be true. He didn't even like her. "What happened—what the hell happened?"

And so he heard the story of his wedding night.

Adam Falconer had found Teura several weeks before, although he did not know it. Just before Christmas he had met Carey Wyeth at Joshua Paxton's white frame house overlooking Matavai Bay, for it was there that she had gone that night so many weeks before, wrapped in no more than Hutiti's shredded sails. Joshua Paxton reintroduced them.

"You remember Miss Wyeth? She's just over a long

151

illness. Her brother died a year ago, and . . . what is it, Falconer? You look as though you'd seen a ghost."

Carey dropped her head in consternation. Surely Adam would not recognize her now, not in these English clothes; not with her golden hair close-cropped into little ringlets that spilled about her temples and her ears; not after a month of hiding in Mercy's spare bedroom and scrubbing her skin with lemon juice to restore her fair complexion! Only Mercy, who had kept all visitors at bay, knew the truth; even Joshua Paxton did not. He, like others, believed that Carey had become ill from the grueling months of begging outrigger rides from island to island, following Jonah's death.

Adam, confronted now by the golden curls instead of the eyes, gradually recovered his composure. "Nothing —it's nothing. Miss Wyeth reminded me of someone. A superficial resemblance, that's all." But his face still looked strange and strained, and his eyes, when Carey stole a glimpse from under lowered lashes, were hard and fragmented in the light, like obsidian.

"Maybe it's because we've met before." Her voice was arch, unnatural, and she hated herself for it.

"I remember." At the sound of her words Adam's eyes glazed and became disinterested. "I had forgotten what you looked like."

"You spanked me." She could not look at him; she ached inside. "I think I hated you then."

"Really? . . . . Well, I apologize. Joshua, can I speak to you alone for a moment? About those inquiries you've been making for me . . ."

Carey had already heard, through Captain Paxton, of Mr. Lovell's stabbing, of the search for Starbuck. Was Adam searching, too, for the island girl she once had been? Or was that just wishful thinking? She wanted so very much to think that he had loved Teura. But she wanted even more to be loved as Carey Wyeth. Surely, if she put herself in Adam's way, some spark would ignite.

In the fortnight after emerging from her "sickroom," she tried every wile she could think of to attract him. But he remained at best indifferent to her overtures; and at worst, his scowl, when he saw her arrive yet once more in his path, suggested an active dislike. Carey despaired.

And then Adam started to drink. Suddenly, heavily, blindingly. Why was he drinking? Carey could find out only that Starbuck's body had been found; that the search parties had been stopped; that the *Sweet Witch* would sail within the week. The hint of cruelty about Adam's mouth and his eyes might have warned Carey to stay away from him, if she had not been so desperate. But she *was* desperate: the weeks since she had left Adam's bed had turned a seed of suspicion into a certainty.

Carey was expecting Adam's child.

Mercy, told of this, was willing to cooperate. At dusk on the evening before the *Sweet Witch* was to sail, Mercy lured a thoroughly inebriated Adam Falconer to the white frame house, ostensibly to share a farewell drink with Joshua Paxton. But Joshua Paxton was not there: Mercy had sent him off on some fabricated errand. With a flurry of apologies, Mercy produced a bottle of medicinal rum and vanished, supposedly to search for her husband, leaving Carey alone with Adam. But things did not go quite as planned. In one long swallow of rum, Adam passed out.

"Drat, drat . . . damn you, Adam Falconer!" Carey pulled desperately at his stuporous form slouched against a chair. The plan she and Mercy had so carefully concocted called for herself and Adam to be found in a bedroom, making love. Carey had been sure that in his drunken state he would respond to a direct invitation, and would in fact hardly notice whose bed he was sharing. Certainly, during this past week of excessive drinking he had been sharing many beds in Tahiti, and those quite indiscriminately.

But it was evident that she had been too optimistic. Carey managed to dislodge Adam from the chair, only to have him collapse into a sodden heap on the floor. She tried to rouse him without success, and at last, hearing the sounds of footsteps crunching up the path toward the house, she hastily extinguished the one lamp burning in the front parlor, and wrenched off the pale sea-green dress and demure undergarments donated by Mercy. Her fingers fumbled at Adam's buttons, but it was too late. As the front door opened, she wound her arms around his inert form, bent her head over his face, and kissed him with a fervor she hoped would not seem too one-sided.

"Good God—Carey! Falconer! What's going on here?"

Carey raised her head with a guilty start, and rolled over, pulling Adam's shoulders after her so that he lay sprawled over her nakedness.

"Captain Paxton! Oh dear."

It was only then that she saw the others: Noah and Nate Gordo, who had come with a dim whale-oil lantern to find their missing captain, and had met Joshua Paxton along the way. Carey snatched at her discarded clothes and squirmed out from under Adam's leaden body.

"What are you doing there, you two?" Paxton peered at the dark shapes. With his one good eye, it was hard to see in this light. "What in God's name are you doing? Dammit Falconer, she's a mission girl, and not used to the likes of you!"

Noah was becoming suspicious. He thought the captain was unnaturally slow in defending himself, so with his lamp he moved across the room.

"Sweet heaven! He's out cold. Colder'n a virgin's tit. An' he ain't so much as loosed up his belt buckle."

"Carey," said Joshua Paxton sternly, "did he make love to you or not?"

Carey knew she had lost the gamble; she had nothing more to lose. "No, not here, not tonight. Other times."

"Then, by God, he'll make an honest woman of you!"

"Now look here—" objected Noah.

"Do you want to marry him, Carey?"

"Yes. Yes, I do."

"Marry!" exploded Noah, who knew he must protect his captain at all costs. "Marry some loose tramp who's tumbled with half the men aboard ship! Ask them! Ask them all! Ask Gordo here!"

"Bedded her meself, last week," grinned Gordo.

"An' he ain't the only one'll swear to it! Marry, pah! The Capn ain't marryin' no one!"

"Whyn't you ask the Captain?" slurred a voice from the floor, and everyone looked down in amazement. Falconer had regained wit enough to remember, somewhere in his swimming senses, that he had indeed intended to marry. With a great welling happiness in his

154

heart, he stumbled blindly to his feet. "Whyn't you ask the goddam Captain?"

Noah had warned Carey to stay away from the cabin as long as she was able, and she did. The wait was not so awful, for at the moment her whole being sang with happiness. Her spirits leaped and gamboled as light-heartedly as the school of dolphins she spent much of the day watching. Life was good . . . it *would* be good. This past week had been difficult; Adam had been dreadful. But she knew now that he had cared for Teura, that he had cared a very great deal for Teura. She had heard his drunken ravings, seen his wild rages. And she intended to tell him everything, as soon as he sobered up and made love to her as Carey Wyeth.

At nightfall Noah informed her that Adam was by now reasonably sober, although he still had a fierce hangover. He warned her of nothing else—for how could he tell Miz Carey, whom he personally liked, what the captain thought of her?

But Carey had expected the glowering eyes, and was not alarmed. She closed the cabin door behind her, quietly and firmly.

"Hello, Adam."

He looked at her for several stony moments; then walked across the cabin and circled her slowly, as if inspecting her. At last he stood before her again, and his eyes traveled insultingly down her figure, then back to her face. He hated the fact that she reminded him so much of Teura—that she had always reminded him of Teura, every time he had seen her since that first day, weeks before, at Joshua Paxton's. His mouth twisted: "So you finally did it."

"Did it? I don't understand."

"Come on, Miss Wyeth. Don't play innocent with me. Anyone with half an eye can see what's going on. You've been making a play for me for weeks. Your brother died—I'm sorry for that. You needed someone to look after you—I'm sorry for that. But why the hell did you have to set your sights on me?"

"That's not—" But it was true, much of it. She stopped.

"You've been chasing me around ever since we met at Paxton's house—met again, that is. Well, I didn't much like you when I first met you, and I like you even less now."

"Adam, please—"

"Dammit, you don't have the right to call me Adam! It's Captain Falconer to you."

"Captain Falconer, I can't argue with anything you've said. But we've been married for a full week now. Shouldn't you start making the best of it?"

"There is no best of it. My cargo's already well over-due, or I'd turn right back and dump you in Tahiti. As it is, I plan to leave you in Macao."

"You can't do that!"

"Watch me." His voice was curdled with dislike, and Carey felt chilled by it. But she was his wife now, and long before they reached Macao it would all work out: she clutched that thought to herself, until she heard his next words.

"As I don't intend to consummate this little charade, it shouldn't be too hard to get an annulment."

"You couldn't!"

"Why not? You're still a virgin, aren't you? And don't bother to lie—I can easily find out for myself, right now."

She stared at him, speechless with rage, amber sparks flying from her eyes.

"Noah told me all about the little scene you planned —very provocative. But even you admitted I didn't make love to you that night. You told the others I'd done it before then—and I *know* I didn't. I slept ashore that week, but I know where I slept, and it wasn't with you. There's more than one Tahitian girl who'll vouch for it— would you like their names? And you can say what you like about what's happened this week, in this cabin— you're lying. I've not been capable."

She had indeed intended to lie to him about this past week, but confronted with his direct accusation, her face flamed and gave her away.

"Ah, so I am right. I haven't touched you. You're a virgin—in spite of the fact that you'd have been will-ing to spread your tight little thighs long enough to snag a husband in them."

"How dare you!" Her voice shook with outrage that he should talk so—he, who had taken her virginity from her!

"Look, Miss Wyeth, you tricked me when I was drunk, but you—"

"Mrs. Falconer to you!" she broke in, her entire body trembling with righteous fury. "And I intend to keep it that way. You can't prove I'm not your wife—in *every* sense. It's only your word against mine!"

The twist of his mouth mocked her, cruelly. "Oh, is it?" Suddenly his arms caught at her waist and carried her, flailing uselessly, to the bed. He threw her skirts to her waist without preamble, and when she struggled to prevent him from removing her undergarments, he tore them away from her skin. Then his hands were on her— his hands that she had wanted and ached and longed to feel on her again; but they might as well have been the hands of a stranger.

"Lie still—or do I have to tie you down? I'd like to wring your lily-skinned neck, but I don't want to injure you anywhere else."

Finally, weary of her struggles and afraid of harming her unintentionally, he shifted so that his knees pinned her legs to the bed. Then he took her thrashing arms and trapped them to her side. After a few moments, her resistance abated, then ceased altogether. There was no use, she thought—he was far too powerful, for one thing. And for another, she wanted him to know, to be quite certain that she was not a virgin, that she could not be discarded with some easy annulment.

"Have you decided to do as I say? I want to look at you down there, that's all. I won't hurt you. Would you rather I called Noah in? He's quite capable of doing what has to be done, and he'll be as impersonal as a doctor."

She nodded a miserable negative, shamed by the indignity of it all. Then she turned her head away so that she might not see what he was doing. But she could feel it—feel it with every humiliated pore in her body. His hands spread her thighs apart without emotion; his fingers were clinical in their impartiality.

"Christ!"

She sat up at once, knowing he had encountered no obstruction, and unwilling to let his unfeeling hands stay on her a moment longer than necessary.

"You conniving, cheating little strumpet!"

She huddled her arms around herself to stop the uncontrollable shivering that had seized her. This man with his cold black-diamond eyes and his hard hands was not Adam. He was an unfeeling, hateful stranger, and at this moment she would have died rather than tell him the truth.

Her eyes mirrored the dislike in his, and she tried to put all the scorn of betrayed womanhood into her voice: "What did you find out, Captain Falconer? Am I a woman or not?"

He answered her with a curse, and started to leave the cabin. He badly needed some fresh air and some time to compose himself, for at the moment he wanted nothing more than to throttle this scheming little bitch, and he was afraid if he stayed here he would do just that. God, how he needed a drink! But drink had given him *this*, this wife, this albatross about his neck—and drink, if he kept at it, might make him give in to the demands of his body some night, and use her. Something he intended never to do! No, there'd be no drink.

Just before he closed the door behind him, he swung back on his heel, and said coldly:

"Why the hell couldn't you pick on the man who did it?"

⋘ CHAPTER SIXTEEN ⋙

The gentle breezes that toyed with the *Sweet Witch* for the next five weeks were perhaps pleasant for those ashore, but on a sailing ship the wind could be measured in time, and time in profits. To Adam, anxious to get to Macao and be rid of his unwelcome wife once and for all, it seemed only one more insult—for her presence on board ship set his teeth constantly on edge.

For the past weeks Adam and Carey had shared the confined quarters as though they had been strangers. A dozen times she had started to speak to him, to catch at his elbow, almost as though she had something on her mind. But whatever it was he didn't want to hear it; and he would thrust her abruptly aside, and leave the cabin. He spent as much time as possible on deck. When he saw her hated figure emerging, he would vanish gracelessly and as soon as possible. Let her foist her starved affections on some other soul—Noah, or that young pup Luke Alden, or Jed Lovell, or any other man who was fool enough to pass the time of day with her! As long as she stayed away from *him!*

He could not bear to see her. He could not bear to touch her—even the brushing of her hand against his sleeve was anathema to him.

It was the chance resemblance to Teura—that was the thing that drove him mad, that twisted the knife in his entrails. He supposed that was why he had raced this girl to the preacher on that drunken night back in Tahiti— why he had stood and said the silly words, the words that had shackled him to her, the words that had turned her into a dragging anchor in his life. He wanted to put Teura behind him, to start forgetting her, for she was dead—and the dead had to be forgotten. But every time he saw his wife, he was forcibly reminded of Teura— Teura, perhaps horribly mutilated, perhaps raped, perhaps killed even before the rockslide—and he would never know. His wife was a living reminder, a ghoulish joke that a twisted fate had played upon him.

Even now, as he lay in his hammock, he could hear her moving about the cabin quietly, doing small things as she prepared to extinguish the lamp. He wondered if she undressed in the dark, or if she undressed at all.

Suddenly he knew what he must do if he was to put her out of his mind. It was no more than she would expect, after all. She had tried often enough to get him to look at her, God knows.

He opened his eyes without getting out of the hammock, without even moving.

She was still clothed, but her hands were at her high collar, at the top of a long row of tiny buttons. She no longer teased her hair into the tiny ringlets he had hated. Instead, it was pulled back into a knot on the nape of her neck, and that was what caught the light now—her hair. Her lower lip, caught in her teeth, betrayed her concentration as she worked at the buttons of her dress, and made her look younger. It was the virginal mission-girl look she had had when she first came to the Pacific. How had she lost her innocence, he wondered? Suddenly it occurred to him that perhaps she had lost it only technically—that it had been one of those accidents of nature that sometimes happened. A fall perhaps, or some vigorous activity. If so, he had been doing her an injustice. But she had tricked him all the same, the husband-hungry little cheat, and he did not like to be tricked.

Her hands traveled down slowly, finding and releasing each button-loop. She seemed to be having difficulty. He noted that the fabric of her dress strained against her breasts. At least she did not have Teura's figure. Teura's figure had been much slighter, less full in the breast, more graceful. Also, this girl was taller than Teura— taller by an inch or two. And Teura would have been stifled by such clothes, dun-colored and not particularly attractive, the kind of thing that came out in mission-barrels from England, cloyingly heavy for this climate, and several years after the fashion.

As the dresses grew tighter, Carey had grown more despondent. What was she to do? What *could* she do? Adam's dislike of her was so evident. For some days

160

she had thought he would get over his initial anger; that then, perhaps, he would notice her. But by now she had begun to wonder if she would ever, could ever, attract him. Perhaps he only liked lithe brown-skinned island girls. And she was not a brown-skinned island girl. Soon, she would be little more than a lumpy, shapeless cow. There was no going back . . . the masquerade had been just that: a masquerade, and it could never have been sustained for more than a week or two. Much as she might have liked, she was not Teura; she could never be Teura again.

How could she tell him now, unless he showed some interest in her? If Adam could not feel some kind of attraction for Carey Wyeth—for pale-skinned, pale-haired English Carey Wyeth—there could be no future for them, ever. She had forced him into marriage; she could not force him into love. But at least her child, *their* child, would be born with his father's name.

Each night, when she readied herself for bed, she undressed slowly, while the whale-oil lantern still spilled its antique gold over the shadowy cabin interior. She always waited until Adam returned to the cabin, no matter how late it was. And he always threw himself into his hammock, without even undressing, and closed his eyes at once. He never watched her. She knew this, for she always faced his hammock while she undressed; and hoped.

But she was growing unhappy about her thickening figure. Soon she would not want to face him at all.

"Have you ever gone horseback-riding?"

Carey looked up in some surprise—not only because he had deigned to speak to her at all, but because of the strangeness of the question.

"Yes, some. A long time ago." It did seem a long time ago, an eternity ago. "I used to like it. Why do you ask?"

"No reason." Then, because her hands had come to a halt over the next button, he said: "Go on."

His eyes were upon her, but hooded by the shadows that fell across the cabin. Somehow, from the unpleasant look about his mouth, she sensed that they were cold and appraising; that they were taking her apart and finding her wanting. She flushed, and hesitated.

"Don't stop. You've undressed for me before, remember?"

Carey gave a start, thinking of quite different occasions, until he added: "I'm afraid I was too drunk to appreciate it. Undress for me now."

She had long ago forgotten any feelings of false modesty. Why, then, did her hands tremble and fumble as they fought their way down the remaining rows of buttons—while they loosened the fastenings about the waist? Why did it seem so hard to lean over, to step out of the unbecoming dress? She felt conscious, blushingly conscious, of the thinness of her camisole, of its low rounded neckline, of her burgeoning breasts, of her wildly beating heart. The ribbons that fastened the undergarment defied her fingers, and Adam, lying there with his hands folded behind his head and the implacable twist of his mouth, did nothing to make it easier for her. She had the sickening feeling that he would watch her until she had stripped herself totally naked, and then merely close his eyes and drift into slumber. The thought was degrading. She knew how she wanted the evening to end . . .

She stopped trying to undo the ribbons. Her voice shook a little: "If you want me to take off any more, you'll have to help me."

"You didn't need any help the last time."

"That was different. You were drunk and—and you weren't watching, the way you're watching now."

"You must have wanted a husband very badly!"

"I did."

"Why?"

She paused, and picked her words carefully. How could she tell him that she had not wanted his child to be born a bastard, as he himself had been? "Some people aren't very good at looking after themselves." Babies, for instance, she added in her mind.

"The helpless type. God save us."

"I'm not exactly helpless."

"You are with those ribbons. Come over here and I'll unfasten them for you."

So she went across to the hammock with hope and fear in her heart. She stood very still while his hard sunbrowned fingers deftly undid the ribbons. And she stood still when he took the embroidered straps and slowly pulled them downward, over her shoulders; when he

162

pulled the whole bodice down to her waist, baring her to his view.

She could not look at him. She waited for him to touch her. Surely he must touch her now.

"You have good firm breasts, I'll grant you that." His eyes, still shaded but now visible, flickered over her half-naked form. Only the eyes touched her; nothing else. "You can do the rest yourself."

His voice was flat, unemotional. Demeaned by its tone, she looked at him with the beginnings of anger.

"Don't you have any feelings at all? You look at me as though I were—cattle."

He grinned, a slow unholy grin that was crueler than any she remembered. His hand found hers and guided it, and held it against the stiffness. "Does that shock you? I mean it to. But I don't intend to do a thing about it— not a damn thing. Now get out of your petticoats." He pushed her hand away, discarding her.

So he desired her, but he would not attempt to take her. Yet he *must* take her. She must make him take her. But how, how . . .

She tilted her head provocatively: "Are you afraid to make love to me?"

He looked at her strangely. Where had it gone, that untouched virginal look of a few moments ago? Now her naked breasts flaunted . . . taunted . . . teased.

Then she laughed, the laugh of a hoyden. "I see you are. If you were a real man you'd be out of that hammock and—"

He pulled her head down toward where he was lying in the hammock and kissed her hard, hurtfully. His hands sought and seized and punished her breasts, grown tender with pregnancy. She did not mind, for she knew now that she could goad him into anything. She twisted out of his arms and twirled happily across the cabin. She unpinned her hair and tossed it, tousled it with her hands, her movements deliberately sinuous and suggestive. Oh, *why* was he still lying there?

"Don't you wonder what it will be like? Don't you wonder whether I will use my tongue or my teeth, whether I will leave claw-marks on your back or on your belly . . . whether I will moan out loud and wrap my legs around you . . . aren't you curious at all?"

He looked, and lusted, and hated himself and her.

How could she do this; where had she learned such shamelessness?

"How many men have you done this with?"

"You'll never know, will you? Because I won't tell you until I've done it once more—with you. What are you waiting for?" A petticoat flew into the air, and fluttered to the floor. Then a shoe followed; two shoes—and he did not notice that their sensible heels had added an inch or more to her height.

The tramp, the little tramp, he thought, and he wanted her badly—but she was trying to corner him into this, as she had cornered him into marriage. Her eyes, glancing sidelong over her shoulder, were amber memories; but her body was an uncharted sea, pale, tempting, swaying, seductive . . .

"Don't you make love to white girls, *tane?*" Scorn and sensuality mingled in her voice. "Or are you only interested in cheap little Tahitian vahines?"

He was across the cabin in seconds, half-crazed with lust and anger. He mounted her brutally, like a frenzied rutting animal, and she encouraged him—at first. But moments later she started to struggle.

"Please, Adam—Adam, you're hurting me! Wait I have to tell you something—"

But he no longer cared about anything, and he clamped his mouth over her strangled cries. All that mattered now was the savage need to drive, and drive, and go on driving, until he had vented every last vestige of his awful rage and frustration. Damn her, damn her, damn her, damn her, damn her . . .

CHAPTER SEVENTEEN

"It's smoke all right, by the lord Harry! Send for the captain!"

The *Sweet Witch* was five days out of Macao, passing well to leeward of some lumpy outcroppings of rock that were no more than pinpricks on the navigation charts. They could hardly be dignified with the name of islands, for there was nothing there.

But there was smoke. On the far horizon a thin unmistakable wisp of it drifted slowly upward.

Within minutes Adam Falconer was at the rail, and Lovell too. Lovell was by now thoroughly recovered, although the scars on his throat would always remain a livid testimony to his brush with death.

"Shall we put in, Captain? Could be the remains of a shipwreck."

"Yes, we'll put in with the longboat. But first break out the charts, Mr. Lovell—we'll see what the soundings are."

Within minutes the *Sweet Witch* had changed course, and was picking its way cautiously, under reefed tops'ls only, toward the inhospitable and dangerous shoals.

"Mr. Alden! Take the longboat and six men. See what you can find." Adam Falconer would have preferred to send Noah along, in case there were men in need of medical attention, but Noah was busy below, watching over the girl. God, if only Carey had told him she was pregnant! The mental image of her in his bed, bleeding and silent, did little for his peace of mind.

In the hierarchy of the ship, Luke Alden had moved up a notch since the day he had stood and watched Hutiti's canoe vanish across Matavai Bay. If he had been observant about that, Adam Falconer had thought, perhaps the lad was ready to move upward in the scheme of things. Alden was by far the youngest of the men aboard the *Sweet Witch*. He was not much more than a stripling, but at least he was no longer the raw sixteen-year-old who had come aboard more than two years before. He'd proved himself trustworthy and intelligent, if somewhat close-mouthed. If he seemed to hold himself a little apart from the rest of the crew, perhaps it was because he was the only Britisher aboard; elsewhere in the world the Americans and the British were, by now, truly at loggerheads. Or perhaps it was because the other men were a little afraid of the strength they sensed in his broadening shoulders . . . but Luke, if he had the look of a fighter, did not have the temperament of one. He was slow to anger, and although admiring stories had gone about the ship of one monumental scuffle in port, a year or so back, Luke had never become involved in any of the petty disputes aboard the *Sweet Witch*. Yes, a likely lad—still too young, but the raw material of a ship's captain, some years hence. Why, Adam wondered, had he sometimes decently detected a current of something elusive in those electric blue eyes—a fleeting coldness, a condemnation, almost as if Luke disliked him? Well, settling on the best man for a job should have nothing to do with personal likes and dislikes. So when the boatswain had fallen victim to a chest ailment not two weeks since, and then died, young Alden had been given the job. It was this that had earned him the added formality of Mister when Falconer addressed him.

Luke Alden's eyes scoured the empty, unprepossessing lump of rock. If there was a man alive here, he was certainly not in sight. "Back starb'd, men! We'll swing around to the other side—perhaps we'll find him there."

And finally they found him: half-buried in what little sand could be found for protection from the sun, his tongue blackened with thirst, his pockmarked face blistered. Only his eyes seemed alive, and they were like black marbles, glittering and expressionless in the Oriental face.

"Christ! He's half-dead. A mutineer, d'you think?"

Luke Alden kneeled down beside the man; the glittering eyes followed him. "I don't know. But it would take a hard lot of men to put a living soul ashore on a godforsaken flyspeck like this. Here, hand me that water bottle."

"He could a been in a shipwreck, got carried here on a piece o' flotsam. He's a big, strong-looking fella for a Chink—even if he's more dead'n alive right now."

Several pairs of hands started to dig the man's body out from its self-made grave of sand. "Wonder how he came here?"

"We'll find out when he's able to talk. Give me a hand, will you? He's too weak to walk."

But they didn't find out, not in the time it took to get to Macao. The man had amazing recuperative powers, that was clear, for within three days he showed few signs of his ordeal, but he remained silent. Even Ah Chin, who spoke some Mandarin as well as his native Cantonese, was unable to communicate; and after the first two dogged days of trying, he gave up. Perhaps shock had robbed the man of the powers of speech. Perhaps he spoke some obscure dialect. Perhaps he was a mute. So at last, when the novelty had worn off, he was left in peace. He spent most of his time squatting cross-legged on the foredeck in an inconspicuous place, staring out to sea, moving only when his meals were brought. If he slept, no one could see any indication of it, with his pock-marked face remained impassive; only the eyes watched.

Once the rocky shoals had been left safely behind, Adam forced himself to face the thing he had been dreading—a confrontation with his wife. Carey looked thinner now. Thinner; and there were purple shadows under her eyes, giving them a bruised look in the pinched face. Her pale features didn't change expression when Adam entered the cabin, but she turned her eyes from the skylight and watched, wordlessly, while he approached.

Adam could not pretend to feelings he did not have, but the sight of her bleached lips and lackluster eyes did give him the uneasy notion that he had not been entirely fair with her. And he did believe he owed her an apology, even though she had led him on.

"Noah says you're a little better this afternoon. You were asleep yesterday when I looked in." The night before last, after it had happened, Adam had at last moved out into the crowded officers' quarters, so that his cabin could be used as a sickroom.

"Oh?" Her voice was toneless.

"I'm sorry about the other night."

"So am I. It was a mistake."

"If I had known you were pregnant, I wouldn't have been so—so brutal. I'm afraid I lost control."

"If you had known I was pregnant would you have touched me at all?"

"No."

There was a silence between them, an awkwardness, compounded by both their memories of what had happened. It was broken, finally, by Carey, and there was a trace of bitterness in her voice.

"At least you know now why I wanted a husband."

"I suppose it's hard for a mission girl who learns she's to be an unwed mother."

"I stopped being a mission girl some time ago. But I wanted the child to have a father. I didn't want him to be a—a bastard."

"Wouldn't the real father have been a better choice?" She didn't answer that, so he went on:

"Who is—was—the father?"

She turned her head away. "Does it matter now? Do you care, one way or another?"

"Not particularly. Unless it was one of the men on my ship."

She felt a little bubble of hysteria rising in her throat. Adam, seeing the way her hands tightened over the edge of the bed-cover, began to suspect that he might have guessed correctly.

"Was it?"

She didn't answer immediately, and when she did, her voice was muffled. "It happened before then—before your ship arrived in Tahiti."

He saw she was being evasive, and left the matter. Who could it have been—a deserted gone on the beach in Tahiti, living with the natives? Not Joshua Paxton! Not Mr. Rivers, surely . . . perhaps one of the young Tahitians. They were a handsome, well-built race . . . it was just possible she might have lost her head over one of them. But really, she had every right to be secretive. It was none of his business. At least, not now that he was no longer expected to father a child that was not his own. He changed the subject.

"We'll be landing in Macao in a few days."

"Oh?"

"I'll make sure you're settled there."

"Settled?"

"In a small house. It shouldn't be too hard to rent one furnished. While you're recuperating, you'll need a couple of servants. Then, when you get your strength back, you can think about traveling again—back to England. But don't worry about that now. The first thing is to get yourself well. I think you'll need a couple of months in Macao."

"And will you be there?" She turned her head back to him.

He knew what she meant, for at this moment she made no attempt to hide the soul in her eyes. But he pretended not to understand. "Yes, I'll stay in Macao for a few weeks. It takes a while to change cargoes. But I'll be aboard the *Sweet Witch* most of the time. All my things are here—it's convenient."

She would not plead with him; she was too proud. Now she would have to get used to the pain of losing Adam—and their child. From the beginning, she had told herself that their relationship was a fleeting one, a moment stolen out of time. The matter of a child had, for a time, put a different complexion on things: she had wanted to fight for something more permanent between them. But now, her whole reason for forcing Adam into marriage no longer existed. Without a child she had no hold over him—and in any case, Adam was not a man who took kindly to being coerced. *I won't be run by any woman,* he had said to Teura, *not even you . . .*

And now he had too much to hate her for. She had deceived him, tricked him, taunted him, lied to him, even goaded him into destroying the very seed he had placed in her. There was too much to be forgiven, on both sides. No, he could never love Carey Wyeth. Adam was her past: he had to be forgotten. She forced a note of gaiety into her voice.

"I'll need some new clothes in Macao. Do you mind? I have some money in England. I can pay you back."

What a changeable creature she is, he thought: one moment all eyes, the next moment almost sunny. He had not expected her to take it so well. But then, he hardly knew her. Perhaps in her own way she was as complex as Teura. But he had no intention of finding out.

"Buy all the clothes you want. And, hell, you don't have to pay me back. It's the least I can do. And I'll

169

leave you enough money to book passage to England, as soon as you're feeling well enough. You can apply for divorce there. It's hard to get, but not impossible. I'll send you some evidence before I leave harbor."

"Evidence?"

"It shouldn't be hard. I usually take a mistress in port." He didn't tell her that this time he had decided to take some woman, yet to be chosen, next time he put out to sea—someone to help him forget Teura.

"Oh." Suddenly she felt very weary. Adam was life and strength and the pulse of the Pacific and all the things she wanted, at this moment, to escape . . . "I'm very tired now. Could you leave me?"

Seeing her blue-veined lids flag downward with fatigue, Adam went quietly to the door. After he had left the cabin, he realized that for the first time since he'd met her twenty-odd months ago, he quite liked the girl.

Five days later the *Sweet Witch* found anchorage in the Macao roads. By now Carey was feeling well enough to sit on deck in the sun for an hour or two, while the ship dropped anchor. That first day in Macao harbor, she told Luke Alden she would be leaving the *Sweet Witch* and taking up residence in Macao for a while, before returning to England. Dear Luke . . . she would miss him. He had been a good friend.

"Can I come and see you, Carey? We'll be at anchor here for a few weeks."

"No, Luke. I don't want to see anyone from the *Sweet Witch*. Do you mind? It's just that I'm still not feeling too well, and—"

"Is it true?" Luke broke in, blue eyes bitter, holding her. "What the men have been saying all week—that you lost a child. That *he*—"

"No, it's not true," she said quickly. "How could you think such a thing? It's just a—a woman's complaint, that's all. I don't think the Pacific climate agrees with me. It's too hot, too elemental. I don't belong here, I never have. I'm one of those—" she caught herself. One of those Pacific casualties, she had been about to say. But would Luke understand? She could not bear to explain what she meant, to go through all the things that Mercy had said about survivors. Adam was a survivor . . . Noah . . . maybe, strangely, Mr. Rivers . . . certainly Mercy herself, and Joshua Paxton too. And Luke —would he be? It was hard to tell. She had faced the fact that she was not a survivor herself. But then, she had grown up, and Luke had not. Suddenly he seemed very young.

Moments later Luke left, for the longboat was about to put to shore. It was then that Carey noted for the first time the heavy-set Chinese man whose life Adam had saved. She had heard nothing of the incident the other day, but she knew he was no member of the crew, and she was curious.

Noah told her something of the story the next day. "But we'll never know it all, Miz Carey. By this morning he was gone, without so much as a by-your-leave. Ain't hide nor hair of him anywheres, an' we've searched the whole ship, stem to gudgeon. Musta slipped over the side, silent as you please. Them Orientals is hard to fathom."

By the third day in Macao, Adam had arranged to keep all his promises—the house, the servants, the money. He took Carey ashore and saw her settled in a small but comfortable residence in a good district; gave her the name of a trusted house of merchants who would arrange for her passage to England in a couple of months, when she was strong enough for the arduous six-month voyage; and walked out the door.

Within the week, Adam had also provided Carey with the promised evidence, for he had found a new Chinese mistress, and was living with her quite openly aboard the *Sweet Witch*.

✂ CHAPTER EIGHTEEN ✂

Macao in the year 1808 was a rowdy, pox-ridden, sweaty whore of a city. It was a city of strange bedfellows. British traders rubbed shoulders with Russian diplomats who had signed treaties with their sworn enemy; Spaniards with Swedes; Finns with Irish; lean-hipped Connecticut Yankees with corpulent brown-frocked friars; swarthy turbaned sahibs from India with haughty-eyed Portuguese fidalgos; delicate-boned Annamese from the lands to the south with moon-faced Orientals from the forbidden cities to the north.

Macao was the main port of call for traders into the Orient. All of China, except for the highly restricted port of Canton, was closed to the barbarian devils of the Western world who came seeking tea and silks and rhubarb and other goods that only the Middle Kingdom, with its celestial blessings, could provide. And so Macao thrived.

The harbor was a crazy-quilt of ships, diverse as the men who had sailed them here: The "East Indiamen," those prosperous bulge-bellied British tea ships; the apple-cheeked Dutch merchant ships; the bedragoned Chinese naval junks; the lean, hard, fur-bearing Nor'west traders and hide-droghers. Nearby were anchored the sloops and luggers and schooners that had the speed and the maneuverability to smuggle, to dodge pirates, and to weather typhoons up the China coast. Ancient Portuguese carracks and caravals, some long beyond their sailing days, rotted at anchor, cheek-by-jowl with high-sterned native lorchas, their lacquered transoms bobbing brightly to the breeze. Dilapidated sampans strung their grass ropes along the shorelines, and whole families slept under single shaky roofs. And of course, moored everywhere, were the sing-song boats, the innumerable gilded junks where flower-girls made love, strummed the moon-fiddle, and burned joss-sticks to Cheung Neung, the patron saint of whores.

Macao embraced every vice, every degradation, every form of prostitution. From India came the opium, the foreign mud: dark sticky cakes of oblivion from Patna and Benares and the Portuguese colonies, waiting to be shipped up the coast, against the express orders of the Chinese Dragon Throne. From China came the steaming boatloads of Hakka coolies, to be sold to anyone who could pay the price of cheap indentured labor: and later, if the laborers did not live, there were no questions asked. Girls of all nations poured into Macao—white Russians, Chinese, Malays, Goanese, Moors, Kaffirs, agile French whores. Some came willingly, for there was always work in the innumerable brothels and pleasure boats. Others came not so willingly, doped into submission, for the traffic in women was lucrative, and authorities looked the other way if a little money changed hands. Slave-girls from Macao found their way into countless brothels and well-hidden bedrooms in secreted houses throughout Asia, and beyond. Once they were there, their fate was not to be contemplated, for it could not be changed. They were best forgotten.

A different kind of forgetfulness was to be found in the joss-houses, Macao's famous gambling establishments; and these, it was said, outnumbered even the brothels. Here, fortunes rose and fell, regularly and almost unnoticed, like the waves of the sea; and if one man more or less chose to die by his own hand after losing all he owned at the fan-tan tables, who was to notice? The games of chi-fi and mah-cheuk went on; the roulette wheels spun; the faro cards were turned; for another man could always be found to take the dead man's place.

But there was another side to Macao—long sweeps of green lawn and cool whitewashed mansions, secluded walled gardens and gracious manicured streets. Macao had its respectable homes, and its respectable districts. If some of the inhabitants of these homes paid for them with money made in less than respectable ways, it was something seldom talked about. This was, after all, a world away from the seamy, thriving waterfront—the Praya Grande.

Adam Falconer left the Praya Grande behind him now, and hailed a sedan chair to take him to the eminently respectable district where he had installed Carey nine months before. He assumed she had left for England long ago—or he would have called when he had first reached Macao. But she had promised to leave a message for him with the servants who came with the rented house; and who would doubtless still be there.

He was cheerful, in the best of moods; and he whistled a low tune through his teeth as the sedan-chair bumped along towards its goal. It had been a good year, all things considered. The load of sandalwood he'd brought to Macao from Owhyhee in the Sandwich Islands—or Hawaii, as some people pronounced it—had been snapped up at once by eager buyers. It had been a good idea, that. Although he had traded in Hawaii a number of times in previous years, this was the first time he'd tried dealing in sandalwood. He was sure that within a few years, as soon as the Hawaiians ended this eternal bickering over who should be king, there'd be dozens of ship's captains clamoring for similar cargoes.

He had not forgotten Teura. He would never forget Teura completely. He had, however, at last accepted her death, even though his dreams were still at times troubled with visions of how she might have died. But time had blurred the memory, and the pain. The night with Carey—that brutal, passionate night—had been a catharsis of sorts; after that the wounds had begun to heal.

For another thing, his Chinese mistress had turned out to be a great success, and that too had helped. Mei Sung was a great beauty. She was skilled and inventive and acrobatic in lovemaking; and totally, charmingly, reassuringly predictable in everything else. He didn't quite love her—but he was fond of her, very fond indeed; and he had made up his mind to take her along when he put out to sea again, in a day or two. Tomorrow he would see Mei Sung's owner and make the arrangements. But first he must tend to this little errand.

The seamed old woman who answered the door remembered him, and her near-toothless grin told him so.

"Hello, Ah Fu. It is Ah Fu, isn't it? Have you any news for me? A letter from Mrs. Falconer?"

Mei Sung was worried about her lover. A-tan, as she called him, had been very jumpy ever since he had returned to his cabin aboard the *Sweet Witch,* and she did not know why. As a rule she did not let the moods of her lovers trouble her unduly. But this time, contrary to all her training, she had become very fond of A-tan, although she would not have told him so.

Mei Sung had been trained as a courtesan almost since she could remember. Her own mother, who lived in Soochow, had been a courtesan, a famous beauty visited by men of great distinction. It was not known who Mei Sung's father had been. The birth had been unplanned, and therefore a cause for great consternation. In the normal way, Mei Sung—since she was a girl-child, and unwanted—would have been abandoned in some rocky place to die. But her mother was superstitious, like most of her peers. A fortuitous horoscope had saved the wrinkled swaddled bundle from a slow and painful death by hunger and exposure. Mei Sung had been spared, at the last minute, and put out to wet-nurse with a stolid Hakka hill woman, so that her presence would be neither an encumbrance nor an embarrassment to her mother. It was five years before her mother saw her again, and instantly recognized the fact that she had made an enormous error. Had she kept her daughter, Mei Sung might have become a legendary beauty, even in Soochow, where the females were renowned throughout China for the beauty of their features.

Mei Sung's face was exquisite, a perfect oval; her skin was clear and pale as pearl dust; her hair was black and naturally lustrous; and her tiny hands were like opening lotus blossoms.

But it was too late. The most important part of all was already large and ugly. Mei Sung's feet were now nearly six inches long, almost twice the size of her mother's. Had they been bound at birth—the tendons cut, and the toes painfully turned back under to foreshorten the foot —Mei Sung might have had the tiny lily feet so prized by all but the Hakka people. The oversight was irreversible: Mei Sung's feet could never be saved.

And that had determined her fate. She would be unacceptable to any Chinese man. But there were always the Europeans, the barbarian devils. They needed women too. They did not seem to mind that a girl with large feet did not bob and sway and glide with the undulating grace given only by a lifetime of binding. Some of them even seemed to prefer it.

Mei Sung was sent to Macao, closest European colony to the Chinese mainland. There, under the tutelage of the man her mother had entrusted her to, and to her everlasting shame, Mei Sung had been brought up for the Europeans. Like the other girls in the teahouse where she was taken, she learned to play the wu-jing and the moon-fiddle; she learned the arts of eroticism and contraception; she learned how to use her dark almond eyes and her hands and her moon-shaped ivory fan. She learned how to play at the charming childish games that would keep most men amused for hours; she learned chess and manners and the art of story-telling. But when her luckier companions were taken for lessons in Chinese versifying and the classics, Mei Sung was taught the difficult sounds of French, Portuguese, and other barbarian tongues.

For six years now she had been a courtesan to the foreign devils. Her first lover had been cruel: but there had been kinder ones over the years, and she had grown to enjoy her work, at least for the most part. A-tan was her first English-speaking lover, and her favorite. It sorrowed her that he seemed distraught tonight.

"Shall I sing to you, A-tan?"

"No, not now, Mei Sung." His voice was abstracted, and there was a frown creasing his brows. She smoothed it out with the exquisite pliant fingers that peeped out from under her long sleeves.

"It is werry bad to frown, A-tan." Mei Sung had conquered the difficult r sound, but she still had trouble with the less-used v. "It gives you fierce face—like a dragon, a dragon of dark eyes."

"I am a dragon. Shall I show you?" Adam pulled her into his lap, and bit her ear softly. "I spit fire, too, sometimes."

"Oh, A-tan! Do it more."

"Harder?"

"If you like."

"I like."

"Ouch!" But she laughed, and snuggled up against him, and toyed with his sleeve. "You see? The dragon-line is gone from your face. Now is in my ear."

"A very tasty little ear, too."

"Shall I rub back for you, A-tan?"

Her fingers slid nimbly over the fastenings of his clothes, and in moments he was lying face-down on the bed, while her supple hands worked the tension from his shoulders. For a time he tried to relax, letting the sensations course through his body. But it was no good—the questions still nagged at his mind.

"Do you think you'll ever want to marry, Mei Sung?"

So it was his wife he was troubled about. Mei Sung knew this at once. But his wife was supposed to have left for England, months ago. Had she sent some evil message? Had she incurred many debts? Had she perhaps not left for England, as planned? But Mei Sung knew she must not ask. It would be bad manners. "No, A-tan. I am happy to be courtesan." It was not quite true. She did think about marriage sometimes, but she knew no self-respecting Chinese man would have a girl with feet such as hers.

"Well, don't. Don't let anybody talk you into it—or trick you into it. All it brings is a pile of trouble."

"Aiee yah! No one tricks me into it, damn-right." That was true—for Mei Sung knew she could not marry without her owner's consent, and only after a great deal of haggling to which she would not be a party.

"Don't be too sure, Mei Sung. I got tricked into it."

"You, A-tan?" She was astonished, but she did not let that interfere with the steady rhythm of her hands. "I not believe it. No one tricks A-tan!"

"You haven't met my wife!"

She knew he did not like his wife, even though she had always been careful to ask no questions. Until now. Now, she could see, he needed to talk about his wife. But she could not be too direct, or too unflattering to the woman. That might offend A-tan.

"She must be werry clebber wife, to trick you."

"Clever? That's not the word for her."

"What is word for her, A-tan?"

"There are a lot of words for her, and some of them you would hardly understand. Silly . . . scheming . . . stubborn . . . deceptive. But most of all, a damn nuisance."

"Damn-nuisance, A-tan? Do not think about her, then."

"I can't help it. She's gone."

"That is good, then. For damn-nuisance wife to be gone—you should be werry happy. Anyway, you knew she shall be gone."

"Yes, but she hasn't gone to England. I found out that much. She didn't have enough money."

"But you gave her many cash! You told me so."

"I gave her enough for her passage, and enough to last for several months in Macao. I sent a bank draft to England, too, so she would have money when she arrived there. But she didn't go there." The muscles in Adam's neck were corded with tension. Mei Sung soothed them with her fingertips.

"Yet she is gone. Does it matter *where* she is gone?"

"To me it does. It means she may turn up anytime, like a bad penny."

"How you know this?"

"I went to the rented house today. She was to leave a letter there for me."

"No letter?"

"Yes, letter—but it said nothing. Only that I was not to worry. But I can't help worrying. She was still in Macao a month ago—and she didn't sail for England. She left some things at the house, and she told the servants she'd be back for them. But the letter didn't say where she was going."

"Then ask servants."

"They told me what they knew, but it wasn't much."

"No-good damn-nuisance Chinese servants always know more than they tell. Filthy dung! What did they tell?"

"That her money ran out. That she took one trunk with her and left, a month ago. That she had been gambling for some time. That they don't know where she is—although they think she may have gone off with some Russian she met at the faro tables, in one of the joss-houses."

"Then you must look for Russian! Did they tell you where to look?"

"Yes. I tried—but his servants said that he was not in. When I asked if there was a white woman living in the mansion, they said there wasn't. But I think they were lying. Their eyes looked shifty."

"Ah! Probly she does not wish that you find her, damn-right. Werry best not to worry, A-tan. What name of Russian?"

"Yasikov—Count Vasily Yasikov, something like that. I'll try to see him again, tomorrow."

So she had been right. The filthy-dung servants did know more than they had told. Mei Sung smiled to herself, a smile that Adam could not see.

"Now I rub oil on skin, A-tan."

"Oil?"

"Werry slippery, werry nice."

"Mmmm—what a good idea."

"I think you are happier now. You feel happier in your back."

"I feel happier in my front. You make me happy, Mei Sung. While you're at it," he added, for she had left him in a rustle of silks to fetch her flagon of fragrant oils, "put some on yourself."

Yes, thought Mei Sung contentedly as she slipped out of her richly embroidered gown, she would tell him later —when he was spent and relaxed, and that would fill his cup of earthly happiness to the very brim.

"That was very nice." Adam could feel the drowsiness creep into his limbs, and the peace into his mind. It had been foolish to worry about Carey. She wasn't worth it, and from what the servants had told him, he wondered if she hadn't been behaving like a silly little tramp anyway. From mission girl to gambling runabout to role as some Russian's mistress . . . well, it was her life. Why waste time thinking about Carey when there was Mei Sung, gleaming and graceful under the lamplight, and at this moment in time, very dear to him?

"Coconut oil is better," Mei Sung said thoughtfully.

Adam puzzled over that for an instant, and then laughed. "You have a wicked Oriental mind, Mei Sung. Yes, it would taste better."

"I buy coconut oil in morning, A-tan. I shall go ashore."

"You shall be busy washing your hair tomorrow morning, I think, instead of going ashore." It took a long time for Mei Sung to wash and re-coil her hair; and the oil had penetrated everything. They would both be washing hair in the morning.

"No hair wash tomorrow! Werry bad day for hair wash. Tomorrow I go ashore. Good day for water under bottom. Bad day for water over top."

Adam bit back a retort about the unreliability of sooth-sayers, for he knew nothing would change Mei Sung's mind. She lived her life by horoscopes. Instead, amused, he asked mildly: "What if it rains?"

"Then I stay here and sit in bath," she returned triumphantly.

"Mei Sung, you're incorrigible!"

"You incorrible too, A-tan." Mei Sung did not know what the word meant, but she was sure it was affectionate. A-tan was always affectionate. She slithered into the crook of his well-oiled arm and wished he had not asked to have the light left on. When she was naked it was hard not to look at her big ugly feet—and they looked bigger and uglier than ever now, ever since A-tan had poured oil on them and, to her everlasting but well-hidden mortification, kissed the toes, one by one.

"Stop looking at your feet, Mei Sung. There's nothing wrong with them. Look at mine instead. They're three times the size of yours."

"Werry bad to talk about feet, A-tan! Chinese woman nebber talk about feet." They had talked about feet a thousand times. "Great shame for me, that you see them." It was only because A-tan refused to let her wear socks or shoes in bed that she had to look at them now.

"You have lovely feet, Mei Sung, much nicer than lily feet."

"Woe! With lily feet, Chinese woman is beautiful, with beauty of winter plum blossom in snow."

"With lily feet Chinese woman can hardly stand in snow, Mei Sung, let alone on shipboard. She might as well be plum blossom still hanging on plum tree, for all I care. I prefer your feet. You have tiny perfect feet, and no reason to be unhappy about them."

"I am not unhappy, A-tan. I am werry happy now. I am happy for you. Tonight I am so happy for you that I might forget that I have the feet of a no-good dung-carrier coolie."

He pulled her face into his shoulder so that she could not see her feet, and changed the topic good-naturedly. "Why are you so happy for me, tonight in particular?"

"Because now you will be happy about your wife."

"This is no time to talk about my wife. That doesn't make me happy."

"Heya, it will make you happy, now that she has gone with big-nose barbarian."

Adam knew she was not giving a facial description of his wife's lover; all Russians were referred to as big-nosed barbarians just as all Englishmen were called red-haired barbarians. He also knew that, to Mei Sung, the name of Vasily Yasikov would be virtually unpronounceable. "Why on earth should that make me happy?"

"Because she no more damn-nuisance." Mei Sung felt dreamy, poetic, enormously happy that she was about to make A-tan so content. "Like arrow shot in air, make bow empty for new arrow. Now you can forget."

"But I can't do that, until I know she's . . . Why are you so sure she'll be no more trouble?"

"The big-nose barbarian, of course. Heya! Your wife is not so clebber as I thought, so sorry."

"Whatever do you mean?" Adam smiled sleepily and ran his thumb over Mei Sung's oil-gleaming arm.

"Ha! because big-nose barbarian is white-slabe trader, damn-right! Everyone of my profession knows that."

Then, when he jerked away and stared at her, her beautiful onyx eyes grew fearful with alarm, and tiny pearllike tears appeared and trembled on her lashes, for she had been told that she must not displease this handsome dark-haired barbarian—no, not on any account.

"Aiee yah! What dung did my damn-nuisance no-good mouth speak?"

It was well past midnight before Adam, glistening now with perspiration as well as with oil, found his way back to the Russian's house. It was already too late. Carey was not there.

❧ CHAPTER NINETEEN ❧

It had been that last day, months before—the day the
Sweet Witch sailed out of Macao harbor—that Carey
saw the man again.

She had gone down to the Praya Grande in early
morning, ostensibly to book her passage back to England,
for she was now feeling well enough to think about un-
dertaking the grueling six-month sea voyage. Ah Fu had
gone along as guide and a sort of duenna, for although
the Praya Grande was reasonably safe by daylight, it
was best not to be out alone.

But the real reason for her visit, Carey admitted to
herself, was to see the *Sweet Witch* leave harbor. She no
longer had false illusions about any last-minute change
on Adam's part. She knew about the Chinese mistress.
She knew Adam hated her for tricking him—not only
into marriage, but into the consummation of it. And in a
strange way, she knew that if she had told him the
truth about Teura now he would have hated that too, for
it was only another example of her duplicity. She knew
that she must put Adam behind her. Adam, and Teura,
and the Pacific: the Pacific that had brought her such
passion and such pain.

So, dry-eyed, she watched the *Sweet Witch* leave harbor. When its sails could no longer be seen, she went
with Ah Fu to the shipping office and booked her passage, and paid half the passage money in advance. It was
not known exactly when the ship would leave. There
were no scheduled departures—not in Macao, nor, at
that time in history, anywhere in the world. Ships left
when they were seaworthy, and when they had a full
complement of crew and a full cargo, and when the
weather was promising. But Carey was told that someone would give her warning when the time drew close.

She booked the cheapest passage she could, for she

knew that she had spent far too much on clothes. It was the first time in more than two years that she had been near shops, and shopping had helped Carey escape from the awful ache in her heart. All the same, she had plenty of money, she was sure. The house and the servants had been paid for three months in advance. She need worry only about clothes and food and incidentals. And the balance of the passage money.

She had finished at the shipping office when she saw the man. He squatted by the waterfront, staring impassively out to sea, his back to Carey. At first, her attention was caught by the curious wooden collar about his neck —a sort of portable prison, several feet in diameter. The man's head and his hands poked through holes in the wood, as they would through stocks, and the whole thing appeared to be so heavy that the poor devil who wore it looked as if he would be unable to stand up.

"That's horrible! What is it, Ah Fu?"

Ah Fu, in rather shaky English, explained the use of the *chin* or *cangue* on petty malefactors. Who knows what the man had done? Perhaps stolen some food. Perhaps been found sleeping, drunk, in a dark alley. Perhaps insulted some official. In any case, he would not be freed until his fine was paid.

"But surely they must take it off soon!"

Ah Fu shrugged indifferently, untouched by this minor tragedy. It was none of her concern. "Soon, missee. Man quick-quick die, no chow."

"Die! Why?" And then Carey realized that no man, encased by this curious device, could live for long unless somebody else provided food and water. His hands could reach his mouth—but barely; certainly he could procure no food unless it was placed on the wooden collar for him. Nor could he clean himself.

She walked closer. The odor of his body was ripe. Under the filth and the growth of hair, something about his face looked familiar. Then she recognized him. It was the pock-marked Chinese man she had seen aboard the *Sweet Witch*.

"Adam saved you once. I can't let you die now," muttered Carey, almost to herself, and hurried back to Ah Fu.

Within minutes, she had begged a cup of water from a nearby doorway. Ah Fu, at her orders, found a street hawker and purchased an unappetizing-looking loaf of bread: and this Carey broke into small pieces, and placed on the man's collar, within his reach.

"You can't understand English, can you? But never mind—I'll see if I can't get you out of there."

His eyes stared at her, dark unfathomable ciphers in an expressionless face.

It took a little longer for Ah Fu to find a Portuguese official and bring him to the scene. Although Carey's Portuguese was imperfect, she managed to communicate. It seemed that the malefactor had been caught swimming to shore three weeks before, in an off-limits area, and had been unwilling or unable to give a satisfactory account of himself. It was suspected that he had intended to steal part of an opium shipment. Since then, he had been wandering around the waterfront, kept barely alive by occasional kindhearted passersby. And what Ah Fu had told her was true: he could be freed only on payment of a fine.

To Carey, it did not seem like such a large fine, although the Portuguese official told her that such a man could not earn so great an amount of money in a year . . . in two years. In English currency, it came to about five pounds.

"Why, yesterday I almost ordered a dress that cost that much!" Carey, sick at heart, stared at the official. She thought of how much she had already spent in the exclusive shops of Macao. The dresses, the shoes, the bonnets. the parasols, the petticoats and fine stockings . . . and a man would die for a twentieth part of what she had so thoughtlessly squandered.

She paid the fine, saw the man freed, and returned to her house. The incident was promptly forgotten.

Until nearly three months later. The promised ship had not yet sailed. There had been a series of unfortunate little delays. An epidemic of the flux among the crew; an accident in loading; a discovery that some of the timbers were rotten. Unexpectedly, the ship had to be careened for two weeks. Then the captain came down with a case of food poisoning. Several of the hands were wounded in a barroom brawl. Two of the midshipmen deserted, and a handful of the seamen. Crimps had to be paid to find replacements: and the replacements, when they finally came to from the knockout drops that had been administered, turned out to be totally without sailing experience. The sailing was delayed, yet again, for at least another two weeks.

It was after Carey had paid for another month's rent that she realized she no longer had enough money for the balance of the passage. She was short by about five pounds.

There had been small expenses she had not expected; and they had mounted up. There had been the venerable Chinese practice of "squeeze," adding a little here and a little there to the cost of everything. A trifle more for a pair of shoes she hadn't really needed. A shilling or two when one of Ah Fu's bad teeth had had to be pulled. Oh, if only she had paid more attention to her cache of money! It had seemed like so much, three months ago.

Carey spent some days trying to think of a solution to her dilemma. The shipping company was very polite, but it was not their problem, and they could not make an exception. The passage must be paid for, in full. The British officials were little help: she was married to an American. The American officials were adamant: she was British, and they were not on the best of terms with the British.

In Macao there was little a respectable woman could do to earn money. Women worked—but at what? One look at the floating brothels in the harbor and the blue-door houses of the city told a part of the story. Other women, like Ah Fu, kept their virtue, and they worked as servants, cooks, matchmakers, midwives, or wash-amahs. But their earnings in a lifetime could hardly solve Carey's problem. And who would have hired Carey when she lacked the skills and the strength of a Chinese woman who was accustomed to hard labor, who could be treated like dirt and fed the leavings from the table?

It was when Ah Fu returned one evening, flushed and triumphant after a run of luck at fan-tan, that Carey decided to take her chances at the gaming tables. She was quite aware that she could lose. But if she did, was she any worse off? She would keep her bets reasonably cautious, not risking too much of her dwindling supply of capital.

She won a little; and she lost a little; and she kept trying. Two weeks later, when word finally came that her ship was at last about to leave harbor, her goal was still tantalizingly out of reach. The ship left without her, and she forfeited the deposit money.

After that, she kept gambling, first with thoughts of booking passage on a different ship, should fortune at last smile on her; and finally, when it became evident that it would not, with a kind of devil-take-the-hindmost desperation. Another month's rent had to be paid, and another . . . She still had money, but her goal was further away than ever.

It was at the gaming tables that she met the Russian. He was tall, like Adam; aristocratic in appearance and title; quite good-looking; impeccably dressed; and he associated with the best people of Macao—for by now, Carey recognized some of the consuls and officials and merchants: many of them spent considerable time in the more respectable gaming establishments.

When the Russian invited her to dine with him, she accepted. When he called to take her to a gaming house the following evening, she accepted that too. He told her he was a shipowner trading in the Orient, and she believed him. In time she discovered that he lived in one of the finer mansions of the city, in one of the very best districts. His credentials seemed impeccable, and even if she had thought to question them, she knew nobody else in Macao to put the question to.

She asked the Russian—Vasily—if he could possibly arrange for her passage back to Tahiti. He already knew something of her situation, of the husband she did not wish to see again. His answer had been yes: the next time he had an outward-bound shipment. And Carey did not notice the odd smile that flitted over his face when he answered.

Finally, news came that Adam's ship was in harbor. That evening she told Vasily. After a moment's thought, he invited her to move into his mansion for a month or so—at least while Adam was in Macao. He had many extra rooms, so many that one whole wing of his house was not even in use. He had other house-guests, frequently. His servants were discreet; Adam would not find out where she was.

By now she trusted that Count Vasily Yasikov would not make improper advances. His behavior had been beyond reproach in the three months she had known him. And if by chance she was wrong—why, she could always move out, and find some other accommodation. She gave up the rented house; wrote an uninformative letter to Adam; took a trunkful of clothes and her remaining money—she had had some luck at the gaming tables recently—and moved, gratefully, into the large secluded white mansion.

She was still there on the afternoon that Adam first came to find her.

From her vantage point in the large reception salon off the main entrance, she could see the sedan chair come up the sweeping circular driveway. With a cold shock of recognition, she watched him stepping out of the vehicle just beyond the front door.

"Adam! Oh, no."

The fact that he had not tried to find her in the past month had lulled her into a sense of false security. Informants—Count Yasikov seemed to have many informants—had reported that the *Sweet Witch* was nearly ready to leave harbor. Carey thought Adam must have received her letter long ago, that he had long since given up worrying about her.

She didn't want to see him. Adam was sure to think she was Vasily's mistress, for one thing—not that that really mattered anymore; everyone in Macao thought she was Vasily's mistress. What mattered was that she didn't wish to face the cold indifference in Adam's eyes.

From the front entrance, he would easily be able to see into this room. Yet she didn't have time to return upstairs by the wide circular staircase: he would see her there too. And he would be in the main entrance in a moment. She must find a way to vanish, and at once. Carey's eyes darted around, looking for a quick escape route. Several other doors opened off this reception area. One led to Vasily's study: she couldn't go in there. Where did the other doors lead? Perhaps to a back hall . . . perhaps to the wing of the house Vasily had told her was unused. In any case, it didn't matter. The important thing was to get away from Adam.

She picked a door at random. It was locked. She tried the next: it opened. In seconds she was on the other side of it, leaning gratefully against the jamb, her heart beating double-time.

From here she could still hear the murmurings at the front door . . . Adam's questions . . . the doorman's response. She looked around while she waited. Yes: she must be in the unused wing. This room had perhaps once served as a morning-room or a second salon, but now the windows were darkly draped, shutting out the sun. In the little light that remained, she could see that dust-covers shrouding the oversize furniture, giving the room a ghostly, ghastly look. Despite the warmth of the day she shivered.

At last Adam left. She could hear his parting words; could hear the large front door closing behind him. She decided it would be safe to leave her hiding place. She put her hand to the knob.

But the door was locked. Damn, damn, damn—the latch must have been set before, with a key, but it had failed to click home until after she had come through the door. And now it would not open, no matter how hard she rattled and shoved.

She would have to find another way out.

Count Vasily Yasikov removed his leather gloves and looked at the cowering welt-covered figure before him with something like affection. She had given him some kind of release after all, this little Malayan puta he had kept these past two years.

Once, he would have done something quite different to her. Listening now to her moans and whimpers, he wished he could feel once again the warmth in his loins he might have felt a year ago. But he could still leave the mark of his manhood upon her: a different kind of mark.

He put down the whip and started to caress the welts on her thighs. "Phuong, my little Phuong. How good you make me feel."

Her name meant phoenix. It was very appropriate, he thought: the beautiful bird who survives the baptism of fire. Phuong had been very beautiful two years ago, and she was even more beautiful now, with her criss-crossing of scars—the pale year-old ones and the new, angrier ones—and her soft, liquid Malayan eyes that were looking at him now with nothing more than a sorrowful acceptance. He knew that with her Malay temperament she had an unnatural horror of scars. And yet she had learned to accept . . .

He would not change mistresses: not, at least, while Phuong remained alive, and beautiful. More mistresses meant more chance of talk—and talk was one thing he didn't want; it was bad for business.

The disease had not yet marked her, as it had marked him. At least it had not yet affected his face. It was in remission right now, but the private scars he carried were a constant reminder that it might at any time erupt —might mutilate him horribly, might even drive him mad. It had driven other men mad. When he had learned, some years ago, that he was syphilitic, he had made a study of other men who had purportedly had the disease. Men like Henry the Eighth of England, Ivan the Terrible, first Tsar of All the Russians, and others. Sometimes they became covered with horrible lesions. Sometimes they became paralyzed. Sometimes their personalities changed . . .

He did not think his own personality had changed. The headaches, that was the thing that troubled him now. The excruciating headaches, and the horrifying impotence that forced him to find release in these extraordinary ways he would never have thought of some years ago. In those days he used to enjoy a different kind of dalliance, often with the more beautiful women who passed through his hands.

Women like this sea-captain's wife, Mrs. Falconer. Caroline, as he preferred to call her. Quite fortunate, really, that he had met her that night in the elegant gambling saloon. He had paid court, at first, to squelch any possible loose talk. Rumors of impotence and the French Pox scared away clients; they cast doubts on the merchandise in which he dealt.

After a time, when he had been seeing Caroline Falconer for about a month, he began to encourage the rumor that she had become his mistress. She, hearing the talk, had only laughed. She did not seem to care what people thought. All in all, the arrangement suited him quite admirably.

Normally, it would not have occurred to him to put someone like the Falconer woman into service. Under normal circumstances, it was much too risky. But in this case her husband seemed to care little about her whereabouts, and she seemed to have no other relatives or particular friends. It was a tempting idea. Golden-haired women were scarce in this part of the world, especially beautiful and relatively innocent golden-haired women. Even the white Russian girls he handled were seldom blonde. There were Chinese Mandarins who would pay a small fortune for such a girl. Already he had put out feelers, looking for a buyer.

Whether or not he actually completed such a transaction would depend on whether her husband made any real effort to find her before he sailed. At the moment, there were too many people who might know that she was staying under this roof. But if the husband left he might not return for a year or more—if ever. A lot could happen in a year. A woman could vanish without a trace, like a wisp of smoke, like foam flecks on the sand of a distant shore. Yes, as soon as her husband left, he would proceed.

Count Vasily Yasikov unlocked the chains, and smiled at Phuong almost lovingly.

"Come, my dear. Put on your clothes—I shall have to leave you now."

Carey moved cautiously along the dim corridor, groping her way past the empty suits of armor that stood like silent sentinels watching over her passage. It was dark here, cobwebby, horrible, hateful.

Ahead of her a door opened, and a shaft of light caught dust-motes in the dingy hall. Flooded with relief, she cried out and ran forward.

"Vasily! Oh, thank goodness—"

Then she stopped, for she had seen the purple room that lay beyond the door—and the girl.

"Caroline! What are you doing here?" Vasily's voice betrayed his displeasure, but he made no effort to close the door behind him. He knew it was too late: she had seen.

"I—I—got locked in." Carey backed away from him, staring beyond him, unable to hide the horror in her expression.

"How unfortunate." His voice had become ice, and his pale eyes had frosted over.

"I'm sorry. I—I'll go." But she could not go, for his hand was clamped over her wrist, a vise that twisted and wrenched and forced her toward the horrible door.

"No, Caroline. You will not go. Do come in. I see you are curious about my little retreat. No, don't pull away—that's better. You see, I am not quite a weakling." He closed the door behind her, and leaned his powerful frame against it.

How ghastly! The studded purple leather walls, the dais and the post where the girl had until recently been chained, the rows of whips and crops and other instruments . . . and worst of all, this man surveying her, his silver-gray eyes like chips of ice, his arms folded, his mouth cruel in a way he had been careful never to let her see before.

"Well, what do you think, Caroline? Would you like to live in a room such as this? Phuong doesn't mind. She doesn't mind anything I do to her; do you, Phuong?"

He clicked the lock on the door, and moved a little closer to Carey. A faint menacing smile twisted his lower lip.

"Oh, don't expect her to answer. I had her tongue cut out some time ago. This room is soundproof, but I found her protests distracting."

Carey felt sick with fear and revulsion. "How . . . how—"

"Horrible? My dear Mrs. Falconer! You *are* an innocent. Men do far worse things every day. In every man's heart there is some evil, some perversion, some depravity . . ."

"Please, I've seen enough. I want to go—you must let me go." But he could not let her go now, she knew that.

Yasikov ignored the demand, and picked up a riding crop. As he circled the room, he switched it against his polished leather boots.

"Yes, my dear Caroline, my whole livelihood is based on this dark side in every man's soul. You were too innocent to question that, or you would have found out about my livelihood long ago."

"I don't know what you mean." Her tongue felt cloven to the roof of her mouth; her lips were dry. Did he bring men here to beat this cringing Malay girl with the hurt in her eyes?

"Don't you? Can't you guess? Ah, my dear, all my women do not end up like Phuong, although some of them doubtless do. But many of them live happy, productive, protected lives—pampered even, if they learn well enough how to please." He smiled at her thinly. "Stop recoiling, Caroline. I am not going to beat you. I won't deny it would be a pleasure—but it's a pleasure I can't afford. I must sell you immediately, now that you have seen my small secret. And marking your white skin would only be an expensive luxury."

Carey, her face ashen, was unable to answer.

"Don't blame yourself, my dear child! Whether you had stumbled on my private room or not, it was only a matter of time. I planned to put you in one of my, er, shipments—as soon as your husband's ship sailed. Especially as he has made no move to find you. It was only a matter of days."

Adam! Adam had come looking for her. He would come again. She tried to brazen it out. "He was here, moments ago. He may still be here! He said he wouldn't give up until he found out where I was. I heard him say it."

Too late she realized what she had admitted.

"So he did not see you? How fortunate. Well, my servants will send him away. He may come back—but what if he does? By then, my dear, you will be gone. And all the powers of heaven and hell cannot be moved to find you. He will never find you again."

A little later, in his study, Count Vasily Yasikov entertained one of his more unsavory business associates. The man was a paunchy, sad-eyed Portuguese by the name of Miguel Braga. He was not the Russian's favorite intermediary—the man's manners were coarse, for one thing, and he smelled—but he could be counted on to deal with matters speedily, more speedily than the slow-moving Chinese, who wished to drink tea and niggle over every tiny detail of price and delivery, and who could be baffling in their deviousness. At least with this man, a bargain could be struck at once. And the man Braga had ways of keeping a girl silent and untroublesome until such time as she vanished, forever, into oblivion. After a week with Braga, Caroline Falconer would be telling no tales. Her remembrance of the purple room would be no more than a dream within a dream.

"Your offer is totally unacceptable, Braga!"

The Portuguese trained his doleful eyes on the Russian's drumming fingers. "But my dear Count, I cannot possibly offer any more."

The Count pretended to be incredulous. "For a golden-haired girl? There are mandarins who would pay a fortune for such a one!"

"Then sell her to a mandarin," said Braga mournfully. "Or are you in too much of a hurry? Ah, when people are in a hurry they always call for Braga! I can see why you want to get rid of the girl. She looks as though she will be unusually difficult during the breaking-in period. Such carryings-on!" The English girl had kicked and struggled throughout the examination, despite her chains.

"Pah! Once the habit takes hold," Yasikov scoffed, "she will be no trouble at all. I know your methods, Braga! She will be doped before she leaves here. Within days she will be docile as a kitten."

"The poppy is effective, it is true. But then some men might prefer to have their purchases undrugged. In some of China it is still hard to procure opium, and expensive." Braga pulled at his chin and looked at the Russian reproachfully, as though he were personally responsible for the price of opium.

"The man who can afford to pay the price you will charge can afford to support any habit."

"And of course I will have to keep her long enough to determine whether she has the French Pox."

"You may have my word that she does not," returned the Count coldly. "She has had no venereal contact within the last year."

Braga of course knew that Yasikov was lying. All the world knew that the Falconer woman had been the Russian's mistress for some months now. And they knew that the Russian was syphilitic; he had given the disease to his last mistress, the little Malay girl. It was even rumored that the Malay girl was still in a back room somewhere, and that he beat her horribly. There were few secrets in Macao.

Braga shrugged, apologetically. "Your merchandise appears clean, but I am a businessman, Count. The risk of the pox is too great. I can go no higher."

Yasikov started drumming his fingers again, in an effort to quell the white-hot anger inside him. So Braga knew about the syphilis: it was clear from the price he was offering, from his remarks about the pox. If Braga knew, others knew. Business would suffer. But for the moment he had no choice—he must get rid of the Falconer woman at once. After a moment's silence, he said, stiffly: "It is agreed, if you can arrange to take delivery at once."

"At dark, then. Give her the drugs with her dinner, a double dose for the transfer period. After that, we shall see."

The Portuguese let none of his elation show in his doleful, liquid eyes. He would turn a very good profit on this one, pox or no pox.

It was the vague indefinite stuff of dreams—the days that slid into nights, and the nights that slid into days; the rocking of the sea, and the darkness of the sampan, and the stealing warmth that came over mind and body. When, at first, they had brought the drafts of liquid forgetfulness with her meals, she had not realized what was happening. And then, later, when they brought ivory bowls and bamboo stems and dark sticky balls of paste that bubbled and beaded gently over the flame, sweet flame, she no longer wanted to resist.

Time had become nothing and less than nothing; but it was in fact only a week since Carey had been in the Russian's house. For three of those days she had been smoking the opium pipe.

The voices were unreal, disembodied, and they spoke in Portuguese.

"When will we move her?"

"Right away. The man Wang T'ung wants her moved immediately. And he has said that there are to be no more drugs."

"O, merda! But she will be difficult, for a time."

"Not for long. Three days' habit is not too hard to break. Give her one last pipe, to make the transfer easier."

Carey, although she understood the language, was beyond reasoning it out. She understood only when the opium came, and its warm butterscotch blessing filled her nostrils, and her own existence became flawless, crystal-clear, exquisite, and the rest of the world blurred once more into insignificance. All that followed was a dream: the dark boat trip to another part of the harbor; the arms that bundled her up a covered gangway; the richness of carvings, the gleam of gilt, the soft sensuous feel of silks, and the dark hooded figures that glided in and out of lacquered corridors, hardly disturbing the sweetness of her inner vision.

Until there was no pipe . . . She woke, and her body was pouring sweat, even her hands. Her skin felt waxy, and she shuddered all over, great horrible rending shudders that threatened to tear her body apart. She had gone mad. She knew she had gone mad, for from every direction her own ashen face stared back at her, wild-eyed, distorted.

She was in an octagonal room, in a pleasure boat that was well known to the Portuguese authorities, but quietly ignored—for many of them, well disguised, had sampled its perverse pleasures. It was, although Carey did not know it at the time, a large and ancient galleon-like Portuguese carrack, anchored in the harbor. It had been bought some years before by an enterprising Chinese businessman, and saved from a watery grave. The owner had spared no expense in its refurbishing, and no effort in making sure that his patrons might taste of its wares without disclosing their true identity. The covered gangplank led not only to many rooms like Carey's, but to wardrobe rooms where the patrons of the night donned their disguise, in the color of their choice; and it was these dark-robed hooded figures whom Carey had seen on her arrival, as in a dream.

Huddled on the large soft circular bed, she pulled the yellow-silk covers over her wretched bones, and closed her eyes against the madness of her own reflection, and prayed for someone to come.

Yet for three days, in her misery, she hardly noticed when they did.

It was on the fourth day that she began to understand what had happened. She had been drugged. And she was in a room that was all mirrors, even the ceiling. On a boat at anchor . . . she could tell by the gentle rocking sway. A boat that was used for what godforsaken perverted purpose! There were chains attached to the floor beside the bed, ankle chains and wrist chains, although they did not enclose her ankles or her wrists—not yet. In one corner of the room stood a japanned chest that contained a weird variety of instruments: cruel whips and crops and studded leather collars and other things for which she could not even imagine uses.

Oh, God, where was she? Distorted memories of the past

days came back to her now—the Russian; the purple room; the battered Malay girl; the dirty curtained sampan where she had spent some unremembered length of time; the boat ride by night; the lacquered corridors and the dark hooded men's figures; the slender sympathetic Chinese girls who had come, and bathed her brow and held her head and given her sips of rice wine and water, for the past few days. Or was it weeks? The attendants had been quite kind, she remembered, kinder than the brown-clad stone-faced men, unmasked, who seemed to be guards of some kind, and who were always present on the other side of the mirrored door.

The door slid open now, and one of the Chinese girls entered, bearing a tray. She smiled, not unkindly.

"Missee feel betta?"

"A little. I'm very hungry."

"No chow three days. Chow now, you feel betta quick-quick."

"What am I doing here? What's happening to me? Oh, for mercy sake, help me!"

But the pleas were not so different from those the Chinese girl had been hearing for three days, and she only shrugged as she put down the tray. "Firs' chow, then get missee ready."

"Ready for what?"

The girl retreated to the door on soft feet, and smiled. "Ready for man—ah yiss, need bath." And she left.

Carey's heart stopped for a minute. But what could she do? She was powerless.

The Chinese girl returned with several other female attendants. Carey, still shaky from the ordeal of drug withdrawal, resisted little as they took her along the remembered corridor to another room, and bathed her body and her hair in a large steaming tub, and anointed her skin with fragrance. But when the attendants took her back to her own room and removed her robe and she saw what they intended to do, she started to struggle.

That only brought the brown-clad male attendants —and when she saw them, Carey signaled that she would no longer resist. The men vanished, and Carey allowed the girls to do as they pleased.

They shaved her body, all over. They lacquered her fingernails, and her toenails. They pomaded her hair, and coiled it, Chinese fashion, on top of her head, and fastened it with red flowers and ornate tortoiseshell combs. They powdered her face, very white; and painted her lips and her nipples with a stain of such dark red that they appeared near-black in the mirror. They gave her a kimono that fastened with a broad sash, but it was of red silk so sheer that it concealed nothing.

And then, in spite of her alarmed protests and renewed struggles, they clicked one of the shackles home around an ankle, and left the room.

She was chained to the floor near the bed. She could not even move to defend herself. But at least she had the whip she had hidden beneath her mattress at suppertime. Her shaking hands found it now, and concealed it again, with the handle closer to her hand. And then, with nothing else to do but go mad staring at the stark unreality of her own white, dark-lipped reflection in the mirror, she waited.

The door finally slid open to reveal one of the disguised figures she had seen before in the corridors. This man had chosen purple, although he might as easily have chosen black, or gray, or dark blood-red. His head was hooded like an executioner's, with no more than a gash for the mouth and narrow gauze-covered eye-slits. From a chain around his waist hung a key—to her own shackles, she supposed. His shirt was purple, his trousers were purple, even his gloves were purple.

Suddenly Carey knew who it must be.

"Vasily," she whispered, backing away against the edge of the bed. Vasily . . . the whips in the japanned chest. Vasily . . . who was tall and narrow-hipped like this man. Vasily . . . the purple room. "Don't come near me!"

And for the moment he did not. He stood and contemplated her from the doorway for what seemed an eternity. An eternity in which her fingers ached to find the whip, but he was still too far away, for the moment out of range. Then, slowly, he circled the room, missing nothing—the chest and its contents, the mirrors, the bed, the still-unfastened shackles ready to accept her arms and her other foot. Carey, sitting on the edge of the bed, turned tensely, following his movements, waiting for the moment when he might draw near enough, for she knew that once he had chained her, as the Malay girl had been chained, she could do nothing to help herself.

At last he seemed to tire of his inspection. He came closer. Her fingers sought and gripped the whip handle, and then, when he was halfway to the bed, she pulled it swiftly from its hiding place. It stung through the silence of the air and landed with biting accuracy across his shoulders. She could hear the sharp hiss of his breath. He staggered, recovered, stood for an eyeblink of time, confounded. She struck again, with every ounce of her strength. But already he had covered the distance between them and wrenched it from her grasp. His gloved hands slashed at her, struck her down against the silken bed. Dazed and for the moment defenseless, she felt her free ankle seized and fastened, some distance from its partner. Then the wrists, too, and she lay on the bed shackled, vulnerable—oh God, nothing could save her now!

The whip had cut through the fabric of Vasily's shirt, she could see that. The darker stain against the purple told her she had drawn blood. And she saw by the way his hands gripped the whip that he was enraged. She closed her eyes expecting to feel the full lash of his fury against her trembling flesh . . .

Instead, she felt the caress of cold leather. It was the whiphandle: it pushed aside her kimono, baring the flesh beneath, stripping her of her last skimpy defense. He was torturing her in more subtle ways, putting off the punishment, compounding the terror. The handle was against the flesh of her thighs now, stroking them; and the purple executioner's eyes were watching her. She could not see them through the gauze, but she could feel them—just as, moments later, she felt the leather-gloved hands on her skin. She felt cold all over, contaminated. The brutal leather hands found her paint-darkened nipples and punished them, but not for long—for they returned again to the wide-open softness of her thighs, and fondled the shrinking flesh with no regard for the repugnance in her eyes. And then, ignoring the cries and protests that tumbled from her lips, the man undid his trousers and, without even taking time to remove them, for he was already visibly aroused, he levered his weight over her shackled and helpless form. His sex entered her with no preliminaries, and painfully, for her body was unprepared to receive him. She gave one last throttled gasp before his mouth ground down over hers, and his tongue, like the rest of his body, raped her.

Agony, agony . . . she could feel the anger flowing from his body into hers, and she could do nothing to resist, for the shackles strained at her hands and her feet. But then the fury and the driving and the passion climaxed, and she felt the stickiness between her thighs, and the man at last lay still, sprawled over her. He did not move away at once. Her flesh ached with the indignity of his touch, a repugnant reminder of the invasion she had suffered. Make him go away, make him go . . . but he did not; and she let her mind slip away, seeking refuge in some other level of consciousness. How long he lay there she was never quite sure. The horror of what had happened returned only later, when he had gone, and she became conscious of the flecks of blood against her yellow silk bedclothes. His blood, not hers. She had survived, thank God and she would survive again. So it was possible for the mind to retreat from the indignities of the body . . . There was no hope of escape from this floating hell, not now. There were too many guards. But sometime, somehow, the chance would come, and until that chance came, perhaps she could train her consciousness to flee, even if her flesh could not.

It was this escape of the mind that saved her in the days that followed. When she had been prepared, as always, for her visitor of the evening; when her hair had been dressed and her nails lacquered and her nipples painted; when she had heard the opening of the mirrored door; when she saw whatever shadowed figure the night might bring, she would lie back on the bed and close her eyes and let her mind steal silently away into some secret hiding place. She knew little of the men who came. Only vague impressions of height and size remained. Sometimes, the visitor took his time, and the gloved hands would try to arouse her—and then, escape was hardest. But at other times the man of the evening would merely force his entrance swiftly and savagely, and then, under the thrusting assault, it was possible to vanish into some other plane of existence.

She made no further protests, no efforts at resistance. She no longer thought about things like innocence and purity and fighting back; that seemed unimportant now. She thought about survival. She wanted to survive, and she wanted to survive without being scarred. After the first night, the attendants had taken away the chest of whips and strange instruments, and they had removed the shackles from the bed's edge. She did not want them brought back.

She remained in the mirrored room for a month.

It was a month during which Napoleon's Grand Army became mired in Spain; Austria's archduke prepared a attack the French; Fouché and Talleyrand plotted in Paris against their Emperor.

It was a month during which Macao salons talked not of those things, but of news six months old—and of the fact that the American sealer *Topaz,* stumbling on the mischarted island of Pitcairn, had solved the nineteen-year-old riddle of the missing *Bounty* mutineers.

It was a month during which another Christmas came and went, and Carey did not even know.

Behind the tiny eyeslot that looked into Carey's room, the man who had been watching, on and off, for much of the past month, sat back and let his lips twist into a smile. Revenge had been more than three years in coming. But he was a patient man, a persevering man, or he would not have survived the seven months in the Haitian prison.

Beau Blore did not look exactly as he had three years before. To his impotent rage, his Haitian jailors had shaved his skull, and kept it shaved for all of the seven months as a precaution against lice. Lice! As if he were no better than the slaves who until recently had been in his holds. But he was too clever a man to let his chagrin show, and he had allowed the weekly tonsure without complaint. Then one day he caught sight of himself in a mirror, while being led from one area to another. The lack of hair amused him—it emphasized the bullish set of his shoulders, the tree-trunk of his neck, the hard knots of his eyes. He knew it made him look more frightening. When he put the Haitian prison behind him, he kept the bald skull.

It had been cleverness and patience and the overpowering instinct for survival that had kept Blore alive. Although he was a man of little formal education, he had learned to read and write and work mathematical instruments—all necessities for a ship's captain. He had also picked up a working knowledge of French and Spanish, well larded with mostly curse-words, from his years at the mast and in the whorehouses of Marseilles and Cadiz. Upon arrival in the Haitian prison he had at once offered his services as interpreter and scribe, and his jailors had accepted, for in the struggling new nation, men of any education at all were scarce. He had made himself useful enough that he had remained alive—and unflogged.

The other thing that had saved Blore was the age-old practice of crimping. Every sailortown had its crimps—men who provided ship's crews, however unwilling, for a price. Port-au-Prince was no exception. When, after seven months of incarceration, Blore had heard that crimps were scouring the Haitian prisons for scum to sail a short-handed vessel, he had willingly offered his services, even though he knew it would mean sailing under a black crew with a black captain. That was a trifle that bothered him not at all, for he planned to desert as soon as possible.

He did, and found his way back to England, and, in time, to the other slave ship he owned.

He had come to the Pacific for three reasons.

The abolitionists in England, led by Wilberforce and Fox, had gathered strength during Blore's incarceration. Blore had seen what was in the wind, and shortly after his arrival in the Pacific, the legislation to ban British slave-trading had been passed.

The second reason was that war had made the Atlantic dangerous. Blore was no coward, but he was no fool. He didn't give a damn which side was which, but he did give a damn if he had to risk his own hide for someone else's principles. There were good safe profits to be made in the Pacific, in the trade Blore knew best—blackbirding. So with a wry twist of unaccustomed humor, he renamed his ship and headed for the South Seas. The *Blackbird,* as the *Sweet Witch*'s sister ship was now called, had in a year and a half earned back its own worth down around the islands of Melanesia.

He had come up to Macao because he had heard of the enormous no-risk profits to be made in the Hakka-coolie trade—imagine virtual slaves who went willingly, as if they were hired labor!—and the even vaster profits to be made in the white-slave trade. He had come knowing it was a gamble, and now that gamble had paid ten times over—and not entirely in the way he had expected.

Because the third thing that had brought Blore to the Pacific was Captain Adam Falconer.

He had not needed sailors' gossip to tell him that his old enemy was in Macao. It was not totally unexpected; Blore had overheard talk of Macao while tied to the mizzen mast. Even before the *Blackbird* dropped anchor, Blore had recognized the *Sweet Witch*. He had taken the precaution of anchoring at some distance, behind a screen of stout-sided East Indiamen, lest Falconer should become curious about a ship so similar to his own. Within hours, Blore had set men to watching the *Sweet Witch*, and the captain's coming and goings.

He knew about Falconer's Chinese mistress, Mei Sung. He knew about Mei Sung's owner, Wang T'ung, the wealthy old Chinaman whom Falconer had visited one day more than a month ago, and whom he himself had visited shortly afterward—the first of many such profitable visits. Last but not least he knew about Falconer's wife—although it had taken him a little longer to piece together the information where she was concerned.

And he knew that, of the men who had forced themselves on the unwilling but unresisting Mrs. Falconer over this past month, the most frequent had been her own husband.

Now he had Captain Holier-Than-Thou Falconer exactly where he wanted him.

⚙ CHAPTER TWENTY ⚙

Adam Falconer removed the hood from his head and did not like what he saw in the mirror of the changing room. His black eyes stared back at his own image with self-disgust, a self-disgust that had been growing apace during the past month.

He had not found Carey through the Russian. True, he had rushed back to the elegant white mansion immediately after Mei Sung's disclosure. But, even though the house was still ablaze with lights and crowds were milling around the open entrance, it was already too late to find out anything.

The Russian was dead. The Russian—and the maltreated Malay girl he had kept somewhere in a back room, and had beaten once too often, until at last she ran amok. She had gone mad, first, with a whip wrenched somehow from her captor's hands; then with a knife, found God knows where.

The Malay girl was dead; the Russian was dead; several of the servants were dead. The others had fled in terror, all but one quaking scullery maid who, if she had ever known anything, was far too frightened to remember now. Adam could not even find out if Carey had been staying there at all. Perhaps she had vanished into limbo a month ago, the day she left the rented house.

For several days Adam despaired. For all that he disliked his wife, he could not bear to think of her condemned to the horrors of slavery and all it implied. Inquiries, official and otherwise, led nowhere. But it was important to act before the trail grew cold, before his wife faded into the never-never-land of forgotten women. *Like arrow shot in air,* as Mei Sung had said, vanishing forever.

He found Carey, eventually, in the simplest possible

way. In Macao in the year 1808, perhaps it was the only way.

He bought her.

When the idea came to him, he went to Wang T'ung, the shrunken Chinese entrepreneur whose business seemed to be nothing and everything. Wang T'ung was Mei Sung's owner, a shriveled ancient man who knew all there was to know about the Macao waterfront. In fact, he owned a good part of it—teahouses, opium dens, sing-song boats, and one very special and exclusive floating brothel that had once been a rotting Portuguese carrack. After the prescribed tea ceremony and idle conversation, Falconer arranged to return Mei Sung at the end of the already-paid-for month. He knew he would no longer be able to afford her, for what he intended to buy would be expensive. Then he gave Wang T'ung the exact specifications of what he wanted, and he told Wang T'ung to procure the merchandise, whatever the price.

After a week of waiting, word at last came from Wang T'ung. Such a girl—a rarity in Macao—had been procured. As Falconer had specified, she would not be drugged. She had been moved from another boat in the harbor to Wang T'ung's own exclusive pleasure boat, a place where a man's anonymity might be preserved. She could be taken from this boat at once, or left there—whichever Falconer preferred.

The price was exceedingly steep. It took all of Falconer's accumulated profits, all the proceeds of the sandalwood shipment. It even meant borrowing some money from Wang T'ung, at an exorbitant rate of interest, of course. This Adam did, for the period of a month.

The loan was due by now, but Wang T'ung had promised to renew it; and Falconer knew that at any moment word would be coming for him to go to the private cabin reserved for the owner of this pleasure craft.

The first time he had gone to see Carey a month ago, he had intended only to reassure her, to tell her that he was making arrangements for her to leave this floating prison as soon as possible. He didn't know what arrangements he would make—he only knew that he didn't want her at the *Sweet Witch;* Mei Sung was at that time still installed in his cabin. Nor, with the evidence of Carey's behavior in Macao, did he feel she could be trusted on her own.

He did not know what he had expected to find. A Carey sobbing and shaken by her experience, perhaps. Certainly not that painted whore—that white-faced, black-lipped whore he could hardly recognize as his wife! She had called him Vasily. Had the Russian visited her other times—before his death? How many other men had visited her? He cared nothing for Carey, and yet the thought angered him beyond belief.

She had cost him the profits of a year, and more. She had cost him his hard-won peace of mind. And most dearly of all, she had cost him Mei Sung, sweet Mei Sung, who had mended his grief of a year ago.

When she had struck him, the blood-lust had come upon him. Something black and terrible and uncontrollable had ripped through his veins and his brain. He had wanted to punish her, to lash back at her, even to kill her. And that was why he had had the chest with its cruel contents removed: because he was afraid of what he might do to her in the blackness of his rage.

Over the period of a month he had visited her many times, driven by some devil in his heart, and still he had told her nothing. At least he was confident that no other men were using her now. He owned her—and although he did not wholly trust Wang T'ung, he knew the wily brothel-owner had a Chinaman's respect for property.

Perhaps if she had responded to his caresses . . . if she had protested, something she had never done since that first day . . . perhaps if she had wept . . . if she had done anything but lie there, spread and waiting, passively accepting her fate like some expressionless Oriental harlot, it might have been different. He might have told her before now.

Or would he? By now she had become a fever in his blood, a sickness in his soul. He had put off sailing the *Sweet Witch*. Mei Sung had gone back to her owner two days ago; he could now take Carey to the *Sweet Witch*, for he realized he wanted her badly—but did he want her there after what she had done to him, after what he had done to her?

She was his nemesis, his purgatory, his bête noire. He longed to be rid of her. He abhorred everything she had become . . . everything she had made him become. And yet he could not stop seeing her, this woman he loathed and lusted after.

He looked into the mirror, hating himself, and saw the dark side of his soul.

Blore glanced around the private cabin of the pleasure boat with satisfaction. Yes, it would be a good place to confront Falconer, and a good time. How ironic that it was Falconer who had first led him to Wang T'ung! Blore regretted none of his dealings with Wang T'ung a month ago, although they had cost him a great deal of money. He also expected that they would make him a great deal of money—and even more important, give him his revenge against Falconer.

As new half-owner of this floating fancy-house, he now had access to this private room, and although he suspected that Wang T'ung or his spies would be watching or listening from somewhere, it didn't really matter. What mattered was that revenge was at hand, and that it would be a long, sweet revenge. He had suffered for nearly seven months in that dung-hole of a prison in Haiti. Let Falconer sweat it out for seven months, too. But for him there would be no escape at the other end.

Blore had already sent a Chinese servant to fetch Falconer, who was expecting in any case to see Wang T'ung. The servant returned now.

"Capan Fakona come soon, mass'er."

"Good. Set out some rice wine, then get your yellow skin out of here. Quick-quick dooa!"

"Yiss, mass'er."

Blore grinned to himself. He knew a great deal about his enemy now, a very great deal. He had underestimated Falconer once, years before. This time, he knew, Falconer would underestimate him.

"Ha, Captain Falconer." Blore's normally strident voice was smooth as oil. "Come in."

Adam Falconer stood in the doorway, silent. Shaven skull or no, he recognized Blore at once: remembered the place and the time, and the man who had last been seen with strings of brown hair in his mouth, sputtering with rage and brine. How had Blore managed to escape? What was he doing in Macao? What was he doing *here?* But to give himself time to assemble his thoughts, he pretended for the moment not to recollect. Instead he said, in a puzzled voice:

"I expected Wang T'ung."

"Wang T'ung's not here. You're seeing me instead."

Falconer, watchful, moved into the room.

"Three years is a long time, Falconer, mighty long. Perhaps you've forgotten?" But Blore knew Falconer had not forgotten, that he was bluffing. He pointed to an empty chair. "Have a seat."

Adam ignored the chair that was offered and chose a different one. "Of course I remember you, er—Bore."

Blore felt prickles of anger travel over his skin, but controlled them. He was a patient man. Falconer's deliberate rudeness was only one more insult to be stored in the strongbox of his mind, a debt to be paid later, along with others. He would not give Falconer the satisfaction of correcting the misnomer; he was sure Falconer knew his name perfectly well. "You've had a load o' other things on your mind, Falconer, and I've not."

Falconer snapped his fingers. "I have it! Haiti."

"Great place for thinking, Haiti is." Blore steepled his fingers and, over them, watched his enemy. "You should try it sometime."

"Good swimming too, I believe." Adam's smile was bland, innocent.

"Aye—some people don't sink so easily, Falconer. I'm one of those people just naturally floats to the top, like—"

"Scum?" Falconer broke in with a pleasant smile.

But Blore's tiny jeweled eyes didn't even blink. "Like oil on water, Falconer. I'm Wang T'ung's partner now. You been up to some interesting things, Captain. Mighty interesting things. Specially of late. Aye, I've been keeping an eye on you."

So Blore knew about Carey. "My private business is hardly your concern. I've done nothing illegal."

"No? It's not every man goes from his ship at night heavily cloaked, leaving his nice little piece to sit on her Oriental arse."

And he knew about Mei Sung. But Mei Sung was safe now, back with Wang T'ung. Falconer, silent, waited and let Blore speak.

"Illegal—who gives a sweet damn about illegal? But interesting, Falconer, very interesting." Blore allowed himself a tight smile. "Your visits to this bit o' floating heaven—"

"Are none of your business. What I do here is my concern, nobody else's."

"I wonder if Mrs. Falconer 'ud agree with you?"

Did he care if Blore told Carey? Unexpectedly, the answer in his head came back a resounding yes. But he said: "Tell her if you want, Blore. I discarded her as a wife long ago."

"So you can remember a man's name if the fancy takes you! Well, I'm not planning to tell her anything—not yet. Aye, it's a situation after my own heart. Must have been quite a shock to see what your little mission girl had become! And to answer the question I see on the tip of your tongue, no, I had no finger in putting her into trade. She did it all for herself—she and her fancy Russian friend. Fact is, I'd not have known she was here if you hadn't led me to her. To her—and to Wang T'ung."

"Get to the point, Blore."

"Very profitable piece o' business, meeting Wang T'ung. Now there's a man I can cotton to, Chink or no. Maybe I'll even give up blackbirding, in a year or two. Aye, Falconer, I'm still at it. I even renamed my other ship. She's the *Blackbird* now." He chortled. "But to get your wife—"

"My ex-wife, Blore, or she will be soon. I'll be divorcing her as soon as possible."

Blore went on as though he had not heard. "Easy to see why you dumped her a year ago. Cold as a fish! She's a looker, though."

Falconer was on his feet, rage ringing through his head, all caution forgotten. "You son-of-a-whore bastard, you—"

"Siddown, Falconer! I haven't been sampling the wares. Never let pleasure interfere with profit is my motto. I don't fornicate with the merchandise—it's bad business. But it makes good watching all the same, even if she's about as lively as a piece o' putty."

Adam sank back into his chair, containing his anger. So there was a viewing slit into the room—but if Blore had been watching, it was partly his own fault that there had been anything to watch. You couldn't kill a man for playing Peeping Tom. And he must stay calm: it was becoming obvious that Blore was a dangerous enemy. He

208

took a new measure of the man. Blore was leaning back with an unholy glitter in his eye, like a gambler who still holds the high cards.

"Aye, I can see why you left her. Beats me why you were willing to pay such a high price to get her back."

"I'm not taking her back, Blore. I told you that. I'm sending her to England to get a divorce. So if you have any thoughts of using her against me—"

Again, Blore ignored the interruption. "A very high price—and for what? Strange—for I hear your Chinese mistress has twice the tricks, and you were mighty down in the mouth to see her go. But you did pay the price. Perhaps a bigger price than you reckoned." Blore fell silent, savoring the moment.

"Go on," said Falconer dangerously. So the high cards were about to be played.

"You borrowed money from Wang T'ung. He had a note."

Falconer didn't answer, but he noticed the past tense of the verb.

Blore went on. "I bought the note from Wang T'ung. Paid through the nose, I did! Aye, it cost me a packet, but it was worth it." He held up a piece of parchment with Wang T'ung's chop mark on it. "Note's due tonight, Falconer. In one mucking half hour."

"Wang T'ung said he would renew it. A Chinaman's word is as good as his chop—even a tricky old fellow like Wang T'ung. That's why I'm here, to sign a new note."

"Is it now? Well, it's not Wang T'ung's note anymore. It's mine. And I can hardly be kept to Wang T'ung's word, can I? If I mean to keep a promise, I generally put it in writing. I've signed nothing."

"Wang T'ung wouldn't sell you the note unless you kept his word for him."

"Maybe." It was true—Wang T'ung had insisted that his word be honored. "How d'you plan to pay me, Falconer?"

"You know I can't—not tonight."

"What d'you aim to give me for the note, I wonder? The *Sweet Witch*—or Mrs. Falconer? Either 'ud do me fine. I'm not partial—black-slave trade or white-slave trade, it's all the same to me."

"You dirty scum!"

"Not so fast, Falconer. I haven't earned your insults, not yet. As it happens, I plan to keep Wang T'ung's word for him. Business before pleasure! I'm aiming to renew your note. For seven months. That's longer than Wang T'ung would have given you."

Seven months . . . what was going on in Blore's scheming head?

"Seven months is how long it took me to get out o' that pisshole of a prison in Haiti, Falconer. Seven months—you couldn't get a better deal! But at a different percentage."

"What percentage?"

"How about a thousand?"

"That's robbery!"

"No it's not, Falconer. There's Chink loan sharks charge as much—more, over seven months."

Adam knew that was true. "I don't need to borrow for seven months."

"And I'm not willing to lend for less. You've got no choice, Falconer—time's near up on this loan. I've been downright generous, considering there's no security on the money. You might take your tail out of Macao harbor and vanish up your own arse."

Only a slight narrowing of the eyes betrayed Falconer's fury. This would surely mean losing the *Sweet Witch*. In seven months, even with the lucrative sandalwood trade, his profits would not come near to covering Blore's demands. Nor could he pay tonight. And that was what it came down to: losing the *Sweet Witch* tonight, or in seven months. He made the only possible choice.

"Make out the papers, Blore. I'll sign."

"They're already made out. Aye, Falconer, I know you right well. Well enough to know your mind before you do! A lot comes clear when you spend seven months in godrotting hell."

Blore looked over the piece of paper with no attempt to hide his satisfaction. The money would be nice. But he intended to get the money—and revenge too. He had not revealed all his cards yet.

"By the bye, I aim to take delivery of the money elsewhere. I'm not much of a reader, but I can read this." His stubby finger moved over the just-signed note. "Says here—borrower to make delivery to the lender *in person*. As the lender I'm here to tell you that my person won't be in Macao in seven months. I'll be back to blackbirding in the South Seas. You'll have to make delivery to where I aim to be."

So, thought Falconer with a rush of anger: the high card had been played, at last. He was angry that he had been tricked so easily. Blore meant to get the money, and the *Sweet Witch,* and probably to kill him into the bargain. But he let none of these thoughts show in his face.

"You tell me where, Blore."

"I'll think on it and let you know in a day or two. I'll send you a note. Best not leave harbor till you get it."

Falconer stood up, impatient to go. He had a bad taste in his mouth, and a strong desire to knock the smirk off Blore's face. He strode to the door.

But Adam was wrong about one thing: the high cards had not all been played.

"Falconer!"

Adam stopped at the doorway, aware, too late, that Blore had more up his sleeve.

"About that little matter of security for the loan. Perhaps I was lying when I said I had none. You paid top money to save a woman you care shit-all for. Wonder what you'd do to save a woman you do like?" Blore paused dramatically, and rubbed the side of his huge jaw, and then, when he saw that Falconer would not ask, he went on: "Already guessed, have you, Falconer? It's true —I took possession of Mei Sung yesterday. For the next five years—and I paid a pretty penny for her too! No telling what could happen to her in seven months if you don't show. But you'll show, won't you? Aye, one thing sure I know about you, Falconer. You've got scruples. Scruples!"

The raucous sound of Blore's laughter followed Adam into the corridor. He stood white-knuckled, controlling his anger and his outrage, composing himself. One thing was evident: he would have to take Carey back to the *Sweet Witch* tonight. She was no longer safe here, in spite of Wang T'ung's promises. Things were bad; they could hardly be worse.

But at least he had seen Blore's hand.

Carey lay on the yellow bed, struggling to let the empty spaces of her mind keep control for a little longer.

But it was no good; the trick would only work for a time. Reality clawed its way back into her consciousness.

When she heard the sound of someone at the door, she thought at first it would be one of the attendants, the Chinese girls, who were usually quite kind. She looked up into the mirror's reflection with a wan smile—and her heart stood still.

"Adam," she whispered, and whirled to face him.

"Is it such a shock to see me?" he asked, for she had gone white, dead-white, even under the makeup.

Why had he come now, of all times? She had prayed for rescue—but she had not expected Adam to be her rescuer. That he should see her now, with the telltale marks of another man still on her robe, still on her bed . . .

"You don't look very glad to see me." His voice was cold, his eyes disdainful. They swept the disorder of the room and missed nothing.

Faint, Carey sat down on the bed's edge. Her mind reeled. Oh, God! What Adam must think of her . . . how awful that he should find her here. A wine goblet was on the table beside her, and because for the past month Carey had been suspicious of renewed attempts to drug her, its contents remained untouched. She reached over to the tray and took the goblet of forgetfulness into her trembling hands.

He watched and said nothing, but closed the door behind him. She drained the glass and at last found the strength to speak. "How did you find me?"

"I bought you."

She stared at him, disbelieving.

"I've come to take you from here, Carey. Back to the *Sweet Witch*."

"The *Sweet Witch?*" she repeated stupidly.

He frowned. "There's no other place to send you."

"The *Sweet Witch*. Oh—" She wanted to laugh and to cry. The *Sweet Witch* that she had thought she would never see again, and Adam was taking her there, although he looked as though he didn't really want to . . . Was it relief that was sending strange messages through her nerve endings? Her insides felt all jumbled with contradictory feelings, feelings that would vanish as soon as the soothing potion took hold. She huddled her arms about her chest and rocked back and forth to ease the agony.

Adam eyed her near-nakedness disapprovingly. "I've brought the clothes you arrived in. And you can wear my cloak."

Wasn't he going to ask her anything about what had happened to her, how she had come to be here? To find her after nearly a year of absence, in a place like this, and ask no questions? To stand there so coldly—while she longed for him, ached for him to take her in his arms. She wanted to cry against his shoulder, to sob out her relief, to let her tears wash away the days and the indignities and the memories of other men, men she had hated . . . and yet he stood still, doing nothing. She started to tremble all over.

"Adam, please—oh, please hold me. It's been so hard."

He stood and watched, hating this woman who had put him in Blore's power, who had cost him not only Mei Sung, but perhaps also the *Sweet Witch*. And if Blore had his way, his life.

"Put your clothes on." He threw a wrapped package toward her, and she made no effort to catch it. Too many wild and uninhibited sensations were shuddering through her limbs. She hugged her pillow and, despite herself, felt her body wracked with dry sobs.

"Please, Adam, help me. I don't know what's wrong with me."

Seeing her writhings, he became suspicious and walked over to the tray. He picked up the glass; sniffed it; tasted its contents on his fingertip. Then he looked at her white and tortured face, and something like pity replaced the anger in his eyes. So Blore had been wanting a show.

"They've put something in your glass, Carey. An aphrodisiac. A love potion. We'll wait until the worst passes. You'll be all right."

"Hold me, Adam. I'll be all right if you hold me." She clutched at his leg and clung to it, but he shook her away and left her, ignoring her agonies.

"Adam, for mercy's sake! Help me. Make love to me."

But he would not. Instead he walked around the fringes of the room, peering at the high cracks where the mirrors joined. At last he found what he was looking for. He took a clean handkerchief and stuffed it into the crack. But

213

were there other viewing slits like this, he wondered? He continued to search the mirrors.

"Have mercy, Adam! Help me, help me, if you have any compassion at all!"

She understood nothing of what he was about: it seemed cruel that he should be so cold, so distant, so inattentive, when she needed him so much. Her body was on fire for him, torn with convulsions, totally abandoned to unchecked passions—and he, having circled the room, was doing nothing, only watching her from a distance. She could see his tall impassive form mirrored, distorted an infinity of times in the all-encircling mirrors. She twisted. and moaned, and turned, but her eyes could not escape him, any more than they could escape her own white-faced writhing image. Adam just stood there . . . and the unfamiliar hands that clawed at her black-nippled breasts were her own, and the alien arched body was her own, and the beseeching bizarre whore's face in the mirror was her own, and Adam did nothing but watch.

And that was what she always, to her horror, remembered about the mirrored room—Adam, with his dark unfathomable eyes, doing nothing; while she heaved and panted on the hated yellow bed, and saw, reflected a thousand times in the inescapable mirrors, the image of all she had become.

Adam need not have worried about the viewing slit into the room. Blore had long since left the private cabin, and it was occupied now only by Wang T'ung. Wang T'ung was not interested in the peephole. He had seen too many shows in his lifetime, and had he wanted to watch he would have arranged something infinitely better—something more acrobatic, with more girls, and more interesting perversions.

Wang T'ung picked up his eggshell-fragile teacup and sipped at it delicately, letting the warmth and satisfaction seep through his frail body. He had come a long way from his humble beginnings in Soochow; how far could be seen by the silken stuff of his embroidered robe, and by the gold caps on his teeth.

It had been very interesting and very profitable, this duel between the two barbarian Americans, and he had turned it well to his advantage. He had already made a lot of money; and he would make a great deal more.

He had done well to send Mei Sung off with the black-haired one for the past year. He had been looking for a ship's captain just such as this, a captain bold enough to accept difficult assignments, and principled enough to be trusted implicitly. Mei Sung's report had been good. Yes, he had chosen well.

Of course, for the money, other ship's captains could be found who would take the risks. But many ship's captains might sail away with the cargo and never be seen again, for if they evaded the port authorities, and if they—miraculously!—escaped the lurking danger of pirates, they might yield to the temptations of their cargo.

He would have to mislead Falconer a bit, of course. The man with his strange scruples might otherwise refuse to take on the cargo. It was a good joke that it was Russian money, money made by men like the dead count; but it was also true enough that the shipment had been arranged for by the Russian government. Russia and Portugal were at the moment on different sides of this incomprehensible war being fought halfway around the world. The Macao authorities would rub their hands with glee at the thought of confiscating such a cargo.

Yes, Falconer was the man. That Blore intended a swift end for him some months from now was of no importance to Wang T'ung. By then the shipment would have changed hands; Falconer's usefulness would be finished.

Nor was Wang T'ung unduly concerned that Blore had made threats about Mei Sung's safety. The smelly barbarian was only bluffing, as he, Wang T'ung, might have done in similar circumstances. It was not that he trusted Blore. In fact when Blore had first started to bargain for Mei Sung in earnest, Wang T'ung had been very reluctant. He remembered how cruelly her first lover had treated her; since then he had been very careful to put her with men who were more considerate.

But Blore had persisted; had finally offered a truly enormous price. Wang T'ung, after closing his eyes and thinking about all the ramifications for fully half an hour, had finally agreed, on condition that Blore also buy an expensive half-interest in the mirrored pleasure boat—a partnership calculated to keep Blore beneath his watchful eye.

Blore had agreed with alacrity. He knew a profitable concern when he saw one. As new half-owner of the pleasure boat, Blore had done some things of which Wang T'ung did not approve. Sending other men in to Falconer's wife, for one: when Wang T'ung had heard about that, two days ago, he had put a stop to it at once. For Mrs. Falconer herself he had no particular compunction. But women were property; and a man's property was a sacred thing, to be used, bartered with, traded away, sold for profit, or simply ignored, but never to be violated without the owner's permission. To think that men like Blore called the Chinese heathens!

And yesterday, when Mei Sung had finally been delivered to Blore, Wang T'ung had at last disclosed several things that would absolutely ensure Mei Sung's safety for all time.

He had told the truth about his own relationship with Mei Sung—that she was his own great-granddaughter, the daughter of his daughter's daughter, and his favorite living relative. To a Chinaman, family was a matter of supreme importance.

Then he told Blore about the first man who had maltreated Mei Sung. How he had been found in the Portuguese colony of Goa, thousands of miles away; how he had been brought back to Macao; how he had been lodged in an isolated place with some of Mei Sung's numerous cousins and uncles.

And finally Wang T'ung had described, in luxuriant and lurid detail, exactly what had happened to the man then—which parts of his body had been removed, and how, and in what order, and over what period of time.

CHAPTER TWENTY-ONE

The sunlight was a balm to Carey's scrubbed skin—the sweet golden sunlight, which she had thought she might never see again. She stretched her face upward to feel its healing warmth. Little winds ruffled her silky combed-out hair, and the *Sweet Witch* swayed gently at anchor, and the air smelled marvelous—clean, tangy, perfumed only by salt and the good tea-smell of the cargo, and the faint lingering aroma of sandalwood that had until recently occupied the holds.

She was trying hard to push the memory of the past weeks from her mind. It had helped that Noah and Mr. Lovell and Luke Alden and others of the crew had seemed glad, if surprised, to see her back aboard the ship. They did not know where she had been, of course, and that helped—allowed her, at times, to pretend that all that had gone before had been a bad dream. When she saw Adam's unyielding face it was harder to pretend, for in his eyes she saw the hated knowledge of all that she had become. But Adam had been avoiding her like poison. For the past three days, ever since her return, he had not come down to the cabin until after she was fast asleep.

It would help, too, when the *Sweet Witch* sailed. She tried not to look too closely at the other ships at anchor, tried not to speculate which one it might have been. She did not even want to look at the Macao shoreline, nor to go ashore. Adam had managed to retrieve her trunk from Vasily's house. She knew now that the Russian count was dead—that the poor battered Malay girl had killed him, finding retribution at last, at the cost of her own life.

She hated the Macao clothes now. The extravagant gowns seemed an affront, an all-too-painful reminder of her own foolishness and of what it had led to. She was unaware that the yellow dress she was wearing, much prettier than any she had owned before in her life, made a very attractive picture as she stood at the ship's rail.

Luke Alden, watching the flowing sun-dappled hair and the slender figure and the expression on her face, almost that of a child discovering for the first time the wonder of life, thought she had never looked more beautiful, or happier—for the moment, at least. He felt the familiar tightening in his throat. He had thought he would not see her again. In his heart nothing had changed. But Carey had changed—how or why, he was not sure. In spite of the expression on her face right now, she was not the same sunny-eyed innocent she had once been.

"It's quite a sight, isn't it, Mrs. Falconer?"

Carey's eyes came open and she turned to the tall young seaman with a warm welcome. Dear Luke Alden —so real, so reassuringly the same, so solid. He had broadened, grown older and more self-assured in her absence. Like her, he had only just turned twenty. But he was no longer a boy. She knew he was unswerving in his devotion to her.

"Why, Luke, you don't have to call me Mrs. Falconer. You've never called me that before. I'd rather you called me Carey, as you've always done."

"Perhaps your husband would object."

"It's me you're addressing, not Captain Falconer. Now say it again, properly." She encouraged him with the sunny tilt of her head—oh, it was good to feel warmed by a man's admiration again, a man who knew nothing of her past!

Luke smiled easily, and repeated her name. "If you insist, then. Carey."

"Were you admiring the view too, Luke?"

"I was admiring you. You look beautiful. Like sunshine."

"I'm sure you say things like that to the girls in every port." Carey laughed, delighted at the compliment. Oh, it was good to laugh again—to have reason to laugh again!

Adam Falconer, coming upon the pair from behind, heard the words and the laughter, and saw the tilt of the heads, the golden one and the copper-colored one. An unreasoning rage seized him. He had just received the message about where he was to meet Blore seven months from now. It was bad news—and it was Carey's fault. She had made it all happen with her foolish, free-wheeling behavior. How dared she flirt, so easily and so casually, after all that had happened! And the blackness in his heart, the blackness he had been struggling to put behind him for the past three days, came over him again, undiminished in intensity.

"Don't you have anything better to do with your time, Alden?"

Carey started guiltily at the sound of Adam's voice. She turned to face him, moving a little apart from Luke Alden as she did so. The laughter died in her eyes and on her lips; her face became closed and wooden—and Adam saw that too, and hated it.

Alden spoke up. "I was just passing, Captain Falconer."

"Well, then, pass on, Luke." Adam's voice was dispassionate for the moment—but once Luke was out of earshot his tone became brutal, abrupt. "Get below, Carey."

"Not right now. I'm enjoying the sunshine." She was annoyed with him, annoyed and defiant. There was no reason she should not talk to Luke Alden, none at all. Adam addressed nobody else in that tone of voice, not even the lowliest deckhand. How dare he use it on her, no matter what had happened! "I'll stay here."

"I said get below!"

"Why must I?" She tossed her head belligerently.

"Because I intend to fuck you."

She gasped; she thought her ears must have been playing tricks. Adam could not have said that—Adam who had once wooed her, won her with his gentleness, his ardor.

"Shall I repeat myself?" His voice was icy. This was not the same Adam. It was an Adam driven by demons beyond his control, driven by self-hatred as much as by hatred of her. "Because I intend to—"

Before he could finish, she fled, face flaming. How could he say such things? When she entered the refuge of the cabin, Adam was close behind. She turned to confront him, shaking with outrage.

"How dare you speak to me like that—and on deck, in broad daylight!"

"Nobody heard. And does it matter that it's daylight? Take off your clothes."

"You wouldn't talk to a cheap flower-girl like that. I'm still your wife, no matter what you may think of me."

"I imagine you've heard worse language. And from now on you're not my wife. I discarded you as a wife, long ago. Now you're my whore—I own you."

"Own me!"

"Yes, Carey, I own you. In this part of the world that's quite acceptable. I paid a great deal for the privilege. I even had to borrow a great deal of money. And for something I didn't even want! So far it's been a bad bargain. Now I'd like to see some value for my money. No more lying back like a stone-faced expressionless Canton whore who can be had for a few yen. I paid top dollar for you, and I don't want to make love to a block of ice."

An awful suspicion came over her. "Did you—were you one of them? *Were you?"*

He didn't answer her directly. He hated himself too much right now; and he hated her, he wanted to punish her for forcing him to do everything that he had done, for forcing him to feel everything he now felt. He evaded the truth. "There was a viewing slit into the room, Carey."

She buried her head in her hands; her brain reeled; but remembering the way he had pushed his handkerchief into a crack between the mirrors, she knew he was telling the truth.

"Take your clothes off, Carey. Paint yourself for me. Your breasts, your face—and be quick about it."

"I can't make love to you now. I can't!"

"Can't you? A few days ago you were begging for it. You're a whore, Carey. Whores make love to order— when their masters please, not when they please. You'll undress yourself, and you'll make yourself beautiful for me, and I don't want any fighting, and I don't want any arguments. For the price I paid for you I could have had a hundred of the best courtesans in Macao. My last mistress cost a lot less, and she was worth a lot more."

"Why didn't you keep her, then?" Carey's head came up, and her eyes sparkled with an amber hate-filled anger.

"Would you rather have stayed where you were?"

"Yes!" And at the moment, she half-believed it.

"Really? Well, perhaps you belonged there, at that. Are you telling me you want to go back?"

"No," she admitted reluctantly, after a moment's pause.

"Then do as I say. There's makeup by the mirror. I bought a large supply, enough to last for a long sea-voyage." The line of his jaw was hard, merciless; and she found no pity in his eyes.

"You can't want to see me—that way!"

"Yes, Carey, I want to see you—that way. Put your hair up too."

When she declined, he ripped the clothes from her body; when she resisted, he flung her on the bed and pinned her there; when she refused to paint her face and her breasts he did it for her. Her struggles caused the makeup to smear badly, but he did not care—for he did it not because he needed arousal, but because he needed to shame her, to debase her as she had debased him. And then with hellfire in his heart and damnation in his head, he took her savagely. It could not be called the making of love, for this was not love, but hatred.

But when he lay, spent, he had still not exorcised the demons from his soul. He resented her frigidity, her unresponsiveness that had made his own passions seem so brutal, so animalistic. She had not even begged or wept—that would have made her seem more human. Even now that it was done she lay with her eyes closed, her face emptied of emotion, as it had been so often in the past month—as though her mind were somewhere else altogether. He wanted to reach her: to hurt her: to tell her of his hatred, as though that would excuse all his bad behavior. So, lying between her legs, he whispered into her ear the black thoughts that raged in his heart:

"From now on, Carey, I'll take you when I want—and where I want, and as often as I want. Because that's all you're here for, do you understand? When I say get down to the cabin, you'll go to the cabin. When I say paint your face, you'll paint your face—and your breasts, and any part of your body I choose. When I say open your legs, you'll open your legs—and you'll do it willingly. You're a whore, Carey, nothing but a whore, and you're not even very good at it."

CHAPTER TWENTY-TWO

"I don't understand it—don't understand it at all." Jed Lovell frowned as he watched the port officials clamber back aboard the lorcha that had brought them to the *Sweet Witch*.

"Routine search," replied Adam Falconer off-handedly. His eyes were on the sky, not on the small boat.

"For the third time in five days? And they said they'd be back tomorrow." Lovell ran his fingers round under his collar. It was oppressively hot and sultry: the calm before the storm. There was little wind yet, but the wind would come soon. In minutes or in hours: but it would come.

"Tomorrow? Well, tomorrow is another day." Falconer sounded abstracted. "These petty officials—nothing better to do with their time, I suppose."

"Looked to me as though they expected to find something on board."

"It's just the usual red tape. Stop worrying."

An awful suspicion took hold of Jed Lovell. "You haven't brought anything aboard that you're not telling me about?"

"Opium, for instance?" Adam laughed. "Set your mind at rest, Jed. I had an offer—a very good offer—to run a shipment up the coast. Perhaps I should have taken it. We could've all retired on the proceeds from two or three trips like that."

Lovell relaxed a little. He wouldn't have expected Adam Falconer to accept opium as a cargo, but this sudden interest on the part of the Macao officials was making him nervous. The other night, Falconer had sent all hands, himself included, ashore. Only the captain and Noah had remained on board—and of course Mrs. Falconer, but she had been in her cabin.

"Anyway, Jed, the Portuguese authorities would hardly

get nervous about opium. Shipments come and go all the time. It's not illegal here. Now if we were up the coast, at Canton—"

"We've been in harbor too long, far too long," exploded Lovell, voicing the other thing that worried him. "We could have left a month ago. First you spent weeks going off God knows where at night. Then Mrs. Falconer comes aboard, and we've done nothing but sit here since—another two weeks."

"Have patience. We'll be standing out to sea very soon."

"Not with the look of that." Lovell squinted at the heavily overcast sky. "Barometer's falling, too."

Falconer ignored the gloomy forecast. "Stop looking so morbid, Jed. We'll have no more trouble."

Lovell looked doubtful. His unpredictable captain was up to something, of that he was sure. It promised to be an unusual voyage: the extra ship's biscuit, the extra pickled cabbage and salt pork, the extra chicken coops with their squawking burdens, and particularly the warm clothing. Yet Falconer had said they would be staying in the Pacific, although he had been unusually close-mouthed about their actual destination. That, too, worried Lovell. But now, to his surprise, Adam confided in him:

"Alta California, Jed. That's the question in your mind, isn't it?"

Now, at last, Lovell understood the warm clothing. They'd be sailing northward, first, to take advantage of the winds and the ocean currents that would lead them to the west coast of America. "So that's it. It's a long haul."

"Sorry I didn't tell you before. But I didn't find out for sure until I saw Wang T'ung this morning. We have to make rendezvous with a Russian ship. It's coming down from Sitka—from the Russian territories in the Arctic."

"A *Russian* ship? Adam, what are you up to?"

"I'm delivering something."

"What, in God's name?"

"Jed, I trust you, but I can't tell you everything. You're too honest. Your face is like a map, laid out for all the world to read."

"I'll have to know more or I can't sail with you."

"Believe me, it's nothing to worry that troublesome

conscience of yours. It's something for the Russian government. Strictly legal."

"I don't like that, either. I don't trust those Russkis. They've got designs on North America, and make no mistake about it."

Falconer shrugged. He, too, was sure that the shipment was intended to help establish a Russian foothold in the Spanish territory of Alta California: something the Russians had been hoping to do for a few years. He didn't like the idea himself, but for the present he had no choice. "It's the British and the Spanish territories the Russians are eyeing, Jed—not ours. In any case, we're not at war with Russia. Their coalition with England has gone belly-up—and since the Russians signed that treaty with Napoleon, I'd have to say they're on our side. France has been mighty friendly to the United States."

"That doesn't make the Russians our friends."

"They're fighting side-by-side with the French in Sweden. And France is our friend—technically. That makes Russia our friend—technically."

"You're mincing words, Adam."

Falconer sighed. "Look, Jed, personally I think you have a point. I don't like the way the Russians are trying to get a toe in on the West Coast—not at all. But I don't like having the Spaniards there either, and I can't do much about it. Best thing would be if the United States took over Alta California. Maybe we will someday, if we ever get over our growing pains and make it across the Rockies."

"That'll never happen!"

"Maybe, maybe not. In any case it won't happen for some years. And in the meantime I'm being well paid to deliver this, this—message. I need the money, Jed."

Lovell clamped his mouth over his further objections. Was it no more than a message? It was hard to believe. But certainly if there were anything suspicious about the *Sweet Witch*'s cargo the prying port officials would have found it this morning. They'd gone through the hold with a fine-tooth comb. Even the captain's cabin and the men's sleeping quarters had not been spared. All the same, Falconer was hiding something, and he didn't like it. Lovell stiffened and became formal.

"Well, Captain Falconer, I'd best see to having the

hatches battened down for the storm, now that those port monkeys have had their search for the day."

Falconer smiled faintly and copied the businesslike tone. "Do that, Mr. Lovell. And then come back. All the men are aboard, aren't they?"

"Yes, Captain Falconer, as you ordered."

"Good. We're sailing at once."

Lovell stared at him, open-mouthed, and wondered if the captain had lost his senses.

"Well man, why are you standing about? You've been after me to make sail for days."

"But not today! There's a typhoon in the making. Only a madman would venture to sea now."

"Good. Then only madmen will follow me."

Falconer had planned to run for the Balintang Channel, due eastward into the Pacific, and to avoid the treacherous China coast: then to work northward from there. For half a day the *Sweet Witch* spanked along in the increasing gales, tearing off the knots at a fine clip, even with triple-reefed sails. It was a gamble, but with luck he could have done it: if the port officials had not delayed him in Macao; if the typhoon had been further to the south; if he had had one more day . . .

"Sweet heaven! The whole Jesus floor of the ocean!"

But the deckhand's words were lost in the shriek of the winds, and this new wall of water that smashed over the maindeck with the force of a tidal wave. Within seconds it seemed that all the furies of the gods were unleashed against the *Sweet Witch*. Wave after wave drove her deep into the trough of the seas, and her decks were awash with a torrent of swirling, raging waters. The wind had reached hurricane force—a blind, tearing, elemental battering ram of wind that tore loose everything that was not lashed down, and many things that were. Men tied themselves to the spars and the giant capstans, and prayed, and tried to keep the ship under control though they could scarcely move themselves.

"Mizzenmast's sprung, Captain!" Somehow, Luke Alden had made his half-drowned way across the deck; although he hollered at the top of his lungs, his voice was nearly lost in the unearthly howl of the wind and the waves.

Falconer swore through a mouthful of water—not at the elements, but at the thought of what might happen if the ship was dismasted. The wind would shift, later, but for now it was screaming in from the southwest, and if the mizzenmast was to be saved, it would mean running before the storm.

He untied himself, crawled on hands and knees across the deathtrap of the deck, and gave the order. At first the *Sweet Witch* balked and nearly split in two. But at last she began to cut through the waves and soon she was scudding for her life up the treacherous waters of the China coast.

For seventy-two hours the ship drove northward in the teeth of the storm, past the coast of Formosa, and well into the formidable East China Sea. The wind eased at last, then shifted to the northwest, and for some hours battered at the exhausted ship with renewed rage. But this time the punishment did not last for long: they were too far from the eye of the storm. The worst was over. The men, bone-weary, dozed at their stations and then woke to more work—the work of repairing the damage.

"You'd best eat, Cap'n." Noah had come up to the quarterdeck to see his master. He held two dishes in his hands, both steaming-hot and giving off an appetizing smell. Things were returning to normal: the ship's galley was once more in operation; the rigging was being repaired; and Mr. Lovell was ready to take over from Falconer.

"Thanks, Noah." Adam accepted one of the dishes gratefully. "How are the wounded?"

"Bruises, mostly. One thumb bust. One shoulder out o' joint—Huggins. Snapped back in like india-rubber, it did!"

"It's a miracle no one was swept overboard. How's the damage below?"

"Some bunged about, but everything as could move was lashed down. It ain't too bad. You best get below yourself, and get some shut-eye. All o' three days now you been on deck, lashed to the mast a fair chunk o' the time. You ain't fit to stand another watch."

"I dozed, Noah, whenever Mr. Lovell took over. What I need more than anything right now is food—and a shave." He rubbed his stubble ruefully. "How's Mrs. Falconer?"

"She's all right—or she was, two hours ago. Got a

mite shook up an' bruised the first day, till I tied her into the bunk. She weren't too happy about that—spunky little crittur, she is! But I been feedin' her reg'lar, and changin' the ropes so they won't chafe too much. I'm off there now, to take her some grub an' untie her for good. I'd a done it before, but there's been the wounded to tend to."

"Is that her dish?"

"Aye."

"I'll take it to her. You get to your own bunk and have some rest. I'll need you later, to help put the ship in order. In a day or two, when things have calmed a bit, we'll need every man jack aboard to fish that sprung mizzenmast. Oh, and Noah, wake me for the next watch, will you?"

Falconer turned and called to the first mate. "Take over, Mr. Lovell! I'm going below."

"Aye, Captain!"

As he made his way down the companion with Carey's meal in his hands, Adam wondered why Noah's words had made him so anxious to go below and see Carey. This exhaustion in his bones, this near-brush with death and the elements, had they weakened his head? Why had he kept forcing himself on her in a kind of animal love-making that was only somewhere short of rape? Why could he never reach her? And why, now, should he have such a sudden attack of concern for his hated and frigid wife?

If Carey had been frightened before, during the hell-swept height of the storm, she was doing a good job of not showing it now. Her face was ashen-pale, but he saw belligerence in her eyes, not fear. They glared at him from between spiky dark-gold lashes.

"I suppose you gave Noah the order to tie me down? This isn't exactly comfortable."

"As a matter of fact, I didn't. I never gave you a thought." He put down the bowl of steaming food, and started to work at one of the knots. Her arms strained at the rope, making the task more difficult. "If you don't relax, I might just decide to leave you there."

She glowered at him malevolently, without answering.

He stopped working at the knot, and looked at her with a surge of irritation. "You're making it impossible, you know."

"Noah managed."

"Perhaps you're more relaxed with Noah."

"Noah's more—"

But the thought was never finished, for her eyes widened with alarm. Adam had pulled a knife, seemingly from nowhere. Carey gaped at it, then at him. The knife, the unshaven stubbled chin, the wind-roughened hair, the dislike and exhaustion in his eyes—it all made him look like a ruffian, and she had a sudden unreasoning fear for her life.

"What—are you doing," she whispered.

"What do you think I'm doing?" Stopped by the desperation in her voice, he paused on the verge of cutting through a rope, and stared at her. "By God, you are scared, and not of the storm. Of me!"

She had closed her eyes, but he could see by the tremble of her chin and by the quick come-and-go of her breath that he had come close to the truth. He put his hand against her ribs. "Your heart's beating double-time, d'you know that? So my icy little wife has feelings after all! I thought you'd lost them all in Macao."

He bent over and touched his lips to hers: an elusive contact, but her eyes flew open and once again her guard was up. She looked resentful and cold.

A slow grin came over his face. "Do you know something, Carey? I'm fed up with the frigid little wife I've had since I took you out of the whorehouse in Macao. If you ever had an honest passion in your body you must have lost it there—for I've seen no sign of it, except the day you took that aphrodisiac by mistake. Perhaps it's time you learned something. There are other kinds of aphrodisiacs—the kind I'm going to use on you right now."

He took his knife and tore her dress raggedly down the front, taking care not to sever the ropes that held her in place.

"How dare you—how dare you!"

His hands worked beneath the ropes, pulling the two halves of her dress apart. "You'll be surprised what I dare. I've had a difficult three days, Carey, and I've a mind to get me a loving wife. One who'll smile when I come to the cabin. One who'll respond when I caress her. One who'll kiss me back—instead of lying there like a lump of clay. I told you, I want my money's worth,

Carey, and I mean it. I won't let you out of those ropes until you're aroused. Well and truly aroused."

"Oh!" How could he be so cruel? There was nothing he could do to make her feel anything for him—no, not ever again! Not after these past painful days, when he had taken her time and again against her will . . . when he had used sex-words and insinuations that had driven her into the inner spaces of her mind, the places where she could escape the knowledge of what he was doing to her. How had she ever loved him? "Whatever you do, Adam Falconer, I'll feel nothing but hatred!"

"Is that so?" He laid the flat of the knife's blade across a nipple, caressing it with the cold steel, watching her reactions with a twisted little smile. "Your body believes me, Carey, even if you don't."

His voice had gone sensual, soft as sin, and the knife moved to the other breast. Carey felt choked with rage and fear and something else—some fire-and-ice sensation that began to shiver through her skin, despite all her efforts to make her mind escape. Yet Adam himself had not touched her—only the impersonal flat of the dagger-blade that was arousing her unwilling response.

"You see, my darling? Your nipples have got a mind of their own. They're hard and pointed and trembling, and I'll wager they feel every little breath that touches them right now." He put the knife down and blew gently. Then, with a thumb barely brushing against each nipple, and his fingers moving slowly on the surrounding flesh, he lowered his mouth to the flat of her stomach, and his tongue drew liquid flame across her navel.

"Adam, please don't!" Her senses swam. It was the first time in these past weeks that he had taken the time to be gentle, even though he was refusing to untie the imprisoning ropes. And it was the first time she had not been able to make her mind retreat at the assault of his body.

"Don't squirm. It won't do you any good." His voice was slow, low, half-muffled against her skin. Oh Lord, what wild and half-forgotten sensations were taking command of her now? And Adam's murmuring voice was making it clear that the torture would go on: "I plan to keep this up for a long time—a very long time. I'm going to make sure that you're thoroughly awakened—that you won't reject me another time, as you've done ever since Macao."

"I've rejected—because you've been cold and horrible!"

"Is this cold and horrible?"

"Please, Adam, your beard . . ." His burrowing face was scraping her skin raw, driving her to distraction, prickling against her soft underbelly.

"Sorry, love, I'm not going to take time to shave. And maybe it will make you feel something through that thick skin of yours."

"Oh!"

His mouth traveled further down, to the golden triangle that tempted him; and now, because the bonds were in his way, he reached for his knife and cut loose the fastening that held her legs together. His fingers found the furrows of her body; then his mouth. She could not have resisted even if her limbs had been unbound.

"Adam, Adam—have mercy. Stop doing that—make love to me properly, if you must." His tongue was driving her wild, making her ache to feel his maleness within her. He sensed her growing abandon in the way her hips strained against the bonds, in the way her legs tried to enclose him. He lifted his head and moved away, leaving her for the moment.

Then he returned once more to slower pleasures. He moved upward on her body, breathed soft messages against her ears, toyed with her breasts, took his time, tortured her with the gentleness of his unhurried caresses. He kissed her hair, her eyes, her cheeks. She moaned, and her head moved under his. His tongue traced the line of her mouth, and he had no need to urge her more: her own mouth, responding, opened hungrily, and her tongue sought his with the savageness of her urgent need—but once again, he pulled back.

"Oh. Carey, you whore—you sweet little whore. You can really pretend when you want, can't you?"

She sobbed and writhed. "I'm not pretending. I swear I'm not. Let me go, please let me go, and I'll show you. I want to make love to you—oh yes, Adam, please. Please kiss me!"

"Beg me," he whispered against her ear; and she did. His lips moved again, this time meeting her mouth more fiercely. But after a few moments he pulled away and laughed softly, triumphantly.

"No complaints about the beard this time? Why,

Carey, I do believe you're beginning to feel something."
His mouth slid down to her body again, to her breasts
and below; and at last, when she thought she would go
out of her senses with the madness of unfulfilled promise, he cut her bonds loose.

"Now you're going to do the work, sweetheart." He
pulled her body on top of his. "There, astride, like
that." He guided her with his hands on her hips. "Let's
see how well you can pretend now—no, not so fast, not
yet. Gently at first. I'm tired, remember?"

But she was no longer to be contained; she was a ti-
gress; she gasped and moaned as her hips ground against
his, and her fingers clutched into the dark mat of hair on
his chest. Then, at the very last, when he saw that nothing could stop her, his hands reached up and seized her
breasts and he allowed himself to go with her, for he
himself had long since been driven to the edge of the
precipice.

At last she lay over him, exhausted, trembling, and
Adam's fingers described slow patterns over the tiny
ridges of her spine.

"Will you always cry out like that at the end, I wonder? My icy whore turned into a proper little savage!
Quite a change from Macao."

All at once she pulled away, and found her own place
on the bed. "Please, Adam, don't mention Macao again.
And don't call me a whore—please."

"I'm willing to make a pact if you are. Will you promise never to be cold again? Will you promise to let yourself go, to do as I ask you?"

"It depends."

"On what?"

"On how you ask me. If makes a difference if you approach me with—well, with feeling."

She could not say love. Since Macao, the word seemed
to have lost its meaning. She was sure that Adam did
not, could not, love her—not now, not ever. And she
was equally sure that she no longer loved him. The
feeling she felt for him at this moment was something
different, something even stronger—a love-hate feeling,
a compound of remembered cruelties during this past
two weeks, resentment that he had so recently forced
her to respond to his passions, and the bittersweet remembrance of what he had once meant to her. More

hate than love—for he had seen her as no man should ever have seen her; he had used words to her that could not swiftly be forgiven or forgotten; he had wounded some very private and essential part of her. She had loved him, once, in another existence, it seemed. Too much had happened since then, too much that could not be changed. But he was still her husband.

And storms could be weathered, just as the *Sweet Witch* had weathered the typhoon. Perhaps there would be peace, and safe harbor, somewhere, sometime . . .

She turned to him, tentatively. "Adam, do you think it could ever work—our marriage, I mean?"

But he was already asleep.

⊂⊱ CHAPTER TWENTY-THREE ⊱⊃

For another week, while the mizzenmast was being repaired and the rent sails were being patched, the *Sweet Witch* made little headway. She was plagued, still, by contrary winds and rains. Neither sun nor stars nor land had been sighted since before the typhoon, and even the most experienced navigator could not have calculated their exact position. Adam knew only that they were somewhere in the treacherous East China Sea, southwest of the Japaner's lands. And so the ship picked its careful way northward, while men kept watch and took soundings so as to avoid the dangers that might lurk unseen beneath the rain-shrouded seas.

Between Carey and Adam, there was now a tempestuous truce, and the others aboard ship noted it. They all knew about the strange black mood that had come over the captain in Macao, and were grateful that it was passing. Some were pleased that Mrs. Falconer, whom he had treated quite unkindly for a time, had been looking a little happier for the past few days.

Now, as the men sat on the foredeck splicing rope and repairing rent sails, they yarned and gossiped; and as Noah was not present, they were dealing with a topic of endless fascination.

"Odd—him leaving her in Macao for near a full year."

"Aye, but it didn't seem so odd at the time. You call to mind how he hated the sight o' her, then? She were poison to him, an' no mistake. Ain't a man Jack counted it strange when he brought the fancy Chinee lady aboard. Thought we'd seen the tail end o' Miz Falconer."

"Mebbe she tricked him again, like she did into marryin'."

"That ain't possible! The Cap'n don't get tricked twice."

"I heard tell she was gamblin' in Macao. Don't seem to care much how the tongues wag, that one."

"Aye—an' she took a lover too. Mebbe that's what tweaked the Capn into wantin' her back."

"True, there's naught like another man seein' value in your property!"

"Still hates her, though. You can spit on his hatred, it's that thick."

"But he can't keep his hands off 'er now, so Gordo says."

"Had your eye to the keyhole, Gordo?"

Someone made a crude joke about keyholes and other things, and there was a round of ribald laughter.

"Wish this mucking fog 'ud go away. Makes me feel creepy, not knowing where we are, exactly."

"Don't gripe. At least this morning the rain's stopped —and the wind."

"Wind might blow the fog away. By jingo, I'd like to see the sun!"

"By noon it'll clear, you watch. Praps today'll be the day the Capn gets a reading."

"Aye, an' it'll be good to sheet home! It spooks me, slimin' along like we was a wounded snail, crawlin' on our belly."

"Hey-o! Do I feel the gawdrotting sun on my gawd-rotting face? And a gawdrotting breeze?"

The men looked out to sea, gladdened by the brief promise—and froze.

"Lookit that."

"Lordamighty save us!"

The ships ghosted out of the lifting mists on the port side. First three of them—then five—then seven, eight, twelve. Their odd-shaped sails swung easily, catching the sudden breeze until it pressed the cloth into layered billows against the bamboo battens. From the masts rippled black streamers, and weathervanes adorned with yellow-eyed fish.

"A whole muckin' fleet of 'em!"

"Pirates, d'you think?"

But there was no more time for conjecture, for Adam Falconer, too, had seen the huge Chinese junks, and already the orders had been shouted.

"Shake the reefs out! All hands look lively—all canvas set! Noah, get Mr. Lovell. Hop to it, Huggins! Alden, issue arms to all hands. Gordo! To the guns."

And in very little time each man was at his station—some raiding the arms chest, some in the shrouds, some manning the carronades. The *Sweet Witch* had only four guns, two each side—not really enough to be running these pirate-infested seas.

Now the schooner was on the port tack, sails taut to the wind, and gathering speed. But it was already too late. The lead junk was closing in, and it fired a salvo across the *Sweet Witch*'s bows. The other junks splayed out, to cut off retreat.

The *Sweet Witch*'s carronades answered the junk's fire, but their range was short, and the first round fell wide of its mark. And now the parting mists revealed a new danger.

"Rocks alee, Capn, two points off the starb'd bow! Rocks—and land!"

"Give them one more broadside, and ready about!"

Again the *Sweet Witch*'s guns let loose, and this time the shots pounded a junk not a hundred yards away. A yawning hole appeared at the waterline of the junk's hull, and water surged through it. Screams reverberated across the space.

"Hard alee!" The *Sweet Witch* swung to her new course. Her sails flattened, trembled, then answered to the wind.

"That'll teach 'em!"

"Good work, Gordo!" yelled Falconer. "Now another round, for that next junk! They can't catch us now."

But the exultation was premature. The damaged junk, tilting crazily, was nevertheless kept afloat by its watertight bulkheads. Its captain, seeing the *Sweet Witch*'s new heading, ordered all hands to abandon ship—but not before they had set the torch to it. There was gunpowder aboard: in seconds the junk exploded into a floating ball of flame, and, reeling drunkenly, wallowed toward the lee shore, cutting off the *Sea Witch*'s line of retreat.

Again at Falconer's command, the schooner changed course to avoid the fireship. His only remaining choice took him directly through the thick of the pirate vessels.

"One more point to windward, Mr. Lovell! We can make better knots than this. Haul those sheets flat!"

And for a few minutes it seemed that they would, indeed, break their way through, as the swiftly-maneuvering junks, swinging almost within their own lengths, parted to avoid collision. But then one of the pirate ships fired at short range. It was a round of dismantling shot—not cannonballs, but great lengths of iron chain that whipped through the *Sweet Witch*'s rigging with the fury of a dozen maddened bulls. Sails shredded and collapsed; a freed boom swung wildly. In seconds the deck was a mass of ripped canvas and shorn line and stunned, stumbling sailors.

On the port side, near Falconer, a low, smallish junk sidled up to the bow of the *Sweet Witch*, jockeying for position as men prepared to board. With a rage born of desperation, Adam grabbed the huge carpenter's maul that had been on deck for mast repairs, and knocked out the retaining pin that held the enormous iron bower anchor. The anchor, hanging from the hull of the *Sweet Witch*, released. The iron chain released with a painful screech, and two tons of metal crashed through the wooden deck of the Chinese craft. The junk split in two as if it had been no more than a reed, and the howls of shocked men hurled into the sea gave Adam a moment's grim satisfaction.

But already, on the starboard side, a larger junk had come alongside, and grappling irons had appeared over the side of the *Sweet Witch*. Men, armed to the teeth, swarmed across the boarding nets; and another vessel came to take the place of the lost one on the port side.

After that it became the confusion of hand-to-hand combat: cutlasses swishing through the air, ancient Chinese flintlocks firing and sometimes backfiring, hand-knives glinting and clashing and meeting bone, men shouting and swearing and sometimes screaming. Then, through the smoke, Adam saw two men dragging Carey up through the hatch.

He fended off a last blow from his attacker of the moment, and threw down his knife. Then he shouted, above the din of battle, an order for his men to cease their resistance. A pair of scruffy pirates seized his arms.

He could see several bodies on the deck, and several parts of bodies. Of his own men, one, two, three dead— at least three. And four of theirs, maybe more. Many wounded, too: sitting and moaning over their wounds.

The men who were still standing were bloodied, most of them. But Noah was still alive and all in one piece—and Jed Lovell, and Huggins, and Gordo. And Carey. More than that Adam could not see, for his eyes were now becoming blurred with blood from a scalp wound.

"Where's Ah Chin?" he shouted.

"Here, Capn." A sorry figure struggled to raise itself from the deck. One hand was wrapped in a piece of dirty canvas.

"Are you all right, Ah Chin?" Falconer could not see well enough to distinguish the wounded hand.

"Damn-right!" Ah Chin had been sailing English and American ships, man and boy, for forty years. He still spoke with a slight singsong accent, but he spoke English as well as any of them. "Mucking debils damn-near got me, but I'm alive. Aiee! Godrotting alive." He sounded shaken.

"I'll need you to interpret, Ah Chin. Tell the man in command that we'll fight no more. But they are not to hurt the woman."

For several minutes a jabber of conversation followed. Finally Ah Chin turned back to Falconer.

"He says Miz Falconer ain't to be hurt, long's you go with 'em and make no trouble."

"Go where?"

"To see their Capn. Their pirate chief."

"Tell him someone must be allowed to tend to the wounded. Tell him Noah must be allowed to move freely." Falconer nodded with his head toward where he thought his manservant stood. With his hands pinned behind his back, he could not wipe his eyes; by now he could see no more than a red blur. He was quite aware that there was no reason for the pirates to cede to his demands—no reason beyond common humanity. It was worth a try, all the same.

"Tell them I'll need you to come too, Ah Chin, as an interpreter. And tell them I won't fight—and to let go of my arms."

When this was translated, the leader of the boarding party balked.

"He says you go alone, Capn."

"Is my wife still all right?" God, he wished he could see—wished someone would wipe the blood from his face.

"Yiss—they ain't even holding her. She ain't hurt."

"Then tell them I'm ready to go."

Just before they manhandled him over the side, he heard a tearing sound, quite close, and Carey's voice.

"Wait!"

The pirates didn't understand the word, but they understood the authoritative tone. They paused. She was only a woman, after all; she could do no harm. And they had been given instructions as far as she was concerned.

Seconds later a soft cloth touched Adam's face. He knew now what the rending sound had been: Carey's petticoats. She wiped the blood away from his eyes. It started to trickle back at once. Then, wasting no time, lest the pirates should become too impatient, she lifted her skirts and ripped off another, larger piece of the white cotton. Quickly she wound it around his head, turban-style, and tucked the ends in.

And as he went over the side of the *Sweet Witch*, only Adam guessed what the others could not—that in the turban's folds she had hidden something.

The pirate flagship was the largest of the junks, an opulent gilded vessel with Chinese characters adorning its masts, and the omnipresent fish-banners flapping in the breeze. It lay at some distance from the *Sweet Witch*. The hands that pinioned Falconer's arms were no longer unwelcome, for he knew he could not have made his way unaided over the side and into the small boat that was to transport him to the flagship; could not have walked, without stumbling, across the huge junk's deck; could not have climbed down the companionway that led to the captain's cabin. He felt disembodied, light-headed, unreal: but perhaps it was as much the strangeness of the scene as the pounding of his own head.

It was a low-ceilinged, large cabin, larger than anything aboard the *Sweet Witch*. Dozens of lanterns swung from above, yet they hardly illuminated the large space that was almost devoid of furniture. It would have looked barren but for the scarlet-and-gold tapestries that hung in hushed splendor from the bulkheads, and the rich brocaded mats and cushions that lay in mounds on the center of the floor. On one large scarlet cushion there was a man sitting cross-legged, Chinese fashion, with an extraordinarily fine chess set before him on a low teak table. The game was half-finished.

The man dominated the empty spaces around him. He seemed to have grown in stature since Falconer had last seen him, but perhaps it was only the effect of the swaying lanterns on the yellow silken stuff of his robe, the one thing that seemed to catch the light in the shadowed cabin. His pockmarked face was no longer totally expressionless. He was smiling, but it was a wary smile, not entirely welcoming, and it did not touch his eyes. The eyes were like black marbles, cold and impervious.

"We meet again, Captain Falconer. I've been expecting you."

"So you do speak. And English, too."

"As you say. Please be seated."

Falconer acknowledged the offer with a solemn bow, and found a cushion.

"You are wondering why I did not speak then, that time you found me on the island? Because I would have had to answer questions. Would you have spoken, in my place?"

"No."

"And if I had spoken at the end—to acknowledge your part in my rescue—I sense it would have cost me dearly. You would have handed me at once to the Macao authorities."

"It's possible." I would now, you pirate scum.

"Ah! Well, a pirate's life is a hard one. It is no more than I would expect."

"You speak English very well."

"As a boy I spent many years on the English barbarian tea-ships, Captain Falconer." His voice changed, and he pretended to cringe. "Yiss, mass'er! No, mass'er! Can dooa, mass'er! Aiee yah, mass'er!" He reverted to normal. "You see? But one can watch, and learn. In those years I learned a great deal about sailing ships, and even more about cruelty and piracy. A different kind of piracy.

"By the way, Captain Falconer, I have been most impolite. I haven't introduced myself properly. Yü Lan is my name." Yü Lan made a tiny gesture with his hand, and shadowy figures started to move in the background. "Do you speak Chinese at all?"

"No."

"Not surprising. Few Englishmen manage to master

the complexities of either Mandarin or Cantonese. Yü is the Chinese word for fish. Captain Fish." For the first time his smile moved upward, and his eyes narrowed. "The fish that never sleeps, Captain Falconer. The fish that never closes its eyes. Amusing, is it not—the fish capturing the bird of prey?"

"Amusing for the fish, Captain Yü." If only his head wound would stop throbbing . . . if only Yü would get to the point.

"Tea will be here at once. You will have tea?"

Falconer inclined his head a fraction. At least Yü Lan did not intend a speedy death for them all. "May I ask, Captain Yü, if you have any medicines that might be sent to my men? Some of them are badly wounded."

"It has been done."

"Thank you. And my wife is aboard the ship. If you would give orders that she is not to be molested."

"It has been done. It was so ordered before we boarded."

Falconer bit back the question: how had Yü Lan known she was aboard? He accepted the cup of tea that was set before him, picking it up with both hands, and praying that he would not betray himself by spilling it.

"It is really too bad you resisted so strenuously, Captain Falconer. So many needless deaths! Did you not notice that our guns were hardly put to use?"

Indeed, Falconer had noticed. The Chinese junks had fired only twice—first, the salvo across the *Sweet Witch*'s bow and then, at the last, the broadside of dismantling shot.

"And yet you sank two of our ships! Very bad manners, Captain Falconer. It's unfortunate that some of your men have died—but then, some of my men have died too. And you have only yourself to blame. It is said in my land that if you save a man's life you become responsible for his actions for the rest of his life. Let the deaths be on your conscience, Captain Falconer, not mine."

Falconer's head throbbed, and his fingers itched to reach for the knife he knew was in his turban. But he was aware that even if he could evade the guards and kill Yü Lan, it would bring only a fleeting satisfaction, no more. There were the others on the *Sweet Witch* to consider. He kept his fingers still, and his voice polite. "It seems that you were expecting me."

Yü Lan didn't answer directly. Instead he picked up one of the ornate ivory chesspieces and fondled its carved surface thoughtfully with his square fingertips. "You have the look of a chess player, Captain Falconer. Do you play?"

"I do." But not now . . . please god, not now.

"Not too well, I think, for at the moment it seems you have allowed your king to be checkmated."

Falconer's mouth felt furry; his temples pounded. "I don't know what you mean."

Yü looked at him unblinkingly. "Don't you? But you do realize where you made your mistake."

"Mistake?"

"You left your queen undefended for too long. Too long, Captain Falconer. A tactical error. Had I not set men to making inquiries about your—ah—queen, perhaps my entire fleet would not have heard the rumors.

"News of a cargo like yours is not so easily kept secret. Normally I would have heard about it, but my men would not. And as they had heard . . ." He sighed, and did not finish the thought. "We knew when you sailed, of course. Unfortunately the *tai-fung* interfered with our plans, and we had to run for safe harbor up the coast. But your ship was sighted heading north. Then again two days ago—but do not be too angry with your lookouts, Captain Falconer. My men are used to these seas, and yours are not." He sipped at his tea, daintily. "Where is the silver hidden?"

"Silver? I don't know what you're talking about."

"Don't you? Well, we shall see. Your ship is being searched at this moment. More tea?"

Falconer declined. "Your spies are mistaken, Captain Yü."

"Of course we shall take the silks and the tea cargo, as well. They are being unloaded now. It will leave you in need of ballast. But that's easy to find, with the rocky islands around here." Yü Lan smiled blandly. "I see by your face that you realize I intend to spare your life. Yes, and I'll leave you your ship, too. A life for a life, Captain Falconer! Soon, you see, I shall have made myself responsible for your actions. For the rest of your life."

Falconer blessed his stars that he had not reached for the knife earlier. He bowed his head: "Thank you."

"To say thank you so often is bad manners—barbarian manners, my dear Captain. Did your Chinese mistress never teach you that?"

"You know a lot about me." Pain, exquisite pain. If he could stop talking he could concentrate on the pain and make it go away.

"More than you would believe possible. Enough to know that if I were to send my men away now, you would not harm me with whatever is hidden in the bandages of your head. Han K'o-fa!" Smoothly, he summoned one of the men who stood nearby, and issued some instructions in Chinese. The man scurried off on some unknown errand. "But I need not send my men away, for none of them understands a word of English. It's quite safe for me to tell you, Captain Falconer, that I would have preferred not to attack your ship."

"Why did you, then?"

"A pirate captain is elected. After that, he remains captain only as long as he has the strength and the face to keep the job. I gained great face by escaping the doom planned for me—not by the authorities, but by some malcontents among my own men. Do you understand face? It is more important than life itself! I would have lost great face if I had not attacked you. The men know that you saved my life; they can understand that I don't want to kill you. But attack you I must, for all the fleet knew of the silver shipment."

"What silver shipment?"

"Ah, Captain Falconer, you have such innocence in your eyes! You should have been born Chinese."

At this moment, the man Han K'o-fa returned with something carefully wrapped in a rather soiled napkin. He handed it to Yü Lan, who folded back the covering. Inside was a small loaf of bread—rather flyspecked and inedible-looking, but unmistakably a loaf of bread.

"My cook is not skilled at this barbarian task. Do not blame him for the unappetizing look." With both hands, as was the polite Chinese custom, Yü placed the loaf before Falconer. Adam wondered for one queasy moment if he was supposed to eat it. His head hurt damnably, and his stomach churned at the thought.

"No, Captain Falconer, it is not for you. A moment,

and I'll explain." He turned to some men who had just entered the cabin. Falconer recognized one as a member of the boarding party. There followed a stream of conversation, and eventually Yü Lan rose to his feet. "You must excuse me for a time, Captain. But I shall be back."

It was nearly two hours before Yü Lan returned. Two hours that seemed like ten. By now, the fire in Falconer's head had become a raging inferno. The hilt of the dagger, if it was a dagger, was wedged against the flesh wound in his head, rubbing it raw.

Yü Lan settled himself on the scarlet cushion. "You don't look well, Captain Falconer. Not at all well. Do you feel all right?"

"Never better," returned Falconer through gritted teeth. He, too, believed in face.

"I'm sorry I took so long. But it was necessary to question your mate. My men had brought him to another cabin in this ship . . . Oh, don't worry, he'll live. And my men are finally convinced that you told the truth about the silver."

"Silver? I don't know what you're talking about."

"No? Well, you may return to your ship now. Your holds are empty. There is no reason to detain you longer. My men will take you back."

Falconer struggled to his feet, fighting the tilt of the cabin. One of the guards, seeing him start to stumble, supported his arm.

"Don't forget the bread, Captain Falconer."

"The bread?" Oh God—if he could only get back to the *Sweet Witch* and lie down, before he disgraced himself.

"Ah yes. My explanation was interrupted, so sorry. It's something for Mrs. Falconer, something I owe her."

Adam looked at Yü without comprehension, but he accepted the loaf that was now handed to him. The guards half-led, half-carried him to the door, and then halted as Yü spoke once more.

"And oh, Captain Falconer, there's another message for her too."

With an enormous effort of will, Falconer turned his glazed eyes back to the pirate captain. Yü's face had become impassive again.

"Tell Mrs. Falconer that I have left a gift for her in the water casks." His expression didn't alter, but there was a strange light in the onyx marbles of his eyes. "What did you intend your men to drink, Captain Falconer? Sometimes there is no rain across the Pacific—no rain at all, for days on end."

CHAPTER TWENTY-FOUR

The thunder in Adam Falconer's head was still reverberating when he came to, several hours later. But now his wound was properly dressed, and Noah was looking at him with anxious eyes.

"How's your head, Cap'n?"

"Exploding." Falconer pushed the word through lips that felt stiff and bruised. "Who's dead?"

Noah named three of the men, one of them the second mate. "That's it for the dead. But Ah Chin lost two fingers. An' young Alden stopped a saber with his shoulder. Hurts some, but he ain't even goin' to notice the scar for all the old 'uns from his floggin' days. A mess o' flesh wounds—but one o' them Oriental gents left us some evil-smellin' muck to dress 'em with, and I'll be jiggered if it don't seem to work." He paused. "Mr. Lovell's comin' along. Rammed splinters up 'is fingernails, they did. Hurts like the ole Nick, but the damage ain't permanent."

Adam closed his eyes wearily over a crease of pain. Let the deaths be on your conscience, Yü had said. They had tortured Lovell, and that was on his conscience too.

"How's Carey—Mrs. Falconer?"

"Nary a scratch. She's up top, bathin' Mr. Lovell's hands. She were a mite upset about that."

"Oh?"

"Aye—an' after being so spunky earlier! Found a nifty little piece o' steel in that head-bandage she fixed you up with." He handed Adam a small and wicked-looking stiletto.

"And the pirates?"

"Took off like bloomin' spirits. Picked up their dead an' our weapons, an' jest vanished into the sea, neat as you please."

Adam's voice sounded tired and toneless. "Send Mrs.

Falconer down when she's free, will you? And where's that loaf of bread Yü Lan gave me?"

Noah found it and placed it distastefully beside the bed. "I wouldn't be eatin' that, Capn. Probly some mucking poison, tricky devils."

"Don't worry. You couldn't force a crumb down my throat. How's the sky, Noah?"

"Rainin' cats and dogs again."

"Empty the waterbarrels, then, at once. And have the men spread the spare canvas to catch rain. We'd best look to our supply of sweet water now, while we can."

Noah was dumbfounded, and ripples of disapproval showed it. "We ain't out o' pirate waters yet! What say they come back?"

"They won't."

Noah was not so sure, and he went off shaking his head. The Captain had outwitted them all—the port officials, the pirates, the rest of the crew, even the typhoon. And yet he looked like he'd just been keel-hauled. And now the silver was to be dumped in plain view.

"Musta been the blow to his head," grumbled Noah, as he went to do his master's bidding.

Another half-hour passed before Carey came to the cabin. Memories of the bloodied desk and the dead bodies and Ah Chin's fingers and Luke's shoulder and Mr. Lovell's hands were still strong upon her. And now this—this knowledge that the thing the pirates had been looking for really existed, all the time. She had been on deck as the water kegs were tilted over. She had heard the shouts of glee as the piles of silver bars grew. How could the men not be upset? How could they be *laughing* —even Mr. Lovell? How could they all treat it as a joke —a hilarious, marvelous, stupendous, colossal joke?

She burst into the cabin and shook the rain off her oilskin cape, and pushed a sodden strand of hair out of her blazing eyes.

"You brute! You callous, unfeeling brute!"

Adam pushed himself up in the bed, and the dark slash of his brows tilted upward to meet the white of his head bandage.

"My. my. You're in a fine frame of mind. Keep your voice down. There's nothing unfeeling about my ears."

246

"You killed them—three of them! You could have killed us all. You knew what those pirates were looking for. Why didn't you just give it to them? Mr. Lovell's hands—" She put her face into her own hands, aghast at the remembered fingernails.

Adam's head throbbed. "I didn't know they intended to torture Lovell."

But Carey would not listen to him. "How can you live with yourself?"

He winced. It was something he'd been wondering for some weeks now; and for more reasons than she knew. But the dead were dead, and had to be pushed into the forgetting places of the mind—the places where you could never really forget, but tried to.

"Calm down, Carey."

"Calm down! Don't you give a *damn* about those dead men?"

"Grieving can't bring them alive."

"And all the crew—up on deck laughing and joking in the rain, as if it were all a romp! Even with blood and bandages all over them! Oh, I *hate* you, Adam Falconer!"

Adam's brow knotted. How could he explain to her that men sometimes laughed because they could not cry? He tried: "Sometimes laughing is the only way out."

"It's monstrous!"

"It's not monstrous. It's the way of the sea. The sea is hard. Men would go mad if they didn't laugh. That's why they tell bad jokes—why they get drunk in port, and chase every skirt in sight—why they sing sea shanties, even when their muscles are hurting like hell and their clothes are caked with salt and their bellies are half-empty and the seabiscuits have got weevils in 'em . . . Oh, I don't know, Carey, figure it out for yourself."

He closed his eyes, crossly, for he could see that she understood none of this. Then, because she didn't answer, he made one more attempt, carefully:

"When men sail, death is always the other member of the crew. The men know that. That's why they're laughing—because they know that next time it may be their turn."

She was silent for a while, then. When she spoke at last, she was calmer. "How's your head?"

"Better, now. It's just a scalp wound. Thanks for the bandage, earlier. I owe you a petticoat."

"It doesn't matter."

"Which reminds me. I have a strange present for you, from Yü Lan."

"Yü Lan?"

"The pirate captain."

"Why would he send a present to me?" Carey was nonplussed.

"You've seen Yü Lan before. Do you remember the castaway? The pockmarked Chinese?"

"Why, yes—I saw him again one time, in Macao."

Adam looked at her narrowly. What had happened between his wife and Yü Lan? His suspicions showed in his face.

She flushed. "No, it wasn't in—that place. It was on the waterfront. He had some awful wooden collar on his neck. I gave him some bread and water and paid a fine so they'd set him free. That's all."

"That's all?" Why did he feel such a sense of relief— why should it even matter to him, after all she had done, all she had been? "Well, it was a good investment. It saved the silver. Yü Lan knew it was in the water casks. But he didn't take it."

A good investment . . . the memory of how much it had cost flooded back to Carey now. Yet Yü Lan wouldn't know that. And he had tried, in his own way, to pay the debt.

"So he did know where it was, all along." Perhaps she had been too hasty in condemning Adam. "But then why did he torture Lovell?"

"To save face. He couldn't appear to let us off too easily."

"But how did he know?"

"He had informants in Macao." Who? *Who?* Only Adam himself, and Noah, had known where the silver was: he remembered the backbreaking night when they had hidden it. He and Noah and . . . by God, Wang T'ung. Wang T'ung! The wily old devil, with his finger in yet another pie. So that was why Wang T'ung had told him Mei Sung was in no danger, despite Blore's threats. What the right hand giveth, the left hand taketh away. Wang T'ung had been making amends for his intended treachery. And even now, Adam could not find it in his heart to be too angry with Mei Sung's owner, for the information Wang T'ung had imparted would be very use-

248

ful later on. At least it would not be necessary, in future dealings with Blore, to take Mei Sung's safety into account.

How, Adam wondered briefly, would Yü make his peace with Wan T'ung for not seizing the shipment? Perhaps Yü would pay for today's actions more dearly than in silver. But the answer to that could only be guessed, and there was still Carey to deal with.

"Here's the thing, Carey: he sent you a loaf of bread." Adam leaned over to find the leaden loaf, and pushed it into his wife's lap.

She bubbled into laughter—and in that moment knew what Adam had been trying to say earlier, for somewhere in the back of her eyes there was the sting of unshed tears.

Inside the loaf was a gift from Yü Lan, a large and beautiful piece of jade intricately carved in the shape of a fish, and suspended from a leather thong. An accompanying note from Yü, also baked into the loaf, told Carey that this was a rare sounding device dating from the Shang dynasty more than three thousand years before. *Long after the last note is struck,* he wrote in English, *the sound of beauty lingers in the air.*

"There's another matter I want to talk to you about, Carey. Something more serious. Where did you get this evil-looking thing?" He pulled the small stiletto from beneath his pillow.

"I—" she hesitated; she didn't want to implicate Luke Alden. So she lied. "It was in my luggage. The trunk you retrieved in Macao. I always carry it now."

"In your petticoats?" What was it in her suddenly guarded expression that reminded him of Teura—Teura, coming back for one fleeting instant from the dead, from that forgetting-place in his mind? He realized he had not thought of Teura for some weeks. Strange—even remembering that his wife resembled her, he could no longer clearly call her face to mind.

"What in hell would you use it for?"

In all truth, she hardly knew.

But Adam, glaring at her, saw the answer.

"Good God—you were planning to use it on me, weren't you?"

She met his eyes, and discovered the truth herself. "Yes. Yes, I was."

⪻ CHAPTER TWENTY-FIVE ⪼

The *Sweet Witch* slid into the dark indigo waters of the powerful Kuroshio Current, and it drove them to the north and to the west. Waters that had been warm became icy and teemed with plankton; winds that had been temperate became biting. The seas remained gray and lumpy under an endless stretch of clouded days.

Salt spray flew and crackled against ice that had formed on sheets and shrouds and spars. Sailors swilled their rum ration to thaw the numbness in their bones, cursed and once more climbed the slippery rigging to knock the ice away, and worked the frozen cracking canvas with fingers that had long since lost all feeling. Sometimes the sun appeared, fleetingly, and then, when the stiffness in their faces became more tolerable, they sang sea shanties that told of warm and willing sailor-town girls with big hips and soft lips, and recounted stories and jokes that shore men would have found uncouth.

The *Sweet Witch* traveled in a great arc that swept across six thousand miles of ocean. Sperm whales were sighted in these plankton-rich zones; and once a school of porpoises gamboled alongside for most of a day. Beyond that there was nothing: no ships were seen—only the roiling, wintry, formidable seas. Yet in this same year twenty whalers battled through this relatively friendly North Pacific Drift to even more forbidding fog-bound shores; the following autumn eight of them came back. The Pacific had given up her riches, and exacted her price.

And in the captain's cabin of the *Sweet Witch*, Carey and Adam skirmished, clashed, joined their bare embattled bodies under mounds of blankets, and clung together in the unyielding Arctic night. Only the air was frigid now.

Eventually, in the gargantuan battle of ocean currents, the bleak northern waters won. From realms where glittering icebergs reigned, from the Sea of Okhotsk and from the Bering Straits, from the cold Aleutians and the glacial Arctic wastes, an irresistible weight of waters reversed the North Pacific Drift and turned it southward, down past a rugged coastline charted by Captain Vancouver not fifteen years before. Now, aided by the California Current, the *Sweet Witch* found friendlier weather; and at last, fifty-three days after leaving the East China Sea, she reached her goal.

"Glad that's rid of." Jed Lovell squinted at the distant departing Russian vessel. "Never thought I'd be so glad to see someone take a pile of silver off our hands. Especially Russians."

"There's good profit for everyone in what's left." Adam Falconer stood beside Lovell at the helm. "A quarter of the shipment—and you'll have a good share out of it, Jed. Enough to take two or three years off, if you want. You've earned it." Falconer, from his own larger share as shipowner, now had enough to pay Blore—and enough to buy another cargo for the *Sweet Witch*.

Lovell considered the prospect. "As soon as those Britishers stop blockading American ports, I might think about it. For now, there's no way to go home—except by land, and to me that's more dangerous than the sea. I'm not much of a land man. No—I signed on with you for five years, and I'll stay. The *Sweet Witch* is a good ship, none better."

"She's done proud by us so far. And she'll do even better. I've a mind to buy some lumber from the mission while we're here in Alta California. There's an idea I picked up from those Chinese junks, and I want to try it."

Lovell, curious, glanced at Falconer's intent face. "Not those damn battened sails!"

"No—a better idea. Watertight bulkheads. All those big ocean-going junks have had 'em for centuries."

Incredulity was written in Lovell's face. "Can't be done. No proper ship has had anything like that, ever."

"But it makes sense. Say you rip a hole in the hull and one compartment floods. The other compartments will still keep the ship afloat—providing they're not damaged too. Besides, the men could use a spell of time at anchor. Where better than Alta California? The mission is friendly, the weather is fine, and the anchorage here is superb."

"Aye—it's God's country, all right." Jed Lovell turned his eyes to shore. They were anchored in the beautiful bay later to be known as San Francisco Bay, not far from the small Spanish Franciscan mission of Yerba Buena. "Wish we could get rid of this damn rock ballast too, and take on a decent cargo."

"I intend to. Tallow and hides. And cereal and wines, if I can get them."

"Perhaps we'd best go southward then, to Santa Clara or San José. I hear the Franciscans in Yerba Buena frown on barter—except for provisioning."

"Officially they do. Unofficially—well, as I said, Jed, they're surprisingly friendly. They deal with the Russians and the British all the time. That's why I sent Noah and Luke Alden ashore—to start talking trade."

"Your wife asked to go with them. Did you know?"

"Did she now?" Adam frowned, annoyed that Carey should have so deliberately gone against his express wishes. He'd told her she could go ashore—later, with him. What was it about her that still made his nerve-endings vibrate painfully, even after these past weeks?

His thoughts were interrupted by Lovell's voice. "You'll not have to worry about your wife for long. There's the longboat now."

Toward shore Falconer could see them: several men plying hard at the oars, and Carey's unmistakable honey-colored head bobbing and glinting in the sunlight. She was talking to Luke Alden, it appeared—talking, and laughing. Why did she laugh with Alden—with Lovell, with Noah? Why did she never laugh with him? Damn it, did she do it to spite him?

But he didn't want Jed Lovell to see his inner rage, so he turned away and said curtly: "Send her to the cabin as soon as she comes aboard."

"Aye, Captain Falconer." Lovell hid his smile. So the captain was jealous again. It was as plain as the nose on his face, and everybody on board ship knew it. Everyone, that is, but Falconer himself.

"Look what Fra Tomaso gave me, Adam!" Carey was still excited as she came through the door into the

252

cabin, but her joy in the recent expedition faded at the sight of her husband's face.

Adam looked at her with displeasure, ignoring the coarsely woven, handsomely patterned blanket she was carrying. "Your expedition could have waited. I intended to take you."

"You've been saying that for three days, ever since we got here. How was I to know you wouldn't decide to sail by tonight? You never bother to tell me your plans."

"Why the hell should I? You seem to do as you please."

"What difference does it make? You wouldn't have enjoyed my company. You wouldn't have wanted to see the things I wanted to see."

"What *did* you want to see? The soldiers of the Spanish presidio, I suppose, in their handsome uniforms." He knew he should not have said it; knew he should have kept the bitterness out of his voice. Why did his intelligence always seem to fly out the window where Carey was concerned? Why could he never conceal his feelings —and what had happened to the self-control he used to pride himself on?

"Why, yes," she said too sweetly. "That's *exactly* what I feasted my eyes on—when I wasn't looking at the winepress, and the weaving shed, and the Indians making pottery." She threw the blanket on the bed, angrily. "I wish Fra Tomaso had given me some pottery instead. I'd break it over your head."

He seized her wrist, and pulled her toward him. She jerked away, but he gripped her shoulders from behind, pulling her close against his already-aroused body.

"Carey," he said fiercely into her hair; then more softly: "Carey."

She could feel that he wanted her, could feel the hardening of his body against hers. But this time she would not give in.

His hands had traveled up to her hair now, and she knew she must move before she herself was on the road to forgetfulness. She wrenched away, realizing too late that he had a coil of her hair wound into his fingers.

"Ouch!" The jolt pulled her back against his body, forcibly. "Oh! How dare you."

"You know very well how I dare. Don't go all virtuous on me, Carey. You know you want me too." His hands had left her head, had come around over her shoulders; and he had cupped them over her breasts, staking his claim. She knew he would soon be able to feel the answer through the cotton of her bodice, and she was angered by his confidence in himself. How sure he was of his powers, how maddeningly sure!

"Not now, Adam," she said crossly. "I'm in a bad mood."

"You weren't in a bad mood when you came through the door."

"Quite true!"

He laughed, and to her surprise left her, and threw himself on the bed. And there he lay, hands laced behind his head, watching her, amusement tugging at the corners of his eyes. His mouth mocked her, sensual, self-assured.

"Do you mind getting off my blanket?" she exclaimed tartly. Now she was even more annoyed: she had expected him to be more persistent.

"Come and get it," he said easily, and closed his eyes.

She went to the bed warily, knowing in her heart of hearts what would come of it; wanting defeat yet not wanting to admit it. She tugged at the blanket, but part of it was under his shoulder. She pulled again, and lost her balance—and then somehow, without conscious intent, their bodies had connected, and his arms were around her, and her mouth was over his. And neither cared any longer whose pride was lost. Their tongues met, and challenged, and trembled, and invaded—and in this war there was no victor and no vanquished, only the moist surrender of the moment. Then, mouths still clinging hungrily, they undressed each other, and their hands started to explore the well-known haunts of passion.

"Move the blanket. It scratches," murmured Adam into the corner of her mouth. She started to obey, to thrust it away. "No, Carey, I mean under us."

After she had done as he asked, he said: "Do you mind?"

"No. It feels wonderful."

"The blanket?"

"No. The way you're touching me. Please don't stop."

He rolled onto his back, pulling her with him. She raised her head an inch or two. "Why did you do that?"

254

"It's time you learned something new now the weather's warmed up." His hands were in her hair again, softly kneading the scalp, and he smiled encouragement into her eyes. "Move your head, Carey."

She obeyed the downward thrust of his hands. Her lips touched his chest, felt the tautness of his body and the little ridges of scar tissue here and there beneath the dark mat of hair, for now she knew their hiding places, every one. Head raised, he watched her progress. She trailed her tongue across the flat of his stomach, feeling the muscles tighten as she did so, and started to move upward again—but his fingers in her hair urged her in quite a different direction.

"Not now, Adam." She pulled away, resisting the pressure of his hands. Yet this was something she had done before, as Teura. But that had been different. Things had been different between them, then.

She could see the naked passion smoldering in his eyes, unconcealed now. "Have you forgotten that we made a pact?"

"There are some things I don't want to do—not yet. Forget the pact. Call me your whore if you want. I don't care anymore."

"For God's sake, Carey, things have changed. I haven't called you that for a long time."

"Not in so many words, you haven't. But you think it —you can't deny you think it. You can't forget Macao any more than I can."

"Look, this isn't going very well. Do you want to make love or not? You know bloody well I won't force you to do anything you don't want to do—not anymore. No matter what happened in Macao."

"So you do think about Macao! I knew it."

"I don't give a damn about Macao now."

"Oh! Well, then, ask me about it."

"No!"

"Why not? Why must it always be there like a wall, between us?"

"Christ, Carey. You made me promise not to talk about it."

"Well, now I want to. I don't want it to be a wall anymore."

"And I don't want to know about it."

"Adam—why not?"

"Because I don't want to know what you've done with other men."

"It wasn't—"

"Stow it, Carey! Keep your guilt feelings to yourself, and spare me the confessions. Do I ever tell you about my other mistresses?"

"You don't have to! I overhear shipboard gossip—about your little Chinese trollop, for instance."

Adam knew a moment of blind rage. "Leave her out of this!"

"Oh! You care about *her*. Was she a virgin for you, Adam?"

"It's none of your goddamn business. Mei Sung's an innocent—a babe in the woods compared to you."

"After six years of being a courtesan?" asked Carey sweetly.

So she had overheard things! Damn that loose-tongued crew. "Mei Sung's gone through a great deal, and you're not fit to wipe her feet!"

"In other words you don't care what I've been through!"

"If I gave a damn about you, maybe I'd care. But I don't give a damn about you."

But when she jerked away from the bed and started to find her clothes, he glowered: "Now where are you going?"

"To find someone who does give a damn about me!"

Adam pulled himself up against a pillow and rumpled a hand through his hair, trying to sort out his tangled emotions. "Christ, I didn't mean that, Carey. It was cruel of me—thoughtless. I don't know what I meant. Let's start all over again."

"Start *what* all over again?"

"You know what I mean. Come back to bed. Let me make love to you."

"Is that your way to solve everything?"

"It's one way."

"Well, this time it won't solve anything!" Viciously, she thrust her foot into a shoe. "Personally, I'm not too keen on making love to people who don't give a damn about me."

"You know I *do*. Anyway, that's never stopped you before—with me, or anyone else."

For a moment she stared at him, speechless with fury.

"For your information, I didn't have much choice in Macao. I just submitted. I didn't feel a thing."

Now, Adam rolled to the edge of the bed and reached for his own clothes. "Ah, Carey, let's drop it. Macao doesn't interest me." He pulled on his trousers. "It doesn't matter what's in your past—it's all forgiven."

"For*given!* Oh, how very condescending of you. How about *your* past? Why should there be one set of rules for you—and another for me?"

"If there are any rules, Carey, you never played by them. I'll admit I haven't led the saintliest of lives." He pulled a shirt over his broad shoulders. "But neither have you—not since the days when you were an untrained little virgin."

"An untrained—oh! I suppose if I'd lost my virginity to *you* you might give a damn for me. That might salve your male pride. Oh—men!" Her fists tightened.

"I don't give a hoot about how you lost your virginity." Or did he? Even as he said it, he knew he was lying. "If that mattered to me, I'd have asked you long ago about who—about that first man."

An odd amber light came into her eyes, and her voice became strange, almost cruel. "Ask me about him now, Adam."

"The hell with him! Carey—"

"I felt something with him, Adam. Do you want to know what I felt? Let me tell you. No, don't stop me! I felt passion . . . and warmth . . . and love, innocent love, fine love, first love, the kind of love I'll never be able to give to any man again. I wanted to bear his child. Lord, how I wanted it!"

For a moment, Adam detected the beginnings of tears swimming in her eyes. Seeing them, he tried to drive down the demons drumming in his head—until he heard her next words.

"You wanted to teach me something just now, in bed. Well, frankly, I've already been taught! Quite thoroughly! Yes, I did things with him because I loved him. I did everything he asked. Everything! And when he touched me my body melted, and when he kissed me I turned to fire, and when he whispered sex-words in my ear I whispered them back . . ."

But Adam had already slammed his way out of the

257

cabin, and the rest of Carey's soliloquy was wasted on the empty air.

For three days now Adam had gone ashore each morning, in an effort to conclude a deal for some cargo with the handful of local traders. The bitterness of his encounter with Carey still rankled. He had not bothered, as yet, to invite her to join him, as promised. Each day the small shore party would push off without her—and she, as stiff-necked in her pride as he was in his, refused to ask permission to come.

Today the longboat was late in returning. When it was finally sighted putting out from shore, the sun was already reddening the western sky. Carey, unwilling to betray the fact that she had given a moment's thought to Adam's whereabouts, kept her back stubbornly turned to the boat's arrival. She was watching Higgins, who had once served on a whaler, as he carved a piece of scrimshaw.

"Aye, 'tis better than twiddlin' thumbs, Miz Falconer. 'Tweentimes there be spells when ye can watch and wait and sight nary a blow. Months at a time—nothin'. Mates get murderous an' men get foulmouthed an' soreheaded. Then all o' sudden ye see twenty, thirty sperm at once, flukes sprayin' twenty feet in the air. Aye, it's a sight! Them's great words: Thar she blo-o-ows! Men make for the davits, an' the boat bottoms spank down on the swells, an' the chase begins."

Carey stubbornly ignored the shore party now coming aboard. "You wouldn't have time for carving, then."

"Nay—for when whales is about, men works till they drop. An' if they drops too easy, like as not they'll feel the business end o' the mate's boot leather." His knife paused in midair. "Beggin' your pardon, Miz Falconer ma'am, but you expectin' the Capn? He ain't aboard that boat."

Carey turned with a tiny premonition of alarm. Noah was coming aboard, and Luke Alden, and three others who had gone ashore this morning. The men looked tired and tense. There was no sign of Adam. She excused herself hastily, and hurried to the group of men further along the deck.

"Where's Adam—where's Captain Falconer?"

Noah's hangdog expression belied his next words. "He's

fine, Miz Carey. Them Spaniards is bunkin' him up for the night, is all."

"Tell me the truth, Noah!"

"He'll be back tomorrow, right as rain. He said you wasn't to fret."

She turned to Alden. "Luke, you tell me. Noah's hiding something."

"Noah's right. There's nothing to worry about. No doubt he'll turn up bright and early in the morning."

But Carey, persisting, turned back to Noah. "Exactly why are they keeping him overnight, Noah? And don't tell me it's for no reason, because I won't believe that."

"They're asking questions, is all."

"What kind of questions? Does it have something to do with the silver shipment?"

"Nothin' that important, Miz Carey. Now don't you fret."

Carey would not be put off so easily. "You must take me ashore at once. I'll see Fra Tomaso. If you won't tell me, I'll find out for myself."

The men looked at each other, and Noah spoke for them all. "Fra Tomaso ain't got nothin' to do with it, Miz Carey. Anyways we spoke to Fra Tomaso. Capn Falconer ain't even in the mission."

"Then where is he?"

"Cain't rightly say, Miz Falconer."

"Noah, that's worse than telling me the truth! Anyway there's only one other place he could be. If it's not the friars asking questions, then it must be the soldiers. They've taken him to the presidio, haven't they?"

And at last, because it could be hidden no longer, the truth came out. Soldiers had seized Falconer and taken him to the Spanish garrison, which was quite separate from the mission. It had been totally unexpected, because for the past few days the soldiers had seemed to be particularly friendly.

"Mebbe too friendly," said another of the men who had been ashore, "now that I think on it. They was yarning and swapping tobacco, them as could speak English. An' they was asking things about the ship—who was on board, how long we was staying."

Noah looked daggers at the man who had spoken. "Think it's the trading, Miz Carey. Ain't legal to trade hereabouts. But we ain't bought nothin' yet, so they got no call to keep him. He'll be back tomorrow with a smile on his face an' a yarn or two to tell. Then we'll wonder what all the fussin' was for."

And they didn't tell her that it was Carey herself, not Adam, that the Spanish soldiers had been asking questions about.

Adam glared at the scarred face before him and spat the words, in Spanish. "You're insane, Fuentes—insane! Of course I won't do it."

"No? Well, we shall see."

The scars on Lieutenant Fuentes's face had healed badly. Great ugly weals pitted his forehead and cheeks, and one horrible gash ran from his brow, down between his eyes, and along one cheek. That side of his face was very nearly immobilized, and when he smiled, as he did now, the muscles didn't respond properly. Only the pale-blue eyes remained unchanged since the day when Carey had dashed the mirror into his face—that, and the abnormal length of his bone structure. It was for this reason, Fuentes knew, that she had not recognized him the other day in Yerba Buena, even though she had glanced right in his direction. And then looked away quickly, as people always did now.

Well, she might have forgotten him, but Fuentes had not forgotten her. Not for one day, not for one hour, for more than two years. He could not see himself without remembering her. He could not see a mirror without remembering her. He could not see the horror in a stranger's eyes without remembering her.

He had recognized her at once. But he had been too startled to react immediately—and in any case, he could hardly have seized her within the mission compound, for the priests would not have allowed it. But he had set his men to finding out more. Who she was, what she was doing here, how long she would be staying here. They had been careful with their questions, but it had been easy enough to find out what Fuentes wanted to know, for when a golden-haired and beautiful woman appeared out of nowhere in a fleabitten Indian mission like Yerba Buena, it was perfectly natural for his men to ask questions. Fuentes had set a watch to see if she came ashore again, but she had not. Finally he had grown impatient, for the captain and commanding officer of his contingent was only to be absent for three weeks, at a mission to the south. Fuentes was in temporary command: and his captain, once returned, could not be expected to understand or condone his need for revenge against the English girl. There would no longer be any excuse for belligerence toward the English, as the Spaniards, having themselves been attacked by the strutting little emperor, were no longer on Napoleon's side. Of course there could be other excuses for punishing the girl, but first Fuentes would have to convince her pigheaded husband to send for her.

"If by tomorrow you still refuse to send for your wife, I shall have to think of other measures."

"Think away."

"Captain Falconer! You seem not to realize that you were arranging to trade in contravention of our laws. All things produced by the mission—the cattle, the hides, the wine—belong to the Indians. They are held by the church in trust, and cannot be sold. Food for your own needs: that is all that can change hands."

"Then arrest your holy brethren."

Fuentes ignored that, and drummed his fingers on the rough-hewn desk that stood between them. "It is a very serious charge against you, Captain Falconer."

"I haven't traded a damn thing but talk, not yet. You can't arrest me for taking on water and food stores and a little lumber for repairs to the ship. In any case others trade here all the time. That Russian ship, for instance."

"That Russian ship, I hear, came to grief further up the coast. A little matter of bad navigation. Perhaps it is a sign from the Almighty, no? Perhaps he is displeased with his servants for shutting an eye to what has been going on with the Indians' common property. Perhaps we shall have to be more stringent in future."

Falconer's eyes blazed back belligerently. "In that case you can't possibly want my wife. She's done no trading at all."

"I am told she was seen leaving with something. A blanket, I believe."

"She didn't trade for it. It was a gift from Fra Tomaso."

"But it was not Fra Tomaso's to give. Perhaps you don't understand me, Captain Falconer. You say she didn't trade for it. Would you prefer to admit that she stole it?"

"You're playing with words, Lieutenant. What do you

want with my wife, really? Where do you know her from?"

"Did I say I knew her? As I told you, Captain. I only want to talk to her, to question her—no more. Send for her and you will be allowed to leave."

"Go out to the *Sweet Witch* and question her there. I'm sure she'll return the blanket. If that's what you want."

"You're a very stubborn man, Captain Falconer. Well, tomorrow we shall see. I learned some very interesting techniques in the Philippines—very persuasive. Would you like me to tell you about them?"

On the *Sweet Witch*, Carey waited. Mr. Lovell, Luke, Noah—they were all adamant about refusing to let her go to the Spanish presidio to plead Adam's case. A shore party, headed by Noah, came back without success. And although the returning men tried to put a good face on it, the news was not encouraging. Even Fra Tomaso, at the mission, admitted that the soldiers were quite within their rights to detain the captain—although the good friar had sent messages to Lieutenant Fuentes, and was personally doing all he could.

A second day dragged by, and against the shore party returned empty-handed.

"Is there any word, Noah—anything?"

"No word, Miz Carey. Only that the Capn says he's right as rain, and you ain't to leave the ship."

"Surely they'd let me see him! They let you see him, didn't they?"

"Ah—not today, Miz Carey. Nossir! Spoke with him through a grating, is all." It was not true: the soldiers had let him in to see Captain Falconer at Fuentes's express order, but Noah knew he could not tell what he had seen. "The sojers ain't gonna let you see him, Miz Carey. Not for love nor money. Said it right out, they did!"

Nor was that the truth: but Captain Falconer had said it, and that was what counted.

"Did he get my note?"

"Yes, Miz Carey."

"And he didn't write one in return?"

"Guess he didn't think of it."

"Nothing? No letter at all?"

"No, Miz Carey."

Carey turned away, despairing, and headed for the companionway.

She groped her way down the steps, reminding herself that she did not even love him any more. But she turned back almost at once, for it occurred to her that it might help if Noah took a note from herself to the Spanish soldiers, and another to Fra Tomaso. Perhaps the friar could be persuaded to come aboard and see her . . . perhaps the soldiers would listen to her pleas. It was worth a try, and if Noah would agree, the notes might yet be delivered before dark.

And so it was that she arrived on deck in time to hear Noah's conversation with Mr. Lovell. The two men didn't see her: they were standing at the rail, faces to the shore.

"Was it true, Noah? No letter at all?"

"Twere only a small lie. Letter for Miz Carey, sure enough, but it ain't from the Capn. It's from that hell-faced Spanish loo-tenant. I dasn't show it to her. Capn Falconer ain't never keel-hauled a man in his life, but he'd be willin' to make an exception in my case if I was to give her that letter."

"What does it say?"

Noah dipped into his jersey and fished out a small, strange-looking rectangle that was neither writing paper nor envelope. But somebody had written something on it: Carey could see that, even at a distance.

"Don't say much—jest that this mucking Fuentes fellow is still waitin' for her to come an' see him, an' he'll send her another note like this every day until she does."

"Any more?"

"A postscript. Says she might be int'rusted to know what this note is writ on." Noah pushed the note at Lovell with anger and disgust written on his loyal face.

"Tell me, Noah, I can't speak Spanish."

"Curse those bloodmucking pirates for takin' our bloodmucking arms! It's writ on Capn Falconer's skin."

"Ah, so you're conscious again, Capitan. That bucket of sea-water on your back did the trick very nicely."

"You bastard." The words were ground out from a mouth swollen and dark with dried blood. The black eyes burned like coals in Adam's bruised face.

Fuentes's scarred face twisted into one half of a smile. "Salt has a way with raw flesh, does it not, Captain

263

Falconer? Be thankful that my men have tied you face-down. You would be even less comfortable with your spine against the rawhide of the bed, I assure you."

Fuentes walked across the beaten earth floor of the tiny two-roomed adobe hut that was a short distance from the barracks. He prodded at the prone figure with his boot.

"Don't pass out again, Capitan, or you'll miss the little treat I have in store for you. Manuel! Tell him what you just told me."

"Sir!" Manuel snapped to attention. "We were watching the shore, as ordered, when the woman was sighted, swimming in by moonlight. I came on ahead with the news. The others will be bringing her up directly as soon as she has had time to dress herself with the wet bundle of clothes she was carrying."

"Hardly necessary," said Fuentes dryly. "Her husband has seen her naked before. And so have I."

Adam closed his eyes against the dim swimming room. So Carey had known Fuentes. And not from Macao, he was sure. Fuentes had come directly to Alta California from the Philippines: Adam knew that much from the conversations he'd overheard. When and where had they met? What had there been between them? If he understood, perhaps he could think of some way out of this—but he did not understand, and the fact that Carey was about to come through the cramped door made it even more difficult. Damn! How had Noah and Lovell let her get away from them?

Carey, arriving in the doorway, was aghast at what she saw. She pulled away from the guards and ran to where Adam lay. Her clinging clothes left a wet trail over the packed mud floor.

"Adam—what have they done to you?"

Fuentes broke in. "Come away, Mrs. Falconer. Your husband is all right. Tell her you're all right, Capitan."

"I'm all right, Carey. Why the hell did you come?"

But Carey was no longer looking at Adam. She was staring at Lieutenant Fuentes. His voice, remembered from the nightmares of two years before, had caused her to look upward—and then she had seen the pale blue icepick eyes, and she had been sure. But she had not guessed how fearful the scars would be.

"I see you remember me now, Mrs. Falconer, even though I've changed somewhat. The other day in town, when you saw me, you looked away. Is my face so awful to look upon? Yes—I see it is."

Oh God, thought Carey, why did I come? She scarcely knew. She had thought she would find Fuentes; offer her body to him; secure Adam's release for something that was, after all, not so very difficult to give. She had not realized that the Spanish soldiers would find her swimming to shore. And now, seeing Fuentes, she wondered if he would be so easily satisfied. But there was no going back . . . and the venom in Fuentes's voice was confirming the dread in her heart.

"If my face is terrible, you have only yourself to blame. Look at me!" His hand came up and held her chin so that her eyes could not escape the scarred flesh. "Look! Does it fill you with revulsion? Does it make your skin crawl—as one lady of the night so charmingly told me? Look at me!"

She looked, and perhaps, if she had not been so cold with fright, she would have felt pity. But there was no pity in his blue eyes.

"So now you know why I wanted to see you." His fingers left her chin and moved down to find her unresisting hand. "Come—there's another room. You wouldn't want your husband to witness this little reunion, would you?"

"Let him go. This has nothing to do with him." Her eyes sought and clung to her husband's bare and bloodied back, and then to his bruised eyes, seeking something—strength, perhaps, or love. She saw only pain and rage.

"Oh, God, Carey . . ." But Adam, who had been ebbing in and out of consciousness for most of the past day, could help her no more. His world had once more gone black.

"Your husband can do nothing for you, Mrs. Falconer. There's no use kneeling down beside him. He'll be sent back to his ship in the morning, have no fear. And who knows? Perhaps if I'm through with you I'll let you go then, too."

"Adam—"

But she allowed herself to be led into the other room; and when Adam's limp form was carried down to the shoreline in the morning, she was still there, and so was Fuentes.

Adam Falconer lay in a fevered delirium for another day and another night, while the men of the *Sweet Witch* tried in every way possible to get Carey back. The shoreline remained guarded by soldiers, as did the presidio itself. Noah and Mr. Lovell went ashore and made representations to the mission fathers: the brethren could do little against the secular authority of the well-armed soldiers, but they did send swift horses to the neighboring mission, normally a day's journey away. Luke Alden went with this contingent, seeking the absent captain of the presidio, on a forced ride that lasted all night and left the horses lathered with sweat.

On the second day of Carey's absence, the good Fra Tomaso, begging the forgiveness of his maker, smuggled some weapons to the anchored ship. Men made plans to use them; but in the end it was not necessary. Luke Alden's mission returned, successfully.

From the *Sweet Witch,* the men could see a small boat put out from shore near sunset, and they recognized at once the golden-haired figure that Alden was carrying. With him was the Spanish captain, and it fell to Noah, who understood the language, to listen to his apologies.

"I came at once, of course, when the message arrived. A woman! Lieutenant Fuentes has exceeded his authority —far exceeded his authority. You must rest assured that none of you will be bothered again as long as you remain in Alta California. The woman will be all right, I'm sure of it. As for the lieutenant—the ex-lieutenant—his punishment will be decided shortly. I assure you it will be severe. Please accept my humblest apologies."

The Spanish captain told them no more of what had happened. Nor did Carey. The men of the *Sweet Witch* did not press her. They moved Captain Falconer—whose raw back was starting to heal, although he was still fevered into Mr. Lovell's bunk, and Carey into the captain's cabin by herself. And once she was settled there in safety, she would allow no one to touch her, not even Noah.

Within two days Adam was well enough to understand what was happening. Somehow, through his delirium, he had managed to learn that Carey was safely back on the *Sweet Witch*.

"What the hell did he do to her?" Adam took the trousers Noah held out to him, and pulled them over his long well-muscled legs. At least there was no raw flesh below his waist—nothing that made it difficult for him to sit down. At the moment, he was grateful that he was sitting down, for the effort made his forehead break out in sweat.

"She won't say, but she's walkin' and talkin', so she can't be too bad hurt."

"Is her face marked?" That had troubled his fevered dreams—that Fuentes would mark her face as fearfully as his own was marked.

"Nary a scratch. She's shook up, is all."

Adam felt relief flood through his veins. "How in hell did she know Fuentes was wanting to see her?"

"She couldn't a known, Cap'n."

"If I thought you'd said anything to her, Noah, I'd personally beat you to a pulp."

"You ain't fit to beat nobody to a pulp. Leastways, not yet."

"And why in God's name did you let her ashore? You had my orders, Noah!"

"Nobody knew she could swim, Cap'n, or we'd a kept closer watch. English girls ain't able to swim!"

"That's one English girl who is. Help me into my shirt, Noah."

"Careful now! Don't want that bandage knocked about."

Adam winced as the shirt came over his back. "Tell Mr. Lovell I'll see him after I've talked to Carey. Tell him I intend to make sail for the Sandwich Islands—tomorrow or the next day."

"Ain't no problem with stayin' here now, Cap'n. That son o' satan Fuentes, he's been stuck in the pokey. An' that Cap'n's been right friendly—sendin' men to find out how you and Miz Carey is doing. He says trade all you want, nobody's to stop you. An' Fra Tomaso's been out to pay his respecks, too."

"They may not stay friendly for long." Falconer didn't explain what he meant, but Noah, who knew his master well, understood.

Carey was sitting on the edge of the bed, staring into nowhere. She looked paler, somehow, but composed. Adam went to sit on the bed beside her, and Noah left.

"Are you all right, Carey?"

"I'm all right." But she was not: he could see that.

"What the hell did he do to you—that Fuentes fellow?" She remained silent.

"Did he hurt you?"

"I'm all right!" She gave a nervous half-laugh. "How many times do I have to tell you?"

"What did he do?"

Again she didn't answer. But her hands, tightly clenched in her lap, told a part of the story.

"Carey! Talk about it. It'll be better."

"He . . . forced me. What else would you expect?"

"Damn his filthy hide! He deserves to die."

When she sat looking at her knuckles without speaking, Adam said again, more gently: "Carey, talk about it."

"Why? Do you want to hear all the dirty details?"

"Oh, Carey, you know what I mean. Talk. Get it out of your system."

"Does it matter to you that I've been raped?"

"Of course it matters!" Christ, it mattered . . . he had known all along that this is what must have happened. But the confirmation of it left a bitter taste in his mouth. A sourness and a rage.

"Why? You've done it yourself." Her voice had a hysterical edge.

"That's different. Oh, God—" But was it so different? And she didn't even know about the first time, the time in the mirrored room.

"Is it?" Her eyes accused him. At the moment she hated men, all men. They took, and took, and took . . .

"It's different because I'm your husband." Adam said it without really believing it, with the cold sinking knowledge that it was not so different.

"And that makes it all right for you, but not for him."

"Look, I agree I should never have taken you by force after Macao, but—"

"But you did. And the word is rape, Adam. Rape! So don't ask what Lieutenant Fuentes did to me. You already know. In your heart of hearts you know."

The black rage, the bloodlust, the ringing hatred in the ears, the unreasoning need for revenge—yes, he knew.

268

Oh God, he thought, will I ever live it down? Am I any better than that swine Fuentes? "I was afraid he'd mark your face."

She looked at him strangely. "Would it have mattered to you?"

"I couldn't bear to see you scarred."

"Well, you won't have to." She gave an odd little laugh. "But that's a strong statement, isn't it? From someone who doesn't give a damn about me."

"You know I do give a damn. I went through hell that night they brought you in. Oh, Carey, why did you come ashore?"

"Do you really think I expected to be caught—to be taken there?" Her throat went tight for a moment, as she remembered the lamplit adobe hut, the cold earthen floors, the terror. Then she found her voice, and tried to push away the memory. "Is your back all right?"

"It's healing."

"It looked dreadful—raw—horrible."

"It wasn't so bad."

"That's not true! You were unconscious."

"Not all of the time, I wasn't—God, Carey! That was the worst. Coming to and hearing no sounds. I didn't even know if you were alive or not. Or if you were still in that back room."

Her silence told him nothing, so he pressed her: "Were you still in that back room?"

"Yes."

Yet he had heard no screaming, no crying out. Perhaps she had gone into that trancelike state he used to see in her.

"Carey—" He reached out as if to take her in the comforting circle of his arms, but she pulled away.

"Please don't touch me. I'm not—clean."

"I don't give a damn if you're clean or not." But with the effort, his own wounds had started to trouble him. He left her alone, but his eyes had become black pools of pain. "Oh, Christ."

"Perhaps I'd better call Noah."

"No, don't call Noah. Not yet. I have more questions to ask."

Please don't let him ask, she prayed, please don't let him ask . . . Adam stood up and started to pace the room like a caged tiger.

"You had met him before."

"Yes."

"And you gave him those scars."

"Yes." She held her breath, waiting for his next question.

"When did it happen? Where? What did you do to him?"

Perhaps he was not going to ask.

"I threw a mirror in his face. It was on an island . . . long ago. When my brother was still alive."

"You must have had a good reason!"

"I did. Or it seemed like a good reason at the time. Perhaps it wasn't. I was only guarding my virginity." She started to laugh again, half-hysterically. "Silly, isn't it! My virginity."

He came close to her and, seizing her shoulders, started to shake her. "Carey!"

And when she continued to laugh wildly, he slapped her once, brutally, across the cheekbone. She sobered instantly, and pinpoints of shock touched her eyes.

"Carey, you're all right. Do you understand? You're all right. You're safe now. We'll sail from here at once. We'll go to Hawaii—with a fair wind we can be there within three weeks. You'll like Hawaii, and we'll stay there for a while. You'll never see the man again, I promise you."

Something in the steely quality of his voice told her his intentions. She huddled her arms about herself and started shivering.

"Adam, promise me you won't."

"I don't know what you mean."

"You've already got your revenge. He's wearing it on his face. He has to wear his face like a prison, for the rest of his life."

"He's an animal, Carey. Subhuman."

"Promise!"

And because he could see she was getting upset again, he gave his word: and for the first time in his life, he did so with foreknowledge that he had no intention of keeping it. But in the end he did: for the next night, when he stole into the Spanish encampment by dark, he saw soldiers building the gibbet, and heard them talking about the hanging that was to take place at dawn.

At the risk of being discovered, Adam stayed hidden in the presidio until well after sunrise. He did not leave until he saw Fuentes's lifeless body being cut from the noose—the noose that had released him, at last, from the prison of his face.

⚔ CHAPTER TWENTY-SIX ⚔

The green serrated outline of Hawaii thrust itself majestically against the dazzling blue of the noonday sky. And in the distance rose Mauna Loa, cresting two and a half miles into the sky. The cap of the volcano smoked eerily and silently into the cloudless blue, adding to the dreamlike quality of the scene. The air was soft and fragrant, and no breeze disturbed its gentle warmth. As the *Sweet Witch* lay rocking gently at anchor, Adam went ashore to find sleeping accommodations. "You'll be happier on shore," he told Carey. "Already, several canoeloads of island girls are taking up residence on the *Sweet Witch*. You'd feel out of place."

"I wouldn't be shocked. I've seen too much."

But she gave in easily. If she had misgivings, they were soon set to rest by the sight of the dwelling-place that had been provided for her use and Adam's. The hale, as it was called, was set in a soft and fern-fringed valley. Glossy yam vines and lush ti leaves clung to the hillsides, and thin streams of icy water coursed down the steep inclines and collected in a hidden pool warmed by the hot sun. Although Carey had seen few flowers elsewhere on the island, here there were more—hibiscus and trumpet-shaped kou, spiky silversword, and the pale pua-kala poppy—their odors mingled with the haunting and pervasive perfume of sandalwood.

Adam decided that he and Carey would stay here through the month it would take for the men of the *Sweet Witch* to cut and haul sandalwood down from the high hills where the tall trees grew. Just as time had healed the scars on his body, he hoped that Hawaii might heal the scars in Carey's mind.

But they were not healed, not yet: for when the air grew velvet with darkness, and he went to take her in his arms, she twisted away from him and would not let him near.

"Please, Adam, no."

"Carey, what happened in Alta California? Why won't you let me touch you?"

"I don't feel like it."

"Carey, I'm not going to force myself on you. That's all over with." It was true: the dark side of his soul was no longer in command. Where he had once felt only hatred and sexual torment and the need for revenge where his wife was concerned, he now felt another emotion—compassion.

"Carey, I'll hold you. I'll do no more."

"No, Adam—not now. Please leave me alone."

And after that, for the next month, he did.

Carey slid into the still waters of the hidden pool. Her sprigged muslin dress, one of several brought ashore from the *Sweet Witch,* lay over a low bush by the water's edge. She no longer had fears that anyone would come upon her private retreat without warning. Several Hawaiian warriors guarded the entrance to the valley to ensure her safety. They never came closer, and the approach of anyone other than Adam was announced by a weird hollow warning note sounded on a conch shell. Adam had been away all this past week, somewhere to the north, visiting King Kamehameha at his summer palace. For the moment, she felt quite safe from prying eyes. After several minutes of stroking lazily across the pool, she rolled onto her back and floated with her eyes closed, enjoying the restorative balm of the clean sweet water.

The month in Hawaii had healed many wounds. Even Adam seemed kinder and more considerate now, when she saw him. She sensed that he no longer hated her: something had burned the hatred out of him, and perhaps the passion too, for he had made no more moves to assert his marital rights. She did not feel ready, yet, for deeper thinking on the subject of what the future might bring. She wanted only to think of the beauty of this unrecapturable moment, and the satiny water that slid over her skin like a soft caress . . .

"Oh . . . Adam!"

It was a shock when the familiar head emerged beside her, for she had not heard him splash into the pool. She gasped and choked, and flailed for a moment, and then she caught her breath and started to tread water.

"Adam! I didn't hear you."

He made no effort to touch her, but she was supremely conscious of her own nakedness, and of his, shimmering through the distortion of the water.

Adam grinned easily and raked his hair, gleaming and tousled from the underwater swim, away from his forehead. "It's a perfect day for a swim. And a perfect place." ·

Carey started to stroke toward shore, but his hands came out and seized her, and pulled her closer to him in the water.

"Let me go, Adam."

"Carey . . ."

His arms were gentle, as gentle as the water. He eased both their bodies for a short distance until his feet found the rough volcanic stone of the bottom.

"Carey."

And because he held her without doing anything else, and because the water concealed many things, she did not pull away from him at once, as she might have done on shore.

After a time he could feel her body begin to tremble. She would not allow herself to relax. But some of her fear was ebbing away, and he could feel it go. Still, he made no further move except, with one hand, to tilt her head against his shoulder.

She was like a vulnerable wounded bird, he thought. Where had the hard-faced harlot gone—where the ardent tempestuous woman who had fought and stormed and loved her way across the North Pacific? Had they been mere illusions? Was this an illusion too—this tremulous, fragile creature who felt as though she might break beneath his hands?

And Carey, with her head resting against his broad accepting shoulder, wondered too. Part of her begged permission to respond to him, but her mind denied the impulse. His nearness was like wine to her swimming senses, but she knew where it would lead, inevitably. Already, although he had made no overt moves, she could feel the demands of his body.

"Please, Adam, let me go. Leave me while I get dressed." And she tried to pull away into deeper water.

But his mouth came down over hers, drowning her protests; and if he had been brutal or insistent or angry or possessive, as he had so often been in the past, it would have been easier for her now. But his tongue and his lips were liquid fire, melting her bones, igniting her veins, destroying her carefully constructed defenses. His hands were in the tangles of her wet hair, then moving against her chin and her eyes and her cheeks and the hollow of her throat; and the words he breathed into her ears were the words he might have whispered to a frightened child —comforting words, caressing words, tender meaningless words.

And when at last he carried her toward the shore, and laid her down on the fine warm sand at the water's edge, she forgot to protest at all, for her lips clung to his with a thirst that could no longer be denied; and his hands were surging over her breasts and her back; and his knees were parting the thighs she had thought no man would want to part again. Impatient now, he moved his body over hers while the water still lapped over them; and together, for a time, they escaped their memories.

But while he lay, still a part of her, the realities returned to Carey.

"Adam, please go now . . . leave me. I want to get dressed." She tried to shift her body, but she was imprisoned by his weight.

"Carey, it can't matter that—" And suddenly the awful suspicion came to him, and he rolled away from her, but kept her shackled with his fingers. "Carey, lie still. I'm going to look at you—at your body. You must let me."

She struggled, but when he found what he was looking for, she ceased to fight and hid her head in her hands.

The bruises had long since vanished, but the marks were still there: thin scars that scored the flesh between her thighs, a reminder forever of the cruel indignities to which she had been subjected. Someday they would fade to white—already they were fading—but for now they were still quite visible against her skin.

Adam's hands traced the lines gently, betraying with his fingers none of the anger he felt in his heart.

"Carey, why didn't you tell me?"

"I didn't want you to see. It looked so awful."

"It doesn't look so awful now. Scars fade. I should know. And they'll fade more with time."

"It's not just the scars. It's the fact that every time I see them I remember. That's what he wanted. He wanted me to remember—everything."

"Tell me the things he wanted you to remember. Tell me what happened. Otherwise you'll never forget."

"It hurts to think about it."

"You'll think about it less if you talk about it now."

And because his hands were still gentle on the marks of her thighs, and because his face and his voice betrayed no revulsion, no rejection, no anger, no emotion, she began to tell him.

"The first night it wasn't so awful. When he touched me I—I retreated into a private place in my mind, a place I learned to go to, long ago, in Macao. An island of the spirit—somewhere he couldn't follow."

Somewhere she couldn't be reached: Adam remembered.

"I hardly knew what had happened—hardly knew what he had done. But whatever he did to me, it didn't satisfy him. He wanted me to respond . . . wanted me to do things . . . wanted me to fight him. He wanted me to know . . . wanted to see by my eyes that I knew. That's when he started to hurt me. And that's all."

But when Adam remained silent, for he knew it was not all, she at last told him about the others who had used her body when Fuentes was through with it.

And when she had told him everything, Adam, to hide the black storm in his eyes, bent over and kissed her scars and the hidden softness of her thighs. His gentleness washed away some of the hurt and some of the humiliation, and something inside her began to heal.

↜ CHAPTER TWENTY-SEVEN ↝

Adam's week-long absence at King Kamehameha's summer palace to the north had paid off. After much talk, Kamehameha had agreed to lend Adam one of his ocean-going double canoes, and a skeleton crew of four, in return for the weapons the *Sweet Witch* had acquired in Yerba Buena.

Only to Noah did Adam reveal his destination. "The Dangerous Islands, Noah. Now you see why I don't want to take the *Sweet Witch*." The Tuamoto Archipelago was called dangerous for good reason: those reef-strewn waters could rip the undersides of a vessel to shreds, and at that time the cloud of coral islands was still poorly charted.

"Three thousand miles in an open canoe!" Noah wagged his head. "It ain't possible."

"The Polynesians have done it before." Adam neglected to add that it had been perhaps five hundred years since a trip of that distance had been made.

"You'll be needin' one man from the *Sweet Witch*," said Noah firmly.

"Yes, Noah. But not you. You'll go with the *Sweet Witch* and look after Mrs. Falconer."

For once Noah swallowed his objections, for he knew by Falconer's expression that they would not be heeded.

"Luke Alden, Noah. I'll take Luke Alden. He's too young and he's no replacement for you—but you're the only man I can trust to look after Mrs. Falconer."

Noah nodded with chagrin.

For several days now, Adam had spent much of his time with the Hawaiians, readying the double-hulled ocean-going canoe for its long voyage to the south. In truth, it was not one canoe but two, joined together by cross-booms and a platform between the twin hulls. Masts on the central section supported two enormous claw-shaped sails like upside-down triangles. It was forty feet long and provided more than ample space for six men and all necessities.

There were supplies to be laid in: great piles of drinking coconuts and dried bananas; poi, fermented so that it would keep on the trip; breadfruit and dried fish and sweet potatoes. Coops of Polynesian chickens were chosen, and a pair of hardy razor-backed pigs. The claw-shaped sails were patched and strengthened, and the sennit ropes that tied all parts together were checked and tightened. With only six men aboard, there would be room for all of them to sleep in the relative comfort of the hulls—where, although it was wet, there was some shelter from the seas and the winds.

In most of these arrangements Adam was dependent on the expertise of the Hawaiians, especially Koolau, the navigator who would have to plot their course according to his knowledge and his ancestors' knowledge of the winds and the tides and above all the stars. That Koolau spoke some English was a bonus, but he had been chosen for other skills—skills even Adam did not have. His was a lore learned from a thousand years of seagoing men—a lore in which any clue could be a matter of supreme importance. The flight and the height of birds, the sighting of certain fishes, the shapes of clouds and the color of their underbellies, the feel of the sea that tells of land resistance in the offing—each must be noted, and weighed, and interpreted.

Koolau had not been to Varua, the island of their destination, before. Nor had he been to the Dangerous Islands. But he had sailed once, some years before, as far as the Marquesas; and with a confidence even Adam did not feel, he plotted his course, using a map tied together with bent sticks and strings and bits of shell—a map such as his grandfather had used, and his grandfather's grandfather before that, back to generations when Roman triremes hugged the shores of the Mediterranean.

Adam divulged none of this to Carey, for he wanted her to remain unaware of his preparations. He spared her what time he could. Although he was careful to conceal it, the things she had told him had filled him with pity, frustration, rage—and other emotions he could hardly define to himself. Why did he care so much? What had she become to him? Was he growing to want her as a wife despite himself—despite everything?

Perhaps: but it was not something to be contemplated now, for Varua lay ahead. Varua—and Blore. It was important to reach Varua well before Blore's deadline, and for now there was no time for gentler pursuits and finer feelings.

But he made love to Carey again, lingeringly, under a night hushed and breathless with stars, and then they curled up together among the ferns and mosses along the water's edge, not even troubling to put on their clothes or to return to the hale.

Carey lay awake for a long time, recalling that Adam had once told her that he wanted to make love to her under the sun and under the stars and in the open air, as he had done in these past days. But he would not remember, for she had been Teura then.

And at that moment, in that soft and dreaming night, as she lay drowsy and contented in the circle of his arms, and grateful for an understanding she had not expected him to possess, she fell in love all over again.

This time she knew there was no need to even think of telling him about Teura. She was aware that Adam Falconer had at last fallen in love with Carey Wyeth. Now it only remained for him to discover that fact for himself.

The note from Adam came at sundown the following day, delivered by Noah. It told Carey little: only that Adam would not be sailing with the *Sweet Witch*, for he was setting off at once on a journey in one of the Hawaiian double canoes. There was no word of goodbye, only a simple apology that he would not be seeing her for a few months. Carey's world crumbled about her ears.

"The Cap'n'll meet us here in about six months," Noah elaborated, seeing her distress. Then he added, not realizing how little comfort the *Sweet Witch*'s destination would give Carey: "Soon's we get back from Macao."

"Macao. Oh—" Carey's throat tightened, and she moved so that Noah could not see her face. But when she turned back she seemed quite calm. "How soon will Adam be leaving?"

" 'Bout an hour. It's them crazy kahunas, the priests." Noah rolled his eyes. "Makin' all kinds o' speeches, an' ceremonies, an' readin' the omens in the sky. Capn's kind o' frettin' to be off, but no ways he can get them to hurry up with that muck. Reckon an hour don't make much difference, though, what with a long trip like that."

"A long trip? Where to?"

"Cain't rightly say, Miz Carey."

And with the note, there was something else: some papers, signing the ownership of the *Sweet Witch* over to Carey.

"Noah! Why has he done this?"

"Don't rightly unnerstand it myself, Miz Carey. Truth is, he loves that ship more'n any crittur alive. Present company exceptin', needless to add."

"Noah, you're hiding something. He must have a reason."

"I dunno why he's done it, Miz Carey. I'm as flummoxed as you are." She saw, by his eyes, that he understood no more than she did.

"I've got to talk to him before he sails."

"He ain't too keen to see you. Not partic'lar for goodbyes, the Capn ain't."

"But to go like this—"

And suddenly she knew that Adam did not expect to live.

Noah went on, not noticing her sudden silence. "He said as how I weren't to allow you to leave this valley. No ways!"

"Noah! Don't you see? Adam expects to die."

"Miz Carey, you've gone plumb crackerbrained! Don't even think such things."

"I don't *think*. I *know*. Why else would he sign the *Sweet Witch* over to me?"

"Hunnerds of reasons." But he could not think of one. And slowly it dawned on him: that Miz Carey must have guessed a truth that Falconer had hidden from everybody, even from Noah himself.

"I have to see him. You have to help me."

"Miz Carey, I ain't able to." Even in the anguish of his realization, Noah could not think of countermanding his master's orders.

"I love him, Noah," Carey said simply, and Noah, who had known for a long time that this was so, said nothing. "You must help me."

"He ain't a man to change his mind too easy. An' he's been cogitatin' on this trip for months."

"Do you know why?"

"Not a hunnerd percent. But it's to do with some money he took a loan of back in Macao. Partic'lar close-mouthed about it, he was."

Oh, no, it couldn't be the money Adam had borrowed to buy her. It couldn't! But she knew it was. Macao . . . it loomed in her life like a giant evil shadow, its clutching tentacles still reaching across the miles and the months.

"I think I can change his mind, Noah, if you help me to reach him." She sensed this was not true: but Noah didn't need to know that. "You can hide me in the canoe. As soon as it's put to sea I'll talk to Adam—convince him somehow to turn back. Don't you see he'll *have* to turn back if I'm aboard?"

"Miz Carey, I—"

"Promise!"

Noah's misery was transparent. But in the end, his concern for Captain Falconer's life was greater than his sense of duty. And so, some minutes later, at the darkened shore where torchlight flickered over an assemblage of be-feathered Hawaiians gathered to see the priests read the omens, Noah created a small diversion. Waiting for the right moment, he directed everyone's attention to the crater of Mauna Loa, which was shooting a fiery omen of its own into the night sky.

And while all eyes were turned shoreward, Carey slipped across the shadowed beach and clambered into the great twin-hulled vessel, and made herself small beneath some canvas laid aboard to protect the supplies.

⚔ CHAPTER TWENTY-EIGHT ⚔

The craft had been at sea no more than fifteen minutes when Adam found Carey in the cramped belly of the leeward canoe—quite simply by stepping on her, and causing an involuntary gasp.

"Carey! Good God."

As she emerged sheepishly from under the canvas he had yanked away, she could sense the blazing fury in his eyes, even though she could see only dimly in the starry darkness that enveloped the swaying canoe.

"What the deuce are you doing aboard?"

"I'm going with you, Adam," she said as bravely as possible.

"The hell you are! I'll have Koolau change course and take you back to shore right now."

"No, Adam! I won't sail with the *Sweet Witch*."

"You'll have to," he returned grimly.

"I can't go to Macao without you." Carey kept her voice lowered, so the others could not hear: she was only too conscious of the shocked reactions of the Hawaiians and Luke Alden. "I *can't*, Adam. I could face Macao if you were there. But not by myself. Let me come with you."

"In an open canoe? It's no trip for a woman."

"*Please,* Adam, *please.* I don't mind the open canoe. I won't complain."

"Believe me, Carey, this time you'll be safe in Macao. Noah has orders to look after you. Wherever you go, he'll go too."

"You can't be so cruel, Adam," she said; and some note of desperation in her voice stopped Adam just as he was about to issue the order to Koolau.

At this moment Luke Alden, who had heard few of their low-pitched words, came over the cross-booms from the windward canoe.

"Captain Falconer, sir! Shall I ask Koolau to put back to shore, or to the *Sweet Witch?*"

"No, Luke," said Adam, making up his mind in that moment. "Mrs. Falconer doesn't want to go to Macao."

"Sir! You said this would be a dangerous trip."

"Luke, go away."

"You have to put her back to shore," said Luke stubbornly.

"Mister Alden!" Adam used the formal shipboard form of address, expecting it would result in unquestioning obedience.

But Luke remained insubordinate. "You can't let her come, Captain."

Carey intervened. "Please go away, Luke. I want to talk to Adam alone."

So at last Luke went; but not without a burning resentment that added itself to the strong dislike he already felt for Adam Falconer.

"Adam, you won't regret it," Carey promised as soon as Luke was out of earshot.

"I already do," Adam said roughly. But he gave no order to Koolau; instead he lowered himself into the bottom of the canoe and pulled Carey down beside him.

She nestled into his arms, content with that, and Adam fell into a brooding silence which Carey dared not break. For a while they sat together watching as the fiery rise of Mauna Loa gradually fell away into the distance.

"Adam, where are we going?"

"South to a coral atoll. An island called Varua." She gave a start. "Varua" meant "spirit" in Tahitian. An island of the spirit: perhaps she had been meant to go there, all along. She returned, quickly, to her other question:

"Why will it be dangerous?"

"Coral atolls are always dangerous. That's what the whole group is called—the Dangerous Islands."

"There's more to it than that, Adam, or you wouldn't have put the *Sweet Witch* in my name."

So it wasn't just Macao that had gotten her wind up. Curse her for being too damn smart for a woman; now he'd have to tell her at least some of the truth. He grimaced. "You might as well know, Carey. There's a man I'm to meet there, a man named Blore." He glossed, quickly, over the reasons for meeting Blore; the reasons for Blore's hatred. "He plans to kill me. Would you rather turn back now?"

"No."

"I won't let him kill me. I'll think of a way. I have some advantages. He expects me to arrive in the *Sweet Witch*. And with luck we'll be there early—perhaps three weeks ahead of the time I'm to meet him."

"Then you'll have three weeks to get ready for him."

"No, if all goes well I'll have a week, maybe two. He'll arrive early too." But he didn't want to think about Blore now. Varua was more than a month away.

"Adam—you're not too angry with me?"

"I'm furious. Tomorrow I'll show you what a tiger I am when I'm furious."

"No, really."

"Yes, really."

And in truth he was a little angry, but he was also secretly pleased, for the despair that had gripped him for the past few days had vanished.

He would think of something. He had to think of something.

By morning, the mildness of the night wind was no more than a memory. The dawn was overcast, and soon whistling gales battered at the canoe as she turned to gain her easting. For three days as they headed east, and for a week after that as they plowed southward, huge jets of spray volleyed and thundered over the cross-booms and the platform connecting the two joined canoes, and breaking waves swept the length of the open hulls. The men no longer paddled, for the giant sails drove the boat relentlessly, spilling the worst of the squalls out of their curiously curved tops.

Koolau and the other Hawaiians, working in gales that ripped at their long-suffering skin and tore the breath from their lungs, relashed the cross-booms with fresh sennit ropes, while Adam moved to the helm and strained at the steering paddle.

Carey, unneeded for the moment, huddled in damp and aching misery in the belly of one canoe. Luke, unskilled in the art of tying sennit, joined her.

"He should never have let you come!" Luke spat the words out at Adam Falconer's dimly seen form at the aft of the central platform.

"He didn't have much choice." Carey forced the words out through chattering teeth. Despite Adam's raincape, the wind and the wet penetrated her very bones.

"If he'd cared for you at all, he would have seen you safely on the *Sweet Witch*." Luke made no effort to conceal the anger that had been building in him.

"Luke, you know that's not true. Now, please—"

"Carey, he's been treating you badly for years. I've known it ever since the day you got into that outrigger canoe, and I saw the look on your face. And then when he married you—"

Carey stared at him in shocked disbelief. "What are you talking about?"

"On Tahiti. I saw you, Carey. I knew it was you."

"But you only saw me for seconds!"

"True. But I went to the mission house later. Mr. Rivers told me that you had gone to Mahi Mahi with your brother. Then I was sure."

"But you've never said—I didn't know."

"Does it matter now? At first I thought you were dead, just as he did. Then when I saw you again . . . I can't tell you how I felt."

"Luke, Adam doesn't know this. I intend to tell him someday. But I don't want him to hear it from you."

"I've told nobody and I never will. But if he loved you a tenth as much as I do, he'd have seen the truth for himself long ago."

"Luke! You mustn't say things like—"

But just then an enormous wave towered above them, and shattered over the boat. For an instant it seemed that everything was awash.

"The animals!" screamed Carey against the howl of the wind. Already, Luke and Adam and the Hawaiians were diving for the cages that had broken loose. But it was too late. Another wave lashed across the platform, and one of the pens was swallowed into the sea in a swirl of vanishing foam. Only the half-drowned chickens remained, their cage tilted crazily and nearly smashed against a pile of coconuts in the far canoe. Several terrified birds clawed their way out of the splintered bamboo and vanished over the side.

Within an hour, near nightfall, the fury of the squall abated. The boat, relashed and secure, was once more on a true course. The wind steadied and the waves subsided, and the men, exhausted, took stock of the damage.

The seas calmed; the clouds cleared. Stars, a heavenful of stars, promised fine weather. Foam, glowing with phosphorescence, christened each bow; and the joined canoes dipped and swayed under the vault of the spangled sky.

Adam and Carey sat together for a time before curling up, each in their own space, for the night.

"How far are we from Varua, Adam?"

"We're nearly halfway now."

Halfway. As far to return as to go on. "Will it matter —losing so much food?"

"With so many fish in the sea? Of course not." But Carey by now understood Adam well enough to know that the tone of his voice was too light.

❦ CHAPTER TWENTY·NINE ❧

On the fourteenth day of their voyage, Carey woke with a languorous warmth in her limbs. She had been dreaming of golden English meadows and silent sunlit days—and for a moment, in the twilight zone of drowsy awakening, it seemed that the dream had come true.

Three days of sunshine had dried nearly everything, but that was not what had caused the dream. Then she realized: there was no movement, none at all, and almost no sound, save for an irregular snoring that came from the other canoe, and the level rise and fall of Adam's breath close to her ear.

Very gingerly she extricated herself from his arms and crawled to the entrance of the ramshackle shelter that Adam had at last, with calmer weather, constructed. Tactfully, the other men had taken to sleeping in the other canoe—all but Koolau, who remained at the helm.

The sun was just rising. It was a fierce and astonishing sunrise, building faery castles of the few puffy clouds in the distance. The horizon, unbroken by waves and the pitch and fall of the boat, seemed limitless. There was no wind. None at all, not even the faint stirrings Carey remembered from other times of being becalmed at sea.

And now, as if to signify that others were waking too, the snoring ceased abruptly. Somehow, in the odd stillness, the double canoe seemed vulnerable, eggshell-fragile—an unreal ark in an unbounded motionless world. The sails drooped, lifeless, not even whispering in the driftless air; the creak and groan of complaining sennit was no longer heard; the water lay like an eerie mirror to the sky. The whole world had grown empty and blue and silent and extraordinary.

Then she heard Adam stirring. He came up behind her, yawning and tousling his hair and scratching at his two-week beard, and the strange feeling of aloneness and smallness and eternity passed.

"What's happened, Adam?"

Adam's sea-sharpened eyes scanned the horizon. If he was troubled by the awesome spectacle he took care not to show it. "The doldrums, Carey. We're in the grip of the doldrums."

She had heard of the doldrums, of course—that shifting, unpredictable belt of calms just to the north of the Equator, where vessels could be becalmed for days, even weeks, at a time.

"How long will it last?"

"Who knows? A week, two, three. We'll wait and see."

"We can't just sit here, Adam!" She kept her voice down, but the alarm in her tone could not be concealed. The food had run very low. In truth, there was only enough for another day or two, and already the rations had been cut. "We have to do something."

"What do you suggest we do, then?" Adam's voice was light. "You can't fight the forces of nature, Carey. You have to accept them."

"We could paddle!"

Adam had gone to the stern and was checking the fishing lines. They remained slack, hanging limp in the water. He concealed his frown before turning back to Carey. On the cross-platform Koolau stirred and shook himself out of his hammock, and the murmur of wakening men disturbed the empty air.

Adam no longer troubled to keep his voice low. "Paddle? We will if we have to, but that's a last resort."

"But—"

"Stop fretting, Carey. Come on, help me put together some breakfast."

From the other canoe, now, came more sounds, pleasurable sounds, and laughter—laughter for the goodness of the sun, for the warmth of the day, and for the prospect at last, of a swim. The Hawaiians, at least, were not worrying about tomorrow.

But four days later there was little laughter. The fishing lines had come up empty. Pangs of hunger had started in earnest, adding their burden to tempers already taxed by the sameness of the sky and the sea. A coconut shell, thrown overboard three days before, still floated beside the boat as if held in aspic: it had remained so motionless that its upper side had grown dry and blackened in the sun.

Occasional almost imperceptible puffs of wind were still moving the boat slowly toward its goal, but that seemed evident only to Koolau and Adam. The others—Carey, Luke, the Hawaiian crew—began to feel an immense sense of aloneness on the limitless Pacific. Their eyeballs and their brains and their stomachs ached. Two of the Hawaiians exchanged words over an imagined slight. Luke Alden, even-tempered Luke Alden, turned on the man whose snoring had become unbearably loud in the long night silences. Adam lit into one of the young bronze-skinned giants who went seeking food in the sea with no more than a horue-board and a bone knife in his hands, and strayed too far from the boat; and in this Koolau, who had remained above all other fights, supported Adam. Although no sharks had been sighted, they remained an ever-looming presence.

Twice, showers materialized out of nowhere and dropped a curtain of warm, unslanted drops on the canoe; then, by nature's sleight-of-hand, vanished as quickly. Carey's skin burned and peeled badly in the almost incessant sun, and this new misery took some attention away from the empty hurt in her stomach. She bathed in the still seas, and emerged modestly to a shielding raincape held by Adam. She occupied her hands and her mind by ripping what remained of her dress into squares of cloth to use as pareus, and the change of clothing helped to lift her spirits somewhat.

Only the water supply was plentiful now. Adam guarded the precious store of remaining coconuts and oversalted fish with zealous attention, and even took to sleeping draped uncomfortably over the lumpy supplies, abandoning the shelter he had shared with Carey.

It was this that led to Luke Alden's next outburst—this, and a temper frayed by sleeplessness and hunger and the maddening monotony of the sky and the sea.

Adam had been doling out the day's supply of food.

"Here, Alden, hand out the rations, will you?" He indicated the carefully halved coconuts and the scraps of fish that had been set out for distribution.

"Hand them out? I can hardly see them," Luke grumbled. He could not help it: the habit of obedience was giving way to stronger impulses, as if his long-nourished hatred of Adam Falconer had been feeding on the emptiness in his entrails.

"Get on with it, Alden," Adam's voice was firm but not unkind. Luke was young, after all. Still growing up. Adam had begun to regret his choice.

But the kindness in Adam's voice only triggered the explosion that had been building up in Luke for a long time.

"To hell with you, Captain Almighty Falconer! Standing over those supplies as if you bloody well owned them." He too had grown a new beard on his chin, and it seemed to bristle now, red-gold, belligerent, the heritage of some hot-tempered ancestor.

"Luke," warned Adam mildly.

But Alden's temper, slow to be aroused, was not so easily appeased. "You're a tyrant, Falconer. Proud, selfish, arrogant, bloody-minded! Just look at the way you treat Carey. As if you owned her too."

"Stop it, Alden."

"You're starving her—starving her by inches! And I don't mean for food. I mean for affection."

"That's enough!"

"You treat her like the dirt under your feet! I've ached to say it since the day you married her. And now we're no longer captain and crew, *sir*—we're two dying men, on a god-cursed speck of a boat in a god-cursed empty ocean, and I don't give a damn any more."

"Alden! Grow up."

"God knows why she's stayed with you. Through everything—more than you know! And you've been too busy hating her to see the truth."

"Luke!" Carey flew forward and seized his arm in alarm, for she sensed that he no longer had control of his words. "Please stop at once."

But Adam pulled her away roughly. "Stay out of this, Carey. It's man's business."

"You don't love her, Falconer, and you never have! You don't know the first thing about her. Have you ever looked at her—really looked at her? Well, look now, because she's going to die soon. We're all going to die soon."

"Shut up, Alden. You don't know what you're talking about."

"Oh, God—" and Luke, with an unreasoning rage in his eye, swung at Adam. The first blow, unexpected, connected; the second was parried. But Adam didn't want a fistfight, not now. He dodged another blow.

"Simmer down, Luke!"

But Luke would not; he came at Falconer with murder in his heart and the skill of a born fighter. And in the next moment he found himself over the side of the canoe.

"Adam!"

But Carey's warning scream was hardly needed, for already Adam was reaching out and yanking Luke from the water. He and Carey had seen what Alden could not: the triangular rise of dorsal fin that told of a shark's presence.

Within seconds Luke was back in the boat, sodden and no longer swinging, but only partially chastened.

"Luke! There was a shark—"

"Leave me alone, Carey."

He sat dripping for a few minutes and then, without another word, stood up and started to distribute the morning's rations to the other canoe. When he had finished, he returned and looked at Falconer with still-unfriendly eyes.

"I meant it, Captain Falconer. We're just two men now. And if I can take her from you, I will." He picked up his own food and turned to go, then added over his shoulder: "I'm sorry for hitting you."

"Forget it, Luke. That's quite a left you've got." Adam rubbed his bruised jaw.

Luke moved away, then turned back. There was something he had to know: he'd never been bested in a fistfight before. "How did you—"

"It's an old Oriental art, Luke. If you ever fall out of love with my wife, I may teach you."

Luke turned away, scowling. But the wry smile on Adam Falconer's face showed some measure of satisfaction. It took a man to apologize without taking back his words. Alden had grown up. Maybe he had been the right choice after all.

Two days later the fishing lines brought in a twenty-five-pound mahimahi; and as if the heavens and the deeps had decided to smile on them, within minutes an octopus, projecting itself through the air, landed in the boat with a series of violent sneezing sounds, and lay snuffling and snorting and wriggling until one of the Kanakas made short work of it with his bone knife.

While Adam sliced and set the octopus to marinate, Carey cooked the mahimahi with shredded coconut over an acrid fire of coconut shells. The smoke stung her eyes and her nostrils and left smudges on her skin, and she did not care, for tonight they would sleep with full bellies.

Sunset, after they had eaten, had never seemed more beautiful.

Adam, seeing Carey turn to watch its dying splendor, joinied her at the edge of their shelter. Luke and the Hawaiians, groaning with satisfaction, had already settled in the other canoe. Even Koolau had vanished—for with no wind, there was no need of his hand at the helm. For the moment, all was silence and radiance in an infinite untroubled sea.

"That was a fine meal, Carey."

When she did not answer, Adam looked at her more closely; and then pulled her into the crook of his arm.

"Silly woman," he said gently. "What are you crying for?"

She allowed him to brush away her tears with his fingertips. "I cry over all the wrong things. I always have."

"I've never seen you cry before." And with a kind of wonder, he realized that it was true, although he remembered, still, the time she had nearly cried—during that last terrible fight. "What's causing the tears now?"

"The sunset. It's so beautiful—and so swiftly over."

What had distressed her that day? It wasn't just the bitter words they had exchanged. There had been other fights, dozens of them, many equally bad, and none of them had driven her even close to tears. She hadn't cried when her child had been lost. She hadn't cried after Macao. Even after California, there had been no tears. What had been different that day? Had it been over that first lover of hers—the one who had left her with child? For the first time he considered how she must have felt— abandoned, pregnant, in a strange land halfway around the world from her birthplace.

Was Luke right—had he never understood her? Where he had once thought her hard as nails, she had been vulnerable. Where he had once thought her cold, she had been passionate. Where he had once thought her unfeeling, she had been sensitive. He tried to remember all the women she had been, through the years. The stiff-spined conventional virgin who'd flouted his orders, and defied the Tahitian vahines—no, by God, she hadn't been conventional, not even then. The flirt who had tricked him into marriage, driven to God knows what desperation. The teasing, taunting hoyden who had provoked him into making love to her, against his will. The silent, accepting woman he had left in Macao. The brittle stone-faced harlot. The ardent lover who, awakened, had abandoned herself to tempestuous passion. The vulnerable creature she had been after California. The woman she was now . . .

But there was a link lost somewhere; something that would make all the different women one—something that, if he had the clue, would make all the pieces fall in place.

"Only sunsets?"

"And other things—things that make me happy."

Why had he never tried to understand her? It was his pride, his damnable pride. She had been a thorn in his self-esteem. She had fooled him, more than once: no other woman had fooled him.

"Do you always cry when you're happy?"

"No—well, yes, sometimes."

"You can't be happy very often, then."

"I—oh, this is a silly conversation, Adam."

Luke was right: he had never really seen her. And in the instant before the sun slid into its sea-bed, he tried to look at her, to really look at her.

Her skin was parched and her nose was sunburned; there was a smudge on her cheekbone from the cookfire; her hair hung in a golden tangle halfway down her back. There were still some stubborn saltwater sores on her hands and on her feet from the days of unending storms, and her fingernails were broken from working around the boat; and she was thin, painfully thin, after this week of hunger and the two difficult weeks that had gone before. He thought she had never looked more desirable.

"You're right, Carey, this is a silly conversation. We shouldn't be talking at all. There are better things to do."

And he pulled her into the makeshift shelter and made love to her, as though for the first time.

They crossed the Equator. Soon after that, the air

stirred with welcome news: they had met the southeast trades. The canoe had escaped the doldrum's clutch. The sails filled and foam slid past the twin prows; the sailors set to work with a will, and the travelers sped southward over a kindly sea.

Now they no longer sailed by night, for there was too much danger of damage from a shoal or coral reef. Koolau remained awake through much of the darkness, reading the signposts of the night firmament, and judging their position. He thought they would reach Varua within two days, maybe three.

By the next day, when the occupants of a sighted island confirmed their position, Adam Falconer knew that he could no longer put off the confrontation that he had been dreading for this past week.

"Carey, come and sit down. I want to talk to you."

And Carey joined him willingly enough, although she wondered why he looked so tense. In spite of the lengthening beard, she could see the tight corners of his mouth.

"Parles en francais, ma petite. I don't want anyone to understand." Adam nodded imperceptibly toward the omnipresent Koolau sitting patiently by the helm. The others, in the far canoe, could not hear.

Carey opened her mouth to answer, then stopped herself. If she spoke French now, it was possible that Adam would recognize the remembered inflections of Teura's voice. Not that she would have minded, now, if they had been alone. But this was neither the time nor the place. She answered him in English.

"I don't speak French."

"What, then? Spanish, Italian, Portuguese?"

"I'm not too fluent in Portuguese."

Adam made the choice and switched easily to Spanish. "Carey, there's something—two things—I want to talk to you about before we reach Varua. First, there's something you have to know."

She answered him in the same language. "It sounds dreadfully serious!"

"It is, Carey. It's about Macao."

Oh, no, she thought—not now. She didn't want to think about Macao; she had hoped that Adam was growing to forget it. She stirred restlessly. "Do we have to talk about it?"

"Yes, we do. You wanted to, once, and I refused. I had a reason for refusing."

"But why now?" She could not completely conceal her anguish. "Now—after all these months?"

"Because there's something I don't want you to learn from anyone but me." Blore knew too much about Macao, and the knowledge was a weapon in his hands. Yet this was hard, telling Carey—harder even than Adam had imagined it would be. "I visited you in that brothel, even before the day I took you away."

She stared at him, doing nothing to make this easier for him.

"I made love to you there, a number of times, incognito. I couldn't help myself. I didn't intend to, when I first went. I intended only to tell you that you wouldn't be harmed—that I had bought you. The man who owned that boat arranged it for me, took you there for safekeeping. I couldn't bring you to the *Sweet Witch* at once—there were reasons." He didn't tell her that the reason had been Mei Sung: but perhaps she guessed it. "I intended to tell you all that at the time, but when you lashed out at me with the whip—"

She had gone chalky white under her sunburn, the color drained even from her lips.

"It was you."

"Yes, it was me, that time."

"And it was you who had me taken to that place."

"Yes—from whatever other godforsaken brothel they already had you in. God, Carey, don't look at me like that! I've punished myself a thousand times over. Even when I was taking you, I loathed myself. There was something angry and hateful and hellish inside me, a demon in my soul. I wanted to punish you, to make you suffer as you had made me suffer."

"Made *you* suffer—oh, God!"

"At the time I thought the demon was inside me because—I'm not sure why. Anger, revenge, frustration. But now I think it was really something else—the thought of the other men who had touched you. When I saw you painted and powdered and near-naked in that mirrored room, I nearly went out of my mind."

"So it was you that night. It wasn't Vasily." She gave a strange strangled laugh.

"Your Russian lover was dead by then. But you called

me by his name, and that was the other thing that drove me into a frenzy."

"But he wasn't my lover—he had never been my lover. I thought it was Vasily that night and—oh, Adam, I wanted to die. I wanted to die!"

"I'm sorry. About that—and about the other times I came to you."

"Oh, God." She had buried her head in her hands, but now she looked up. "Don't you see, Adam? You were the first to visit me in that place. There had been no others before you. And I hadn't been in a brothel. I'd been in an opium den—a sampan."

"What do you mean?" A cold hard knot of something coiled into his stomach. This was a possibility he had never reckoned with. He should have known to expect the unexpected.

"If you'd taken me away with you that night I wouldn't have been—wouldn't have become a whore. A puta, Adam!"

"Don't use that word!"

"Why not?" Her voice now had a hysterical edge. "You've called me that word often enough. And it's the truth. That's what I am—what I was. A puta—a cheap puta who lay back and spread her legs for anyone who cared to take her. For anyone—for all the others who followed you. After that first night it didn't seem to matter anymore. I only wanted to survive. And you were the first, Adam. *You* made me a whore."

"Carey, I visited you again—often—after that first night. Remember, I'd bought you. There weren't any others."

"Don't lie to yourself!" Carey's overwrought voice rose, drawing the attention of Luke and the Hawaiians in the other boat. It was as well she was still speaking Spanish.

Adam remained silent, suffering his own particular brand of hell. The moment of hysteria had passed. When Carey finally spoke again, she sounded tired. "There were others."

"Maybe you're mistaken," Adam insisted, as much for his own sake as for hers. "You told me once that you used to vanish into some secret place in your mind—that you hardly knew what was happening to you."

"I always saw who came through the door." An immense weariness came over her, remembering. There had been men of different shapes, different heights. Once three men had arrived together, and she had been sure, even then, that it was the guards. A frequently recurring tall figure—the one who had tried to arouse her. That had been Adam; it must have been Adam. Would the others have taken her, had she resisted, struggled, cried out—had she done anything but lie there, passively accepting?

"Carey—" Adam reached out as if to touch her, but she shied away.

"Don't touch me, Adam. I'm dirty. Your dirty little whore!"

She stood up, and as if there had not been six pairs of eyes upon her, she unfastened the square of cloth that covered her, and shucked it into the bottom of the boat, and dove naked into the crest of a wave.

⚔ CHAPTER THIRTY ⚔

At first it was only a wind-trembling of green shimmering
at the outer limits of vision. Then, as the graceful high-
sterned twin canoe approached, the lush forms of tropical
trees appeared—pandanus and fragrant tafano and beach
umbrella; gnarled wind-twisted mikimiki; and everywhere,
tall graceful cocopalms, dipping their fronds and bending
to breezes that swept in over the vast spaces of empty
ocean.

To the windward side of the island, a line of spume
marked the rust-red reef where waves four thousand miles
old met their doom, and dashed themselves to death, and
exploded skyward in mighty geysers from hidden time-
worn caverns in the coral. But there was easy passage on
the lee side, where a narrow channel opened outward to
the sea; and it was through this channel that the double
canoe, after more than a month on the open ocean, at last
entered the lagoon of Varua.

Within the necklace of coral, the water changed and
became less restless. The interminable blue of the water
turned to green. In the center of the lagoon lay the motu,
or island, itself, its sandy rim an astonishing white.

Carey trailed her fingers over the canoe's side with a
twist of remembered pleasure. The lagoon of Mahi Mahi
had been like this: sparkling-clean and unsullied. But that
had been long ago—so very long ago.

"Look, there's a parrot-fish!" She pointed at the blue-
green shape that zigzagged lazily by, perfectly visible in
the transparent waters. "Oh, Luke, we'll have to go for a
swim!"

"That sounds great, Carey." Luke's hand reached for
hers in the water. He meant what he had said the other
day: he had every intention of taking Carey from Adam
Falconer if he could. Something drastic had happened be-

tween them, he could tell that—but two days before, when Carey had gone for her startling swim, he had been able to understand none of their conversation. "We'll race each other to the reef."

Carey laughed and splashed him, but she allowed his hand to find hers. "Winner take all?"

Adam, who had been watching the shoreline, overheard and frowned. Carey had been totally unreachable for two days now—so unreachable that he had had no opportunity to talk to her about the other thing he had had on his mind. But he would not stand by and see his woman taken from him.

"You'll swim with no one, Carey, until we've found out whether the lagoon is safe."

"Is that an order?" she retorted impudently. "Because if it is, Luke and I shall see that we break it as soon as possible."

"There could be sharks."

"Sharks! Luke, do you hear that? Adam's afraid I might be eaten by sharks. Or are you afraid of something else, Adam?"

"Carey!" But Adam's warning was ignored.

"Luke saw me naked the other day, so it can't be that. And think of all the other men who've seen me unclothed." She addressed herself to Alden, sweetly. "Did you know that other men had seen me unclothed, Luke? Seen me—and more? Adam doesn't mind. He arranged it, once."

Luke's face mirrored his mixed emotions. This was not the Carey he loved, this brittle woman with poison in her eyes and venom in her heart. What had come over her? And Adam Falconer was looking at her with an odd expression that was half anger and half something else. What had happened between them over the years? How much did he really know about Carey? He recoiled, instinctively, and she felt it in his fingers.

"Luke!" She reclaimed his reluctant hand and held it to her breast. "Adam's quite prepared to share me with other men. He always has been."

"Good God, Carey!" Adam seized her furiously and pulled her to her feet. "Have some shame!"

She matched him glare-for-glare. "You taught me not to have shame. Now I have none at all! I'm only waiting until we get on dry land, and then I intend to take Luke into the bushes and teach him everything I know. Everything! Which, if you'll remember, is quite a lot."

For a moment it seemed that Adam was going to strike his wife. But at that moment a call came from Koolau; he was pointing excitedly to shore.

Adam wheeled around to face the beach. "So it is inhabited!" He added a silent curse against himself for allowing Carey to distract him just as they were entering the lagoon. It was an unforgivable lapse. Thank God this was not Blore waiting on the motu, but a scantily clad cluster of Polynesians who had emerged from the trees—probably from a group of huts that was not visible from here. Lord, what things Carey drove him to!—and only two days ago he'd sworn to himself that he'd not show her the black side of his temper ever again.

He had not thought the island would be inhabited. His own charts had told him it was not, and he had been sure that Blore would not want witnesses. But then, perhaps when Blore had last seen the island, it had been empty. The Polynesians, a migratory race, often abandoned a motu where the food was running out, and found themselves a new home.

Adam glanced briefly at Carey, his self-control regained. "Your plans will have to wait, Carey. I'll need you to translate. You're the only one who speaks Tahitian."

"If you insist," she returned coolly, and sat down again beside Luke, to wait until they arrived at the shore.

The headman of the Varuan Tahitians was a gray-haired patriarch by the name of Tu. Adam had guessed correctly: this was a handful of nomads, a family group who moved from atoll to atoll, from motu to motu, hunting for food and the oyster-pearls that white men seemed to prize so much. There were twenty of them in all: half a dozen men, three children, the rest women. They had been living on Varua for no more than five moons.

"Tell him there will be trouble here, in about half a moon," Adam instructed Carey. "Ask him if his people could move to a neighboring atoll for a time, and take you with them."

She glared at him belligerently. "I'll ask no such thing."

"Forget the last part, then."

She translated.

"Tu says they have been thinking of moving. He says it is a bad reef—a dangerous reef. Three of their young men have died already."

"Ask him why."

"Tu says there are barracuda in one of the places where the pearl oysters are found. That is how one of their men died—savaged by barracuda. But they can kill barracuda. Since then, they have killed most of them. That is not what troubles them now."

"What troubles them, then?"

"It seems they're concerned about a moray eel who lives near the other pearling area. He is a big fellow, an old fellow, a wily fellow. Tu says no one can dive safely when there is a moray in the reef. The divers have been hunting him for many days, but this eel is too clever to take the bait. It was he who killed the other two divers."

"Ask him if there are sharks."

"No sharks."

"Ask him if there is fresh water."

"Tu says not. But there are many *nu*—green drinking coconuts. Usually they bathe in the sea. But if they wish to sluice their bodies in unsalted water, they dig a well into the white sand of the beach. The water that seeps in is filtered by the sand. It's good for bathing, and other uses."

"What is there to eat?"

Again, Adam watched while Carey gathered the information from Tu. "Tu says there is no shortage of food. Fish and shellfish. Lobster. *Kaveu*—the giant robber crab that climbs trees and feeds on coconuts." Her eyes, stony, dared him to remember. "Some wild pigs, probably brought by a former inhabitant. Many cocopalms. Wild greens, roots, and a few yams—also planted sometime in the past."

"Ask him where we may build our shelters."

"Tu says they will help us to build shelters, as we have just finished a long and arduous voyage. But he wants to know how many shelters."

"Tell him two shelters. One large shelter, for five people. One smaller shelter, for two people, away from the others."

"Which two people?" The words were simple, but her tone conveyed the insult.

"Just translate, Carey."

But when the crude cocopalm-thatched shelters started to take shape, an hour later, there were three of them, all side by side, and Carey took possession of the smallest.

⚜ CHAPTER THIRTY-ONE ⚜

Carey saw the outriggers pull away from the shore: saw Luke Alden sitting alone beside the water. Conscious that he had been avoiding her, she sought him out deliberately now.

"Come for a walk with me, Luke."

"I'm busy."

"You don't look busy."

He put down his whittling knife, and his blue eyes meeting hers seemed somehow older, colder. "To tell the truth, Carey, I don't know what you're trying to do, but whatever it is, I don't like it. I don't want to be a pawn in your game."

"It's not a game." But her eyes fell. "It's not to make Adam jealous. He won't even know about it. He's gone to watch the islanders hunt the moray eel. And the eel's lair is to the windward side of the island—he'll be gone for an hour at least, maybe two."

Luke looked at her, trying to see her, really see her, as he had told Adam Falconer to do. He knew now that a veil of illusion had blurred his vision all these years. To him, Carey had seemed golden, inviolable. In these past few days he had begun to see that the gold was dross; that part of Carey had been in his imagination. He said slowly: "I've loved you for a long time, Carey. Perhaps too long."

"Do I take it you're turning down my offer?" She tried to keep her voice light, but it shook nonetheless.

"That depends on why you're making it."

"Because—because I want to find out what it's like to make love to someone other than Adam." *And because in my heart I have never been unfaithful to him. And because in his heart he has never believed I was anything else. And because I must do this now—or die inside, with the memory of too many indignities.*

303

"I thought you already knew what it was like," Luke said, mindful of the things that had been said over these past few days.

"Not really—oh, Luke, this is hard enough for me. Don't make it harder." Then, when her words were greeted by a long silence, she added: "Please, Luke, come with me—help me."

A year ago, six months ago, even six weeks ago, there would have been no hesitation. But now—did he want to destroy the last of his illusions? If he still had illusions, they were in the trembling of her voice, in the twisting of her fingers, in the way that her eyes avoided him at this moment. "I don't make love to other men's wives, Carey. Are you telling me you plan to leave him?"

"I was hoping you'd help me decide."

Luke's eyes searched her face for a few more moments. Then, unsmiling, he said: "Really, Carey? I think you've already decided."

By the time Adam and the others returned to the beach, Carey had joined the Tahitian children in a hunt for shellfish along the water's edge. Luke Alden was nowhere to be seen, nor did he turn up again until dark. Adam tried to fight the question that gnawed at his vitals.

But Carey met his eyes levelly. Surely, he comforted himself, she could not have been unfaithful to him this afternoon, and faced him so unflinchingly now.

"Have you seen Alden about?" he asked, with as much lack of concern as he could muster.

"No. Not since shortly after you left," she said coolly, and turned her attention back to the wet sand. "How was the hunt?"

"No luck. But it was interesting to watch. I've never seen men hunt the moray eel before."

"Oh?" Her tone invited no further description, but he wanted an excuse to keep talking to her; any excuse. He persisted.

"They use themselves as bait."

She pounced on a shellfish, and moved further along the shore. He followed her, slowly.

"They put splints of wood along one man's arm, and wrap bandages around it, as if he had a broken limb."

"Really?" But her voice was indifferent.

"He dives down and—"

"Why are you telling me this?" she broke in. "I don't really want to hear."

"Because it's—ah, hell, Carey, it's because I need to talk." He dropped his long limbs to the sand and skimmed a stone viciously out to sea. "Blore will be here in a week or so. I have to decide what to do—how to trap him."

"You'll think of something." Her voice held a touch of sarcasm now, but she came to a halt and stood watching him. "You always do."

"If I'd brought more men—"

"There'd be more to die."

"D'you think I don't know that? Why the hell else would I send the *Sweet Witch* back to the China coast?" He glared at her, forgetting his private vow to be patient with her, under all circumstances.

For a moment, but just for a moment, she felt a twist of compunction. "I'm sorry," she said stiffly.

"Christ, so am I. I'm sorry most of all that you're here —that Luke Alden is here. I should have come alone."

"Listen to the brave man talk!"

"For God's sake, Carey! I can understand that you're bitter, but can't we put it aside for a week or two? There are more pressing problems."

"Like a man who wants to kill you? I don't consider that a pressing problem."

Adam's jaw worked, and it was a moment before he answered. "He may try to kill us all."

It was the first time he had admitted that to her, and even though she had suspected as much long ago, the revelation chilled her. Slowly, she formed her answer.

"I don't die so easily, Adam. I'm a survivor." And when she had said it, she suddenly knew it was true. She remembered what Mercy Paxton had said long ago about the Pacific and its survivors and for the first time she was aware of something diamond-hard inside her, some core of cold strength. It was something she had recognized in Adam, long ago. But she looked at him now with a dawning awareness, a new objectiveness that was devoid of emotion. And perhaps, in that moment, began to understand something of the reasons for his behavior. "You're a survivor too."

Adam saw that she was not, for the moment, fighting him. He lowered his guard a little, and let some of his worry show in his eyes. "This time I'm not sure. We all die, sooner or later."

"You sound like a fatalist—like my brother. Predestination! That's why he made me come to the Pacific. It's all nonsense."

"Perhaps he was right. Perhaps you were meant to come here."

With a start, she remembered her own fleeting thoughts on the subject more than a month earlier. The island of the spirit: what irony!

"I don't believe that. I should have stayed in England." But she sat down on the sand, not too far from him.

"But you didn't." Adam rolled onto his back and laced his fingers behind his head, and looked at the fat-bellied clouds drifting by; and he felt strangely happy because Carey was beside him, and because he was reasonably sure she had not been unfaithful to him with Luke Alden —not yet. "Your brother—you never talk about him. You've never told me about that part of your life. The time when he was still alive, and then after he died."

"You wouldn't be interested."

"Try me."

"I'd rather not."

"I need to think of something besides Blore."

"But you have to think of Blore!"

"I'll think of him later. Right now I want to think about you—about those months."

"I don't want to remember that part of my life, any of it." Her voice had gone suddenly vicious.

For a moment the sky seemed painfully blue: Adam closed his eyes, and his brow creased.

"Why not, Carey?" he said mildly.

"Oh—" She wrenched herself to her feet. "I don't feel like talking any more, that's why."

His eyes had opened at the sounds of her restlessness, and he looked at her from some unfathomable depths. "Don't go, Carey. I need you."

But she had already started across the sands. For an instant she halted, and looked back at the taut muscles, the well-knit length and strength of him, the hard line of his bearded jaw, the self-assurance of him. Adam needed no one—not her, not anyone.

"Oh—why don't you go find a moray eel!" and with

that she turned and ran the rest of the way to her grass hut.

He didn't follow her: God knows he wanted to, but perhaps the time was not ripe yet. She had still not worked out the bitterness inside her—and Adam knew, from the dark demon-ridden periods in his youth and in Macao, that it was something she must do for herself.

For the moment, his mind cleansed of the cobwebs that had been tangling up his thoughts, Adam was able for the first time to concentrate on the problem of Blore. He rolled into a sitting position: cross-legged on an uncluttered beach, the best possible place for thinking.

Once again he went through what he knew about Blore, what Blore would expect him to do; what he guessed Blore would do. Yes: there would be ten or twelve men in Blore's shore party. He'd bring no more; he would have to leave some crew with his ship. All the same, there would be too many men to out-fight. Could they be ambushed? Perhaps in the stand of pandanus trees? Those twisted spine-bristling aerial roots, where the giant-clawed robber crabs made their home, would be an ideal place for an ambush.

No: Blore would be only too aware of the possibility of ambush, especially once he had found clues that others had arrived first. And he would find clues. It would be impossible to hide the evidences of habitation—the native huts, the tidy coral paths, the broken coconut shells and spent lobster claws, the miscellaneous debris of everyday life that only time and tides could thoroughly wash away. Besides, Blore would have planned an ambush himself: possibly in the same pandanus grove.

What weapons could be constructed of the things that were found on the island? Sticks . . . stones? There were few rocks, and most of these were chunks of coral torn from the reef in long-forgotten storms. Some were immovable, the size of a small house; others were small, too small to be of much use. Not against firearms and cutlasses. Blore's men would come well-armed.

No, there was nothing dangerous on the island. Only in the lagoon.

Suddenly Carey's parting words came back to him. *Go find a moray eel.*

The moray eel trapped itself. It was too strong and

too wily to be taken by force, or by ordinary bait. But it had a fatal weakness. Once it locked its enormous ugly jaws over a victim, nothing short of the victim's death could unlock the viselike grip. The Tahitians had learned to use this weakness. One man would splint and bandage his own arm as bait, as Adam had described to Carey. The bandaged arm would be waved in front of the moray's lair: sometimes it was taken, sometimes not. The bandages held no particular appeal to the moray's sense of smell, although the moray could occasionally be fooled if the bandages had been rubbed in old fish-slime. If the bait was seized, the Tahitian, using the enormous swimming strength and breath-holding ability it had taken a lifetime to acquire, would push off from the bottom, and surface with the brutish trunklike body thrashing from his splint, irreversibly fastened by its own jaw. Others, standing by in canoes, would kill the repulsive and now-muzzled creature. The living bait, the swimmer, would slip his unharmed arm out of its protective covering; and there would be occasion for much laughter and many congratulations all around.

That afternoon Adam had dived down to watch the hunt; he had seen the cruel gemlike eyes of the eel glittering out from the lair in the jagged coral. But today the creature had been too crafty, or too full-bellied, or too patient, or too suspicious of the bandages, to take the proferred bait.

Blore was crafty. Blore was tenacious. Blore was patient. But Blore was not full-bellied. He was hungry for revenge.

Blore would bite. And in the end he would trap himself.

☙ CHAPTER THIRTY·TWO ❧

Carey looked out to sea anxiously. The ship that had appeared hull-down on the horizon first thing this morning was now lying hove-to just beyond the reef, and she could no longer dismiss the certainty that it must be the man Blore, the man she had never met, the man who had led all of them to this remote Pacific atoll like some evil beckoning star. There was no going back now, no escaping.

Adam was coming up the beach toward her now, loping almost lazily along the sand.

She came to meet him, anxiety written on her face.

"There's nothing to worry about. You're to stay on the beach, and stand just near the trees, where Blore's men can see you clearly from the boat. Over there." He pointed to a huge coral rock just to the fore of the fringing cocopalms. "It's beyond firing range. On no account go any closer to the water, or any closer to the trees."

"Where will you be? And what if they come to get me?"

He ignored the first question. "They won't come to get you. And they won't fire at you. But they'll send a man and he'll give you a piece of paper, and you're to destroy it. Read it first to make sure it's the note for the money I owe Blore. It'll have my signature on it."

She nodded, wondering how he could be so sure of everything, and repeated her other question. "Where will you be?"

He tilted his head at the Hawaiian double canoe that stood, ready to push off, by the shore. "I'll be at sea. I have to deliver the silver to Blore." A pile of silver bars was quite visible on the cross-platform between the joined canoes. "I'll be nearby long enough to see that you come to no harm. Call out when you've burned the note. I'll hear you."

"Adam—" The words ached inside her, and she could not find them. But her eyes spoke for her, and told him that he had at this moment been forgiven, for everything.

He grinned encouragement down at her. "Don't worry about me, little one. And one other thing. After Blore's longboat has vanished, Tu will come to you. Go with him. He'll be taking you to sea, too. All the Tahitians will be putting to sea in their outriggers."

So he had thought about their safety. But how could he be so sure that Blore's longboat would vanish?

She started to ask, but he interrupted her. "I don't have time for answers now. I'll explain later. Luke and I must be gone before Blore gets near the beach."

"Please take care."

"I will. You too—and remember you're my woman." He would not say goodbye; he had always hated goodbyes. They sounded so final. And if he kissed her it would have made things even more difficult. But there was one more thing he wanted to say, in case he was not around to say it later. His knuckle came up, gently, under her chin, and he smiled into the amber-flecked eyes.

"I love you, Teura," he said softly.

It was the first time he had told her that, and for a few moments it was all she could think of. By the time she realized the exact import of his words the double canoe had already slid into the lagoon, and was fifty yards from shore.

CHAPTER THIRTY-THREE

To Blore, entering the channel, the few figures on the motu of Varua were no bigger than bird-droppings, even through the telescope. But he could count them perfectly well. There were six figures pushing off in that strange native craft with double hulls, such as he had never seen before. Probably coming to meet the longboat. From here the beach itself looked deserted—no, by damn, there was another moving speck over near the trees, half-hidden by that big coral rock. It would be a few moments before Blore was close enough to shore to see more: he cursed that he had decided to leave the stronger telescope aboard ship, so that his men might watch for signs of the *Sweet Witch* on the horizon.

The fact that the island had turned out to be populated, after all, was no more than a minor hitch in Blore's plans. These cursed rootless islanders were always moving from place to place. But it wouldn't be a large population: probably just a wandering family group. Varua had no fresh water, none at all, and could not support many people for any length of time. It was one of the reasons Blore had chosen the island. Disposing of a few Polynesians would be easy business, pleasant business almost, a foretaste of greater pleasures to come.

Of course there was the possibility that Falconer might have arrived first. But Blore was ten days early.

Revenge would be good! Already he could feel the taste of revenge in his craw. He had plotted, waited, and hungered for this revenge. Falconer would pay for every past insult—with his money, with his ship, with his life.

But the big double canoe was not coming to meet the longboat after all: that was strange. It had skimmed halfway across the lagoon, then veered off to one side, as if waiting for his own slower approach. Why? It wasn't typical native behavior, and for the first time Blore felt the stirrings of apprehension. He began to watch the double canoe more closely, and urged his oarsmen onward.

Something on the connecting platform of the twin-hulled canoe gleamed in the sun. What was it? And was that a red-headed man in the prow—a *white* man? Blore cursed. As his own boat came within hailing distance of the craft, he saw that he had guessed correctly.

Falconer had beaten him to Varua. Until now, his enemy's teak-tanned face and dark hair had been less distinguishable from the others in the canoe, but once he had found the hated form, there was no mistaking the set of those shoulders, that black thatch of hair—in spite of the beard Falconer had grown. Those others, they were surely Polynesians. Blore with his sea-honed eyes could see them all now, quite clearly, and his finger itched on his musket trigger. The canoe remained just out of range.

"Blore!" came the hail he had been expecting. Yes: Falconer's voice.

"Where's the *Sweet Witch*, Falconer?" shouted Blore.

"What does it matter to you? I've brought your money."

"Where is it?"

"Here—with me in this canoe. Look at the cross-booms, Blore."

So that was the metallic glint in the sun. Good, solid silver bars. Blore could see them quite clearly now. Silver bars. Forty, forty-five . . . at least fifty of them. A small fortune. Yes, all that Falconer owed him, perhaps more.

Falconer called out again. "Have you brought the paper, Blore?"

"Of course I've brought the bloody paper! What are you up to, Falconer?"

"Send one man to deliver the note to my wife. She's standing on the beach. Then you can have the silver."

Blore turned his gaze to the beach once more, remembering the lone figure he had seen earlier. Yes, by God, Falconer's wife . . . he could recognize her readily enough now, by the golden shimmer of her hair. Wrapped in one of those skimpy cloths, as if she were any mucking native. But then, he'd seen her in less. Falconer's wife—what a stroke of luck. She was standing quite alone near the trees. Unprotected.

But would Falconer leave her unprotected? Blore's gimlet eyes scoured the sand and the land and the trees more closely. There must be more men from the *Sweet Witch*, somewhere, hiding. He thought he detected a suspicious trembling in one of the bending cocopalms. Not wind: the movement was too sudden. Was it a trap? Had Falconer thought to leave his wife ashore as bait? Blore directed his oarsmen to pull closer to the shore. It would be safe to go as far as the water's edge. They'd still be out of musket-range there, even if Falconer had planned an ambush.

"You can't fool me, Falconer! I see men in those trees . . . muskets."

"None of my men are in the trees," came the answering shout.

But Falconer was lying, Blore could see. The morning sun laid long shadows on the downward-shelving beach, and even where there were no telltale stirrings in the trees, the shadows told a different story. Men—and muskets.

But the woman was out in the open, closer to the shore. It would be easy enough to shoot her, or to threaten to shoot her, once a man had her within range.

As if Falconer had read his thoughts, the shout came: "Harm her and you'll never get the silver, Blore! I'll dump it in the deep waters of the lagoon, right here. It'll be sixty or more feet down, and guarded by barracuda."

Blore considered that for a moment. He'd seen the long menacing shapes of barracuda in the lagoon a year ago, when he'd first scouted Varua. He knew a little of their habits, as did any seaman in the South Pacific. They were more feared than sharks in coastal waters. But they'd stick to the deeper parts of the lagoon. Of course, Blore mused, there was always the possibility of keeping those natives alive, of forcing them to dive for the silver, later. But silver, or anything that glinted, would attract barracuda—and barracuda would attack, even without that provocation, in deeper waters. There would be little hope of getting the silver up. His own men, those who could swim, would not be capable of diving that far. He himself could only manage a depth of twenty feet or so, and he was a good swimmer.

So, for the moment, it seemed best to give in with good grace—with the appearance of good grace.

"Do it now, Blore, or I'll dump the silver here anyway! I'll give you ten minutes."

"How do I know you won't do it after the note's delivered?"

"You have my word—and your threat about Mei Sung."

Blore considered that for a few moments. Falconer would lie, would resort to trickery and treachery, but he was one of those men who was stupidly scrupulous about protecting womenfolk.

"First I want to know where the *Sweet Witch* is!" yelled Blore. "If I don't get that silver, she's mine!"

"I'm not sure where she is."

"I don't believe that, Falconer!"

"Probably in Macao—or the seas near there."

"You're lying! How did you get here, then?"

"I came in this canoe, from the Sandwich Islands."

Blore laughed, a nasty chortling sound. Now he knew Falconer was lying. So the *Sweet Witch* was nearby. Would be coming back for Falconer, as Blore had anticipated. Falconer had lied about the men in the trees . . . he had lied about the canoe . . . he was lying about the *Sweet Witch* too.

"You're a fool, Falconer, and a liar!"

"I'm not lying about the ten minutes, Blore. Get a man to shore with the note. I'm counting."

So Blore did as he was directed.

Within minutes the call came from Carey: the note had been destroyed.

Blore stood up, legs planted firmly in the longboat, and once more resumed the shouting dialogue. "Now, how about my silver, Falconer?"

"I intend to dump it."

"Damn your eyes, Falconer! So much for your word! But I've witnesses to say that you welshed on your debt. The *Sweet Witch* is mine."

"I said I wouldn't dump it *here* and I won't—not in barracuda waters. It'll be in fifteen feet of water, Blore, where your men can easily see it, and dive for it."

"Curse you, Falconer!"

But already the double canoe had turned its sails to catch the breeze, and there was little Blore could do but order his men to follow. The swifter sail-powered canoe made little effort to escape for the moment, staying only just out of range, and leading them the length of the lagoon.

"What the hell are you up to, Falconer?"

"I've told you, Blore!"

"Then get to shallow water and dump that silver—fast! Remember, any trickery and Mei Sung will die. She's aboard the *Blackbird*."

"I won't forget. Neither will Wang T'ung, if she comes to harm."

"She doesn't belong to Wang T'ung any more. I bought her outright. And what's more, Falconer, I married her. She's my wife now."

"By God! Is that so?" Falconer was genuinely astonished.

"Dump the silver! It's shallow here."

"I will, in seconds."

"Why not now?"

"Because I intend to come out of this alive, Blore! I've picked a place where this canoe can get over the reef."

"Tell me another one, Falconer!" scoffed Blore. "How do I know you're not planning an ambush?"

"If you're afraid of ambush, Blore, keep your eyes on the island!"

The gap between the boats had grown now, for with the brisker breezes on the windward side of the island, the canoe had picked up its pace. The waters, too, were choppier. And now Falconer was doing as he had said he would do. The double canoe came about just this side of the reef's breakers, losing for the moment its heading. Blore urged his men to new efforts. Closer, closer . . .

Falconer and the copper-haired man with him were dumping silver bars into the lagoon. Ten, fifteen, twenty, thirty . . . But Blore's boat was close now, within range. He lifted his musket.

"Fire, dammit!"

The thunder of Blore's weapon rang through the lagoon. But Blore's men, who were forced to drop their straining oars in order to find their own muskets, were unable to do so as swiftly as Blore would have liked. Thirty-five, forty . . .

The double canoe hesitated for a few moments on the

brink of the reef. Luke Alden swept off the last of the silver bars; and then, when the Hawaiians saw the comber they had been waiting for, their paddles flashed and Adam turned the sails to the wind, and in a thunder of spume and a swirl of spray the brave canoe escaped into the open ocean.

A volley of musket-shot followed them, but the choppiness of the lagoon made accuracy difficult. Then it was too late. They were out of range again.

Blore, cursing, put down his musket and stared at the retreating canoe in frustration. Revenge had been so very close. He couldn't possibly take the longboat over the coral. It would have been dashed to pieces; men would have drowned. Perhaps that was Falconer's plan. If so, it had failed.

Falconer's wife was still on the island, and Falconer's men. Falconer would hardly abandon them: he wasn't the type. Even if Falconer escaped for the moment, he would be back with the *Sweet Witch*. And Blore could wait.

Blore looked down into the lagoon. The silver lay there, easily within reach, scattered over the sand and in the coral heads. No more than fourteen or fifteen feet of water, as Falconer had promised. The silver was safe there: it would keep. Blore decided to direct his men back to the ship at once. Even though the native canoe seemed reasonably swift, it was no match for his *Blackbird*. He could catch up with Falconer and have it done with, once and for all. Blore started to give the order: then stopped.

All at once he knew he was doing exactly as Falconer wanted him to do. Falconer was using himself as bait. Bait to draw the heavily gunned vessel away from the channel entrance . . . just as he had already drawn the longboat along the lagoon. Blore swore softly, angered that he had not seen through the ruse earlier. It would take him at least fifteen minutes to get back to the *Blackbird*. Falconer had been giving himself a head start. The damn trickster had gone out into the open sea and he intended that Blore, in the *Blackbird*, should follow him. And while Blore's own ship was away giving merry chase, the *Sweet Witch* would return for Falconer's wife and his men . . . in response to a smoke signal, probably. Maybe Falconer even had a plan for getting the silver back: men hidden on the island, not far from here.

Blore smiled to himself, a cruel knowing smile that twisted his lips without touching his eyes. How well he understood his enemy! But this time Falconer had out-foxed himself.

"How many of you sons-of-bitches can swim?" he roared to his crew.

Two or three voices went up, without enthusiasm. They'd heard the warning about the barracuda. But they wouldn't dare lie to Blore, or they'd be spread-eagled over the grating without a moment's hesitation, and too many of them knew too well the taste of the lash.

"You, Mr. Larsen?" He addressed himself to the first mate. "I didn't hear your voice. You swim. Modest as a mucking maiden, aren't you?"

Larsen confessed reluctantly. "Didn't think you'd want me, Captain."

"I don't pay you to think! Get your goddam trousers off. And any of you sods fancy enough to wear rings, stick 'em up your arse. This water's shallow for barra-cuda, but anything shiny is going to bring 'em. Take your shirts down to wrap the silver in."

The water here was clear, in spite of the swell that came over the reef. It was possible to see for some dis-tance through the lagoon. There were no barracuda nearby, none at all. Nor did there seem to be much ma-rine life of any kind, beyond a few gaudily striped and inoffensive wrasse: a matter which might have given Blore pause, had he known more about the interrelation-ship of life around the reef. The wrasse were tolerated by all other fish, even predators, because of their role as nibblers of parasites and cleaners of teeth.

"Shake a leg, you sodding sons-of-bitches! We'll sight those frigging 'cudas if they come within twenty yards. What d'you think this is, a ruddy picnic?"

Four naked men slid unwillingly into the water, and within minutes the silver bars had started to come up.

The twelve men who had been left minding the *Black-bird* had been given strict instructions about what they must do if they sighted the *Sweet Witch*. But there had been no instructions about outrigger canoes—especially outrigger canoes loaded with those natives who had for some reason just climbed down out of the cocopalms, and one golden-haired woman. In any case, the canoes were too small to make a decent target for the large guns, and too far away for muskets. The second mate let them pass to sea, unmolested.

But this other canoe that appeared, now, from the far side of the atoll—that would bear watching.

"D'you think it's the same sodding canoe that Captain Blore was taking after?" It was only two or three minutes since the longboat had vanished from view, and gunfire had been heard.

"Looks like the same one. I say we give chase." This was the gunner's mate.

"Doesn't look like we need to." The strange-looking craft was drawing nearer. "Wish we knew why Captain Blore was following it."

"Aye—and why the musketfire." The gunner's mate was nervous, trigger-happy. He wouldn't have minded laying a broadside to this larger craft, which was a better target—but he needed the word from the second mate. "I say we take 'em."

The second mate held the spyglass to his eye. "Those clowns don't even have muskets, from the look of it. Must have been our own men firing. Four brown devils . . . two white men. But they're not trying to get away— just sitting there." He put the glass down, with a worried frown.

"Mei Sung!" Falconer's voice rang clear over the wind. "I want to speak to the captain's wife—to Mrs. Blore. Mei Sung!"

At this unexpected turn of events, the men aboard the *Blackbird* looked at each other in bewilderment. What were they supposed to do now? Blore had anticipated nothing like this.

Nor, in fact, had Falconer. He had intended only to sail away, screened by the island, and rendezvous with the outriggers farther to sea, as arranged. But then, he had not known that Blore had married Mei Sung.

Aboard the *Blackbird*, the first mate had reached a decision. He addressed himself to one of the lesser seamen.

"Fetch Mrs. Blore, at once. Maybe there's a message from the captain. And hurry it up, you oaf!"

But Mei Sung had heard some of the commotion, and

was already tripping her dainty way up the companion. She came across the deck with a tiny-stepped swaying walk, in fair imitation of a woman who had had her feet decently bound.

"What for all-a shout?" she asked in her pretty singsong voice. "I hear name of Mei Sung. Someone call Mei Sung?"

"Aye, Mrs. Blore." The second mate swung around and pointed to sea. Mei Sung went to the rail. "That man in the canoe—he called for you."

"Mei Sung!" came Adam's voice again. "We're coming alongside. Tell your men to relax."

Mei Sung thought she recognized the voice, but borrowed the mate's spyglass, to be sure.

"A-tan!" Her mouth curved with pleasure, and she repeated the name in a high-pitched voice. "A-tan! What for you here? What joy! You come close, we talk, hey?"

And with that reception, Adam was fairly certain that it was safe to come alongside Blore's ship—as long as Blore's longboat remained out of sight.

"Tell your men to put their muskets away, Mei Sung. Tell them I'm not the man your husband is looking for." Falconer grinned easily. He had spoken no lies to Blore, but he could lie when he had to. "Tell them I've been helping your husband."

"Is true!" Mei Sung promptly ordered the putting away of firearms. The men of the *Blackbird* who had no grounds to quibble with her judgment in the matter, obeyed, although with some reluctance.

"It's damn good to see you, Mei Sung," said Falconer affectionately, once the firearms had been stowed, and the canoe brought closer. He had almost forgotten how beautiful she was—how pearl-pale, how almond-eyed, how willowy.

"Damn-good to see you too, A-tan! Werry hairy chin, heya!"

"You remember Alden, don't you, Mei Sung?"

"Yess." She smiled at Luke, whom she remembered only vaguely from her days aboard the *Sweet Witch*. Then Adam introduced her to the others in the canoe, and suggested that she ask the crew of the *Blackbird* to step out of earshot. Again they obeyed, with misgivings.

"Has Blore been treating you well?" Adam kept his voice low.

"Is husband," she said cryptically, but then smiled, and added more revealingly: "For Chinese wife with big feet, is werry all right husband."

"He hasn't been beating you?"

"No," she lied. Once, when Blore was drunk, he had forgotten the shadow of Wang T'ung. "But if he did? All good Chinese husband beat no-good Chinese wife."

"You're not a no-good wife, Mei Sung. You're too good for him. A damn sight too good for him! Do you want to come with us? We'll take you away—get you back to Wang T'ung, somehow."

She considered the offer. "No. Wife's place is with husband. Wang T'ung sells me—I not his now. I cost many cash," she said proudly. Blore had paid Wang T'ung a great deal for the privilege of marrying her—a very great deal. To Mei Sung it was a point of honor; it was the price of a high-born virgin with lily feet. Mei Sung had no idea that Blore had decided she was a good investment, considering Wang T'ung's assets; and if she had been told that, she would not have believed it. Mei Sung knew that she was Wang T'ung's great-granddaughter, but she also knew what Blore did not yet know, what Wang T'ung had been scrupulously careful not to tell him: that under Chinese law and custom, she would inherit nothing.

"You're sure you won't come with us?"

"Aiee yah! I think you miss Mei Sung a little, A-tan. Werry good times, heya?"

"It was good, Mei Sung, but it's over now. If you come with me I'll take you back to Wang T'ung—no strings attached."

"No string attach? Not unnerstan'. Anyway, I stay."

"Can you borrow a spyglass from your crew, Mei Sung? Otherwise I'll have to leave at once."

"What for spyglass? What for you go?"

"Just borrow it and then I'll tell you."

She did, and returned in moments.

"All right, Mei Sung. When you see signs of your longboat returning, you must look through the spyglass and tell me if your husband is in it." Mei Sung, from her vantage point at the *Blackbird*'s rail, would be able to see long before Falconer.

"What for he not be with boat? You talk damn-crazy talk, A-tan."

"I can't lie to you, Mei Sung. Your husband may be very sick by now." He didn't mention that, with luck, Blore might even be dead.

"What for sick? What he do?"

"I imagine he's gone for a swim in the lagoon."

"Swim! That damn-fool talk, A-tan."

"Just keep your eyes open, Mei Sung. If he's not in the longboat you must remind your men at once that we had nothing to do with it. That we've been here all along."

But Mei Sung was not so stupid. She looked at Adam appraisingly, and stated the facts as she saw them, without emotion. "You kill him, A-tan. How you kill him?"

"No, Mei Sung. He was alive a few moments ago. If anything kills him it will be the lagoon. But if he dies you'll own this ship."

"Chinese woman owns nothing!" she averred incredulously.

"Wrong, Mei Sung. You're not Chinese any more. You married an Englishman. A barbarian devil! But it's given you some rights. If he dies, the *Blackbird* is yours. Remember that! The men will have to obey you, if anything happens to your husband."

"Heya, where you get chopsticks in head, A-tan?" But she trusted and believed him, and for one unforgivable moment she almost hoped that A-tan was right—that her husband had indeed gone swimming in the lagoon.

With only four men diving, Blore was becoming impatient. It was apparent that the barracuda were paying no attention to the swimmers, who were moving slowly and carefully and keeping a close lookout for any untoward appearance in the water. Half the silver bars had been recovered—but it was a slow business, slower than Blore would have thought, what with having to conceal each bar in cloth before coming to the surface. And his men were not the best swimmers—not used to holding their breath for any period of time. Winded now, they had to spend some time clinging to the gunwale of the boat between dives. Curse them for being so bloody cautious! It was easy to see that they were exaggerating the dangers—that even he himself had worried needlessly. There was nothing dangerous down there. Yet the men were moving at a snail's pace. One man, Ord, a particularly poor swimmer, was gasping by the edge of the boat. A second, the best swimmer, was farther afield near the reef, where some of the bars had landed. Two others had just gone down again—Blore could see them clearly through the water—and they were heading for some bars that had wedged themselves among the branches of a fernlike coral head.

It was a particularly beautiful coral head of a flaming crimson shade. But Blore did not notice its beauty, only that three silver bars had been trapped in the graceful branches, and that it might be a little tricky to get them out. The swimmers tugged at some of the coral fronds and broke them off; then finally surfaced with two of the bars. After a short rest, they returned below to dislodge the third.

Hurry—why the Christ couldn't they hurry?

"Ord!" Blore cried to the man who was still recovering at the edge of the boat. "Get the hell down there and give them a hand!"

"Yessir!" gasped Ord, and took a gulp of air into his pained lungs.

But just then one of the two men came racing from below, like a cork under pressure, and his scream could be seen in the uprush of bubbles even before the sound of it came to the waiting boat. His partner followed, only seconds behind.

"Sweet Jesus!" Ord exploded the air in his lungs, and stared, pop-eyed.

And Blore and the rest of the men stared. What had come over the divers? Especially Larsen, the mate—he wasn't given to irrational behavior. And yet there hadn't been a thing in the water, not a damn thing.

"Get those sods over the side—into the boat!" yelled Blore above the agonized yowls of the men. "Shut up, Larsen! Shut up, damn your eyes! What the hell's wrong with you?"

And the two swimmers garbled out some words about the coral. Only minutes had passed since they had first scraped the coral. Yet already, it was plain to see, they were not exaggerating. Great weals and welts had erupted on their bodies, like whiplashes. One of the men fainted as he was pulled into the boat. The other's lips were blue, flecked with spittle; he was in shock.

Curse the luck! It must have been something poisonous in that coral. Flaming red . . . like fire. Blore could see another spectacular frond of it, half concealing another silver bar. They'd give that one a wide berth, and forget the other bar here, in this coral head. There was still plenty of silver, and the rest of it lay over nearer the reef, which was quite a different color of coral. The fourth swimmer had already touched it several times with impunity.

Still no sign of barracuda.

Ord was clearly not competent to go down again, Blore could see that. He had started to heave with fright, great dry retching sobs that told of his terror at the fate that had so nearly been his.

"Bloody yellow-belly," muttered Blore. Curse it—now he'd have to go down himself, for one man could not do the work alone. He snarled: "Get out, Ord, you fathom o' bilge water, and stop slobbering! Goddamn nance! I'll have your hide for this." And with several more oaths that did nothing to assuage the diver's panic, Blore shucked his own shirt and pants. He took one more thorough look-about to see that the barracuda were still keeping their distance, and lowered himself into the waiting lagoon.

Blore sucked in a breath on the surface near the reef, and dove down for yet another bar. He had sighted one lying on a ledge of coral not far from this place, at one of those yawning black gaps that appeared here and there in the reef's wall. The first time he had passed such a gap, a little distance from here, he had been startled. Great eyes had stared out at him: but then he had recognized a giant grouper, and he had sloughed off the moment of unreasoning primitive panic, and returned to the hunt. Cowardice was not one of his failings.

So he reached for the bar, cautiously but with no particular warning bell sounding in his head. It took several precious seconds to wrap the silver bar in the dark cloth of his shirt. By the time he had done it, he was running somewhat short of breath.

And in the instant that he became conscious of the jeweled eyes watching him, it was already too late. His scream never reached the surface. Only the great uprush of bubbles marked the beginning of his death, and the slowly spreading stain of red in the turquoise waters of the lagoon.

"Who do you see in the boat, Mei Sung? Look carefully. It's important—if your husband is there, I'll have to be off."

"Five, six, seven row—all low-down no-good sailors. No husband." By Chinese custom, Mei Sung could not utter her husband's name.

"Any more?"

"Two—no, three sick. Werry sick! One name of Ord. One name of Larsen. Firs' mate."

"And the third sick man. Is it your husband?"

"No. No husband. Great woe!"

"Ten men, then? And two men missing. You're sure?"

"Yess."

"One of the missing men is your husband?"

"Yess."

"I'm sorry, Mei Sung." And he was, in a way. "Your men will have seen by now, too. Tell them what's happened. Tell them that the *Blackbird* belongs to you.. That they must do exactly as you say."

And while she did, Falconer mused to himself which of his traps had done for Blore.

Not the silver seeded into the fire coral. That would be the sick men in the longboat. They would live, but their agony would be indescribable.

So it had to be the silver bar that had been so cautiously placed by the moray eel's lair. Either that or the tiger sharks that Luke Alden had lured into the lagoon. They had not been enormous sharks: in truth, they were smaller than the few barracuda that were left in these waters. But they would come, more swiftly and more surely than any barracuda, at the first sign of blood in the water—just at that very moment when the watchers in the boat would be reacting with panic, and not keeping watch at all.

And as he had said to Mei Sung, he was truly sorry, sorry that he had not been able to think of a more humane way.

CHAPTER THIRTY-FOUR

"So that was Mei Sung," said Carey thoughtfully. They had just left the side of the *Blackbird*, which would stand at anchor until dawn. Luke Alden had gone aboard to stay on as captain, and look after Mei Sung.

"Jealous?" Adam's smile teased her, gently. The sun was sinking rapidly in a purplish blaze; moments from now the sudden tropic night would enfold them in darkness. The double canoe slid through the channel and winged gracefully toward the white and waiting shore of Varua.

"Of course not," returned Carey airily, but it was not quite the truth. Mei Sung had been dainty, ladylike, fragile, exquisite, ageless. Porcelain skin and an entrancing smile. A formidable rival. "But I can't think why you had to talk to her for so long while we were waiting at the rendezvous."

"Were you worried? I told Tu not to let you fret if I was late." The outriggers had spent nearly three hours just over the horizon, where they could see the *Blackbird*'s masts without fear of being seen themselves. Three long anxious hours, before the double canoe had finally made its appearance.

"What makes you think I would worry?" In truth she had been sick with fear. "You're far too sure of yourself, Adam Falconer."

"You're quite right." And he took her comfortably into the crook of his arm. "Very sure."

As if by mutual agreement, neither had mentioned Adam's parting words of the morning. Each was hoarding the thought of the discoveries that would be made later, by dark, when they lay entwined in each other's arms.

But at the moment Carey had not quite forgiven him for the anguish of the long wait at the rendezvous. "You might have explained what you were doing."

"Would you have approved?"

"No. What if Blore hadn't fallen into your trap? What if he had followed you?"

"If he'd tried to go over the reef, his boat would have been ripped to shreds. If he'd gone back to the *Blackbird*, I'd have had a head start."

Blore had been right in part of his thinking. Adam himself had been the real bait—but there had been the other bait, the silver. It had only been a matter of waiting to see which would be chosen. Either way—barring the unforeseen—the chances had been excellent.

Carey was not convinced. "Even with a head start, that was a terrible risk! Does the *Sweet Witch* really mean that much to you?"

"Which sweet witch?" He curled a tendril of her hair around his finger, and planted a kiss on her nose.

"Is that all I get? You did a better job when you kissed Mei Sung goodbye."

"You are jealous, you little vixen! Just remember that I kissed her *goodbye*. I wouldn't do that to you."

Carey was a little mollified, and decided to be generous. "She's very pretty."

"I can't argue with you."

"And very sexy," she admitted more grudgingly, begging for a denial.

He remained silent, and she pulled away with a momentary surge of annoyance. "I see you can't argue about that either."

"Should I? I'm sure she and your young friend Luke Alden will have a very sexy time together."

"Adam! She's far too old for him," she said with a touch of spitefulness, remembering that Mei Sung had been a courtesan for six years.

"D'you think so? Mei Sung's eighteen."

"Eighteen! Oh—" Suddenly, her own troubles seemed less important.

"Chin up, Carey, Mei Sung doesn't have to do anything she doesn't want to this time. She's her own mistress now. But I recognize that look in her eye. She pretends a true Chinese disdain for barbarian devils—and underneath it all, she adores them."

"Some of them."

"Some of them. I think your friend will qualify."

"*My* friend!" But the turn of the conversation had made

326

her a trifle uncomfortable, and she quickly changed the subject. "Look, Adam," she said, pointing to shore.

While Adam and Carey, in the Hawaiian canoe, had been at the *Blackbird*, the Tahitians in their outriggers had returned to Varua. Those who had been ashore had not been idle, Carey could see.

"They're planning a tamaaraa—a Polynesian feast, I'm sure of it." From here they could see the torches, still unlit, that had been set along the beach; the spreading of large glossy leaves to serve as tablecloths; the mounds that showed where the himaa, the earth-ovens, had been dug. Laughter chimed across the water. Two sturdy children, shouting with glee, darted in and out of adults' legs, while their elders looked on indulgently, and gossiped and laughed and told ribald jokes, and recounted for the hundredth time the happenings of the morning, and only wished they had been there to see.

Adam frowned. This wasn't what he'd had in mind at all, for the next few hours. "Blast! I can think of better ways to celebrate."

"We have to attend, Adam. This will be in your honor."

"Any excuse for a feast! They should have waited until they caught the moray eel."

"You never finished telling me how that's done."

"Same way you caught me, Carey." In the last violet-tinged light of day she could see the way his eyes crinkled, forming little laughter-lines, the way they darkened and danced with hidden fires. "You just stayed stubbornly in view and let me do the catching."

The banquet was over. Groaning with satisfaction and unbelievable quantities of food, men and women reeled to their feet and cleared away the remnants of the feasting. Koolau and the Hawaiians pulled Adam aside, wanting to relive once more the excitement of the day and their part in it. Carey watched him go with regret—but she knew that men needed this time apart, this male togetherness when tales of great exploits were retold and savored and told again.

So, content to have an hour or so for the meal to digest, she sat alone on the beach under the flickering torches, and watched and listened. The headman Tu, elder of his tribe, had begun to mutter in a trancelike voice. Then, when the other Tahitians stilled their chatter to hear, he began the chant. Guttural sounds emerged from his crêped but still-strong throat. It was an ancient ute, a Tahitian ballad that told of great exploits of other times—of men, of ships, of victories, of the Great Ocean of the Blue Sky, of the islands that lay sprinkled over it like so many grains of sand. Tu told tales of the dim origins of Polynesian man, tales a thousand and more years in the making. Other sounds in his throat, wavering falsetto notes, mingled with the deep. The audience swayed, hypnotized, visionaries for an eyeblink of eternity.

But at last the chant came to an end. The primeval spell was broken; the ghosts of the past scattered silently into the night. Had they been dreams? Now instruments appeared—crude instruments, fashioned of the indigenous things of the atoll.

And to the throb of drums, the indescribable throb that became a fire in the veins and a fever in the brain, the Tahitians began to dance under the stars. It began slowly; but soon dances as old as all race-memory pulsed through their ankles and their wrists, their hearts and their hips . . . dances that spoke the language of love in a land that had no written word, where there were no symbols to describe the act of love beyond the doing of it. The wildly abandoned tamaure and hura, the heva and the upaupa—undulating, unabashedly sensual, arousing beyond belief.

And when she could bear the madness in her blood no longer, Carey looked around to find Adam.

He had vanished.

For one awful moment, she thought he might have been led off—as others were even now being led off—by one of the Tahitian vahines. But then she knew.

She came to her feet, and left the torchlit beach behind. In the darkness, without a lamp, she had a little trouble groping her way toward the waiting huts. But Adam had set a coconut lamp outside in the clearing, and its uncertain light served as a beacon.

Inside his hut, there was another lamp burning. Adam was sitting on a pandanus mat, still fully dressed.

"I thought you'd never come." His eyes reflected little pools of light from the smoking coconut.

"You should have spoken to me when you left." She stood in the doorway, strangely hesitant now.

"I wanted you to come to me. Of your own accord."

"How long have you been here?"

"About fifteen minutes."

"Think of the time we've wasted."

"I've been thinking of nothing else." And they both knew that he did not mean fifteen minutes.

"Oh, Adam." She came down on the pandanus mat beside him, and clung to him, totally unashamed of the emotion in her voice and in her face. "Adam, I—"

"Hush." He put a finger to her lips. "We'll talk later. There are some things that can't be said in words."

She knew it was true: and she started to say them, with her hands and her hips and her lips and her heart.

"How did you know about Teura, Adam? When did you find out?" The coconut lamp had burned itself out; the drums had at last grown silent. They lay clinging to each other, lovers who could not bear to waste time in sleep. Already, at Adam's insistence, Carey had told a slightly altered version of how Starbuck had died, how Teura had survived. "When did you find out?"

"It was on the trip down from Hawaii—that's when I knew."

"Did, did—was it something someone said to you?"

He knew she meant Luke Alden, and wondered why she avoided his name. In the dark, he could not see her face. "Yes, but not directly. He told me I'd never looked at you. It was the truth." He paused, then plunged on, recklessly, mindful of the thing that Carey had just let slip, inadvertently—that Luke had known about the masquerade. "Carey, I have to know. Tell me and I give you my word that I'll never mention it again. Did you have an affair with Luke?"

"No." If she had had to lie, she knew that Adam would have sensed it now. How grateful she was that Luke had seen what she herself had been too blind to see! Until today, until this morning on the beach, she had not been sure of her feelings. Dear Luke . . . she had so much to thank him for. "There was nothing between us, Adam."

She could feel the tension go out of his limbs. "Go on," she urged, glad of the curtain of night. "Tell me how you knew."

"I realized Luke was right, that I'd never really seen

you. It came over me when I saw you crying that evening, over a sunset."

"A silly sunset? Do you mean you knew everything that night?"

"No. It wasn't that easy. But I did start to look at you, really look at you, for the next few days. I'd seen so many different sides of you—and I didn't really understand any of them." He hesitated for a moment, wondering how he could explain. "Have you ever looked into a lagoon through a piece of glass?"

"No," she admitted.

"Well, it was something like that. I'd seen the different surfaces of you. Rippled by rain, torn by storms, ruffled and shimmering in sunlight, sometimes just glassy and untouched. But even on the stillest day there's always some distortion . . . some trick of the surface that conceals a part of the truth beneath. Under the surface the lagoon doesn't change that much— oh, sands shift and coral grows, but imperceptibly."

"How can you say that—knowing about things like the moray eel!"

"We all have some ugliness hidden somewhere." Unwillingly he thought about Macao, and wrenched his mind away. "But I'm not talking about the sealife. I'm talking about the lagoon itself. Once I had the knack of looking beneath the surface of you, I began to see things that hadn't been clear to me before."

"And you saw something you hadn't seen in all these months of being married to me? I'm amazed."

"I must admit I was helped by the fact that you were wearing a pareu for the first time in nearly two years, and that your nose was sunburned, and that your hair was hanging halfway down your back. When I married you, it wasn't. But even at that time I'd noted that you had Teura's bones and eyes. It's part of why I refused to look at you for so long— part of why I hated you."

"But after all that time how could you suddenly be so sure, so very sure? I thought you'd forgotten Teura."

"In a way I had, but not completely. Your image was superimposed over hers in my brain, although I didn't realize it until recently. It was in thinking about you, not her, that the thought first came to me."

"I'm not sure what you mean."

"One thing I saw in all the different Careys was that

she didn't care too much for the proprieties. A girl like that—like you—would have carried a fatherless child, and to hell with the consequences."

"But I didn't want the baby to be fatherless," she protested with a twist of long-forgotten pain. "I remembered what you had said about being a bastard—how you had felt."

"Yes, but—would you have tricked any passing man into marriage, just to provide that father? I didn't think so. And if so, there would have been easier targets than me. You had to have a reason for your choice."

"It could have been a schoolgirl crush."

"That occurred to me, of course, but I soon saw it was impossible. You told me back in Alta California how you felt about your first lover. I should remember—I was jealous as hell! Could you have felt like that, and still nourished a crush on some man who'd done no more than paddle your pretty bottom? It was the one piece of behavior that didn't belong. For you, it would have to be a man you loved as much as that first man—or nobody."

"How astute of you to see all that! You must have been very pleased with yourself."

"Not half as pleased as I was with you. And just to be sure, I set you a small trap—and you fell for it, hook, line, and sinker."

"What?" She was astonished. "I don't remember any trap."

"You refused to speak French to me, remember? Nice little English girls aren't brought up to speak Spanish and Italian, and God knows how many other languages, without speaking French. It was a two-way trap. If you spoke French, I'd know. If you refused to speak it, I'd know."

"How stupid of me."

"How stupid of me, not to have seen much sooner. It would have saved an awful lot of hating."

"Oh, Adam." She turned her face into his shoulder, remembering. Had it all been to no purpose? She had to know. "I thought of telling you the truth a thousand times. When we were first married—and even before that, when I was still Teura. Would it have changed things?"

He was silent for a time before answering. "I'm not sure. I'd have been very angry that you had tricked me into thinking you were an island girl. I don't like to be tricked.

I might never have wanted to see you again. Pride is a terrible thing—a curse."

She had been holding her breath, and now she let it go against his broad chest.

His fingers moved comfortingly in her hair. "Does that upset you? I'm sorry. I'm trying to be truthful, Carey. I loved Teura—but not as much as I love you. And remember I had told you things, thinking you didn't understand English—things I'd never told to anyone, not even Noah. Things I still wish you didn't know."

"I love you more for them," she whispered.

"Carey—Teura." He tilted her face up to his own, and tasted her mouth, lingeringly. "Do you realize we don't have to be back in Hawaii for four months?"

"Maybe Koolau will want to return at once."

"I don't think he'll be in any hurry. Didn't you see him with that pretty Tahitian girl?"

"Yes. I saw them go off into the bushes."

"Making babies."

"Adam—"

"The answer is yes, I do want to."

"That's not what I was going to ask. Must you always be so clever? I was going to ask if you weren't anxious to get back on the *Sweet Witch*."

"Same answer, Carey." He came up on one elbow and kissed her more thoroughly, and she could feel the renewed stirrings of his body. "My own love, my only love . . " he whispered.

And then, because the words he had said to no other woman in his life seemed to come more easily in the language of love, he murmured into her ear: "Je t'aime, je t'adore, mon amour, ma vie . . ."

And for a time they both forgot the other witch, the wild and sweet and terrible and seductive witch that had ruled their lives for so long. But under the eternal wheeling stars, the Pacific glittered and pulsed and surged and crested, and survived a thousand little deaths against the reef, and swept uncaringly on.